CW00972862

One-Inch Punch

by

Oran Ryan

A SEVEN TOWERS PUBLICATION

Published 2012
By
Seven Towers 4, St Mura's Terrace,
Strangford Road, East Wall, Dublin 3, Ireland.

www.seventowers.ie
info@seventowers.ie

ISBN 9780957151086

Copyright © Oran Ryan 2012

All rights reserved. No part of this book may be reproduced or utilised in any form or by any means mechanical, including photography, photocopying, filming, recording, video recording, or by any information storage and retrieval system, or shall not, by way of trade or otherwise, be lent, resold, or otherwise circulated in any form of binding or cover other than that in which it is published, without prior permission in writing from the publisher. The moral rights of the author have been asserted.

Cover photograph © Sarah Lundberg: Window in the ruin of Rathborne Candle Factory, East Wall Road, Dublin 3. (Taken on a Nokia E5 Mobile Phone)

Set in Garamond 10 Pt. on 100 GSM Munken

Dedicated to

Sarah S. Lundberg

1.

I, Gordon Brock, married twice, divorced once, IQ 170, former psychotherapist, author, father of three, had come down to Dublin for my usual bout of apocalyptic Christmas shopping. There, after two decades, I once again met Ed Frasier.

O'Connell Street was filled with twisting crowds when I met him. I watched the busy people pulling and bumping like dodgem drivers on amphetamines they moved.

That day, and the days before meeting him, I felt someone was watching me. If you think someone is watching you, then someone is generally watching you. Then I thought, perhaps I am depressed. It's not uncommon, this depression feeling. There's a dark dark somewhere, I thought, despite the lights, the crowds, and the glorious freezing Christmas theatre. I couldn't be objective.

The sense of being watched had started down on the farm with Lucia and the kids. And it continued in the city. Then I got my answer. Someone really was out to get me. As I passed Clery's Department Store, I met Edward Frasier. Again.

"Well shave my head and call me a pop tart! Gordon? Gordon Brock? Is that you?"

Ed Frasier was a surgeon now. He looked good. Lean. Hard. Handsome. Tall. Empowered. Ed wore strong shoes that kept out the chill underfoot, a heavy woollen buttoned-up coat, leather gloves, a soft cap tilted to one side, and the smiling affected optimistic manner of a successful professional shopping for loved ones. He looked well. His face now had crow's feet. He had scalpel deep lines from cheek bone to lantern jaw. His tight blonde hairline was receding just beneath the soft slightly tilted cap, and the ghost of that huge bony body I remember from when we were young. He had broad straight shoulders. He had long arms and legs. I thought of him as a kind of warrior, a battle-hardened navy SEAL, a marine, a fighter. Not a surgeon. Not a healer. I still felt the old dread and hate as I looked into those cold blue eyes and heard that clear crisp voice, as cutting as the frosty air that, despite previous years of unseasonably warm winters, seemed to promise more cold.

Frasier put down a pile of paper shopping bags and put out his gloved hand for me to take. Then he stopped, removed his glove and put out the hand in a more formal, gentlemanly way.
"Put it there," he said, wanting me to shake hands.
"Ed," I said coldly, not taking the Evil One's hand.
I went to walk on by, but it was the way he put out his hand that stopped me, daring I not take it, daring I defy his charm and goodwill, daring I refuse him. Then, smiling a little less broadly, he dropped his hand.
"How are you? It's good to see you after, how many?" He said.
"A lot," I said harmonising the chill of the air with the ambient temperature of my voice. Twenty years, I thought. No, longer. Far too short a time to not see Ed Frasier.
"What are you doing now?"
Nothing, I thought. Then I thought of another word.
"Shopping," I said.
Now, that's just being negative, I thought. You, Gordy, are buying gifts.
"You still have that wit, that singular sense of humour, Gordon," he said.
"Thanks," I said.
"You know what I mean."
"I do?"
"Sure! Whatcha doing this weather? Where are you at?"
"Thanks Ed. I'm doing 'stuff'. Christmas stuff."
"And?"
"I am doing what millions and millions of parents and family people do at Christmas: suppressing their loathing of the commercialism of it all, and trying to be loving."
"That's good. So, what did you go into after college?"
"I became a psychotherapist."
"You like that?"
"It's dismal. I quit. Became a writer."
"I see."
"How's Rachel? I read her novel. It was good, too autobiographical to be believable, though."
"She'll be, eh, delighted to hear that. I will send her an e-mail. She is living in Florida, last I heard."
"She broke up with your Dad?"
"Oh that's a while back now." Ed said.
"Wow. That I did not know. I mean your Mom and he broke up and

then he hooks up with Rachel Morrison and, well—"
"She lost her medical license."
"Well, I guess chronic substance abuse does have its downside."
"Don't do this, Gordon."
"Sorry. I guess I never liked her. She was mean to me."
Ed changed the subject.
"You know I'm in London now?"
"I see. Weren't you embarrassed at how Rachel portrayed your Dad? Angry? I would have been angry."
"It's a good job. In London," Ed said. A silence followed.
"Youknow,"Isaid."I think this conversation is going just super,don'tyou?"
I went to move on, but he stopped me.
"Please take your hands off the material, Ed. Ok?"
"Sorry. Look I wanted to. I think we should have a talk. One talk. Just the one?"
"What?"
"You are down the country somewhere, living on a farm? You don't come up here much."
"How did you know that?" I asked.
"Ever heard of the Internet?" He grinned.
"Ever heard of- oh forget it. Yes I have heard of the Internet. For god's sake!"
"I'm in London now, took the necessary exams, thoracic surgery. I am glad to have met you. Let's go somewhere. Catch up?"
He touched my elbow. But I didn't move.
"If you ask me, the chances of us meeting without the use of researchers, or private detectives, and a careful planning of the right moment at the right time of year, well it's simply astronomical."
"Would you have a few minutes to talk?"
"How did you find me?"
"I didn't look for you."
"Of course you didn't."
"I didn't!"
"Not to worry. God loves a trier. Are you attached? Married? Kids?"
"Married. With three children."
"Good. It's extraordinary how that changes us. We start off being a little bohemian and free, after all life holds so many possibilities. And then we start having children and family need us to be there for them and we are. We are there for them. Reliable. Consistent. Caring."
"That's true," Ed smiled and nodded.
"And we love them. And we are responsible, earning a regular wage, paying for everything, loving them, and we think ourselves

enlightened."

"Oh, I know," Ed said, looking a little quizzically at me.

"And then the years pass, and our self-centered, ungrateful offspring who are too stupid to realise we have mortgaged our peace of mind for their future, comes home with a Bassett Hound called Maude, and says they are engaged, or worse, in love."

"That's not funny," Ed said." Its sad, actually."

"I mean something like that could ruin a very carefully crafted career and reputation."

Suddenly, and understandably now, he was hurt, and angry. Now he was disappointed in me.

"Gordon, it's impossible to believe a person could have your talent for hate. I'd better be going. I'll see you. It was nice to meet you after all this time, I think. I hope you are well, you and yours."

"Enjoy your life," I said.

Frasier went to pick up the bags that he had neatly deposited like sentries between his two boots. Across the street beside Eason's Bookstore yet another Christmas charity choir began ironically singing 'O come all ye faithful, joyful and triumphant' to the inconsistent rattle of a tambourine. The lights from the trees along O'Connell Street winked on and off. Car lights reflected off the decorations gleaming in stores. I looked at the glittering trinket decorations, how they were suspended between lamp posts and hung across adjoining streets. I glanced across at the choir, amazed I could hear them from across the street, irritated at how cocktail party hearing could be so selective in the midst of this Christmas din.

"No, I want us to talk. I understand why you are being deliberately provocative like this. Look, I have a conference in an hour," Frasier said." If you like, we could catch up and have a quick drink."

"What?!"

"Have you got all your shopping done?"

"No," I said.

I thought how it would be easier to pretend. To smile and wave and shake hands and fight the deepening chill of the early afternoon with the warmth and the cheer of the Christmas shop windows. Ed shifted from foot to foot, still smiling but only occasionally looking at me. Ed was watching the swell of people flow around us. We moved nearer the shop window, filled with elves conversing with centipedes with hookahs in golden caves replete with glistening silver and scarlet and gold wrapped bow-tied, big, shiny, inviting Christmas gift boxes.

"So?"

"Tell me, it's a little near Christmas for school, don't you think?"

"It's only for a few hours, Gordon."

"Okay."

"I suppose you have collected a few doctorates at this stage, eh?"

"No, not really," I said.

"What about all those self-help books you churned out, eh?" Ed said.

"They were money-makers, and mostly rubbish."

"I thought they were quite good, some of them."

"I gave it up."

"Ah, why?"

"Because, Ed, they were rubbish."

"So what are you doing?"

"Working on a kind of fiction thing now. Have been for years."

"Ah. How's that coming along?"

"I suddenly see an end in sight."

"Ah I see. Well, then. Can we go indoors? Eh?"

"Why?"

"Because I'd like to talk to you, Gordon."

"I don't know about that, Frasier."

"You sound bitter," he said.

"I'm not bitter. I'm just miserable," I said." How is your Dad this weather?"

"He died last year."

"I heard. Sad news."

"You bastard!"

"Listen, Ed…"

"What?"

"I don't like you. Please don't talk to me ever again. If you see me, just walk on. I am operating here under the purely hypothetical assumption you have a mind of your own. You do have a mind of your own? Is there a mind left after all that passive learning? All that ambition? That need to please?"

"Please, just listen to me. Just shut up and listen? Please Gordon? I know you don't like me—"

"Er, no."

"And I understand."

"I refer you to my previous impassioned diatribe."

But Frasier was always tenacious. He persevered.

"It's cold and it's Christmas. And we haven't seen each other in over twenty years."

"Good!"

"And we have, as they say, history. What do you say we take a time

out for a while, go somewhere and sit down and have a drink and let me say my piece?"
"No."
"Please Gordon. Ten minutes?"
"No."
"Ten minutes and you need never see me again for the rest of our natural lives."
"I'm calling the police."
Frasier looked at the passing people with their chatting and their shopping and seemed a little lost. Then he smiled and, reaching out to me said:
"I need to talk to you. Okay?"
"No."
"It's Christmas. Goodwill and all that."
"I see. Goodwill, hum. Let me think that over for a millisecond. Hm, let me see. Oh, there- I have it – Er, No!"
"Come with me, Gordon Brock. Ten minutes, Ok?"
"'No' is not a word that really seems to penetrate, is it?"
"Go on."
"Let me put it to you this way. I do not, will not, cannot and will not ever meet with you, talk to you and/or have any kind of interaction with you not now. Not ever, never. If your major organs failed before me, I would rejoice. If your very being and memory were erased from history, it would be a rather happy thing. Now please fuck off and stay in the perpetual state of fuckedoffness!"
Frasier smiled a little, steeled himself, and in a pleasant voice said:
"Look, Brock, there's a nice warm bar just two minutes from here, ok?"
"Go fuck yourself, Frasier, OK?"
"Please?"

2.

I walked with Frasier to Arthur's pub on Sackville Place and we looked for a spot to sit down. On the television Tiger Woods was scoring another triumph. Customers sat with pints of beer and ate turkey and ham and Brussels sprouts and mashed potato. The air was suffused with the invigorating smell of steaming hot food and Guinness on tap.

"He's quite the genius isn't he?" Ed said.

"Tiger Woods?"

"Tiger Woods. I love him. If I were gay, I would marry him and have his children."

"He is arrogant because he cannot allow himself to be aware of the possibility of failure he lives with every moment of his life. One slip and down he goes," I said.

"Like you," Frasier said.

"Really?"

"Yes, really," Ed said.

"Why really?"

"Because Woods has achieved his potential."

"Ah, I see. We are back to that. Look, seeing as we are here, what would you like?" I asked.

"A cappuccino."

I turned to the bar woman, who smiled and nodded to me.

"Cappuccino and a hot toddy please. And a bowl of soup too. Oh and I am going to go for a few of those little bread rolls I saw in that big basket by the bar on the way in."

"Great."

The waitron scribbled furiously.

"And some butter?"

"No problem, I'll get it sent over to you. Take a seat. Anything else?" She smiled.

"We have," I said. "Taken a seat."

"So I see," she said.

We had acquired a corner seat, far from the bar, beneath a cool light in the nether ends of the pseudo old world pub, which was filled with old lanterns and old suitcases and fake musical instruments and old motorbikes mounted on the wall and worn out advertisements for carcinogenic cigarettes and how Guinness was really good for you. We sat in that pub, miraculously near the fire, and I looked into Edward Frasier's eyes and he looked back at me.

"Frasier?"
"Yes?"
"I have a question."
"Sounds portentous," he said.
"So," I said, "How long have you been watching me?"
"I'm sorry?" He said, raising his eyebrows and smiling meekly in mock shock.
I said:
"You waited until you had an opportunity to accidentally-on-purpose bump into me and here's the soup, oh and the drinks too."
"Eh, no I didn't, er, follow you, Gordon. We met by accident. Wow, paranoid man. You are not that important."
"Absolutely, Frasier, absolutely. I am insignificant to you. Hence your burning need to talk."
I looked into the steaming hot soup and broke a little of the fresh brown bread that came with it and smiled a thank you to the woman who brought it, ignoring the nicely warmed bread rolls that sat in a nice bowl beside the brown bread. Ed tipped her generously when I tried to pay. He sipped his cappuccino and winced.
"How's the cappuccino?" She asked.
"Almost undrinkable," Frasier said.
"I see. We will sort that out for you, sir," the woman had not left.
"Soup's good. Toddy is excellent, by the way," I said.
"Great."
Then suddenly the waitron had vanished to another table with Frasier sitting in front of his rancid coffee.
"Soo, Eddie my sociopathic interlocutor."
"What? What the fuck did you just call me?"
"I said, 'so Eddie, my sociopathic.'"
"What? Fuck you."
"Tell me. How long have you been an alcoholic?"
Ed didn't answer. He flushed with an angry embarrassment.
"Fuck you," he said. "I came here to make peace."
"I imagined that to be the plan. There are things that can't be fixed."
"Very emo of you," Ed said.
"Not so much emo as true," I said.
"It's also not so much a plan as a wish list. It's Christmas."
"Made a searching and fearless moral inventory of yourself, then?"
"This is such bullshit. I am wasting my time," Ed said.
"You are wasting time, our time."
"You are still a child, Gordon Brock, an angry hurt child."
"And you are a psychopath, Edward Frasier, a cruel heartless

manipulative generally unpleasant —"
"You just called me a sociopath, and before a psychopath. Isn't there a difference?"
"Absolutely."
"And? Go on!"
"Well, Ed. You see, the two words are spelled differently. That's a difference. They both refer to you. Everything has and always will be about you. In your mind the entire world exists to bolster your egomania. People exist to reflect upon and serve your fractured self."
"You never made peace with who you are, Brock. You had potential."
"I am not sure what that means."
"It's a quote from one of your books."
"Really, and you were dumb enough to read them?"
"Er, yes. A few of them were good, actually."
"No, no they weren't. I have made my own way, and I am not answerable to you for my history."
"No-one said you —"
"But you know your story, don't you?"
"Don't go there —" Ed began.
"I mean, Ed, you did well. You always got great marks. You brought home the results. You made your parents proud. And then suddenly someone new comes along. Someone smaller. Someone less well adjusted. Someone who succeeded without even trying."
"So, Gordon. Supposing that's true?"
"Oh Ed, I know that's true,"
"Ok, you're right. I was jealous of you. For all kinds of reasons. I accept that."
"You do? Well that's just great."
"What have you done with your life, Gordon? I mean really?"
"That's none of your business. Really. None. You turn up in my life after decades and you ask me questions like that?"
"You became a therapist. You wrote self-help books. What about those novels you wrote afterwards? They were really good. I mean you couldn't help yourself. You packed those crappy self help books full of useful insights and deep learning."
"So what?" I said.
"So what? Are you so blind you can't see the truth about yourself? You were brilliant. You had real genius. You churned out those books without a second thought. You took the easy route because you pitied yourself and you let your demons get the better of you."
"No. You must have someone else in mind"
"Yes! There was no end to what you were capable of."

"I had no such gifts. You mistook good parenting for the kind of gifts one sees maybe once in a lifetime. I was not that person. You believed the hype and you demonised me."
"Yes, I did. I demonised you because you dazzled. You dazzled and you wasted it. You crashed and burned."
"You shot me down," I said.
"Yes."
"Yes?"
"Yes, I did. I shot you down, Gordon."
"But you didn't see me burn. You don't know that. Tell me, Edward the confessor, have you admitted to God, to yourself, and to another human being the exact nature of your wrongs?"
"Have you? You never learned to forgive. I understand that. You need to forgive me!"
The question hit me. Ed looked calmly at me.
"Sometimes, Gordon, I think intelligence is wasted on the intelligent. You are a fucking idiot."
"True," I said.
"You're divorced."
"Who isn't these days?"
"You have two children,"
"Three. Remember my oldest son, Joshua? He works in insurance now. Doing well. The other two are still in school."
"Okay, three."
"Good."
"All of whom are troubled."
"Eh, no, they are not troubled. They are relatively happy and rather loved."
"You are living on some farm in the middle of nowhere with someone who you only occasionally get to see," frasier said.
"Wrong again! I have a close personal relationship with Lucia. Tsk, tsk, Ed- Who are you paying for your information?"
"What? Nobody! You are so paranoid!"
"Whoever they are —"
"Nobody, Gordon, you crazy-. You need to file all this away. Get over yourself. Forgive and forget."
"They are obviously overly fond of the old Bolivian marching powder."
I mimicked a cocaine sniffing action with my fingers and nose, and chuckled.
"I paid no one. I was always interested in you."
"Sounds somewhere in the realm of restraining order, Edward

Frasier. Do I need to make a call?"

I made a loud hailer shape with my two hands and leaned near Ed Frasier. Then I said:

"Dr. Edward Frasier, now hear this: It is not simply that you tortured me. It is the effects of that torture. It's the kind of carnage it wreaks on one's person, one's family, and life, and capacities to make friends and form bonds. It's what it does to one's self-belief, one's capacity to think clearly, one's tendency towards illness and dementia."

"Get over it, Gordon. You are not unique. I am here to make amends."

I sat back and smiled sunnily at Frasier. His brow was furrowed. He was sweating and pale. I said:

"And you know what, I just think that's super, Ed. It's really heartening. Except it's an illusion. There's no such thing as making amends. It's a religious delusion."

Edward ignored that and, as the waitron passed us, he turned to her and said, "Hi," and smiled at the girl, who smiled back. "Can I just say something?"

"Sure," she said.

"There is something terribly wrong with my coffee."

"Okay we can change it." She said.

"Sorry to trouble you," Ed said.

"No problem," she said.

She took it back.

"Okay, Gordon. I just, I just wanted to make amends to you. I beat you," Frasier said.

"No, really? Good heavens! Did you really? You beat me up? You know I'd forgotten. I'd say it must be all the brain damage. Must be why I failed so terribly in life, chose badly in friendships, and hate the living sight of you, you pompous supercilious, holier-than-thou, judgemental, hypocritical creep."

"I deserve that."

"There really is no talking to you, is there?"

"I nearly killed you. I accept that."

"Yes, indeed you did. That is correct. Daddy would indeed be proud of his son's forthright honesty. Now, you could say I could have killed you too, but then what happened in the garden, well, it was an accident…so, Dr. Frasier, the charge is attempted murder."

"I could have killed you."

"Ditto. We just covered that ground, you motherfu..."

"There is no way I can go back in time and take away what happened."

"You know something, Frasier, I am working on that." I pointed to my cranium and, tapping it a bit, said: "Trained mind, you know. Plenty of money and time on my hands. The pleasures of bourgeois intellectualism."

"Hah, that's funny." Frasier gave a fake chuckle. He suddenly stopped himself grinning, and went on: "And I am not here trying to make excuses for what I did."

"That's equally heartening."

"I am here to unequivocally apologize."

"Great. I am so happy for you. Apology accepted. Now go away and never come back. And keep your private detectives with their electronic snoopers and brothel creeping secrets off my private turf."

"If you want to file charges against me, I will plead guilty."

"I would rather detail your crimes in print. How about that?"

"Okay."

"So, you are okay with my writing about you?"

"Yes."

"Everything you did."

"Yes."

"And you are aware of libel laws and all the rest?"

"Yes."

"Right, okay. Are you insane?"

"You seem to think so, Gordon."

"Frasier, people will know it was you."

"I know."

Ed sobbed a little, and then suppressed the sob. His chin trembled a little. Then, centering himself, he spoke calmly:

"I want to make amends. I have carried this guilt."

"And you want me to take the pain away."

He reached out to me across the table, his voice trembling. I instinctually withdrew, as if he proffered me a potent toxin. He went on,

"If you want me to pay you reparations for the damage, I will. Or call the police."

"Don't be ridiculous! There's a universe of difference between justice and the law."

"I know we were very young at the time and I —"

"Why?" I asked.

"What?"

"Why did you nearly kill me?"

The renewed coffee arrived with a flaked chocolate stick on the side and a small apple Danish by way of apology.

"I thought I answered that. The jealousy thing, I guess. I guess. I was

a bastard, that's why."
"Mmm, interesting and accurate technical term."
"I was evil." He took a draught of the creamy cappuccino, softening the lump in his throat.
"You believe in evil?" I asked.
"I believe in evil."
"What is evil?"
"The opposite of love. What I did, I did out of envy. I envied your gifts. I disliked your, well your difference."
"You mean hate. You hated me and were a bigot."
"What?"
"Hate is the opposite of love."
"We're not talking dictionary definitions here, Gordon!"
"Beg to differ, Doctor Frasier. Saying evil is the opposite of love doesn't actually unpack any real information."
"Fuck you!" He snarled, then he calmed himself, and smiled a little. "You are a twisted man, Gordon Brock."
"Thank you, Ed. Okay then, this meeting is over. You have done your twelve-step thing and I am touched to the core. Now, as I said before in so many ways, please leave me, alone!"
I glanced at my non-existent watch.
"My heavens, will you just look at the time! I really got to go, Ed."
"Sure you do. Do what you do so fucking well! Run away!"
"Nice seeing you again."
"Right. Charming."
"I wish you well."

Ed looked askance at me. He wanted conflict and I was too frightened of the truth. He wanted the real deal between us to emerge from the dark of our denial. He wanted us to sit together in the snug for the Christmas hours and forensically trawl over the details of our differing biographies, talk about his career in London, all the monies he made, his marriage, his children, the death of his parents, his incipient alcoholism, my divorce from Martha, my affair with Lucia, how he hit rock bottom, how the very core of his life and marriage and career buckled under his addiction, all the terrible cruelties he inflicted on others to do well to get on, while I talked about my depression and my failure to achieve anything despite my much vaunted gifts, how I took my doctorate then went in to psychotherapy. I wrote self-help books, made money, then disappeared off the grid. He wanted us to communicate. What we have here, I thought cinematically. What we have here is. What we have here is a failure; and I saw it. I saw that cool hand look, the sad angry look of insupportable disappointment.

I knew it. My ex-wife used look at me like that too.

This is what that look said to me:

'Why won't you talk to me? Why won't you do the right thing and connect with me? After all these years. After the offspring and the days and the hours of worrying and solving things together? Why don't you connect? Don't you want love? Don't you want to be loved and to love? How could someone so gifted be so stupid and alone? What's wrong with you?'

I did. I wanted to. And because I wanted to, I would withdraw. As soon as I began to feel the near irresistible gravitational pull of personal investment, I would withdraw, because to not withdraw would be to suffer destruction, the insupportable pain of annihilation. Once they found me, found out who I was, they would get me. They always did.

"Don't do this, Gordon."

Ed understood what was happening. I smiled bashfully, and then, assuming a serious look, I said.

"What?"

"Don't walk away. Don't play the burn-out."

"The burn-out? Thank you."

"A burn-out, a fucked up, burn-out genius,"

"I'm no genius. And have you ever thought there are some things that can't be forgiven?"

"No, I wouldn't be here if I thought that"

"Please fuck off, as a personal favour."

"A sad burn-out."

But he didn't go. He shook his head and sipped his cappuccino. Our voices were beginning to rise. Faces were turning discreetly towards us. I smiled at Ed and said.

"You are assuming that I have something to contribute, or want to contribute."

"Now that's delusional thinking."

"Ever think that might be a waste of time? Ever think that most of everything lovely and worthwhile dies before ever flowering?"

"Even if that were true, it doesn't matter."

"Oh really?"

"Yes."

"Why? Because you say so?"

"You failed yourself."

"That's for me to decide," I said.

"Don't blame me for what you became."

"I have a file on you, Ed Frasier. I'm gonna get you."
"Fuck you!" Frasier yelled. Suddenly both of us were standing, with the table, the soup, the cappuccino and the hot toddy between us, in one of those Hollywood face-off moments. Ed towered above me. I pointed between his eyes and said,
"Remember Edward Frasier, you got yours too. You got your punishment from your higher power."
"I have no idea in the wide —" Then he knew. He got it. He heard my message. He looked at me with horror. He knew. Got him, I thought. A small smile played on my lips.
"Ever wonder why the culprit never got caught? Eh?" I said. And I walked away.
"We need to finish this!" Ed yelled after me.

Because I could not stand the truth, because I could not stand the weakness and the surrender of reconciliation, because I could not let go of all that happened, because I had not forgiven either of us for all that we had done, because I nurtured my guilt like a new born lamb, because I loved my hatred of Edward Frasier, I walked away.

"No wonder your life is in the toilet!" He yelled after me, and tossed the soup bowl on the ground in a burst of rage that would no doubt be talked about at his next encounter group meet. On hearing the clatter of a soup spoon on the pub's stone floor, and the cessation of background noise, I stopped walking away. I turned and said:
"You know something, Edward? I like you. You're not like the other sociopaths that St. Raymond's moulded. I mean, don't misunderstand me; they all were successful professionals, just like you, all good ruthless citizens. But what I like about you is, despite all the soul searching and the therapy, you still want to kill me. And I like that. You're not like the others, Mister Edward Frasier."

And he didn't say another word, and I left. As I turned to go, I saw him as he shook his head and got his stuff. I assume security staff escorted the well-heeled doctor to the door. I was long gone by then, returning to my guilty compensatory shopping and depressive thinking.

3.

I stormed out of the pub. Then I turned left, walked back onto O'Connell Street. I was feeling crazy. I was struggling to regain self-control. I felt more hatred in my heart than I ever considered possible. And, worse, I still had that horrible feeling of someone watching. Someone saw into me. Someone saw beneath the gifts I had bought for Christmas. I felt eyes watching me. Those eyes saw underneath the clothing that protected me. Those eyes saw that I was wrong and that Ed was right. I felt that even the most cursory glance at my basic credentials, a quick glimpse of facial structure, of hair, choice of language, clothing, beneath the brain that thought and dreamed, beneath all my signs of life, that Ed was right about my failure to achieve my potential.

And because Ed was right, he should suffer for this truth. I fantasised the punishment I should mete out for his hurting me by reminding me of this truth was death, or perhaps something worse than death, a state which inevitably brings an end to pain. Yes, I thought, I should kill him, or better still, I thought, as I window-shopped for the apocalypse, as I looked for happy Christmas seasonal gifts, I made a list and checked it twice.

My Christmas List: Torturing/Killing Ed Frasier

1. Put him in a position where he remains alive, yes, but he has to kill someone he loves. Maybe, I thought, as I bought chocolates and perfume and cuddly toys, maybe if I put him in a position where he either has to kill himself, or someone he loves.

2. Or make him long for death, I thought, as I smiled at a beautiful child talking with her mummy who kissed her and gave her hot chocolate as she stood in front of an outrageously overpriced Christmas toy store, as street traders sold batteries and tinsel and chocolates and toys and Santa hats and wind-up planes and cars, I should give him a choice where he either kills his wife or himself.

3. Or, I thought, maybe something better. I imagined Ed Frasier put into a position where he watches his family conduct their lives happily, but he is absent. Perhaps Ed is watching his family live on a television screen in a dank underground room, and his family are there on screen and carrying on happily obliviously and I walk into the room and Ed is all bound up and I propose a choice. Either Ed kills me or I kill his

family. No, I thought. Forget that. I might have to carry out my threat. He might care more for himself than his family.

Note: all these delusions involve hurting people other than Ed Frasier in order to hurt Ed Frasier. That's fucked-up.

And I took myself back to the hotel, threw the gifts I had bought on the floor and lay on my bed and I looked around the room and I remembered Dad, my Dad, David Brock. I remembered his death, his sad, peaceful, beautiful, hospital-bed death. I thought about that for a moment, then fixed myself a drink. I poured a large brandy, put on some mind-numbing television, and rang Martha, my former wife. Martha is my present wife, Lucia's, half-sister.

"Hi Martha, it's Gordon."

"Gordon! Happy Christmas. How's life in the depths of the forest?"

"Good. You coming over this year?"

"Not this year. I'm with Joshua and Penny in Galway."

"Lucia and I will miss you. I must give Joshua a ring, see how my handsome successful, good-looking boy and his wife doing."

"We will miss you too. Give my love to Lucia. How's Lucia?"

"Okay, fine, thanks for asking. You are not going to believe who I met."

"How's the writing? I really loved those novels you wrote. I never told you that, but they were good. And the reviews were good."

"Busy. I think I have an ending in sight."

"That's great! When can I read it?"

"I dunno."

"Sorry, I side-tracked you. But I have some fantastic news. Joshua has been promoted."

"I see."

"You don't sound too excited, Gordon."

"I am. I am delighted. Has he been promoted into management?"

"Yes!"

"Wonderful!"

"Who did you meet?"

"I just ran into… nobody really. I must tell you about my new book. It's an autobiographical piece, fictional really."

"Now I am really curious. Go on, who did you meet?"

"I ran into Ed Frasier."

"Really? Wow!"

"Really. Yes, really."

"That is amazing, Gordon."

"He was following me."

"Wow, that's scary."

"Oh yes, he is completely insane. But I realised something. I realised I have been lying to myself all my life. I realised that what he said about me is true. I realised that I have to tell it as it is. I have to tell."

"Go on," she said.

4.

Martha and I had sex the first time we met. I was overwhelmed on meeting her. At the moment of seeing her, I knew we were meant to be together. I had no doubts whatsoever. At the time of coitus, I was supposedly in an exclusive relationship with Lorna Burroughs. At the time, though I felt mega-guilt over betraying Lorna, it didn't stop me seeing Martha. I was living with Lorna in a big old tumbledown house that doubled as consulting rooms for psychotherapy clients. Martha, my future first, and only, ex-wife, was, at that time, living with the loathsome, arrogant, condescending, awful human being, Dr. Richard Smith. Martha subsequently broke up with Richard, while I, not being the breaking up kind, preferred to let matters dissolve between Lorna and me. But Lorna wasn't one to let matters easily dissolve. She fought to keep me, and the more aggressive she became, the more I withdrew. The situation got ugly towards the end.

Speaking of things getting ugly, Richard, the other person in this love quadrangle, was, like Lorna, someone who never really got over breaking up. Richard Smith never got over breaking up, with Martha that is. Despite the commanding ego one encountered on meeting him, the bass voice, the handsome, rugged, earthy features, the ready smile, the apparently indomitable will, here was a vulnerable and uncertain person. Afterwards Dickie meandered through several marriages and casual affairs, like a lonely explorer looking for a lost self in some vast continent. He remained, from what I hear, as arrogant and hostile as ever and so rarely made meaningful connections with others. He holds some towering position of authority in oncology in Cork.

Moving on, though: Martha, on the other hand, didn't get lost in this little relational tsunami. Her relationship with Richard was a mixture of intense erotic passion coupled with the happiness associated with being in relationship with someone who was beautiful and intelligent and charming and an achiever and successful and well-connected. Dr. Richard Smith came from a good family in a good area of Dublin. Richard came from a family who had money and an attractive family home that was decorated with exquisite taste. Richard had parents who were simply delightful and loving and moral and liked opera and read good books. They were people who aroused suspicion and gossip and dislike because of their goodness and morality. Richard was close to his parents and to his relatives. Richard remembered happy childhood holidays in the sun. Richard had done well in his exams and succeeded well without appearing to have tried too hard, and despite all this catalogue of overwhelming achievement, Richard Smith said he loved Martha Reynolds. Richard wanted to be with Martha. They were engaged to be married. But, in the end, she married me. And, after she married me, she got bitter about Richard. I didn't like it much, this bitterness. She used say things like: 'Richard was someone who, deep down felt everyone was entitled to Richard's opinions', which, from what I recall of his character, was totally true. When Martha said this, she made sure she was in the company of people who would repeat her comment. She also made sure her voice was like ice, the kind of icy ironic voice that mimics a sense of self-possession without the burden of actually having to maintain such a difficult characteristic. And Richard, who would hear these comments back, would get dreadfully upset, for he didn't like this pretentious verbal cut and thrust channelled via the social network of innuendo, the gossip cyberspace. Despite treating her disdain with a little light wit, Richard, as I said, was someone who hurt easily. Prickly and self-loathing. As you may have gathered, I really didn't like him. Richard knew intimately Martha's inverted snobbery, her social ambitions. He knew Martha was afflicted with the delusion that social advancement led to a better life. She never lost that delusion, even after Martha left Richard for me.

I said to her:
"You are being a snob and an idiot, Martha. Richard's name is, well, just his name. It it his public credential hiding an innate sense of inferiority, his need to go up the social and professional ladder, and his unhappiness at succeeding without really trying. He was the ordinary extraordinary Richard Smith who had made it big. Let him have that and let it go."
"He told me over the phone I must be clinically insane to hook up with you. He said you were an incredibly fucked up genius."
"Really? Probably a bitter man. I imagine he hates to lose." I said.
"I didn't know I was a kind of prize," Martha said.
I didn't answer. I thought of her as a prize, and felt guilty and paranoid about that.

But, before we finally got together, Martha liked the social circle Smith was peripherally touching. She liked striding in this Dublin Valhalla, maybe I should call it Tir Na nÒg, mixing with the immortals, even if Richard was not yet one of them, even if she, Martha, was only a visitor, for now.

Before Martha met me, she and Richard were very committed to each other, devoted really. They were engaged to be married. They were sharing a home. Moreover and unusually, at least among the couples I knew, they even shared bank accounts and money, and took strifeless holidays regularly together. They met each others' parents and, after a proper length of time, Richard proposed to Martha during a lobster dinner at McGinley's Restaurant off Baggot Street. It's gone now, that restaurant where Richard waxed Joycean and talked about 'Baggot Maggot Street' and talked about everything with his own personal sense of omniscience, filled with clever subconscious metaphor, choosing the moments where it was appropriate to insert into the conversation a sufficiently intimidating, but not too supercilious, cultural, historical, or philosophical reference; for Richard enjoyed his own erudition, and liked to remind others in his company how well educated he was, how intelligent he was, and how the burden of his own potential weighed him down. And Martha looked down at the dinner and didn't like lobsters: clawed crawlers, creatures with creepers at home at the bottom of the sea, in suits of armor tentacling across the ocean floor, packing fashionable battle proof Kevlar for crustaceans, civilizations – living, marrying, eating, sleeping in another world, a world other than our own. It's like Dublin High Society, she thought. O my god, did anyone hear that, she thought? No, that was a thought, she told herself, and looked self-consciously at her future ex-fiancé. Let them be, the lobster people. Let them over populate, she would think. There are other predators that can eat them. She looked guiltily hungrily at the claw cuffed lobsters as the waiter politely expertly held one in each hand. Now madam, pick your next victim. Those pink creatures with feelers. Creeping along the sand. Striding Atlas-like along the bottom of the world. Water world on their back. It's too awful, the death I chose for them. She thought- we are mostly water too. Or were they brown? No pink. Colour not particularly an issue when one can lay the code of which we are made, line after line of letters and in the end the difference is all somewhat digital.

"That one", she pointed. Kill him. Kill him until he is dead. For a moment Martha imagined being boiled alive. The slow awareness of rising temperature. Thrashing around in a liquid that is cooking you and one that doesn't really have a very high boiling point, either.
"You were meant to be a vegetarian," Richard said, reaching over and with immense tenderness, stroking her hair.

"How did you know what I was thinking about?" She asked.
"I guessed."
"Is it oversensitive to worry about the death of other creatures? When I was little, I remember hearing crying at our front door. And there was this beautiful little black cat crying and mewing at the front door. My parents wouldn't let me take it in. I cried myself to sleep for days and days afterwards, thinking about where that little cat went."
"That's very sad. That's what I love about you. You are so sensitive and deep and thoughtful and caring."
"Really?"
"It's kind of why I do what I do. Because —"
"But," Martha interrupted. "Don't you do what you do because it was expected of you?"
"No."
"Oh. Can I ask you something?"
"Sure. Go on."
"When you have a patient anesthetized in front of you, do you think of them as living?"
"I do. But I am more concerned about getting it right and working well."
And she looked at his face, his hands. Those surgeon's fingers, she loved them, her heart on his sleeve.
"Okay", she said. And she could hear the ocean calling. And they served Mister Pink. Mister Pink, he dead. And she cracked his shell. Yummy.
"The food is delicious," Martha said,
"It's tasty because it's flesh", he said.
"It's tasty because our brains are programmed to like it," Martha said.
"What if it was human?" Dickie said.
"Why are you doing this?" Martha asked, feeling a dread rise within her.
"What?"
"Aren't we supposed to be on some kind of date, Richard?"
"Yes."
"I mean do we really need to talk about eating human flesh?"
"Two million years ago, we developed tools strong enough to be able to get at the organs and the muscles of other animals."
"Well thanks for sharing that grossness, Richard."
"It's what triggered our brains increasing in size."
"That's fascinating darling."
"I mean our brains only take up five percent of our body weight, but they consume twenty percent of our calorific intake."

"What a waste of energy."
"Okay, what if the human flesh were served in an acceptable manner?"
"Er, no."
"Why not?"
"Richard, for God's sake!"
"Sorry, you are right."
"This is hard to cope with, even as a thought."
"But Martha, many species eat their own kind."
"I don't, okay?" Martha said, getting less hungry.
"In the wilderness, when it grows dark, creatures eat each other, sometimes their own offspring. The amount of suffering in nature is simply unthinkable."

Martha didn't flinch. She looked at him, for a moment afraid he was serious. Then Richard cracked a mischievous smile and they laughed out loud as people looked at them with more than a pinch of disapproval. And then the onlookers returned to their own absorbing table conversation, the restaurant overburdened with moneyed guests and condescending waiters, whose constant attentions and overpriced fare gave an air of nervous liturgical gravitas to the evening that the guests handled with the same gentle indifference they wore as beautifully as their designer casuals and caring smiles and gentle, artful conversation.

"Such a pretentious little place," she said.
"I think I chose it."
"Yes Richard, You did."
"Social aficionados."
"And this is what you want."
"What? What do I want?"
"Well, I guess, to be part of the group that makes the decisions."
"Power?"
"Isn't it, Richard?"
Richard didn't answer.
"People are here to be seen to be here," Martha said, annoyed he wouldn't be honest with her, musing on a life spent as the appendage to an egomaniacal politically-minded, career-obsessed, self-advancing social climber, then suppressing the sense of disapproval of that part of him and wondering about their mutual future, and if he loved her, and her said he loved her, she needed assurances.
"Ah, you mean you want to be like them," she continued.
"No I don't!" He snapped. "What about you?"
"So? What about me?" She leaned closer, almost hissing at him.

"You're the social climber here, not me!" He said.
"Maybe not any more. Maybe not since I got to put my hand inside the cage of upmarket life. Maybe I got bitten."
"I see. Well these people are my friends."
"These people don't know you, Richard."
"I see."
"But I do."
"Okay," he said.
"Okay, then, let's get a take out, go home, and have sex."
"Look, we have ordered. And we are already eating!"
"So?"
"So, let's finish our meal, and not come back. Okay? Will that satisfy you?"
"Oh, we'll be back here. You like this place."
"Look, we can go anywhere you want, really Martha. I'm not that attached to the place."
"I know that. I mean, I think you believe that."
"So what's the problem? I mean, I thought you liked this place."
"I mean I do. I know we come here a lot, but —"
"And?"
"It's just hard to relax in and enjoy yourself when there is such an amount of ceremony around having your dinner. I just prefer somewhere quiet, or something."
"There's a difference between dining and having your dinner," he said.
"I mean it would be nice if you'd mentioned that before we booked the place, wouldn't it... Martha?"

Perhaps that's why he chose this place, she thought. Or was it me? No, it was him. A flash of rage, a sense of suffocation, a fury at herself for inflicting another's will on herself yet again, as she looked across at this beautiful man with his delicate regular features, this gateway to a better life, as though suddenly, for the briefest moment, her anger had burned away the mirage his beauty had for so long sustained, his slim near perfect doctor's hands, beautiful body, his eyes so dark, so intelligent, so hurt and so alive, and that winning smile that was not simply the product of careful dentistry. You just knew how lovable and special Richard was. He had been talking and talking, as was his habit, a practised conversationalist, talking about this and that, then, with the same degree of casualness he discussed shopping for socks and underwear and wine, he started talking about love and marriage:
"Do you know why people marry?" He asked.
"You know the answer to that," I said.
"I am asking what you think, he said.

"Love?"
"I don't think so. Anything else?"
"No, do tell."
"Because they want to," he said.
"Fascinating. That's —"
"I think so."
"I thought people married for love, and security, money and stuff like that."
"Love is chemistry," he said." It's programming."
"I'm looking forward to following the program."
"Look, I am not specifically talking about our relationship."
"You mean our chemical bond," Martha said.
"I'm not discounting —"
"Really?"
"We feel incomplete if we don't pair off. All that bohemian crap about living together for a time then moving on to the next love affair leads to middle-aged misery and loneliness and empty-headed nonsense about freedom of choice."
"I think you are over-thinking this."
"Maybe I am."
"Can't we just-?"
"Absolutely. Sorry, I just don't know how I got into this."
There followed a minute to two of respectful silence, but Richard couldn't stop talking about what was on his mind.
"It's built into being human. And it does as much damage as it does good."
Martha tossed her lobster back onto her plate. Put her shoulders back onto her soft chair and looked angrily at him and said:
"Do you want us to break up?"
"No!"
"Is that what you want? Because you are going the right way about it!"
"Who said anything about that? Jesus!"
"You just dismissed our entire life together."
"Eh? No- no I didn't."
"And you reduced love to a reflex!"
"I didn't really. I said it was a very complex thing. I said it had a physical and non-physical part. I discussed a theory about relationships. I might be wrong."
"Well, thank goodness for that, Richard! Maybe you are!"

And he smiled and didn't answer. It is impossible to know for sure whether he loves me, Martha thought; or why I should doubt he loves me; or whether worrying about something I can never know for sure is really the right way to carry on with a narcissist like Richard Smith. Looking at him there in the restaurant, sipping wine and smiling, eating, it was all so unclear, so difficult to follow a thought down these blind alleys of feeling. You can't think this through; she declared herself bankrupt of vision. It's like asking if there's a god, she thought. She looked down at her body, just for the briefest second.

"Is everything all right, darling?" He smiled, noticing her pain.

"Sure."

"Sure?"

"Yes, fine."

"I'm a condescending, arrogant…I don't know why I say these things. I don't mean to dismiss anything."

"No, no. No, you're not. You were just talking."

"Sorry. That's my biggest personal shortcoming."

"What?"

"My tendency to use words. Worse, I tend to use words in sentences. It's appalling, really. I should shut the hell up and listen to people."

And Martha smiled and kissed Richard. This is why he loves me, she thought. He loves me because I look like this. I am attractive. No, no how could I think that? I'm beautiful, an appendage to his identity. No, not that. He loves me for who I am. Maybe. If I were scarred and dowdy would he love me? I will say yes. I will say yes, because he loves me. Because I love him. Because I am impulsive. Because I can't be alone. Not that I am alone. Not that. No.

And, on the way home, they stopped the car in the Phoenix Park and made love up a quiet drive. And she drove home slowly and they watched the lights tracking the passing cars, feeling somewhat stoned.

5.

GETTING AHEAD IN THE LUCRATIVE BUSINESS OF PEOPLE MANAGEMENT

I met Lorna Burroughs at a seminar. I remember the title of the seminar. It was Getting Ahead in the Lucrative Business of People Management. We got talking because of mutual interests. We were reading the same books. She was reading the same books as I was because she was completing her degree in some aspect of psychoanalysis I had no interest in. I was doing a doctorate. We began to date. We talked a lot. We laughed a lot. We realised we were in love. It felt right, the two of us being together. We began to make plans for a life together. We moved in together. I did not question this natural progression, this caring, warm, enriching, fulfilling, happy, stimulating love we had. I did not feel any angst about the meaning of this relationship in relation to any other relationship one might have, this coupling. It seemed a pointless thing to try to search for meaning in one's shared history with another person, as if, amidst the billions that were born and died, that it might be possible one would encounter the predetermined perfect life partner in one single person. Lorna and I seemed to fit. I guess I found a more compatible partner when I met Martha Reynolds, and even more so with her half-sister Lucia, though I know writing this might cause Lucia pain.

Lorna and I were, for the time we lived together, compatible. Then we grew apart. I was unfaithful to her. That was my way of trying to break free. The problem was Lorna needed more than anything to be needed. She shielded this desperate need beneath a hard outer shell of independence. She was brilliant, fragile, vulnerable, sensitive, artistically inclined, self-absorbed, slightly depressive, intellectual, and, infuriatingly, needed to possess the beloved as much as she hated her dependence on being so possessive, so controlling. For Lorna, power and love, I think, were the same thing. For her, if one were in control, then one could love. This was something I discovered only after a year or two. It poisoned things between us. She sought power, amassed qualifications, took over conversations, interrupted constantly, pretended to love the social swirl, threw lots of parties she hated really, and enjoyed a wide circle of friends to whom she was obsessively loyal. She did those things that took away her sense of isolation and insecurity. She did things to fill her gnawing hunger, that sense of loss one noticed in her expression. She was something of an infomaniac, always reading, and though absorbed in books, was hypersensitive to changes around her. Nothing in our home could be moved without her agreement. 'I live here too, you know,' she would say. She seemed to sense almost telepathically what I was thinking. That upset me, this listening to the secret transmissions of my soul. I don't have a soul, I would think, I am an accident, a clever concatenation of clever accidents making a random me. I never wanted to hurt Lorna, which made it all the worse, which meant there was no easy, cowardly way out. Ending, like any execution, was cruel and unusual. Any last words? I thought. I ruminated for a long time on how to break free of her. I feared we might have a child together. Then I worried, I would never be free.

I said: "You kill the thing you love."

We were lying on the floor, half dressed on the carpet of our beautifully understated living room, replete with serious books and tasteful art, after unplanned sex."That's Oscar Wilde," Lorna said. "De Profundis."

"Bingo," I said. "Mind of the librarian," I said.

"Thank you; you say that with much irony in your voice." Ready reference, head full of data going nowhere, I thought. She's lost in a forest of misinformation. A mapless Blair Witch seeker.

Lorna rolled over, and, leaning on her elbow, her curls falling over her face began self consciously rubbing the hair on my chest as though looking for the vital organs underneath. Then she looked at me so closely, my eyes, my face, my shoulders.

"Well?" She said. "What's wrong?"

"Nothing. And you?"

"Something is wrong, with you," Lorna said. "Tell me."

"Nothing is wrong. I hate my job. I hate what I do. Nothing I write is going anywhere and I don't have an exit strategy. I don't want to be an academic. I don't want to be a therapist and yet I am really good at it. I am bored and frustrated and depressed and sometimes, to be honest, a little suicidal. Oh, and I really fucking hate my own self-involved depressions.

"Your body is so furry," she said.

"Really?" I said. "That's a really helpful response."

"The missing link. My missing link, so furry, I love you. Don't worry too much about your angst ridden musings. You are a genius. You will come up with a really clever solution." And she nuzzled her face into my chest and stomach smelling the smoky smell that was so distinctly mine.

"Yes, I love you too."

"You are so lean," she said. "I wouldn't call you thin. More like lean."

"Yes," I said. "But I was thin when I was younger. Too thin."

"Did you have a good appetite when you were a boy?"

"I did."

"I did too," she said.

"So you had a good appetite when you were a boy," I said, grinning.

And she pinched me mischievously.

"Noo," she smiled.

And we chuckled and we lay there till it got cold, for she did not warm me. At the time of our lovemaking, the one I just described, I had not betrayed Lorna. I had not been unfaithful. But, after I had sex with Martha, I guilt fantasised a proposal of marriage to Lorna. It would be a particularly beautiful proposal, filled with authentic love and a desire for a happy life, enacted in a rural setting in August, everything a deep verdant evening, with crickets making maraca sounds and wood pigeons cooing and a harvest moon silvering the heavy whispering leaves, a weighty presence of self renewing life. Look – a fox in the undergrowth, squirrels, rats and robins scuttling about. I see the fox, it's hard, fearless stare penetrating like a shaft from a longbow, then it is gone. Anyway, back to the guilt marriage proposal, and here we go. It's time to ask the big question:

"Lorna, my love."

She looks so beautiful tonight, so desirable.

Pause.

"Will you marry me?"

And then I stopped the fantasy. Now hold on there, pilgrim. I need to analyse the situation. Dredge some meaningful self-understanding from something which is definitely not quite right.

Questions:

1. Will I ask her because I have betrayed her? (Guilt)
2. Should I just go on until I know the right thing to do? (Hope)
3. Why would I go on with someone I obviously do not love? (Reason)
4. Look at other options:

Option (a) I'll ask her because she loves me. And love should be enough. (Romantic)

Option (b) I can sense her love and its ferocity terrifies me. (Pragmatic)

Option (c) The "Let's do lunch, let's talk it out in public," strategy.

Useful create a relaxed social environment where honest, unthreatening interaction can occur. (Therapeutic)

Problems:

The problem is how?

What words will I use?

Will the ruth about me make things better?

Will forgiveness? [1]

1 A brief epistemological interlude about words and what is beyond words before we move right on.They say you get past words, and beyond words comes the unknowable and you learn to sit there, just sitting there, as they like to cryptically put it, and then it's still, or maybe one might call it stillness, and sitting there in the stillness, you just know. How do you know you know? Or, more to the point, how do you know you do not know what you do not know? This is confusing. They say you know you know the unknowing, that which is beyond words. No external reference. Just seeing. As though today were any different and just sitting would take away that peculiar version of blindness and stupidity that makes me, well, me.

6.

I met Martha because of Bobby Lydon. Bobby Lydon worked as a divorce lawyer. Bobby was a man with all the charm of a hooded cobra. I mean he didn't look like a hooded cobra. But he was a nasty human being. Maybe, though, if I had never met Bobby Lydon through Lorna Burroughs, then I might not have met Martha Reynolds, and then never met her half-sister. Tricky situation.

Before I went to the party on the day I would meet Martha, I sat with my friend Seán O'Gorman, someone I met in college. Occasionally we got together. Seán O'Gorman was a long-time colleague, an ex-Jesuit, and a better human being than I. He looked like an aging Gandalf in an ill-fitting suit and snow white open-necked shirt. He sat there with long hair brushed away from his eyes, a long greying beard, and a bald patch at the top of his oversized head, and size sixteen black shoes. Seán, my friend, had a real gift, whereas I had training and knowledge and experience. I was sitting with him, the smell of perfumed café bodies and the mutterings of shopping conversation all around us.
"It's eleven in the morning, Gordon."
"That sounds like the title of a song," I said.
"- and you are irritatingly silent today."
"I know."
"What's the problem?"
"I have to go to a soirée with the most obvious corporate psychopath I have ever known, who happens to be a good friend of Lorna's."
"Well that should be fun. Tell me all about it, okay?" O'Gorman said.
"Okay then. Let's do dinner next week. Okay?"
"Okay then, I will see you soon."
And Seán ambled off as I did, moving his huge shoulders with each measured step, and I felt a certain loneliness seeing him go, as if this was the only person I ever felt completely at home with.

Usually I brought a paperback or magazine to get me through social gatherings. I always felt intense guilt and self-loathing at the annoyance and boredom I inevitably felt after a certain point in being around people. Sometimes I found other dysfunctional ways to cope. I would provoke or insult someone, in order to start an argument. I would sullenly withdraw from the discussion. Or, as on this occasion, when I couldn't leave, I would play a mental game. I was playing the game of Contrast and Compare. Contrast and compare O'Gorman and Lydon: Aside from the more obvious marked differences in physical dimensions – Seán over six feet in height, Lydon five foot eight inches. O'Gorman- homosexual. Lydon- heterosexual. Lydon ten stone in weight. O'Gorman at least sixteen. Seán was undiplomatic and direct. Lydon when not using expletives, had the right word for every moment. O'Gorman was well-read to the point of being a polymath, kept his knowledge to himself. Bobby let most know his moderate learning. Seán was self-possessed. Bobby was possessed. Seán was a friend for life. Lydon had too many friends. Bobby Lydon was a solicitor. Seán O'Gorman was a healer. Lydon was a predator. Seán was generally quiet. Lydon was a noisy manipulator and social climber.

But this was pointless, I thought. No games, not even Contrast and Compare worked. I hated this place. The game got dull. I felt annoyance building. Then I saw Lydon's cat looking resentfully at me on the sofa and stomped off amidst the conversing crowds. I wanted to stomp off just like Peaches the Cat.

Bobby lived with his fat imperious self-satisfied cat Peaches, who seemed to barely indulge Bobby's need to have somewhere half decent to live. Then I thought of how O'Gorman had finally settled down in his house in Tallaght, and, as I tried to be polite and make conversation, I tried to remember Seán O'Gorman's partner's name[2] I couldn't for 'the life of me remember the goddamm name. What was wrong with me? How could I forget the name of such a sweet man? What was it?

Anyway, so it goes. Lydon had made a pot of vegetarian chilli and had invited over one hundred and fifty or so few very special friends, thirty or so of whom turned up, as well as other clichéd people he hardly knew, they who turned up uninvited and came on over for food and drinks and generally descended on his apartment, eight or nine staying the obligatory hour and going on to other parties or meetings or family obligations. Peaches, in a fit of pique, climbed into a press in the kitchen in protest and refused to leave until every guest had gone. Bobby fed her in the press and brought her favourite toys by way of apology. She seemed placated, like some jealous lover who would not share her man or personal space. Then she curled up and snoozed.

2 Sean O'Gorman's life partner was called Gregory James Pritchard. Born 15/7/2---- to Phyllis and Rupert Prtichard, at Manchester General Hospital. Moved to London at age 14, Educated in St. James Public School, eventually qualified as an architect. Also holds advanced qualifications in modern dance (non-professional). Moved to Ireland after the death of his parents, mainly for career reasons. Met O'Gorman at a Poetry reading.

Friends brought wine and beer and desserts and snacks, and complemented him on his immaculate home and the delicious smell of food that wafted through his bright clean rooms, with their tasteful paintings, and panelling and reconstituted wood doors built from railway sleepers and old ships. Fabulous, they said. Simply Fabulous. I looked around, and liked the place, and looked at the old, weathered, reworked, reconditioned, chemically treated floor boards, deep treated wood like flat sculptures that carried deep within their fibres memories of other lives and shipwrecks and images of the old man and the sea and twisted Gothic souls forever drowning beneath the fibres of the boards. Dammit, I thought, I could be sitting in a bar chatting about nothing, watching that huge hairy, craggy mountain called Seán O'Gorman, passive smoking his cigarettes, listening to him, a not so ex-Jesuit. I could be having something akin to fun with my former Catholic companion, having a real conversation. God knows, I see so little of him. God knows, we are, both of us, too busy. God knows, I miss the time had nothing but time on our hands to do better, less useless things like be friends to each other. God knows, I wish I believed in something.

And I got more irritated as I watched Bobby as he worked the room, perpetrating an irresistible charm offensive. I watched Lydon socialize from the tall grass of another group I was standing in, while I stood sighing and ignoring the babble and wishing death would come right there right then, I saw Bobby smiling and talking to three people at once, the mark of nervous perspiration on his collar, signalling his inner pain. You are your pain, I thought, as someone tried to say something him, the woman who came with the doctor, but he didn't reply. Well hello, I said, my whole body aching as I saw her. She was gorgeous. She walked away. I watched her. All I could do was watch this person move. I watched her face, her lips, her hips. Everything about her was intoxicating.

I looked at the huge television.
"Bobby?" I said.
Bobby spun on his heel like some dancer and smiled and put his hand on my shoulder. Shall we dance?
"What can I do for you, my friend?"
"Bobby. I am worried about you."
"You are?"
"I am."

"Fuck, I got no problems, Gordon."
"Oh you do, Bobby."
"I do?"
"You do."
"I do? Fuck me!"
"No thanks."
"You're the shrink. What problems? Talk to me. Give me the details."
"If I were to scan your limbic system —"
"My what?"
"Your limbic system, Bobby."
"Limbic. Is that some kind of exercise regime? Some kind of tree hugging half-assed wheatgrass-drinking yoga system?"
"In your brain. The limbic system is part of your brain."
"Ah."
"There we would find problems."
"So there something wrong with my mind? You saying I got brain damage?"
"Now you have it. No flies on you, Bobby."
"You telling me I got brain damage, you fuck?"
"Well, a part of your brain, the part that empathises, it's not working properly. It's actually what makes you so effective."
"Fuck you. You a doctor? Eh?"
"Well, no. I guess I never bothered. Too lazy I guess. Too apathetic. I mean, you must have been a bit concerned there was something wrong."
"No."
"I mean deep inside?"
"I said no, Brock! You deaf as well?"
"A kind of inner absence."
"No, Brock, actually."
"Come on, Lydon. You must know. I have been watching you. The ready smile, those vacant watchful eyes, the faint hint of sadness and self-pity in all you do, the nice sharp modern home, the sense of your expensive clothing, worn more as a costume than an expression of self. The sense deep down there's something missing. You are trying too hard. You don't feel a thing for these, your so-called friends. You're too clever for that. You know you are lacking in empathy. You know you are performing a kind of role? As if every move and word spoken might be a constant search for the right person who might help you? Someone or something to help you find just what is missing? You know? As though you were a kind of stranger in your own life? Someone or something who might give you the next step up that all

important ladder, a move to the next job? The next important client? The next valuable contact? You know? I mean, there are winners in life and there are losers? Nobody wants to be a loser. We all know what happens to losers in life. They lose. Don't they? And, after they lose, what is there left? What is there for us to do? We simply discard them like the trash they are. What is important in life is success. Real success. Success, and power, oh and not to mention success. Isn't that right? Eh Bobby? We need the right friends. The right contacts. Money. Position. Connections. I mean it's the law of the jungle."

Bobby peered coldly at me for a while. Then he said:

"That is fucking funny. You know that? You are a funny fucking guy, Gordon. A fucking funny guy. That's a really fucking good joke."

"Thank you."

"A fucking cool fucking. I mean did you memorise it, all of that, from some movie or something you read?"

"No. I kind of rolled with the moment. I can roll with the moment. I roll."

I moved my finger in a circular moment in demonstration of my rolling skills.

"Jesus, that is fucking sad. You could be out there curing diseases or solving crimes."

"Maybe I am."

"Instead you're fucking with me. Trying to undermine me. You are garbage, Brock. You are a waste. I don't know the fuck what Lorna sees in you. Fuck you."

"You know something Bobby, you are cool. And the thing about being cool is you play this role all you life. Everyone in your pretentious group is —"

"Do me a favour? Stay the fuck away from me. Okay? Everyone acts."

"I'm not."

"Right now if I had a fucking butcher's knife I would fillet you like a motherfucking executed deer."

"O-okay. Woow violent imagery. That's a lot of bad blood you got flowing in your veins there Lydon."

"Really. I'll fucking kill you, or I'll have you killed. I will fuck you up. Think I can't fuck you up?"

"I believe you are good at that."

"You are garbage, Brock."

"And you are a psychopath, and should be stopped. People have tried to kill me before by the way."

"That doesn't surprise me at all."

"And they failed."
"Well, that's sad, Brock. That's fucking sad. The world would be a better fucking place without you."
"And believe me, Bobby, the person I am talking about really tried —"
"Brock, I don't care. I really don't give a shit any more. The only troubling fact is that saint did not succeed. You are the worst kind of waste of space: someone with real ability just pissing it all away."

Lydon dismissed me with an enraged look and stomped away. We didn't speak much after that, neither that day, nor any day after, even during any of the other casual social situations in which we encountered each other.

But, at this particular social situation, the guests settled down on the comfortable sofas and nibbled the snacks, then ate the chilli as some movie credits rolled and the guests told Bobby how good the chilli was, but the movie was terrible and the great big screen was too big and too overwhelming but amazingly clear, crystal clear.

At first I liked the movie- Kubrick's last, generally awful, film. How the mighty had fallen, I thought. I ate chilli and sipped beer and watched on, knowing the beer would gave me a nervous headache in an environment like this, that I had a low tolerance for alcohol anyway.

So I ate a little more and I got up and went to the kitchen to wash my plate, despite the existence of a large dishwasher. I wanted to get out of the room and be alone for a while, and drink a lot of water and look for aspirin to counteract the tingle I felt behind my eyes and in my forehead, a pain borne from the twin devils of fear and a lingering terror of the void beneath and beyond all things; a pain that would grow into a sickly headache. I walked to the kitchen and saw Martha coming from the toilet. I saw Martha and she saw me.

I have often wondered what people, especially Martha, saw when she looked at me, this strange shy, over-thoughtful, tortured thin man someone had told her was a psychotherapist. He had something, something interesting, she thought. We smiled at each other.
"Hi there," she said.
"Hi" I said.
"Hi," she said.
"What's up?" I said.

"Well," she said. "You are the one being miserable and picking fights with the host. He is a ruthless-."

"I hate myself. I can't stand it. I planned it. I hate him. I can't stand ... ordinary things. I can't have a civil conversation. I can't cope with."

And she smiled and I smiled, like a fool smiles, as only I, the fool, can smile, and she put her hand on my chest, as though to stop me passing by, or start my heart, and I felt the shock when she put her hand on me and I grabbed her and we kissed and it was as though my clothes, my chest, my skin and muscle and bones were penetrated, the energy, the force burning through me and she was inside me. Started my heart, I thought, after a lifetime of just having a pulse. Electroconvulsive. And, holding hands, we went into Bobby's bedroom and we had sex. No conversation, no preamble, no explanations. There was no time to take off clothing. We fumbled with zippers and buttons and in between thrusts tried not to crease clothing or leave marks or make much noise. She began to groan as we made love and I put my hand on her mouth and she pulled it away.

"Don't!" She said.

"Okay," I said.

"I need to," she said.

"Sorry," I said.

And the orgasm came so fast, like an electric jolt, the rush of feeling so unexpected. Like coming home. Like suddenly, after careering through a lifetime trying to know a point to everything, suddenly feeling it, feeling centered. Like someone striking a match and seeing a clear light after a lifetime's twilight. White lights appeared and disappeared before my eyes. Cocaine Morphine Drowning Dead Loss of Oxygen, I thought. And we separated and she looked at me, deep into my eyes, and she kissed me and she smiled and I smiled and I knew it was love and she put her arms around me and kissed me again, and she fixed herself and then she left. Her body was so perfect, I thought. Perfect. I imagined my hand brushing against her cheek, pausing along her hips, along her neck, her breasts and stomach, just to kiss here, then there.

Martha smiled took a card out of her jeans and put it in the top pocket of my jacket. I looked at it later, after she left. Martha Reynolds, one three five three oh nine six. Her number.

"Call me," she had said as she walked away.

"You are such a fucking cliché," I had said. And had she laughed. I remember seeing her go as one watches a dream fade into the unconscious, and I watching the way her body moved as she went back to the television room. Then afterwards, twelve minutes later, after a trip to the bathroom for a quick wash, I returned.

"Where were you?" Lorna asked.

"Oh, having sex with someone, some total stranger, very relaxing you know." I said. And everyone chuckled, and we watched the movie.

And I took aspirin and I thought: I am so ugly. Lean and ugly, like some Beckettian refugee. Brain in a vat. Just kill me, I thought. Bullet in my head. I am merely a mind that thinks. I make concepts. I describe. What am I? What am I doing here? How did I get here? What is this thing I am doing?

The story line of the movie, if it could be called such, displayed Tom Cruise's taxi cab entering the gates of the dark Gothic, surreal, reinforced steel rococo, over-embellished gates of the mansion. This was the secret location of the masked ritual orgy, which was weird and ironic and made excruciating viewing. Such a bad movie, made by a genius past his best work, I thought, and I watched Cruise walk through the rooms where people were fucking. Maybe they were making love, but it looked like fucking. Is there a difference? I was glad the room was darkened, and despite the initial complaints about the film, a dozen were huddled around the giant screen and I had joined them, sitting beside Lorna who hugged up to me, and I was embarrassed, feeling sweat trickle down my spine and my palms dampen. I worried if I smelt any different. I worried if I should have washed myself more, if anyone with heightened senses could detect the smell of sex. So I pulled away gently, and Lorna put a proprietary arm around me and snuggled up to me once more. Are there any vampires in this room? Werewolves? Mutants with heightened senses?

I didn't see that Bobby understood what had happened. Bobby was sharp, sharpest tool in the social tool box. Mind of the detective, and, in his group, a social crime had been committed, a sex crime. With just a casual glance at Martha and my comings and goings, he saw what was going on. Bobby conducted his group with the same non-committal efficiency as he would any other pressing matter, manoeuvring friends and acquaintances together, ensuring an atmosphere of positive friendliness and warm chit chat with a strong focus on career and networking without making it all too obvious. Lydon did not start out as a divorce lawyer, but he became adept at such matters and became known as one, image supplanting his other interests and skills.

Eventually, at about seven in the evening, we made our escape, driving home, I seeking to vent about how awful the day was, how awful the people at the party were, and, if I were honest with myself, how guilty I felt about having sex with Martha Reynolds.

"Who is he seeing, by the way?" I asked Lorna as we drove.

"Who is who seeing?

"I have to tell you something, Lorna."

Tears filled my eyes. I blinked them away.

"What?"

"I, I don't like Bobby."

"Okay, but why are you so upset?"

"Who is Bobby seeing?"

"I don't know. He is keeping it secret."

"Surely," I had said, "Surely we should get to eventually meet his significant other'?"

"It's nobody's business but his. What do you have to tell me?" Lorna said, as we drove home.

"I feel terrible."

"About what? Are you seeing someone else?"

"No, I mean I don't think I can go on being a therapist. And by the way relationships are, by definition, public property."

"Nonsense, Gordon!"

"They are communal."

"Why are you so angry, by the way?"

"I hate those gatherings. Anyway Lydon —"

"Bobby."

"Bobby Lydon talked all the time, in tedious generalities," I said.

"No he didn't. He was polite!"

"About this apartment, this furniture, the television, the neighbours he blocked from buying next door, politics, and sex. He made endless off colour jokes about sex."

"He did?"

"Yes!"

"Are you sure?"

"I wanted to put two in his chest!"

"Wow! Violent imagery from my psychotherapist lover partner! Okay! Bobby's naturally shy. I know you don't like Bobby."

"Lydon hates me! He wants to gut me with a fillet knife like a deer carcass!"

"What!? That's ridiculous."

"No, not it's not!"

"Yes, it is!"

"You are over-loyal. So loyal you are blind to the awful friends you keep."

"That's not true, and really offensive. Jeez! You are so arrogant!"

"Anyway, Lydon is too hyper competitive and narcissistic to be anybody's friend. And he threatened to kill me."

"What? Oh, you know, Bobby!"

"He is Satan. Full of empty promises. Lydon is a corporate psychopath!"

"You should be less judgmental. Bobby is a loyal friend to me."

"Really?"

"Really. Give people the space to say what they need to say. And I like Bobby."

"The only thing he needs to say is whatever gets him what he wants."

"What a refreshing attitude."

"Rather."

7.

One night, I called Martha up using a public phone that had its glass smashed. I mused on the smashed glass on the phone box. Maybe the smashers do it for a bet. I imagined the phone vandals as I fumbled for a coin or a credit card:
'I say, Theophilus, I bet you five Thalers you won't smash eighteen phone boxes before the twenty fourth of the month.'
'Eighteen, you say?' Theophilus asks, and stops beating up a policeman.
'Indeed, dear fellow,'
'You know something Larry; I will take you up on such a fun wager. It will be a marvellous party.'
'Well let's get to it, eh? Larry, do pass me my favourite axe, will you?'

Or maybe it's out of a desire to know, the pursuit of science that makes the smashers smash. Tiny shards of glass like crystals were scattered all over the pavement, all of them refracting the lights of cars and streetlight lamps as I rang Martha's telephone number. Maybe they have an interest in physics and discuss Newton's optics around the campfire as they roast some vagrant for dinner. But this time the discussion wasn't between Larry and Theophilus. It was between Lucky and Teddy.
'Mercury's perihelion was a problem for so very long. Wasn't it Lucky?' Teddy the cannibal says. Lucky the cannibal is tucking into the vagrant's meaty thigh. Juicy.
'Indeed,' Lucky answers, finishing her plate as she smiles seductively across at Teddy. Having tucked into roast vagrant, she was definitely feeling frisky.
'Until Einstein, that is,' she said.
'More meat, my love?'
'No thank you sweetheart; I have computations to finish for tomorrow's lecture.'
'Good for you,'
Lucky answers as her mobile phone rings.
'It's Daddy. I forgot. I've a book report to do.'
My fantasy continues as I discovered the pay phone still worked, despite the best attempts of the imaginary cannibalizing quantum physicists. And, as I imagined a group of cannibals discussing the perihelion of Mercury, Martha answered.

"Hi," I said.
"Hi," she said.
"So, how are things?"
"Okay, good" she said. "So..."
"So," I said.
"So, why are you calling me?"
I felt my mind freezing with shyness and uncertainty.
"Because."
"Because?" Martha said wanting to make me work hard for the privilege of a relationship with her..

"Because, I think about you most of the time. Because making love with you for those few minutes at that party was the happiest time of my life. Because, despite all my reservations about the meaning of love and whether or not it's possible to love another person, I knew the moment I saw you that you were the one, though the idea of there being a 'one' in the midst of a rapidly over populating planet is something of an absurdity. Because I want to be with you and I know that, despite all the horrors and the trauma that are going to ensue from our being together, the breakups and the betrayals, however wrong it might seem to others, or how others might judge us, that it is the right thing to do, at least in the way anyone can understand right from wrong."

And she hung up, which did not come as a huge shock, in retrospect.

And then I smashed the phone until it was in pieces. So that's why so many of them are broken, I thought. The callers get hung up on by prospective lovers. Then I went to another phone and rang her again.
"Do you want to meet up?" I said.
"I don't know," Martha said. "I don't want anything big to happen."
"Too late," I said.
"Also, I can't talk now."
"Meet me," I said. "We should, we should meet."
"Why?"
"I want to see you. And the fact you are playing this bullshit-passive-aggressive-geishaesque-seductive-hard-to-get-thing means you want to as well."

Martha didn't answer for a while. I waited for her to answer and watched people drive up to the Chinese take away across from the particular phone booth I was talking at and go in and collect take away meals, as the impassive till person handed out meals and took more orders. It started to rain. Oil mixed in with leaves blew along the street. Suddenly the street seemed darker, the groups of people malevolent.

I felt cold.

I thought of reasons why Martha and I should meet.

Because the self we present to people exists in the minds of people. (Problem: maybe we don't really exist for each other.)

Because I felt a connection beyond this imaginary self, this self I am talking to you with, writing these words. I felt there was something beyond it. I felt it during sex with Martha, and I wanted to go back there with her.

I want to know Martha. I want to know you, Martha, as an Other. I want something real and I am willing to work for it. Something akin to pain. Something richer than pleasure. This disease. This love.

Physical attraction. Sex. Because your body is perfect and I want it. Toned. Perfect and not perfect. Because perfect does not exist. Because your skin is like cream. Downy down. Soft rabbit like. Kitten. Because I am obsessed. I fantasize scenarios. Because I want to kiss you.

Because.

I need to talk and say nothing.

Because I want to get drunk and stoned and lose my mind and other instruments of torture like my body and myself and my history. I want to have a minute that is unlike like the many other thousands of minutes I have lived[3].

As Martha was taking the call from me, the loathsome detestable Richard came into the bedroom looking anxious, saying he had to go out.

"I have to go out, sweetheart," Richard said. "Who is on the phone?"

"Telephone Company. Offering us some deal. Wanna talk to him?"

She held up the receiver to Richard. Richard took the phone.

"Hello?" Richard said.

"Hi, Is this Mr. Smith?" I said.

"It is. It's Dr.. Richard Smith, actually."

"Sorry Dr. Smith, I do apologize. We will update our databases accordingly. My name is Angelo. At Arc Communications, we are prepared to offer you substantial savings on your land line as well as a competitive rate of …"

"Sorry, I have to go." And Richard handed the phone back to Martha. Martha didn't hang up.

"How long do you think you will be?" Martha asked.

"I don't know - a couple of hours. These Thai massages," he said,

3 Humans live around 39,420,000 minutes (given a ballpark average lifespan of 75 years) – allowing on reasonable nutrition and little or no proximity to a theatre of war. Or one might just get lucky and live a long life.

running his fingers through his hair, wrinkling his nose and forehead. He smiled then frowned, as though savoring the words he had just spoken, as though replaying a melody he had just composed, then relaxing as he came to a conclusion, happy, with his work.

"They take as long as they take."

"I guess."

"I mean, this particular individual, she literally pulls my fingers and cracks my knuckles, she stretches my limbs, once or twice I wept a little."

"I see. Very intense."

He smiled, and then kissed Martha lightly on the lips.

"The masseur insists on unblocking my blocked energy centres."

"I see," Martha said. "Blocked centres. Sounds intense."

"Don't be negative," he said.

"I'm not being negative. I mean, if it helps you. I know how badly stress has been affecting you. I know a lot of people who have been, well, conned by all this alternative therapy."

"It isn't 'alternative', it's 2500 years old."

"Maybe it's a very old con game."

"Well, I don't think it is. Oh, I nearly forgot-,"

"Forgot what?"

"Philip Sound."

"Is that a real name?"

"Do you think I make up the names of my friends?"

"No Richard. All I am saying is that I think that's a very unusual name."

"It isn't an unusual name. It's the name of one of my oldest and dearest friends."

"You never talked about him till today."

"Oldest and dearest friends. Who happens to have a very large company that is in the process of being bought by an unimaginably larger company and is going to make him unimaginably wealthy. I went to college with him. I roomed with him. I stayed in his parents' houses. We are like brothers."

"So how come I never ever met this Philip Sound and how come you never mentioned him before?"

I was listening in to all of this, much to my delight.

"I did!"

"Oh, Richard?"

"What?"

"Aren't you going to be late?"

"Someone I know very well wants to meet you. Philip Sound wants

to meet you. You have been talking and talking about getting out of the place you were in, doing something more interesting and more challenging and here is your chance. He's got a company that needs people like you. Someone with your repertoire of talents. Ok?"
"What?"
"I said...well you heard what I said. I met Phil for a drink last night, and we got talking. And I mentioned you and he said he would be very interested in meeting you."
"I am perfectly capable of getting my own work."
"This isn't anything to do with-."
"I don't know, Richard. Maybe. Right now, I'm going out for a drink with Suzy."
"Really, can I come?"
"What about your massage?"
"It can wait."
"No, go for your massage. You would hate it if you came. Apparently a crowd are getting together at Zanzibar. Kind of a girly thing."
"Fair enough. Think about what I said. Philip Sound is the kind of guy you want employing you. He is a good guy."
"Oh really?"
"Really Martha."
"Then I must call him up."
"I know you are unhappy where you are."
"I know you are looking out for me, Richard."
"No, Martha. How could I possibly be looking out for you? I mean I love you and I want to marry you, so of course I want what's worst for you."
"Lose the sarcasm, Richard."
"Sorry, whatever the hell, his company is expanding, or being bought over by another one, or something. He explained it to me but I stopped listening to him."
"You said that," Martha said. "About the company expanding, and you never listen anyway. Anyway."
"What?"
"I won't last long there."
"Of course you will. I have to go. My massage awaits."

8.

Richard had left and we were still on the phone to each other. I kept putting change into the phone. After a while Martha came back on the phone.

"Hello?" Martha said.

"Hi, hi there. That was fun," I said.

"You are still there, then," Martha said.

"Well, that was kind of special," I said. "Take the job. You will make a lot of money."

"Unwanted career advice," Martha said.

"Okay. My bad."

"So, what happens now?" Martha said.

"I want to sleep with you."

"I see."

"Or more precisely, I want to have satisfying sex with you."

"Well, we do have to be precise, don't we?"

"The kind that doesn't involve esoteric techniques but gives a feeling of happiness, and, afterwards, causing both parties to fall asleep, a peaceful restful sleep, I said"

"You really are not like anyone else I have met," Martha said.

"Sorry," I said, suddenly self-conscious and embarrassed, aware I had crossed some line somewhere that I shouldn't have.

"It's very funny, actually, in a slightly disturbing way. Why?"

"Why what? You have lost me."

"Why do you want to have that kind of sex?"

"It's a question of desire, attraction, and sleep deprivation. I don't know. Is desire the same as attraction? I don't think so. Is attraction a question of chemicals? I imagine us having breakfast somewhere, possibly, followed by a walk in the park and then maybe a silly movie possibly afterwards having the kind of non committal non defensive conversation that real couples have."

"Wow, that's fascinating, Gordon. I mean you really know how to over think a moment" she said. "Does the movie have to be silly?"

"Yes. Absolutely brainless."

"Okay."

We repaired to a hotel room. Unlike with Richard, Martha had nothing beautiful to look at - at least not physically. I was thin, as though something was consuming me, preventing me from filling out.

"You are very thin,"

"I am. And you are very beautiful, not in the willowy beautiful that you get in European art movies, those females that you fear might break in a high wind, with arms that are bird leg thin, and that slight wan thin untouchable body that might disappear in a breeze, but strong, sexually self-aware, beautiful."

"I see," she said.

"I take it I might have overstated matters and given too many references."

"Something like that," she said.

She told me I seemed weighed down with a raw intelligence that killed my faith in humanity, tortured by human frailty in the chambers of my heart, over-intense desperation buried beneath calm, warm, impassive gaze with the occasional smile.

I was immediately, absolutely, terrifyingly in love. This beautiful creature, I thought. Something had happened.

"So where is this going?" I said.

"Well I think I am going home," she said.

It was raining heavily as we left the hotel. Small hailstones hopped off the taxi we took back into town. The taxi driver was somewhat talkative. He ushered us into the taxi like a sheepherder with lost lambs. He wore bottle end spectacles and had a big toothy smile. I liked him immediately.

"Bad night," said the taxi man. "Bad. Bad. Get in folks. Get in. Get in. Good. Good. Where can I drop you folks?"

A clap of thunder rolled like barrels down a sidewalk. Very J. D. Salinger, I thought. We gave directions, and then sat in silence as the taxi man talked about the damn weather and his son who was going to make a fortune playing in this band called the Soul Guerrillas. "Genius, my boy," he said. And, as the taxi man continued worshipping his son in his son's absence, I reached over and took Martha's hand. She played with my fingers, looked at me, then looked away, and the warmth crept up my arm, and my heart started again.

"That jolt. Ride the lightning, Frankenstein," I said. "Man made monster. God made man."

"What?" Martha said.

"Nothing," I said. "Sorry."

"For what?"

"Saying something that makes very little sense."

"You apologize a lot, Gordon Brock, for a shrink."

"I am not a shrink. I am a board certified psychoanalyst, also a psychotherapist, and it's not my calling. It's merely what I do for a living."

"I'm just saying you feel sorry too much."
"This is your stop. I will see you soon," I said.
"Tell me the truth. Why all the apologies?"
"Now you are being unreasonable," I said.
"Tell me this is real," Martha said. She looked closely into my eyes, the hail and slush hopping off the roof of the car.
"You will get my cold," I said.
"I already probably have it," she said.
"It's as real as it gets," I said.
"Okay then," Martha said. And we kissed in the cold slushy hail and then she was gone in doors to Richard and I went home.

The house was dark when I got in. I felt unsteady on my feet as I came through the hall, over sensitized to the sounds I made, the space I occupied, a sense of subterranean disturbance. Lorna had left a radio on. I could hear it off in the distance. She listened to the news. Read three newspapers daily. I went into the kitchen. Jazz music played through the stillness of a scrubbed midnight kitchen. Outside the clouds began clearing and a huge cold moon was hanging there in the recently cleaned atmosphere. I looked at the kitchen surfaces. Spotless. She always cleaned when lonely. I made myself a cup of tea and self-consciously sipped it while listening to the Continuo Sessions on the radio: 'Well this is Chad here on FM one ninety seven point three and it's a rainy night out there and we have a message from Jim in Rathfarnham. Don't take the N4532 as there is an overturned truck and he sends his love to Peggy his lovely wife. 'I love you Peggy' Jim says. Ah now that's sweet. It's great to be able to spread the love. Speaking of spreading the love, I will be playing so many great tunes between now and two, here on the very best of the continuo sessions and that was the Giles Peterson Four playing the Cosmopolite Blues. Good word that. Who thought that up? Huh? Mail me in here with your very own newly made up words. I love that. Is that a real word. 'Cosmopolite? Text me or call us here and tell us what's happening for you. We'll be right back here after these messages. Don't touch that dial. We've got something really special coming after the break.'

Then came the commercial break, with advertisements for wine, beers, movies, new bars, and the very best place to buy sports gear. I looked out the kitchen window and saw off in the distance someone's light on, a person peering over a desk, writing something. I took two aspirin, an anti–flu capsule I found in the medicine cabinet, switched off the radio, and went upstairs.

Lorna was asleep, almost missing there in the midst of the uncharted expanse of pillows and duvet. I climbed into the bed beside her and lay on my back, knowing somehow I would have to tell her, if she didn't know already, about Martha. I crossed my arms in Bella Lugosi imitation and slept soundly.

9.

The morning in work after that stormy Bella Lugosi night, I had three patients, then two more in the afternoon. The light between the curtains crossed my room. It bounced off the floor I had sanded and varnished. It reflected off my couch, my desk. It touched my pages and pages of notes, the only thing that remotely interested me in that room. In the theatre of therapy, props were critically important. I felt it important the consulting room give an aura of relaxed non-minimalist, unself-conscious tweedy-professorial-comfortable-with-my-body-make-yourself-at-home-with-couches-to-sit-on-patterned-throw-rugs-and-prints-hung-on-the-wall-enlightened-environ.

Between clients, I took out my notes and read. I sipped my coffee and read. These weren't patient or client notes. These were notes I was making for a book. And, in these notes, I saw a first chapter coming together. I had a picture in my head of the entire trajectory of the book. I would write in between clients. I would be witty and edgy and provocative. I would make money. It was impossible to find the time to write, except in between patients. I made notes and waited for the time to come when I could see fewer patients and write. Then the phone rang. It was Lorna.

"Hi. You were in late."

"I know. I'm sorry. I drank too much."

"That's okay."

"I'm meeting Bobby for lunch."

"That's just great, great. You must hate your life!" I said.

"Gordon, don't do this."

"I mean goddammit, there has to be a name for what's wrong with that man. Wait a minute. Wait, I think I got it. I know: Corporate psychopath.[4]"

"Don't say that!"

"Sorry."

God, I hate that man, I thought. The doorbell rang. I buzzed Mark in.

"Sorry Peaches, I've got my ten o'clock just in. Hi Mark. Come on in."

"Doctor Brock," Mark said as he loped across the door, a tall man with

4 Corporate Psychopath: Someone who works in the business or professional milieu who exhibits an abnormal lack of empathy, coupled with a marked capacity for amoral conduct, yet who gives all the outward signs of a normal well adjusted person.

gangly limbs. I didn't really like being called that. I think he had checked out my credentials somewhere and had counted my doctorates. What a waste of time.

Mark had a formal demeanor to him, a very tall man with huge shoulders and gym built body, and a Harry Potter scar in the middle of his forehead where his mother glassed him when he was twelve. Usually the children of army types make model citizens or addictive rebels. Mark fell roughly into the former group.

"Gotta go. Love you," I said.

"Love you too," Lorna said.

"Sorry about calling what's his name a corpor —"

But Lorna had hung up. And as Mark, my ten o'clock, sat and talked and wept about how his father beat him and his mother tried to seduce him, Bobby Lydon held a meeting with Lorna. He had called Lorna because he wanted to tell her about his suspicions of me: 'that damn Gordon, who thinks of no one but himself and manipulates everyone'.

But Bobby Lydon wasn't sure right there, right then, that he was doing the right thing. Before he met Lorna that morning he was taking a meeting on what he usually took meetings about- divorce settlements. His clients, a former couple, future ex- wife and husband, Murphy and Murphy formerly of 21A West Maddox Place, were disputing the division of their house and a small cottage outside Westport, they had, during their years together, bought and renovated. Lydon, as I heard it, was representing the male of the party, the Mr. Murphy. The meeting took longer than expected. It got bitter and vicious. Voices were raised, tears and recriminations, shouts and waving arms, accusations of infidelity, insensitivity, lack of emotional intelligence, excessive drinking, telephone calls from withheld numbers with the other party suddenly hanging up, unexplained receipts from hotel rooms, claims of friends sighting either party out on the town, claims of workaholism, refusal of sexual relations, and Bobby, who was feeling an unusual amount of internal pressure anyway, got very exasperated. He was worrying about having to give bad news to a good friend just after the meeting, and was feeling pretty tense. He lost his temper.

"Please!" He said. "Motherfuck! Fuck! I mean, really! This has to fucking stop! Jesus Fucking Jones! You're behaving as though you were still married. This is a meeting to decide the division of property. It's not a fucking therapy session!"

Rachel Sawyer, the lawyer representing the female Murphy, the one doing most of the accusing, saw that her friend Bobby, who was representing the male Murphy, saw Bobby was pretty messed up. She was a good friend of Bobby's. So she drew a line underneath the meeting, and suggested yet another meeting next week to finalise matters. She had to be in court that afternoon. Everyone agreed- a little intimidated by the unexpected outburst from Bobby, who normally remained very controlled during client meetings.

Afterwards, feeling raw and angry, Bobby went to lunch to meet Lorna, stomping down Grafton street, turning left down Duke Street to Gotham Restaurant, to see Lorna, who was at that stage strung out on five espressos and an overwhelming sense of apocalyptic doom.

As Bobby met Lorna, Martha Reynolds was sitting talking to a friend of Richard's, Philip Sound- approximately one hundred and fifty yards from where Lorna was meeting Bobby in the Gotham Café on South Anne St.

Martha and Philip sat in Bewley's Café and restaurant, out front in the coffee area, and Martha, unaware that other matters of non-peripheral significance to her own life and destiny were being worked out so very near to her, focused on Philip, unconsciously trying to become the kind of person he wanted her to be. And Philip Sound was watching Martha's body language, carefully searching for tells, for signs of weakness. Sound was spouting clichés that were really irritating Martha:
"We are looking for someone who could head up our management team, help take the company into a new stage of development. Someone dynamic. Resourceful. With leadership skills. Help grow the business. We'd be interested in offering you a contract, compensate you for the big change in lifestyle and responsibilities. Think about it. Give me a call."

Then Philip Sound gave her his card and left the table. 'For contract, read: 'suicide note'', she thought. 'These bastards won't get me. I'll get them first. Suicide. Too much money offered initially means something's wrong. And this, this is a very big contract for someone Philip Sound (what kind of a name is that?) doesn't even know. Maybe this is a setup. I don't know what kind of a set-up but this is too easy. A guy I never met in my life (how is that possible if this amadán is so close to Richard?) comes up, not to me, not to my secretary, but to Richard and suddenly I am getting offers for a job. A set-up. Definitely a set-up'.

Bobby had walked into Gotham Café Restaurant. Gotham was his favourite restaurant. It was a place he used eat wonderful pizzas and gaze mesmerized at those fantastic covers of Rolling Stone Magazine framed and hung on the walls. He remembered those times, when he was on dates, or alone in the evenings, late and tired after hours of crushing work. He would come in here and sit and eat pizza and look at the walls and want to be one of those people on the cover of Rolling Stone. Then, returning to the there and then, he saw Lorna. She looked awful. Bobby kept thinking about how terrible Lorna looked and that he felt somewhere he was supposed to care but he couldn't muster the emotion. He tried, but he couldn't.

Lorna was thinking about Gordon, her Gordon, how late he came home, how alone she was, how he had, in the past few weeks, really changed. How he was absent, well even more than usually absent, even when with her. Something was apocalyptically wrong.

Bobby came near.

"Hi Lorna, sweetie, you know what? I've just been at the worst fucking meeting of my entire fucking life. You have no fucking idea how neurotic ex-husbands and wives can be. I lost it. Totally lost it. I said: 'This is not a motherfucking encounter group,' I said. 'What the hell is this?' I said. I was so fucking angry. My counterpart, she saw what was going down and do you know what she did? She fucking killed the meeting. She totally fucking rescheduled. She didn't say anything, but I knew she thought I blew it. She was being nice, thank God. Could have beat me up over it too if she was so inclined. We could have tied things up if only I'd kept it together. But enough about me. Fuck me. You doing okay? You don't look so hot, what's wrong? Eh, sweetie?"

Lorna's hand was shaking. She was sipping espressos. This was bad. Her face was pale and she kept looking away. Bobby put his hand on her arm but she pulled away.

"No touching? Sorry about that. I am a touchy feely kinda guy. Okay, okay. Take it easy. What's on your mind, sweetie? What are you – worried about – someone? Gordon?"

She choked back a sob, and nodded.

"Okay," he said. "I'm sure everything is fine."

I can't do this, he thought. I can't tell her about. It would kill her. Or not, he thought. It may or may not kill her. But then Brock is a scumbag. Tricky, he thought. Fuck it, he thought. Let's do this.

Bobby rather wanted to kill me. And, because he wanted to kill me, his tone became soothing, sensitive, conciliatory even.

"Honestly. Sweetie. I love Gordon like a brother. I would never do anything to hurt you or him."

Lorna's eyes narrowed and looked into Bobby's.

"You hate Gordon. You always have. What do you know? Did something happen?"

"Nothing. Gordon loves you, and would never —"

"If you know something you have to tell me."

"Look Lorna, I wouldn't tell you if I knew."

"I have to know and I want you to tell me now. What happened? Tell me!"

"What are you doing wearing these fucking clothes? Eh Lorna? They are not nice. You always look good. Now you come wearing these rags. Let me buy you a new outfit."

"Don't do this. Don't change the subject!"

"I am not changing the subject. But what is with this repressed school uniform look."

"Tell me! Bobby!"

"I saw him fuck another woman. I happened to go into my bedroom for a magazine. I opened the door and they were doing it on the bed. It was Richard Smith's fiancé, but he's fucking his massage therapist. There, I am sorry to be the one to tell you."

"Oh, my God."

10

It was after two o'clock.

I should be in work, Martha thought, that crappy job I hate. Meeting at two thirty. She rang Richard. And left a message:
'Richard call me. I had this meet with Sound. He offered me a job.'
No answer.
Martha had been ringing Richard since Philip left. "Call me Phil."
No answer.
She found Philip Sound personally and professionally loathsome. Something reptilian about that man. The kind of man who would hand you a misfiring weapon in a fire fight. 'Here you go, solider. Defend your team, with this piece of shit weaponry.'
She had already called her office and told them she had to go home.

But Richard wasn't answering the phone. She was enraged. She was going to get him.

11.

While all this was going on, I sat in my office in front of my notes. It was two fifteen in the afternoon. I couldn't read. Or at least my brain wasn't registering the signs on the pages of notes in front of me. Head filled with notes. Fragments. I had twenty pages of notes in front of me.

There was only distant sound of traffic in the background. Occasionally the tinnitus rush and crackle of blood passing semi-circular canals in my ear disturbed my confusion. Phantom limb phenomenon. Something that isn't there. Hiss and crackle of badly tuned radio. Infections of the ear canal. Free association to give the impression of relaxed self-possession. Also demonstrates I know a lot of stuff. Dysfunction. Next patient: fifteen minutes. Fletcher, who, as a child, saw his mother murdered. Life, therefore, was murder. He wrote murder stories. I liked him. I checked my notes and read once more a quick précis as to why I became a therapist:

1. I became interested in the vast and largely unregulated literature.
2. It gave me access to the contents of others' lives without personal involvement.
3. It's a lucrative business, a veritable secular priesthood, with many social advantages, for instance, working alone, and with lots of time off for private pursuits.
4. I get to control my schedule.
5. I am good at it, in as much as one can be good at something which is so unquantifiable and subjective. (Also shown in the way I have never once had a complaint made about me)

12.

I became a psychotherapist because of an interest in the literature (I'm also qualified as an analyst). My interest in the literature came from my own experience of being in therapy as a child. My experience of therapy as a child, being largely bad and very expensive, negatively impacted me. It led me to believe in the importance of appearances rather than the reality of things. It led me see the need for belief systems that offer hope, hope in the possibility of human healing. I saw that once we change how we see our reality, that human is a matter of what one really wants, that death is the only certainty.

But back to therapy. My being in therapy as a child emerged from my own childhood traumas. My childhood traumas came from two things, the fact that I was smart, and the fact of Ed Frasier - which is a way of saying I was the dumbest smart kid you would ever meet in ten lifetimes, capable of complex cogitations but unable to navigate my way through the dangerous terrain of human relationships. Lucia says she still sees the terrified little child in my devastating remarks, my preemptive verbal strikes against folks I see as threatening.

Speaking of threatening, I met Ed Frasier when I was a boy. I would go to other peoples' houses, friends of my parents, and play with their sons and daughters. When I was a boy, I tried to make friends. I was encouraged gently, lovingly to go out and seek friends, to play with others, make connections and experience the personal intellectual and emotional growth concomitant with making friends. I loved to play in the Morrisons. The Morrisons were friends of Mom and Dad. They were the kind of friends Mom and Dad liked to have.

The Morrisons were, like Mom and Dad, good people. They were people who had done well. They had a steady income stream, remained employed, had not broken any major laws, and lived in a well maintained house in a nice neighbourhood and had a relatively stable relationship. They were people who pulled themselves up by the bootstraps and retained their integrity. They were fit, wholesome, warm, witty, emotionally independent, ambitious people. They made few demands on their friends. They made little fuss of their success. They were honest and caring and generous. They had been through so much. They had survived, stayed together, and done well.

Rachel Morrison was a recovering alcoholic MD and her husband a businessman who had come perilously to financial meltdown, but was now operating a profitable import-export business, with some shady associations on the side that made some questionable transactions on his balance sheets that tax consultants and forensic accountants made a small fortune making appear entirely above board. Perhaps this was one of the factors that cemented the friendship between the two families. They had money, but not too much, or at least had the appearance of not having too much. They were neither too clever nor too dull, which was important, at least to Dave. For Dave, my Dad, he neither feared they were thinking ten steps ahead, nor did he have to simplify every conversation for the sake of friendship. It was, all in all, a good match. They gave what was needed without any substantial threat.

Finally, and most importantly for Daddy Dave, rather than Mommy Lucy, the Morrisons came from the right stock, no hidden agenda, no secret past.

"I was going to drop Gordon over."

"Over where?"

"To the surgery. He is doing a liver transplant."

"Dave, there's no need for that."

"What?"

"Being an asshole"

"Lucy, sweetheart, it was a stupid question."

"Why are you so hostile?"

"I am not hostile."

"You are hostile. Hostile and impatient and sarcastic."

"Where else does he go on a Saturday? To the Morrisons. That's where he goes. He doesn't have any other friends."

"Making friends can be really painful."

"Except if you count his classmates, and most of them hate him."

"They don't hate him."

"He embarrasses them. I'm glad we got him out of that school."

"I am. Look, Dave, sweetheart. He doesn't need a lift. He can cycle over there. He is eleven years old. It's like, 20 minutes, by bike."

"I don't like the traffic. It's really dangerous. There are three main roads..."

"Gordon needs to negotiate the traffic."

"Gordon will never be able to negotiate the traffic."

"If you over protect him, he won't."

"That kid lives is his head so much he would mistake an unpinned

grenade for a small pineapple."
"And he is perfectly capable of the twenty minute cycle to the Morrisons."
"No way am I letting him."
"You are over-protective, Dave, really, you know you are."
She nodded solemnly as she looked at her husband. He gazed bashfully for a moment at his cooling cup of tea.
"I am. Yes I am. And you have to realise he is not like other kids."
"Don't treat him like a freak."
"He is not a freak!"
"It's the worst thing you could ever do."
"He is sensitive."
"He is also manipulative."
"Way too sensitive. And it's only because the Morrisons are good stock that I let him up there."
"Who said they were from good stock?"
"Look."
"What?"
"Don't do this."
"Do what? You judge everyone from the standpoint of lineage and reputation."
"That's a gross generalis-"
"You don't know the Morrisons like I do."
"You have big issues about your social position. I know that. You know that. Because of what happened to your Dad, which was a terrible injustice.We have talked about it and I don't think we need to drag up the whole issue of your past because we are —" [5]
"Oh, shut up, Dave! You are as sensitive as they don't come!"
"What did I say? I thought we talked about this."
"You need to think!"
"Think?"
"Yes, think!"
"Okay. On the whole subject of thinking. Is there anything you think

5 Melvin Brown, Lucy's father, my grandfather, was fired from his post as second assistant senior accounting technician grade one, because of company fraud that, though innocent, so it was claimed, ruined his reputation. One Monday morning Melvin was told by his bosses that he had ten minutes to vacate the offices of Smith and Smith and Smith. Apparently they accused him of stealing from the company, misappropriating funds, indulging in illegal accounting methods. That, for the most part, was the end of his career. Like many summarily dismissed from posts of consequence, his firing, killing his confidence, inevitably marked the end of his life, his potential, his inner resources. So Melvin, my mother's father, lost his pension, benefits, and his company stocks, within a year of that terrible day. It marked the family, and had a powerful effect on my mothers self-confidence and sense of her social standing.

I need to think about in particular?"

"You need to be less of a jerk."

"Can you maybe unpack the whole notion of my being a jerk, perhaps?"

"You need to be less pompous, condescending, supercilious, less sarcastic, and a little more loving in your words."

"So you think I am unloving, or that I don't love you."

"I never said you didn't love me."

"It's just you are impatient and angry and a little condescending."

"I love you more than anything. Sorry about that. Did you ever think about this."

"You even sound edgy and angry when you are apologising."

"Sorry about that. The origin of the phrase 'chip on one's shoulder'. You know 'so and so?' well he or she has a real chip on her shoulder ."

"Shut up Dave, okay?"

There was no point in Melvin suing his bosses when they accused him of stealing, and then fired him. He could have, of course. But Melvin knew he would lose, even if he won. He knew how vindictive his bosses were. He knew they would wait in the proverbial tall grass and make Melvin suffer in some unspeakable manner, or worse, make some member of his family suffer, if he sued them. Maybe Melvin thought about it, but he was temperamentally a self-deprecating type who loved chess and crosswords and spent time alone, and alone, his anger congealed, and he got angrier and more bitter following his leaving the company, eventually spending years moving from job to job, the family passively suffering the prejudice of living in their neighbours' and friends' suspicions and the memory of their former relative affluence.

"Look, you need to like face the truth."

"That he was a crook?"

"Well."

"Is that what you are saying?"

And then Melvin became ill with the psychosomatic stress of it all, and kept it secret, bottled up the pain to grow death within him from it. Then, as disaster has its very own tracking device, Melvin suffered a heart attack while starting his car to leave for work one afternoon. He was late for his late shift at some car wash where he had a temp job. Dead at the wheel, head tilted forward in obeisance to the unsupportable strain of blame and a guilt he could neither defend nor explain nor articulate, though no charges were ever filed against him.

"Anyway, how could Melvin not see what was going on?"

"Well he was obviously an idiot!"
"No, Melvin was really really smart, like his daughter and his grandson, a lot smarter than…"
"So he was a crook."
"He had to know where the money was going."
"Maybe they kept the information from him."
"How could he not know where the money was going? How could you keep anything from Melvin Donnell?"
"Maybe he was a fall guy, then."

Because this sense of deprivation drove Lucy to achieve, acquire money and success and to find the right man, or, rather, someone not like her father, Melvin. And Dave Brock, my Dad, turned out to be just that. Dave was the right man. He was the very one to confound her needs and drive her unsuccessfully to be something more than the product of circumstances. Still, for him to suggest the Morrisons were from the right stock was to suggest she was not from the right stock. What David Brock, my father and life partner of Lucy Brock, neé Lucy Donnell, was suggesting, by that rather ridiculously innocent remark, was that his wife, Lucy was retrograde material, comprised of bad genetic code, that she was a loser. Somehow, her husband had stepped on an emotional land mine and confirmed her heartfelt crippling self-impression. It was more than a mere faux pas on Dave's part. He was just not being supportive. In fact, he was being unforgivably insensitive. This truly was a damnable comment, perfect ammunition for control and reproach. She needed to provoke no more. It was just what she wanted him to say. And he always did it, right on time and right on cue, and thus she could relive all her favourite psychodramas in living high-definition colour.

"How can you say that?"
"Say what?"
"How can you stay married to me and continue to have those opinions about people I loved?"
"What?"
"You hear me. How can-?"
"Look, please don't raise your voice."
"Don't tell me not to raise my voice!"
"We can be overheard."
"I don't care if we can be overheard!"
"You really should!"
"No one knows what he went through!"

"I nearly went bankrupt, you know."
"We nearly went bankrupt! We nearly went bankrupt, you mean, you narcissist!"
"I might have an idea just what that's like."
"Sorry, we nearly went bankrupt. Sorry. You are right."
"Don't placate me, Dave. Don't do that."
"I am not."
"You are."
"Not even a little bit."
Dave, my Dad, I think knew he had escaped divorce because of the comfort zones he created, through money and the mostly passive attitude he maintained to my mother's near inexhaustible reservoir of anger, which needed more than the occasional release. I was describing above a time when he was stupid enough to engage with her. Mostly, though, he let her ventilate and occasionally sympathised with her unresolved frustrations.
"I don't mean anything. Look, I'm sorry, darling."
"Darling?"
"They are good people, the right kind of people to have as friends."
"Very funny," she said.
"What I'm trying to say is —"
I was there watching.
"I'm going to go over to Jenny, if you don't mind," I said.
Lucy and Dave gave a small start, and then they turned to me and smiled. Like the Buddha's smile, it covered a multitude of guilt. When you looked at that statue you just knew he had been up to something naughty.
"Sure, son. I'll drive you," Dave said.
"You look busy, Dad. Anyway, it isn't far. Thanks for the offer."
"I'll take you."
"No, Dad. I'll bike it, really"
"All of a sudden, I fancy a spin in the car."
"Okay then, but I feel uncomfortable when you two argue."
"We weren't really arguing, you know," Dad said.
"No, and sometimes we argue. People argue because they get emotional about certain topics," Mom said.
"I know why people argue, Mom."
"And it's important that things come out in the open," Mom said.
"But your Mom and I love each other. So it hasn't anything to do with you, and it's nothing you should ever worry about, ever. Anyhow, people are silly. They argue about all kinds of dumb things," Dad said.

"Right, really dumb," Mom said.
"And I am driving you, so get in the car. And call me when you are done in the Morrisons. I'm hoping for some of their home made pizza. It's delicious."
"I love their pizza," Mom said.
"Food of the gods." Dad said.
"Zeus makes pizza."
"Ha Ha Ha"
"Okay then. Let me change into my runners first. These shoes are not suitable."
"I'll be in the car," Dave said.
I smiled at my mother, who smiled, and blew a kiss at me.
"Okay Dad. Okay Mom,"
I did not talk during the car trip to the Morrison's house. That is, until Dad said something.
"I notice you don't bring books up to the Morrison's, son."
"No, Dad."
"Would you like to tell me why?"
"No."
"Why not?"
"Just 'cause'."
"I need to know."
"It provokes trouble."
"I see. What kind of trouble, son?"
"I don't want to say."
"They don't approve of a person reading words from a book?"
"Maybe"
"Civilization is doomed, son."
"Alan wants to know why I read all this shit."
"Is that what he calls it?"
"That's what he calls it, Dad."
"It looks more like text, to me."
"He calls it shit."
"It isn't shit, son."
"No, Dad."
"And it betrays a level of ignorance to call it that."
"And anyway I like Alan," I said.
"You do?"
"Sure, Alan is cool."
"That's good."
"And we have so much fun,"
"Great. I'm glad."

"So it's a question of a trade-off and it is…" I said.
"Maybe he doesn't know shit" Dad said.
Dad and I laughed.
"Don't tell your mother I said that."
"I won't."
We chuckled again. Dave drove on.
"Son, you have to be yourself. We talked about this. We talked about your abilities. It doesn't make you special or give you any kind of special privileges but you can't hide. Well, people have, you know, but it causes problems."
"What problems?"
"Generally they end up pretty troubled, maladjusted. Here we are."
"That's what my therapist says."
"I think he is right."
"He is so serious."
"He is?"
"Oh yeah. Tom is so serious and he always wears black during therapy."
"Don't condescend or disrespect people. But be who you are. I think that's what Tom is getting at"
"Okay."
"You have fun and we will talk later."
"I know, Dad."
I looked at Dad with such intensity for a moment
"Sometimes you have to lie keep your friends, Dad."
"I know, son. Who are you lying to, though?"
"That's deep."
"Do I know shit or what?"
"You know shit, Dad."
"Believe it my boy. Enjoy your day. I love you, son."
"Bye, Dad. Mom looks really pretty today, doesn't she?"
"She is always pretty to me, son." And I went up to knock at the door.

13.

Lorna was waiting for me when I got home. She was waiting for me, shaking and weeping and waiting and drinking and waiting and chain smoking and waiting and drinking neat whiskey and was getting drunk while waiting.

"You know," I said.

"I had a long talk with Bobby," she said.

"Bobby has issues with long sentences that don't include the word 'fuck', but you know, I gather. I was going to tell you."

"You have been with Martha Reynolds, Richard Smith's fiancée."

"Yes, yes I have."

"Don't! Don't lie. Don't!"

"I won't. I'm not."

"You cynical, cold-hearted selfish bastard."

"I am just being honest. It's true. Martha and I were together, biblically."

"You bastard!"

"Lorna, I want you to understand. It is exactly what you think."

"I am sorry I ever met you."

"I know. Richard Smith has been apparently having incredible sex with his Thai Massage therapist. So Martha is breaking up with him. Martha and I are going to move in together at some stage in the near future. The details have yet to be worked out."

"What, what do you mean?"

"It really wasn't just sex. With Martha. The sex we had was in actual fact an expression of something far deeper and more meaningful," I began.

"I can't believe you. You are fucking evil!"

"I don't know what that means. Calling something I did with no malice aforethought evil points to a non-factual moral status."

"You did this to hurt me."

"No, I didn't. These kinds of things really can't be explained. I mean. I have to be honest, Lorna. I don't think I was ever really in love with you. I mean, we could have married, had children together, moved into middle age, bought a second house, down the country, where either you or I could visit if we needed a break from each other, or holidayed together, over time reached a kind of mutual accommodation in which we lived parallel but separate lives, and, after a relatively lucrative, well-established career with the usual round of disinteresting but eminently safe respectable friends, we could have had something akin to a half-life together. I mean, I don't blame you for this. It's my fault really. I think I kind of drifted depressively into the orbit of a powerful, controlling, passive-agressive female, who reminded me in some way of my mother, well actually not in some ways, but, I guess, in a lot of ways, but I don't know. I mean, when I look at you and talk to you and reminisce about you, you really don't remind me of my mother, I mean honestly. You aren't in any way like her. She was a fascinating woman. And funny. And, she was a lot more open-minded than you. Have you ever considered why you seem to addictively amass information on every conceivable subject just so as you can defend every narrow-minded entrenched position you take?"

And that was the exact moment Lorna hit me hard across the head with an ashtray, not that there were any smokers in the house. It was a frightening change in someone I thought I knew, her face twisted with rage and hurt and bitterness, pain my stupidity and cupidity had caused. She smashed up the place. But I only saw fragments of her breaking up the place. I passed out, you see. Woke up in our bed naked, with no memory of how I got there.

14.

Richard Smith called Phil Sound.
"Hi, Phil".
"Richard, what's up?"
"Did Martha take it?"
"Take what?"
"Did she take the job, you know. The change management job."
"She took the job," Phil said.
"That's good," Richard said. "That's good, isn't it Phil?"
"Yep, I think she has the instincts to be really good at change management."
"She never did anything like that before."
"I know."
"So, how come you, you know, gave her the job?"
"I dunno, instinct, I guess. After a while you just know these things. Sometimes you know you sit there for days and days with these shiny graduates or managers who have worked so hard and are efficient and creative and intelligent and you know those shiny well-adjusted, highly trained highly skilled change managers out there that would sacrifice their firstborns for a chance to be part of the team to manage Leef Inc. as it integrates into Xpex. But I am not looking for an efficient cog in the machine. This takes that extra something, not just graduates with good hairstyles and tight fitting."
"I know. She is special. How long did you interview her for?"
"I didn't."
"You didn't!"
"I know talent, raw talent when I see it."
"That's kinda strange. Phil, we broke up."
"Okay we talked. I mean we kind of talked about stuff. I gave her a kind of outline of the job and she said she didn't want it and didn't care. I made her a huge offer. I want her. Sorry, did you say you broke up? You did what?"
"We broke up," Richard said.
"You stupid prick."
"Yes I am."
"You never could keep it in your pants."
"I know, Phil."
"All your life, all that pompous moralising."
"I know!"

"How are you?" Phil Sound said.

"Thanks, I am pretty messed up," Richard said. "But it was my fault. I fucked up. Don't fire her or anything."

"If I fire her, it won't be because of you."

"Good. And if you hurt her in any way, I'll fucking kill you."

"I know that, Richard."

"Okay."

"I won't."

"That's good to hear."

"Come over to dinner on Friday. You can spend the night. We'll talk."

"Okay. But I have surgery on Saturday."

And Phil and Richard hung up on each other.

15.

"I heard you took the job," Richard said to Martha the day he came to pick up the last of his stuff from her place.
"I did," she said.
"Well that's just great then," he said
"Yes, it is," she said.
"How well does it pay?"
"Really, really well."
"Great!"
"They just threw a fortune at me."
"I see."
"I'm wondering exactly what I have gotten myself into."
"What do you mean?"
"Well, I guess I don't want to go into that, right now."
There was an awkward silence as Richard mechanically took boxes of stuff down to his car. He came back to have another quick look around.
"So, if I see anything else around that isn't mine, I'll get it over to you."
"Actually there is something, Martha. First editions."
"What?"
"I had a few first editions."
"You don't have first editions, she said.
" I bought them and I think I might have left them here."
"You don't have any first editions in our place, I mean my place. You kept all your first editions, the few you have, in your parents' place. You swore you wouldn't have any first editions in any house that you didn't own yourself. Remember?"
"Oh, you are right ."
This actually wasn't right. She kept his first editions on him. Just out of spite.
"And by the way couldn't you have done something less clichéd?"
"Sorry?"
"Couldn't you have done something different? Couldn't you have done something honest and just told me you weren't in love with me?"
"What?"
"Couldn't you have come clean, Richard?"
"You have regrets? Six months afterwards? After all the horrible things you said about me?"

"No!"

"After all the —"

"Whatever you heard, Richard, it didn't come from me. When people break up, there's gossip. People take sides."

"For your information, just because I had sex with another person doesn't mean I stopped loving you. I had sex. You ended it."

"Richard, you think that the rules do not apply to you."

"What rules?"

"The "no fucking the chickens rules""

"I have no idea what you are talking about. I didn't break any rules. I had sex with my massage therapist!"

"And how do you think I felt about that?"

"You were obviously truly disappointed in me."

"You always had such a gift for understatement, Richard."

"You are so right, Martha. You are always right. That's why no one can live with you, not for long, your overwhelming sense of moral purity. Your constant air of disapproval and holier than thou condescension. Everyone will let you down. Because you hold everyone to an impossible standard. Your next man will let you down. Everyone disappoints you. In the end everyone goes to someone who accepts that people are people. I'll send for my stuff. You can keep the books."

"You don't have any books, Richard!" Martha said. "I checked!"

"Fuck you!" Richard yelled.

16.

I remembered Mom talk about how the Morrisons were a nice couple (they weren't really), and their son, Alan, was a nice boy (he wasn't really), my best friend, (he wasn't really), but I loved going there (I didn't, but there wasn't an elsewhere to be).

So I went out into the garden and batted a ball with Alan Morrison. I sort of became friends with the well likeable, sporty, well adjusted, friendly, confident, smart Alan Morrison, two years older than me, by pretending I was just like him. I wanted to be like him. I wanted to have friends. I wanted to feel calm and confident in the company of others. I hid my love of books, my weekends spent alone, my lack of friends, wanted not to be laughed at. I wanted his approval and friendship more than anything.
"So, whatcha been doing lately?"
"Nothing much. TV, I guess." I said.
"You haven't been out?"
"No, but we are going on holidays soon." I said.
"Where?"
"Paris. You like Paris? They are going to stay in Arrondissement 9, where we stayed before."
"What?"
"I dunno. Nothing. It's an area, I think. They like it there. We went there before."
"Hit the ball, Brock."
"The ball, right," I said.
"I'm going off to visit my cousins next week."
"Which ones?" I said.
"What do you mean which ones, Brock? How many of my cousins do you know? Hit the ball!"
"Four. There was a Tom, and Sasha, and Mairead, and I can't remember the last one."
"Conor, he's the one."
"Right, are you going out to his place. Were does he live?"
"His folks own a hotel."
"Salthill."
"You know?" The ball came soaring down the garden. I stood between the swing and the pear and the apple trees and watched the ball whizz through the blue gold sunlit air and hoped this time I wouldn't look

like a complete idiot if I missed the ball once more. I put my hurley stick up in the air and by a miracle I stopped the ball.
"Good one!" Alan said.
I smiled and I huffed and puffed and I lifted the ball with my hurling stick and missed the ball. Then I lifted the ball again, prayed a little, and with great relief, connected with the ball. It went a little low, and a little astray, but generally I managed to return the hard leather ball.
"It's gonna be so fucking cool. He has beer and cigars, and guys give him big tips for errands."
"Hotel, right you said that. Do you smoke and drink?"
Alan didn't answer. I guessed he was posturing, but I couldn't let the smoking and alcohol intake pass.
"I said that?"
"Right. I think you said that. Salthill. Didn't you say that? Listen you want to go for a swim later? I fancy a swim." I said. I was so exhausted with the heat, and the effort of conversation, and I was sweating, the back of my T-shirt was wet. I wished I were fitter. I looked at Alan. He seemed calm. He looked at me, and smiled.
"Sure, sounds like an idea," he said.
"Great!"
I thought of a nice cooling swim, swimming underwater, thinking of the silence, the blue silence.
And then the kid next door came over the wall.
"You guys got another hurley stick?"
"Hey Ed!"
"Hey Alan!"
"Gordon, you know Ed Frasier?"
"No," I said.
"Hi," Ed said.
"Hi," I said.
Alan was looking for a hurley stick for Ed.
"Sorry Ed. No fucking stick."
"Here," I said, handing him mine.
"Thanks," he said. "Weren't you at the Gifted Kids Camp last June?" He looked at me quizzically.
"No," I said, turning away.
"You were there, you lying fuck!" He grinned. "What's the problem Gordon? Think I don't remember? What's the game here? Pretending to be a civilian so you get friends?"
Ed hit the ball. Alan blocked it successfully. It hopped off his stick and bounced once. Alan lifted the ball a half metre and whacked it back to Ed. Their accuracy was terrifying, the skill and physicality of their

play mesmerising. They continued to hit the ball to each other with increasing speed and skill.
"So, Gordon," Ed said.
"What?"
"I got a question."
Ed hit the ball hard. Alan jumped, blocked it with his hurling stick, then let it fall into his hand.
"What?"
I watched Alan toss the ball into the air and lightly tip it back to Ed
"Not so hard, Ed. No more broken windows, capiche?"
Ed nodded to Alan.
"Can you play?" Ed asked.
"Play what?"
"A civilian."
"I come here for fun. Don't ruin it."
"Okay. Hey Alan?"
"What?"
"You got any water. Its like a hundred out here!"
"It's in the tap or in the fridge. Go get it and bring us all out some!"
"Okay. In a minute. Brock, are you ever going to play? Here."
He tapped the ball to me. I threw the ball to Ed, who hit it on the rebound to Alan, who hit it back to Ed and thus I was excluded for another five or ten minutes as the ball ricocheted back and forth from stick to hand to stick until one of the duo let the ball drop there in the afternoon heat, and I ran over and picked it up, nervously.
"Jeez, I am tired," Alan said.
"Pheeew," Ed said. "It's the heat." He went over and sat on the swing, tossing his hurley aside. I picked up the hurley and started fooling around with the ball. I hit the ball around a bit and Alan went inside and brought out bottles of water, tossing one each to us when he came back, then sat and pointed to the swing Ed was resting on.
"That's Jenny's swing."
"Huh, what?" Ed asked.
"I'm just saying. My sister Jenny. She is very possessive of her swing."
"Okay," Ed said.

Just then I lifted the ball once more from the ground and I held it parallel to the flat grassy pear and apple tree ridden really large back garden of the Morrisons, I tapped the ball upwards then let it bounce against the base of the hurling stick. The other boys were not watching. They were talking about school, they both went to the same school.
"So what do you think of the new headmaster. He spent hours talking to my mother, that is as soon as he heard my Dad is a police man. I

think he is a bit of a creep. All the teachers are afraid of getting fired," Ed said.
"Where did you hear that? I hope they get rid of Frank."
"You go to St. Raymond's?" I asked Ed
They didn't answer.
"I'm going there next September, you know."
Then I tossed the ball ten feet into the air. The boys didn't see it go up. There were still talking. Then the ball came down like a stone, and, as it came within a couple of inches of the ground, I struck. The ball made contact with the hurley with a smacking sound and shot at Ed Frasier's head. Frasier didn't see it coming, and it glanced off the side of Edward's head as he was drinking.
"Oh fuck!" Alan said as Frasier started choking. We ran over and thumped his lungs as he coughed up the water.
"I'm really sorry. It was an accident. God, I feel terrible."
"I feel really dizzy!" Ed said. "Brock you are a monumental fucktard."
"Brock, you are a fucking tool, a total fucknuggett. Give me that!" Alan took the hurling stick and threw it near the pear trees.
"Now leave him alone! You have done enough harm. You could have fucking killed him."
"I am really sorry, both of you," I said.
"Yeah, whatever, even if you are a total fake," Ed said.
"What?" Alan looked at me, then Ed.
"Gordon here is a total fake. He is toying with you." Ed was coughing and choking." He is treating you like a fucking plaything."
"I, I —" I was embarrassed, I did not want Alan to know.
"Stupidfuckinfucktardedgoddamotherfuckinsonofabitch," Ed yelled.
"Look Ed, I said I was sorry."
"Yeah. I'm gonna sit here for a while."
"You okay?" Alan asked.
"I'll be okay. It didn't hurt so bad. Just the water boarding experience, that's fucked up."

And Ed glinted a smile at me and I didn't smile back. I had met Ed before at a gifted youngster's work camp. I remembered. He was an attention seeker. I didn't like him there. He was barely in his depth at that camp, with its games and challenges and puzzles and get togethers and discussions and nature walks and debates. Ed was the type of smart gifted boy who was pushed almost beyond his ability, and succeeded beyond either his ability or probably beyond his own expectations. But, as a boy, back in the arena of gifted weekends, where the moderately to profoundly fascinating self-absorbed kids, from the clever to the freakishly smart, sought out each other and, hopefully, bonded, who were being scoped out, trained to compete, trained to fit into the arena of building bigger better bloated economies with self-loathing pathologically shy, gifted kids, I though he was a loudmouth. I though he was dumb. I didn't like him. I stayed far away from him, and that was that. At those weekends and get togethers, there had been no connection between us, no conversation, and I didn't see him again until that day he climbed over Alan Morrison's wall.

And there he sat, sipping water in the hot sun, and Alan went back to batting a ball, and then Jenny arrived, and the first thing she saw was Ed Frasier on her swing.
"Excuse me, 'scuse me," she said.
She stood before him holding Marjorie, her favourite dolly, in front of her. Ed looked warily at the two sets of calm disapproving eyes.
"What?"
"That's my swing!"
"I hurt my head. I need the swing."
"No!"
"My head hurts, ok?"
"Nooo!"
"I'll give it back in a minute."
"No!"
"I'm in pain!"
"Well, go in and lie down! Take a tablet! I want my swing!"
"In a minute, okay?"
"Anyway you were not nice to Marjorie before. You pushed her away!"
Ed pushed Marjorie the glass eyed dolly, and grinned.
"Stop!"
"LEAVE ME ALONE YOU LITTLE BITCH!"
"Hey Frasier, that's my sister, ok? Leave her alone, seriously man," Alan said.
"I hate you!" Jenny said.
"And I hate you too!"
"Frasier, don't fucking talk to my sister like that, now get the fuck off her swing, okay?"
"You are a really horrible, horrible," Jenny said.
"Person?" I said.
"- person," Jenny said. "Person."
Alan walked over to Ed. He could see Ed wasn't going anywhere and pushing only made things worse.

"Jenny, you should go get Mom?"
"Mom's not home," Jenny said.
"Get Dad then."
"Dad had to go to work!" Jenny said.
Alan looked increasingly worried.
"Ed, get the fuck off my sister's swing, you asshole!"
"In a minute. Go play with Brainiac."
"You are a bastard."
"I am dizzy, and my head hurts. I will give the swing back in a minute."
The day was getting warmer, a dry heat, the air tasting of ashes, and Ed looked pale.
Alan walked back to me, but at this stage the game was going into a decline. Partly it was the heat, partly it was Frasier's colour, and partly it was that Jenny wanted her swing and Frasier wouldn't give it to her.
"Alan?"
"What is it, Brock?"
"I don't like your friends."
"He is better than you. Ed told me who you are."
"He is a loudmouth and a bully and he is out of his depth."
"But he is right. Ed told me you are some kind of genius brainiac loser that comes here just to pretend you are a normal person."
"I just want to be friends. I like you and I don't bully little girls."
"That's because you are one, Brock," Ed laughed.
"If you like," Jenny said, "If you like, you can wait by the seat near the other tree. I'll get you a coke. That's my swing. Nobody else's." She pointed to her dolly, "This is my swing. Mummy and Daddy bought it for me."
"Stop pointing at your doll. It's just a doll! And the answer is NO!" Ed yelled.
"Yesssss!" Tears appeared in her shining blue eyes. Her lips quivered.
"Leave me alone, Jenny," Ed said.
"Knock it off Ed! Give her back her swing!" Alan said.
Jenny squealed in rage. Ed reached out, and, using his thumb and middle finger, flicked Jenny on the lobe of her ear. She had recently had gold studs inserted into her ear lobes. The carefully formed tiny punctures were beginning to heal into two near perfect piercings. The impact of Edwards' middle finger against the gold stud caused her ear lobe to tear and bleed. Jenny screamed in pain, held her ear and cried out for her mummy. The little girl ran off. Alan stood in shock, then, turning pale with rage ran over, and leaping onto Ed, landed a punch onto his cheek. He fell off the swing, and Alan fell onto him swinging

his fists hard in rage. Ed recovered quickly, then flipping Alan, began returning the punches hard and fast. I picked up the hurley by the pear tree and ran over. Holding it. Looking for a way to end this.
"Stop! Stop it! Stop it! Fuuuuck!"
Ed Frasier's elbow rose. He was about to deliver another punch. I cracked him with the base of the hurley on his elbow funny bone.
"AAAAAHHH! Fuuck!"
Frasier turned and punched me on the nose. Enraged, I poked him in the forehead with the base of the hurley. He fell back, stunned, and was out cold for a few moments.
"Jesus, Brock!"
"I wasn't thinking!"
"You fucking psycho! You fucking loser brainiac fucking psycho!"
"AUUUUHHHH!"
Ed Frasier stood up and, holding his head, turned, ran into of the house.
"Frasier!"
"ED!"
"Are you all right?"
Alan looked grimly at me.
"We are in so much fucking trouble. We are going to have the police on us now."
"Why? We are children. This was an accident!"
"I have to find Jenny," Alan said." Gordon, you're a moron."

Soon after Alan's mother, Rachel, turned up. She listened to our stories of what happened and why, and took care of each of us. She assured me that though I had sustained quite a blow to the nose, it was not broken, and that Jenny's ear was easily fixed, and that she had only sustained slight tear in to her right lobe, though that was undoubtedly a painful and cruel experience. And I said, yes it was terrible and it hurt, but not as much as it must have hurt Jenny, who was only a little girl, whom I liked a lot, and Alan who was sitting there looking at me with much hostility and saying little or nothing, his head in his hands, and I said:

"You okay?"

"What the fuck do you care?"

"What, why?"

"He kept saying he knew you. He met you at some gifted kids' weekend, and you were at the 'higher end of the scale' and you were a fucking user, and nobody liked you there anyway. That you were a creep. You are a creep, by the way," Alan said.

"I don't know about that," I said, "But I don't like your friend," I said, feeling increasingly alarmed. Then mercifully, the doorbell rang.

"I'll get it!" I said.

"It's okay, Gordon, I'll get it," Rachel said.

17

I watched Edward Frasier's father, Larry Frasier, come into the garden with Ed in tow. Rachel Morrison stood up and tried to kiss Larry. Larry pushed her away.
"What the fuck, Rachel! What the fuck!"
"Watch your fucking language, Larry! Calm down! Think of your blood pressure! Okay? There's been a bit of an incident."
"I heard. How did it happen?"
"As you probably know, Larry, I only just got in."
"So, who was looking after them?"
"We rarely have a problem, Larry. Jane was due in an hour ago. Jane is the housekeeper."
"So, who looks after the children, usually?"
"Where is this going Larry?"
"My son is concussed. There have been fights. Serious fights. This freak here, whom I remember from my son's weekend for the gifted, and following camps, assaulted my boy with a hurling stick."
Larry was indicating at me with his thumb. I retorted:
"I am not a freak, and it was not your son's weekend for the gifted, and as I recall, he only barely got in anyway, and I was protecting my friend, Alan, who was being seriously assaulted," I said. "You should check your facts, Mr. Frasier."
Rachel put her hand up and said to Larry:
"He'll be fine. Don't do the overprotective bourgeoise middle class parent routine with me, Larry! Knock it off. Ed does Karate and what not. Not a fair fight, okay? Ed plays rugby and does martial arts."
"I know Rachel. I am looking for an explanation."
"Why? He will have a headache. He will take a few painkillers and sleep for a few hours and wake up. From what I can gather your offspring here has caused more concussions that he has received. By the way —"
"What, Rachel, what?"
"Where is Mary?"
"She's not here."
"I see."
Rachel looked conspiratorially at Larry.
"Is she- angry?" She asked.
"Very."
"What? Does she know the facts?" Rachel nervously asked.

I didn't know then, but I know now, that Larry and Rachel were secretly seeing each other.

"She knows, but it will be okay in the end."

"I see."

"Or suspects?"

"Okay?"

"So answer me, Rachel, who looks after the kids, usually?"

"Parents or nanny usually. You know that! Look, Ed will be fine. The kid is fine. A few headaches and no anxiety till the swelling goes down."

"I will try to contain the matter."

"Larry, your son is a thug! Wise up!"

"Don't ever talk about my boy like that! He told me that the Brock boy assaulted him!"

"Maybe you should take Ed, get him checked out, and remember to bring an armed guard next time, because children don't run around and have accidents and don't fall down, don't get knocks and cuts and bumps, don't get into fights, okay?"

"Okay, you knock it off, Rachel. I'm sorry. Is he all right?"

"He's got a bump on the head. The other two are pretty beaten up, you know. My son, who is not half the size of —"

"O for god's sake, Rachel! We're going. Come on son. I don't need to listen to this any more."

Larry led his son through the Morrison's house, passed the kitchen, the living room, the toilet, down the hall to their refurbished front door where I calmly opened the front door for them as they left.

"Goodbye, Mr. Frasier," I said

Larry nodded. Then he stopped, turned suddenly, then punched me on the nose. I did not see his hand move he moved so incredibly quickly. I fell back, and landed on the carpeted hallway. Larry looked defensively into Rachel's tear stained, hurt, disappointed eyes, pulled the door closed after him, then walked to his car.

"We should call the police, Rachel," I said. "That man assaulted me."

"That's not going to happen, Gordon."

Just then Jenny came into the hall and watched her mother stem the bleeding.

"Brock!" Alan said.

"Alan?"

"I don't want you here any more!"

"We should call the police immediately, Rachel," I said.

"Sweetheart, the police have already been and gone," Rachel said and continued mopping up operations.

"Poor Gordy Gordy," Jenny said.
"Thanks, Jenny."
Rachel took me into her study. My nose was bleeding again. It would bruise, possibly a black eye.
"That was the second punch on the nose I got."
"Sorry about that Gordon," Rachel said. "Larry can be very protective of Ed. Listen I have to ask you."
"What?"
"What was all of that?" She asked, a look of compassion in her eyes, yet her lips slightly smiling with a cynical twist, her voice as adaptable as an interrogator who uses the emotion necessary to get the subject in question to confess.
"What?" I asked.
"Provoking Larry. You wanted him to hit you."
"No."
I wrung my hands and frowned, stepping back from her.
" I held the door. That's all."
"Why did you hold the door?"
"It's not my fault."
"Gordon, that's something a child would say. Aren't you supposed to be a really clever boy? Maybe you wanted revenge?"
"No, Rachel."
"I think you did."
I looked solemnly at her.
"You wanted to be able to file a police report. Assault charges, right? To get back at Ed for what he did to you and Alan and Jenny?"
"No. That's not true. I held the door and then Larry Frasier hit me. He was the one at fault."
Rachel smiled sweetly at me and moved her well-defined face, her perfect nose and lips, dusted with sweat in her hot afternoon home office. Her face, so well made, seemed more defined than a doll, rendered life-like without the life. I looked at her, and, disbelieving in the reality of what I saw, went on.
"But they might need a statement from you. Daddy will help me do that."
"You might not get the statement you want from me, Gordy. Things don't work to plan."
"I know. I'm sorry."
"Larry's a police officer. A very senior, decorated famous police officer. He has been sick, for the past few months. He was injured on duty. He is very protective of his own."
I didn't say anything for a long time. I was confused and frightened.

My lower lip trembled. I felt tears come from my eyes. I felt so lost, so confused and afraid.

"Now, now sweetie. Don't be like that. Here, dry your eyes." She handed me a tissue.

Outside Alan was kicking a football. I saw Jenny was eating an ice lolly and swinging on her swing. She had changed her dress, her ear all patched up. She wore a bright red floral dress I didn't like. I would always remember her there, but didn't know that right then. I looked at Rachel Morrison.

"You are just like all the rest, Rachel."

"Sorry, sweetheart."

"You took the wrong step years ago."

"You watch your mouth, kid!"

"There's something wrong with this room."

"I see."

"It's too old for a doctor's office."

"You need to learn discretion, Gordon."

"There is no computer." I looked at her through tear stained eyes. "Rachel, what's wrong with you?"

Rachel smiled.

"I'm fine, honey, thanks for asking."

"You are welcome."

"You know, he could have broken your nose?"

"Who? Mr. Frasier?"

"He is a martial artist. He has two black belts."

"One to keep the other up," I said.

"And Larry Frasier did quite a bit of boxing in his day."

"How do you know that?"

"He is a friend of mine. And he is quite the martial artist; though he's recovering right now from a trauma."

"So am I, Rachel."

"You know something Gordon?"

"What?"

"I think I'll give your Mum a call. She will collect you. And we won't say a word about this, okay? I mean you will have a black eye, but well, we can say you got his with a ball on the nose, okay?"

"No, thank you."

"But I think it best you take a break from coming here, just for a while till things settle down. You must have loads of friends, a fine handsome boy like yourself?"

"No. No I don't. I am disliked and resented because I am —"

"Of course you do."

"No, Mrs. Morrison, I —"
"There's a good boy. Okay? Would you like a sandwich and a glass of milk before your folks come?" She asked.
"Yes. Thank you. No milk. Water, please."
"Great. No milk. Water. Great, I'll fix it now."

Half an hour later Dad came and took me home. I tried to call up a few weeks afterwards, but Alan had the flu. On another occasion, Alan was away. On another, it was a family day out. Then Alan was meeting another friend (Frasier) or there was a family event – or they had another appointment. After that, my persistent and desperate calls were unreturned and the few times I turned up that their front door, just to see if anyone was in or wanted to play, turned out to be a deeply humiliating experience. Worse, I was due to go to the same school at both Alan and Ed. After these portentous happenings, I was dreading the experience, without actually acknowledging just how much I was living in fear. I buried myself in books up to the point of going to St. Raymond's, but I knew what was going to happen. And it happened.

18.

And Lorna Burroughs didn't leave in this little house where I both lived with her and saw my patients back then. She wouldn't leave. She remained. She didn't leave the house. We continued seeing each other and most days having breakup sex. Though, after a while the breakup sex became less frequent. Then, after another while that contact stopped. Then, another while passed, and the waiting game began. And when we would occasionally meet, it became very, very awkward.

"Gordon, hi," Lorna said.

"Lorna. Hello."

"What? No kiss?"

She put her arms around me and opened her lips a little to kiss me. I stepped back and turned away a little.

"Don't do that. Don't. Please."

"Okay," she said.

"I, well, you aren't holding any kind of heavy object, and that's good," I said

"I already said I was sorry for hitting you. I think I showed you just how sorry I was!"

"I am still getting headaches."

"I really am sorry. I lost control."

"And you are still living here."

"I know."

"We talked about that."

"And we still don't agree on it."

"We broke up."

"I find that hard to accept. We separated. That's different."

"No, we broke up. That's what's different."

After I broke up with Lorna, she did not leave the house we had shared at Mapleview Avenue. She hovered for weeks wanting us to get back, wanting me to take her back, languished in bed. Occasionally I overheard her weeping, knowing by the smell she was smoking pot, eating chocolates, tormented with guilt at having hit me.

"I think you have been avoiding me," Lorna said.

"Good heavens, have I?"

"Gordon, you are like a child."

"No! I am not!"

"What?"

"I am trying to get you to accept that we already had breakup sex. I am trying to get through to you. I am living with my full-time girlfriend."

"Yes."

"You and I had breakup sex. We had occasional sex. We had rough sex (I didn't like that). We had suddenly-jumping-each-other-kind-of-unexpectedly-sex. We had slow sex. Dress up sex (which was ridiculous). Face it: it is over. We have done every type of sex imaginable. We have had all kinds of talks and conversations. We have smoked pot. Done coke. Gone out to clubs. The experiment is over. It's over. Do you know what would happen to my relationship with my full-time girlfriend if she ever knew about this?"

"What if I were to tell her? Gordon. What do you think would happen?"

"I guarantee you and I would not get together as a consequence, Lorna. Let-It-Go!"

"There's no need to be so cheap and stupid."

"I am not being cheap and stupid."

"You are being cheap, and very stupid."

"I am saying it as it is."

"We did those things."

"Good, then I really am not having psychotic episodes."

"I am not saying we didn't do those things."

"That's gratifying. Now we need to move on. We need to go our separate ways."

"You are reducing what we did to each other."

"Not the case at all," I said.

"You are reducing love to something like porn."

"Porn is good, but it should be regulated more. Look, you should go, and go soon."

"I live here."

"You should move," I said. "I will pay."

"No! I won't let a man manage me out of my home."

"I'm not managing anything! I mean I'm not managing you. Leave!"

"You need to know I live here and I am here."

"That makes no sense. Don't get all metaphysical on me, Lorna."

"I'm not. I love you."

"This is getting creepy and it is getting stalkerish."

"You know you and I were —" she said.

"You need to move on."

"I don't want to. I want you. I want you now."

"You deserve better than me," I said.

"I love you, Gordon Brock. Don't leave me. You and I were meant to be together. We fit. We understand each other. I accept your genius. I know you hate your giftedness. I know you want to be someone other than who you really are. I know you are running away from yourself. There's no need to do this. We could have a very good life together."
"I am sorry, Lorna. I am very sorry. I don't love you."
After that, I mostly avoided her, neither asking her to leave or to stay, hoping by a passive standoff, a cold war, she would leave and the whole awful situation would go away.

But it didn't. I came and went, day after day, occasionally seeing Lorna, encouraging her to just go, to let go. But she persisted. She was a persistent kind of person. Then I came in one morning, and Lorna, stepped suddenly in front of me.
"Omymotherofgod! You scared the fucking bejeezus out of me."
She stood there, looking at me, leaning her face near me, hoping to get me to respond.
"Lorna, get out of my personal space. I have patients."
She didn't answer. She just stood there. I got so angry. I wanted to punch her in the stomach. It would leave a bruise so bad it would make moving about difficult.
"If you don't move, I am going to have to move you out of the way. Please Lorna! Don't fucking do this. Get the fuck out of my way!"
So I shoved her away. She fell over. And I stepped past her, taking deep breaths. My hands were shaking.
Then I understood. Lorna would never get over this. She'll never forgive me. I'll never forgive me. She'll build an altar around what happened to her, and come there to offer sacrifice in her dreams.

After I shoved Lorna like that, she pretty much left me alone. I saw her come and go as I continued seeing patients during the day. At night I was staying over in Martha's place. I drove over to my former home, and took patients during the day. After I pushed her, mostly Lorna wasn't there. I was still getting headaches from where she hit me. I didn't seek medical advice. I should have. A part of me didn't want to know.

So, while I was behaving in the manner of the egotistical self-absorbed reptile, Martha had got decorators into her place and was making a home, clutching the viper I was becoming to her heart. We made love all the time, rang each other constantly when we were apart and, as the builders repainted and rebuilt the apartment, making it suitable for two, I worked quickly through my first book and, as a sideline, continued with this book. I was, in truth, very worried. I knew I was going to be famous. I knew I was going to be rich. I could feel it. I also knew I was becoming a kind of devil. So as the darkness and gaudiness dissolved in Martha's place, replaced with clear lines and bright colours, clear defined lines meeting at right angles, becoming a fit engine for living, I made a list for myself.

Sensory input log: Why I write this:

1. I need to write a work to take revenge on the tragedy of life.

2. I need to hurt those who took away my happiness and made me this monster.

3. I need to use my gifts for the purpose of revenge, (which is not even superficially like 1.)

4. I need to prove to myself I am brilliant, despite having achieved little or nothing.

5. I need to take back lost time. I have this deep rooted fear of Marcel Proust. He haunts my dreams with his opera gloves and his …

"Are you not done with that book, yet?" Martha asked, making me start.

"Eh, no. This is another project."

"Ooh, do tell. Can I read it?"

"Sure."

"You sure don't sound sure."

"I'm not."

"Why? I mean, I will be honest. I have read lots of books for people. They give me their stuff to read. I don't know why they do, but they do."

"I have to warn you…"

"What? I am in this? Am I in this? I am?"

"You are in it."

"I am?"

"Yep. You are in the book."

"You are serious? Why am I in it?"

"Because I love you."

"I love you too. But that's not an answer. That's total nonsense. It's avoiding."

"No, it's not."

"Please."

"Well I don't think it's avoiding. You are important."

"So, I am important?

"Yes, yes you are."

"Is that what I am?"

"Sure you are."

"Gordon, that's how people talk to each other when they can't really find the words. They say things like, 'Darling, you are important'."

"I think I can't, you know." I began: "The idea that I would live without someone like you, now, after you are here and we are here in this big old beautiful place, would hurt so bad I wouldn't want to live. I would retreat into a world of ideas. I would construct theories instead of describing things. So I had to, you know, talk about you."

"I see," she said. Then she started reading. "So you want to 'take revenge on the tragedy of life'. That's incredibly pretentious. What the hell does that even mean?"

"These are notes," I said defensively.

"They don't look like notes. It looks like maybe a second or even third draft. There's a definite style emerging."

"You think so? I don't think so."

"I mean, if you were going to write about me, why didn't you ask permission first?"

"I didn't think I needed to."

"My life isn't public property."

"This isn't history. It's a cross between memoir and a —"

"What about privacy?"

"Look, this is a thing."

"Words are your friend, Gordon. What thing?"

"It's a project I have been working on for years. It's a very personal memoir, a fictional memoir. Reality has been altered."

"I buy that. Then you can edit me out of it."

"I can't, sweetheart. We live in slightly altered reality."

"But anything you write could end up in print. It does. People will buy it."

"Anything I have done thus far is well, mostly academic."

"Jeez, you are an egotist. All that false modesty is crap. You are a genius."

"Don't be a bitch, Martha. I am not."

"You wrote that book in your sleep practically."

"On so many levels. But this one. I swear. This one will never end up in print."

"You are so arrogant, so self-centered."

"I am sorry. I really am. Look, about the other thing."

"What other thing? Oh the book you are secretly writing not for publication where you are stealing moments from my life for your

own use, that?"
"Yes, if I painted your portrait would you object?"
"I might. I own the rights to my own image."
"It's not like you are being portrayed as a psychotic —"
"That's heartening, Gordy."
"Don't call me that."
"What?"
"Gordy. I really don't like it."
"Gordy? It's cute. What's wrong with it?"
"I am going out."
"You do that."
"I will!"
"Okay then!"
"Okay then!"

Bang! I slammed the door and went downtown and had a few drinks at this dirty ancient men's-only-spit-on-the-floor place where I didn't know anyone and they had winter Olympics re-runs showing, and I shambled back an hour later sheepish, and apologetic and, after Martha elaborated on my erratic and unpredictable behaviour patterns, my tendencies to over react and withdraw, and how difficult that made our life together, and I said that I was sorry and then Martha was maternal and forgiving, we laughed about it all.

I knew then I was not the man I appeared to myself to be, and this difference, this secret life, the split between who I appeared to myself to me and who I was and still, to an extent, am, kept me writing this.

But I wrote lies in the books that I kept coming out, that is, until I stopped. I knew my market and wrote what was necessary to sell truckloads of books. It was all total nonsense, but it sounded great. I was a good writer. My work was backed up by interesting well-endowed rigorous research[6] that was such complete bullshit. I wrote how we the therapists impose meanings on the lives of vulnerable impressionable clients and, by extension, on others' lives. I then went further. I figured if you want to really sell well, one cannot take half measures. I said that therapists, psychiatrists, even in some cases entire medical and psychological disciplines are but an extension, a tool of law enforcement, of politics, of religion. I said we had grown corrupt,

6 I only used the research of people who had received the biggest and most prestigious academic endowments, so my work, though complete nonsense, was generally perceived as solid, though a few of the researchers heavily criticised my interpretations of their work.

lacking in vigour and intellectual and moral independence. That we had become like Universities who had received too many endowments from governments and corporations. And then I named names. It's important to name names. I dropped names like a fading rock star reminiscing on times when she once nearly made it big. I talked about the new religion. I talked about how we chose our gods and killed them. I talked about the sacred space of the therapeutic encounter, within the theatre of the room of psychotherapeutic psychoanalytic encounter, we lay down a dogma, a morality, either by our silence or our speech. I talked about the all seeing inner eye, how within the sacred space we made people see themselves, face up to terrible truths, but only in the way we deemed healthy. I talked about the new world order, how soon the entire earth would be turned into one great economic machine, and how we make people sufficiently mentally healthy to work. We oil the wheels of the economic machine. We make well-adjusted functionaries. We label the deviant 'bad', those who will not participate in the great feast of wealth creation and consumption. We also label the co-operative person 'good', but we'll never admit that. We swear an oath that we, the therapists, are honest people, leading other people, our clients, to the door of moral choice, but we never tell them the choices they have to take are already made for them. Who could live with the truth that personal freedom is a myth. Who could live with the truth that they pay us to keep people unhappy and medicated. And people go on being miserable and productive.

And I made a lot of money out of that. I was a fraud. I had constructed a web of lies and half-truths. Everything I did was a lie.

19.

On the evening of the fourth of April 2---- nothing in particular happened. I drove the two point three miles from my Mapleview house where I work and see patients, to the 14a St. John's Terrace Apt 214b, the home I shared back then with Martha. I parked in my designated parking spot. I locked my car and taking some shopping in, walked into the apartment building. Five hundred and five people lived there. Living in such close proximity to five hundred and four other human beings, some rather litigiously minded watchful types, is something of an intense experience. Their cars are expensive. Their lives are expensive. They are kind decent warm trusting caring family-oriented people. I hated them all.

I took the elevator and arrived at the door of my apartment. Inside, Martha was on the phone. She smiled at me, showed me her left breast, winked at me, rubbed her crotch area and continued talking to the other members of her conference call. Martha was regailing them with a story about a person called Greg O'Sullivan. Greg was a former head of accounts. Martha had recently fired Greg O'Sullivan for stealing from the company. No one could figure out why. Perhaps he was unhappy with his job. Perhaps he was bored. Perhaps he was greedy. Martha was in the process of readying Leef Inc. for a corporate takeover by Xpex, a company that aspired to put people before profits, and aspired to grow in its centre the values of truth, honesty, loyalty, and the avoidance of evil acts.

There were two other people on the phone line with her- Philip Sound, her boss, and a third person, whose name I did not catch. But this wasn't fun for her. Martha was nervous and defensive. She was doing what she always did when she was nervous and defensive. When she was nervous and defensive she talked. She told stories. Good ones usually, stories that may or may not have any direct bearing on the actual subject matter of the conversation, but, like any good story they served the purpose of hiding the storyteller in the tall grass of the story, and made them unreachable. Martha was like that, always like a rabbit in the undergrowth. So good at what she did, so unable to define her own needs in the thicket of other's needs that embroiled her, so sensitive and sexy and beautiful and charming and witty, yet so alone in the midst of all the demands placed upon her. I loved her. But then, perhaps I loved my image of her. For in truth, I did not know. Her. I wonder now was I capable of knowing anyone at that stage of my life. When I came in the door she was laughing. She was five months with the company at this stage. I was getting very irritated at the amount of time they took from us, especially with these phone calls.

"Greg was shocked when we used talk about competitors, joking we didn't have to worry about them. That we would eventually buy out the competitor company in a year or so."[7]

"He didn't get the joke?" Unknown Female Voice said.

"Think it offended his politics," Martha said.

"But he stole from the company," Unknown Female Voice said.

"Yeah, but that wasn't why we fired him," Martha said." We fired him because he constantly resisted change and he didn't want to adapt."

"Agreed" Phil Sound said." And our Board went down that road with us on it," Sound added.

"Ha ha ha, you know, they used tell stories about him."

"Really?" Sound said.

"But I shouldn't really talk like this. I mean I shouldn't." Martha said.

"Go on." Sound said.

"Go Martha go!" Unknown Female Voice said.

"There was one I liked," Martha said.

"Go on, tell us." Phil Sound said.

"I gotta go soon, you know." Martha said. "Time to eat."

"Go on Martha, after all those figures and stats, we could do with a chuckle or two, eh?"

Martha rolled her eyes for a moment, looking pained and stressed and angry. I looked at her and clenched my fist in anger at the callers, who were clearly annoying and exhausting Martha, and opened my hands in sympathy to her and I wanted to walk over and disconnect the conference call. Then I saw pages and files strewn everywhere. She had obviously been on the phone for a long long time. Then she forced a smile into her voice and regailed on:

"Greg O'Sullivan was the was the kind of guy, some of his former colleagues would joke, who if he was out jogging, you know Greg used jog a fair bit, so there is Greg is out jogging, jog jog jog, four or five

7 Xpex bought out a Company about once a month, usually one with over 500 employees. Leef had 1,500 or so. After full legal entity change into Xpex, it had shed 700 staff, it's systems streamlined and integrated into the Xpex EMEA Sub Region (Europe, Middle East, Africa) the problem was Greg resisted this integration, despite the fact he was kept on after the name change. Because of his attitude he was let go. He has since taken up chess full-time and earns a modest living playing the game, a pastime up to that point he pursued in a purely amateur status.

miles and there he is, jogging past, for instance, past a Primary School during lunch break, or whatever, and suddenly, like out of the blue you know, a passing petrol tanker hits this fucking huge oil slick and started to skid, and the tanker driver yells 'Get out of the fucking way! Get out of the way! Breaks are gone! Breaks are gone! Moooove!'"
The other members of the conference call were laughing out loud. As was I.
And in the midst of the laugh out loud, Martha moves into the netherworld of her story.
"But the tanker driver can't stop, you know?" Martha says. "And the tanker driver is screaming and banging the steering wheel and the tanker jack knifes, turns over, sparks flying as it slides across the road, smashing against cars, breaks through the school railings, killing everyone and everything in sight, and continues on its inexorable journey towards the school building."
"OMYGOD"
"GOLLY!"
"And the appalled horrified tanker driver jumps out of the cabin of the overturned vehicle and runs screaming towards the school and tries to warn as many of the kids as possible yet the tanker screeches across the school playground, smashes into the school, killing the brave driver, and it explodes into an apocalyptic fireball, and there are hundreds of deaths and fire brigades and ambulances and all those torched crispy little bodies and there stands Greg, looking at all of this, and says to a passer-by, 'well, you don't see that every day' - and goes home."
"HA HA Eh He heee heee"
"HA AHA AAAh haaA"
"HAAAA HAAAA"
"That's the kind of guy he was they would say. The kind of guy who saw what was happening and knew there were some things you could stop and some things you couldn't."
"What a nut!"
"Serious issues!"
Everyone laughs and laughs. Phil Sound interjected.
"Look Martha, really sorry about the call. We all appreciated you coming in on this call on this your day off, Martha."
"You're the best, Martha!" Unknown Female Voice Said.
"These are, well, stressful times and you are carrying a big load. I know you are able to carry this burden of leading the team to rationalize Leef Inc., so it dovetails beautifully with the mother company. We want Leef Inc. to be best of breed. I have word down from Xpex

headquarters, actually I am flying out there real soon to meet with Jim and Emma.
"No Problem Phil," Martha said, "Gotta go, though. Really soon."
"I understand. But this issue was flagged and we wanted our sector to be, if not best of breed, at least way up there."
"Yes." Martha said.
"We need to nail, need to well, ensure that the people we are keeping aren't duplicating work. How's that working out generally, Martha?"
"Extremely well, we are scheduling some more team building exercises, personality typologies, not very expensive, but effective. We have a few occupational psychologists assessing, and we will get back to you, say by Tuesday next week. We are hoping to peel away fifteen maybe twenty percent? There is a lot of unnecessary duplication."
"What's the legal situation with this?"
"There is no legal situation."
"Industrial relations?"
"If you are asking will there be strike action, I don't have a crystal ball. To the best of my knowledge, it's taken care of."
"Okay then. Can you unpack that for us?"
"No, no I can't unpack that for you, except to say that the relevant bodies have been met and serious negotiations are in progress. Listen, I don't mean to be rude. We have been talking around the same subject for the past ninety minutes. Can we wrap this up?"
Sound allowed a small silence to hang before he answered.
"Sure. Okay people, we are closing the meet. Thanks for your input."
The call ended. Martha put down the receiver.
"Bastards," she said.
"Is there anything to eat?" I said, "I'm really, really hungry."
"I'm sure we can find something to eat," Martha smiled.
"Why do you get so many calls?" I asked.
"It's my job. I'm hired to fire as many as I can. Look, why don't we get away for a while, just the two of us?"
"Look, why do you take so many calls from these people?"
"It's my job. Why do you think they pay me all that money?"
"Actually they don't pay you all that much money. You should be earning twice as much as me."
"What are you saying? Are you saying that they got me on the cheap? That I am some kind of two for one job?"
"I know that they are under paying you and considering the kinds of work you do, and the kinds of effort and expertise you are putting into a rather complex situation, and the kinds of travelling you are doing for them."

"What? What are you saying? Are you saying they are conning me?"

"I am wondering how this will end. I am wondering if you have really tied up your contract. I am wondering what will happen to you after the transition is complete."

"Why can't you support me? Why do you never see what I do as important?"

"I do."

"No you don't. You never do. You are always looking at the negative. You are always criticising and undermining me."

"I think what you are doing is really great."

"No, you think I am helping to hack up a company for a bunch of greedy corporate types and you think they are just using me."

"I think they pay for what they get. In the end you can't give them the kind of near religious devotion you give them without them taking advantage of you. Why do you think Phil Sound came looking for you?"

"He wanted the best."

"Why do you trust these people? What did they ever do to deserve your trust? Your loyalty?"

"You just don't accept me. You want someone who lives life your way, according to your standards. You use your intellect to control and dominate people. You crush them with arguments and you have contempt for their stupidity. Sometimes I wonder if you love me."

"Now you are being crazy."

"I always loved you. I always thought you would do something incredible because you are so brilliant and so extraordinary."

"Look, please explain where all this is coming from. Please tell me that you don't really hate yourself so much that you have to find some kind of elaborate excuse for pushing me away like this."

"But you don't want to achieve anything. You want to drift. You want to amuse yourself with writing silly books and reading day and night and sniping at people and ticking over in your practice."

"We have a great life together, Martha. Really."

"I don't know if it's a life at all. I know we live together. I know that. But I don't know if anyone can get close to you without being continually hurt."

"I am sorry Martha. Please don't cry. I am sorry. I don't know what to say except perhaps we should go away to somewhere nice and talk about this. I know I don't want to leave things like this. Really. It's too important and I feel terrible you feel like this. I never want to undermine you. I never knew you felt like this."

"We are always arguing over this. You don't listen. You won't hear me.

You never listen. You think everyone should listen to you, but —"

"I suppose. I'll think it over."

"Please do," I said.

20.

Ed Frasier began his campaign of torture and intimidation not long after I arrived in St. Raymond's Boys' School. At first I thought it odd I didn't see Alan Morrison the day I started in St. Raymond's. Alan was two classes ahead of me, at first. Then Jim Anderson, the headmaster, conferring with colleagues, moved me to Alan's class. That took, I think, about three weeks. I tried meeting Alan a few times during the furore of lunch, but Alan had other things he had to do, so I sidled up to him one day during lunch break when he wasn't expecting it, and I said:

"Hi."

"Hi Brock, what do you want?"

"Nothing. Just saying hi. We're in the same class now, I see."

"Yeah, what's that about, eh?"

"I dunno. Wasn't my idea."

"Whose was it? You some kind of freak? Oh wait, you are!"

"No! I expect it's the Headmaster's idea.

"Whatever, Brock. Can't you see I'm busy?"

"Want to get together after school?"

"No."

"Okay. Why not?"

"I don't, okay?"

"Okay. Why?"

"I just don't like you Brock. Now piss off, okay?"

"Why don't you like me?"

"I just don't. You're a weird person, that's why."

"Has this anything to do with Edward Frasier?" I asked.

"No, it fucking doesn't, it's to do with you pretending to be someone you are not," Alan answered.

"That's not fair. I was embarrassed. I just wanted to play with you as a friend."

"Really? Did you? That's so sweet. Wow, I am touched. Now fuck off, Brock."

Alan was, I remember, playing some kind of computer game, one of those small devices I never got to like much.

"I don't know if I believe you." I said.

"I don't give a shit what you believe, Brock."

"Why don't you give a shit?"

"Brock. Fuck off."

"You always called me Gordon. Now you call me Brock. That matters. Little things like that matter."

Alan stood up and looked me coldly in the eyes. Then he punched me in the stomach.

"Okay, if you want, I will call you Gordon. I always thought I called you either one or the other. Now please, as a personal favour, fuck off. Fuck off Gordon. Gordon, I am asking you to keep a distance from me. Do not speak to me, Gordon. Do not greet me, Gordon. Do not make any kind of friendly gesture towards me, Gordon. Do not pass me notes. Do not nod to me in the corridor, or in the yard, on the way to school, or from school, or if you see me in the street, or at a party. I do not like you, Gordon. I never liked you, not really. You are a creepy person. You don't know how to talk to people. My parents like you. Not me. Now please, Gordon Brock, leave me the fuck alone."

I looked at Alan continuing his game. He smiled to himself.

"This game rocks," Alan said, grinning.

"I can tell you are having fun," I said, as he increased his game score to the hundred thousands, enjoying his own wit, wishing he had a crowd to laugh with him. He kept playing. He had punched me. Then he had gone back to that fucking game. Maybe there was a competition in his group as to who could score the first million.

"You seem to be hanging with Ed a lot, and his group," I said.

"So what? He said.

"He is a viper," I said. I suddenly felt worse, worse than the pain I was feeling right then in my stomach. I was suddenly feeling lonely, so terribly empty and abandoned, like someone waking up lost in a desert, or living alone on an island.

"You mean his crew, Smudge, and the others?" Alan said." Bunch of glue sniffing perverts the lot of them. Better than you, Brock."

"I am sorry I didn't tell you, about myself. I wanted to be your friend. I wanted to be —"

"Normal? You think I don't understand? You think you are special?" Alan said and kept playing, his fingers moving the tiny track wheel as he punched aliens and took down fighter craft, the wreckage and bloodshed spattering virtually along the landing strip in the tiny virtual world across the galaxy.

"Brock, hello Brock. Yoo hoo HEE HAAAARRRR!"

Alan[8] was waving his hand in front of me.

---

8 Alan was afraid of Smudge, so called because of the mole on his face. This was because Smudge was smarter and stronger than he, but felt less than because of the mole. The mole was due for removal, sometime. Eventually Smudge (David Jones) became a theatre director. I do not know if that mole was ever removed.

I don't know what I was thinking at that stage I possibly went into shock. I felt numb, dizzy, slightly disoriented.
"You have been standing there."
"You are no good," I said to him.
"I asked you to leave."
"Okay," I said.
"You know something, Brock, there really has to be a name for what's wrong with you. So fuck off, okay? Just leave me alone. I have enough friends. I never wanted you to play in my garden. My mother wanted me to keep you company. You were a pity playmate. Okay?"
"Fuck you too," I said.
"Whatever. I'm not your Mommy in the new school. Figure it out for yourself."

And Alan Morrison walked off into the school crowds coming and going and shouting and I hated the noise and the crowds. I sat by myself. I was too uncomprehending of what had happened. It would be later on I would begin to feel the overwhelming hurt and devastation that would crush me. It would be later on isolation, after dozens more similar rejections would become so commonplace that I would begin to feel strangely naked without the everyday dull sense of paranoia I felt just going about my everyday life. But there and then I had a salad by myself in the school cafeteria, feeling paranoia rising with the growing noise, increasingly self-conscious, as no one spoke to me. I felt numb, a lengthy prelude to that pain. I ate, rather mechanically. The food felt tasteless. The knot in my stomach made a hard indigestible ball of the salad. I usually loved salads. I took out a book and began reading it. That usually took my mind off things. If I read for long enough, I generally relaxed.
"What's that you're reading, Brock?" Ed Frasier asked, sitting beside me.
"Just a novel. Anna Karenin."
"Is it good?"
"Fascinating. I didn't hear you"
"I can be really nifty, Brock."
I didn't answer. I looked at Frasier. Ed smiled sweetly at me. I managed a nervous smile. I said.
"What do you really want from me? You are bigger than me. You have friends, if you want to call them friends. You have a dad who is a policeman. And you are two years older than me. I am twelve. And you are fourteen. I haven't made much noise in class. I haven't corrected you in public. I haven't disagreed with you or your friends

or embarrassed them. So what could you want from me. I think you are a sadist. I think you are especially sadistic when you come across something you can't control. And you can't control the fact that I am smarter than you. I am afraid of you. But I also am smarter than you. It's not something I am proud of or particularly sought out." I said.
Frasier didn't answer.
I said: "Frasier?"
Frasier stopped smiling for a moment, as though the question disturbed him, then he began smiling again, as though the question had never been asked. I, giving up any hope of ever reasoning with Ed, returned to nervously trying to follow the gist of the novel I was reading. Frasier edged a little closer. The touch of Ed's thigh against my thigh felt like an electric pulse. Ed leaned his face closer and looked grinningly across at his much bemused crew. I noticed Alan was among them, enjoying the show.
"You are reading because you don't have company. Isn't that it?"
I didn't answer. I tried hard to hide the fear I felt in seeing the cold fish-eyed stare in Frasier's eyes. I looked at Frasier's face, his frame, the fact he sat near me, but not so close to imply a comfortable amicability.
"I asked you a very polite question, Gordon."
"No, no you didn't. I want you to go away."
Ed elbowed me.
"Fuck off," I said.
Ed punched me in the ribs, just underneath my elbow.
"I think I did, and I am not getting a verbal from you."
"Not the verbal you wanted, you psychopath. Aaaaaah!"
A second, harder punch landed in exactly the same spot as before.
"I have to say you are not being polite."
"What was, what was, your, q-question?"
"I was putting forth the proposition (do you like that?), Brock- that you are reading because you don't have company. It's a common complaint of academically inclined people."
"I, I'm not academically inclined. I-I like to read. Books are not the end of my search, unlike an academic."
"How old are you, Brock?"
"Just twe-twelve."
If he had told me I was fifty I would have agreed with him.
"Yes, but what you do, all the reading, you know? They call it defensive reading. People do it because they can't really engage with the world, they feel isolated, or can't bond with others. It's a way, how shall I say? It's a way of understanding the world from a safe distance. Like playing board games or living online rather than doing it in the real.

Do you feel like that, Gordon? Do you feel alone in the world? I can help you in that regard. I have friends. You see them over there? At the next table?"

Frasier pointed to a group watching. They smiled and waved, then looked at each other and chuckled knowingly.

"Now, if you like, I can introduce you, end this isolation, improve your popularity, widen your social circle, and introduce you to people who can help you, really bring you out of yourself, even get you laid if you are really lucky."

A loud burst of laughter accompanied the last remark made by Frasier. Ed Frasier grinned broadly, looked knowingly around the room, and smiled.

"Those aren't friends, Ed."

"No."

"They are your tribe."

"Aren't they pretty?"

"Eh, no."

Then Ed reached under the desk and grabbed me by the testicles. I tried to scream, and then noticed I couldn't. Ed had caught me by the throat, which is not a metaphor. Then releasing me from the throat and lessening his grip on my testicles, Ed smiled broadly, and began to make his extended point. Tears streamed from my eyes. I never in my life ever believed it possible to feel so much pain and humiliation all at once. I was in full view of the entire school. Now hold on, I wasn't. Not really. That's ridiculous. I mean. I was in full view of what appeared to be several hundred young people and I was feeling intensely humiliated, embarrassed, and rather paranoid. Dozens were passing and grinning at me and Ed. They knew full well what was going on. They had seen it before. Brock, so they muttered, was obviously Frasier's new bitch.

"Aren't they pretty?"

I couldn't answer with the pain in my testicles.

"Gordon, I'm asking you a question. Aren't they pretty?"

I nodded.

"Now, I want to make myself clear to you. Do not disrespect me, and do not make claims that I initiated your social exclusion, or told friends, like that little fuck Alan Morrison, not to hang with you. I didn't. Make one move, one sign that I have you by the balls, and I will squash them like the fucking grapes they are. Nod politely and smile if you understand me clearly."

I nodded politely and smiled.

"Smiling through the tears. It's definitely mediocre sonnet material.

Now I am going to let you go. You have very small balls, I just wanted to let you know that, and I also wanted to let you know I am going to fuck you up. So far and so bad you will never be the same."

"Frasier?"

A new, older, softer voice, hardly audible above a whisper, but elocuted to a kind of academy of dramatic arts clarity, cut through the gaggle of school lunch verbal traffic. A pool of hush rippled out from the centre of Frasier's naming. Ed and I looked up. It was Brother Frank, Frank Ryan. Even at this early stage I knew about the great, terrifying, brilliant Brother Frank Ryan. Ed let go his firm, crushing, and merciless hold on my testicles.

"I see, Frasier, as ever in your life, you have something of a firm grasp of the inessentials. I take it this is something of a new departure on the ever downward spiral of self-abasement and self-loathing you laughingly call your life. Or, on second thoughts, maybe not."

"No Brother I —"

Frasier stood up. Frank raised his hand.

"Please, please, Edward. I look at you and I feel only pity. You will get yours. And I have my eyes —" Frank pointed two of his long fingers at each of his eyes, and then pointed at Frasier "On you. You know what that means, don't you Edward? It means trouble. Trouble like you could never possibly imagine."

Frank turned his eyes upon me. He saw my tears and he knew what had been happening.

"Gordon Brock, I presume? Report immediately to the nurse's station. Chop, chop, young man. Don't make me have to ask twice. Go!"

"Yes, Brother."

Frasier made to move quietly into the gathering crowd as I ran off, books and food stuffed into my bag.

"Frasier?" Frank snapped his fingers and waved at Ed.

"Brother?"

"Walk with me. Outside. Ignore you friends. Let us indulge in a little communication outside the earshot of your, 'friends'."

"Yes, Brother."

Ed looked grinningly at his crew. They smiled and looked worriedly at each other.

"They can't help you, Frasier," Brother Frank said.

Frasier stepped out of the cafeteria with the Brother Frank. Then Frank stopped and Ed looked at him with defiant look that had an overwhelming fear and respect percolating through it. Frank looked at him for a moment then turned to look around and beyond him, eyeing the moving packs of students for signs of inappropriate behaviour.

"What happened?"
"Sir?" Ed answered.
"What happened, Frasier?"
"Brock and I had a disagreement, sir."
"I see."
Frasier and Ryan walked around the yard. Ryan didn't say anything.
"I have class, sir. I am sorry."
"Please, you are not sorry, Frasier."
"There really wasn't anything in it."
"Oh, but there was, Frasier."
"Really, Brother. It was just a bit of rough and tumble."
"With someone half your size?"
"I know Brother. I am ashamed of myself."
"Oh please, Frasier. Ashamed? You?
There was a silence as they walked past other teachers and students going to and coming from class. Brother Frank picked up the faltering conversation.
"Why pick Brock?"
"It just happened. I really am sorry. I will apologize to him straight away."
"But that won't work. I think there was something in it. So don't be a liar. There very much was something in it. You see, Frasier, there is a recording of what happened. I happened to be in the control room at the time. I saw it. Brock was with Morrison for a time. Then Brock goes to his bag and takes out his lunch and begins eating it. You and your group were watching Brock and Morrison from a distance. Then you go over to Brock and you start talking to him. Then you assault Brock. Then you appear to grab the boy. Then the boy starts crying. Then I intervene. Have you anything to add to that, Frasier?"
Frasier kept walking with Ryan. Ryan stopped him.
"You know something Frasier? I fear for you. I don't like you."
"Sir!? You can't say that!"
"I know. I am breaking all kinds of laws by telling you what an awful human being you are becoming. Do give me your attention. I don't like you because you are cruel. I don't like you because you are jealous and you are too ambitious to do anything other than serve your own needs."
"I could say, sir, that you made inappropriate suggestions, sir. That would be bad for your career, sir."
"And I will fight you, Frasier. There are some things your policeman father and your connections cannot protect you from. Stay away from Gordon Brock. Give him a free pass. You won't win this. He will.

Remember, there is a recording. It can be used."

And Brother Frank walked off.

Ed went back inside. He started shouting:

"Didn't anyone fucking see Frankie arrive?"

No one answered.

"So no one saw nothing? Motherfucking Fuck!"

He gazed angrily at his crew, who looked sheepishly at each other, then giggled.

"You people are like fucking children! I asked a simple question. Answer me!"

Smudge shook his head.

"You said 'nothing'."

"What?"

"You mean no one saw anything. You said no one saw nothing. That's a double negative."

"Whatever, Smudge. You are such a fucking bishop in the church of fucknugget"

"No, dude."

"Don't 'dude' me."

"Look, Frankie Four Faces, he sort of came out of the crowd, kind of beamed in like Captain Fucking Kirk or something"

"Well, you know how tall he is. You can kind of spot him."

"Just because you didn't see him, Ed. And you know how softly he walks."

"Shut up, Smudge!" Ed snapped.

Smudge grinned.

"He really got to you, didn't he?"

"You think that's fucking funny, Smudge?"

"Yeah, sort of. So tell us. What did he say to you?"

"Nothing."

"That was sort of funny. Frankie Four Faces fucked with Frasier. I like that. Alliterative."

"Smudge, there has to be a name for what's wrong with you."

"I'm a friend of yours, Ed. That's what's wrong with me."

21.

Martha and I arrived back from Greece on a Tuesday in November, relaxed and happy. As ever, suspicious of that feeling of contentment, after a few hours, I began worrying about the office and, after we had begun unpacking and had something to eat, and after I had taken a nap, and after I had found a few other excuses not to work, or do anything productive, feeling anxious, I wanted to do something. Then I finally realised the only way I would be able to eliminate my worry over the office and my house and what was happening with Lorna, who was still there after we officially broke up, was by actually going over there.

So, I got into my car and I drove over to the house on Mapleview, and found Lorna gone, and her rooms cleaned out. The downstairs consulting rooms, with their double locked double doors, with my files and notes, had remained untouched, but the house that formerly had that messed up, lived in, slightly dusty appearance from people (Lorna and I) living and shedding dust and hair and skin and those fluids one only cares to think of medically, opening and closing doors and carrying dirt in on their feet and skin and coughing and sneezing and breathing and cleaning and using the space they call home, was just my office with a lot of cleaned out empty rooms upstairs.

Those upstairs rooms had that professionally cleaned, shiny, unlived in look, that gave me a sense of alienation from my own place. It reminded me of those perfectly clean houses where they change the furniture or the flooring or the carpets once every eighteen months, people who get new doors and windows installed every so often, people who give you that sense that they are hiding something, something bad; people who politely greet you, then look away as they pass you by. The fireplaces shone. The windows were perfectly translucent. The curtains and shutters were spotless. She took every trace of our life, our history, from the place, turned it into a cold rental. And it was cold. Not that the heating had been switched off. Just everything was devoid of living warmth, like those paintings that reduce the complexity and contradictory nature of living into a series of hard lines and clear contours. No life.

But I was so relieved the downstairs floor office was still locked intact. Inside, I could hear the phone ringing. An envelope was pinned to my door. Inside the envelope was the following letter:

November 7th--
Dear Gordon,
I want you to know that I am leaving the apartment. I know it is over between us and I do not want you to contact me in any way. I am truly sorry for hitting you that day and, if you send me your medical bills via my solicitor, I'll be happy to pay for them. I assume you won't be suing me, as that would attract negative publicity for a brilliant rising star in the therapy game. I also want you to know that I still love you, despite hating what you did to me, to us. I don't know how this works, if I will always love you, or if, with time, 'clichés notwithstanding' as you would say, love goes away. I think you broke us up precisely because you finally had the happiness you wanted in life, unbearable suffocating happiness, perhaps with someone you least expected to have happiness with. And happiness, to your mind, is for lesser mortals. You believe you are someone searching, always open to change. But, in reality, you are rigid, fearful, judgmental, arrogant and cruel. You are selfish, yet merciless with yourself, so you demand from others the same standards of cruelty and devotion you impose on yourself. I do not think you know what you have done to both of us, Gordon, but what goes around comes around. People like you end up terminally alone.
Yours etc,
Lorna.

My hands shook as I read this letter. She was right about me on many levels, and it was precisely that which hurt. It came from her heart to mine. I rolled the paper in a ball and threw it across the room, as I wept, unaware at the time that, while in Greece, Martha and I had conceived our son, Joshua. I remember, though we hadn't married at the time, the topic arose during the holiday, despite our constant touring and visiting of ancient sights in the boiling heat. I remember drinking vast quantities of water, taking long cold showers, wearing cheese cloth and heavy sunglasses and hats. I remember reading so much about Greece. I remember I drove Martha crazy because I spent most of my time reading about the place, its history, its geography, its culture, its food. I remember the dry stones, making love on the beach. What I most remember was the depths of my desire for Martha, how no matter how much sex we had, how much we were connected, I remember there was this longing and with this longing there came this love, this intense connection this sense of completion, this happiness. It is something I can never forget, lying there in the afternoon, my hands running along her body covered in sweat and just watching the trees moving in a distant breeze, a breeze that never came to visit our exhausted happy bodies. I remember the boiling heat, disintegrating edifices, a timeless beauty shining in the mid day light. Though unaccustomed to the climate, though I suffered headaches and nausea and tiredness because I burned myself out with reading, that time was unforgettable. It was unforgettable because I knew the shallowness of my capacity to love and be loved and that, despite this, this person, this desirable, this extraordinary person, Martha Reynolds, had chosen to be with me. And it was so good, all of it.

One night I said: "I think —"

"What?"

"I think I am not good enough to be with you."

"That's silly, Gordon. I mean, you know that's not true."

We were sitting near one of the acropolises outside Athens after dinner and the conversation had quietened between us. I was somewhat drunk and voluble, and wanted Martha to participate in my ecstasy, but she wouldn't.

"What's wrong?" I asked.

"Nothing."

"I know I have drunk too much."

"So?"

"The wine is really good."

"It still is. They make a lot of this stuff around here, you know?"

"Hmmm."

"So don't be silly and let's have some fun together," she said, dangling her wine glass at me.

"And the company's not too bad either," I said.

She grinned.

"I just realised something last night," she said.

"Oh?"

She took another sip of wine, and then stopped, as if the stuff she had been really enjoying had suddenly gone bad on her, and she was angry with her glass of wine for some reason.

"I didn't sleep."

"Ok," I said. "Why didn't you sleep? What's happening? Why didn't you wake me up? We could have talked."

"It wasn't so bad."

"You don't take good care of yourself, Martha."

"Why?"

"Because you don't."

"Very profound, Dr. Freud."

"Noo, nnnooo, no, no, no. I mean. I mean you think you are taking care of yourself when you are taking care, taking care of others."

"For god's sake."

"I mean, why do you love me?"

"I like your brilliance."

"What about me makes you like me- that I'm smart?"

"I love your passion, your charm, your warmth. Being with you is a difficult, rewarding."

"I love everything about you. But you give too much. You should ask for something in return."

"I know."

"Really. Really Martha?"

Martha became irritated with me, with my disbelief of her.

"Didn't I just agree with you? Didn't I ? Gordon, answer!"

"Sure, sure. I was just saying."

"I know, and I agree with you. I heard you and last night I was thinking about a lot of things, about us, and about my job. I was at a meeting last week. Phil Sound, my boss, had been away. The meeting happened after."

"Look, no offence, but that job you have - I hate it. And I swear I don't care."

"I know that too. But I care. This is important to me."

"Okay."

"And when he came back he was all fired up, filled with evangelical fervour, and he called this big meeting of all the heads of Department and there we were all sitting round looking at each other; each thinking about whatever we wanted to be doing other than sitting in that damn conference room; and then Sound walks and, then there was this live feed.

"Martha, we are on holidays and you are giving me a briefing about your job. That's really weird and obsessive."

"Phil was like an evangelist. He had been to Tuscon, and he had met the head of Xpex Inc, the company taking over Leef, you see."

"I know."

"And they had changed their company logo to green and blue circles to make it more people friendly and there was a new mission statement and it was Phil Sound's job to take the new mission statement and to bring it, so to speak, to us, the management."

"Why? I mean, couldn't he just send a memo?"

"Apparently not."

"Why not?"
"You need core values."
"I like that. Core Values. Like what? Greed and avarice and an endless supply of ambition?"
"Well, Gordon, you know," she began using a friendly emotion free corporate tone, "that the healthiest and most profitable companies define their management systems and corporate strategies beyond that of the mere bottom line."
"Really? That's fucking great honey. Now let's go have lots of sex, how about that, forget the Xpex brainwashing with a lot of fucking."
"But I want to tell you something, Gordon, and you keep interrupting me."
"Eh, no I don't."
"You do. There was this revolving light show. I swear."
"Common brainwashing technique," I said. "Breaks down one's resistance. Like playing music constantly, or listening to sermons, or company retreats."
"See? You keep interrupting."
"Sorry."
"It was a kind of mini-strobe light show going on in the background."
"What? Someone brought a light show into the board room. What kind of an idiot would do that?"
"The attention-seeking kind. It had been switched on by a member of lower level management, really distracting lights flashing all around. Until, eventually, I got up and I pulled the damn plug, and the whole thing went on and on for six hours."
"Six hours! Holy crap! What did you talk about?"
"Open channel communication, barrier-less creative outlets and at the end we all had to stand up and wave our hands in the air and we went off to talk about this new message in small groups."
"That's so beautiful. Heartwarming. You praised the lord for salvation. They really fucking hate you, don't they?"
"Well, they get to send out the message of good will, the decisions you make are guided by the values you have."
"I need more booze."
"Service. Knowledge. Winning spirit."
"Or spirits, like Brandy. Sambuca."
"The Xpex Family, or as they call it, the soul of Xpex, the destiny to work for a higher purpose, ethical competitiveness."
"Man, they really hate you."
"They pay me to take the heat."

"After this job is done, you know the transformation of Leef in to an Xpex associate, you know, will you stay?"
"I don't know," Martha said. "I'm going to have sex, lots of it, coming?"
"I was about to suggest the same thing, you know?"
"I thought you said you didn't feel worthy of me," she said grinning.
"I don't," I said. "But I have that competitive, winning spirit, that can-do attitude."
"I know," she said.

We were sitting in the car outside the doctor's surgery. I was quiet. I wasn't sure how I felt about the news.
"Aren't you happy?" She asked me. "Aren't you happy we are going to have a baby?"
"Of course I am happy. I don't know what kind of a parent I will make, but I am happy."

I wasn't happy. I was miserable. I thought about my future child's prospects, that is, if the child came to term, thought of their hopes and dreams and expectations, their possible health or lack thereof, whether or not they might live to adulthood, the kind of sexual orientation they might have, whether I might be able to sufficiently nurture the child, whether or not Martha and I might stay together, if I could continue to remain faithful to her, whether I really believed monogamy as an realistic lifestyle, what we might do if the child is born with a disability, and that maybe we should really think about buying a house, though I like the apartment. Instead of voicing any or all of these thoughts, I suggested Martha changed jobs.

I said to her, 'Martha, you have to get out of there, I mean the job. It's really stressing you out.' and we would end up arguing about it. I would say, 'I am making money steadily now, taking in more patients, and I have the bones of another book in my head'. And Martha, would say, 'I know', pointing out her contractual obligations to be there for the duration of the changes going on in Leef Inc, and that upper management would be, shall we say, less than pleased should she jump ship, so she was trapped and wished she had thought things through before she signed the contract with them in the first place.

22.

And, as Martha agonized about her job, a bizarre social group came to life in former Leef now Xpex, a group who were subsequently known as the Brunch Committee, comprised of well entrenched, long-term members of the original staff of Leef Inc, seeking a solution to what they saw as their dead careers. These were a group of conspirators who targeted Martha as the source of their ruined careers.[9]

And, as the zygote that Martha and I would eventually name Joshua Brock moved through Martha's fallopian tube to attach itself to her uterine wall, the Brunch Committee formed a plan. They decided to ruin Martha, to terminate her command with extreme prejudice. So, as the first weeks of pregnancy passed, and, as the zygote becoming baby Joshua, through it's gene regulating substances, reprogrammed endlessly dividing cells, deciding on organs, glands, bones and limbs, Eliot Spenser, Accountant grade 7b, degree in marketing and accountancy, married, one child from a previous relationship, non-smoker, social drinker, ambitious without being pathologically so, well socialized without being dependent on the group for his sense of self, who believed in his work and colleague without making a religion of team building, who looked with scepticism on the 'soul of Xpex' mythology that seemed to percolate through new management structure, meetings and literature and memos, who was well-liked without enjoying stardom status, was filled with fear and hate because his pal Greg O'Sullivan, the person Martha told the torched truck story about, had been terminated on what to him was a false charge of fiscal mismanagement, plotted Martha's ruin. Eliot wanted to strike back.

Greg hadn't been fired unjustly. Greg was a thief. Despite hours of discussion, of comforting his friend, Eliot Spenser figured this augured badly for him. One way or the other, Spenser knew that this termination set a precedent for his own career prospects. It sent the necessary message, that he too might suffer a similar unjust fate,

9 Essentially, Change Management involves migrating the assets of one company into another, called change in control (CIC), in this case from Leef to Xpex. Of the fifteen hundred employees in the original company (before CIC), Leef, eight hundred were kept, after the change (Legal Entity Change or LEC). Of those eight hundred, sixty were management. Of the sixty management kept on, thirty were fired in the six months after they signed contracts with Xpex, the aforementioned former head of accounts, Greg Sanders being one of them. These firings bred a hatred of the chief Change Manager for the Xpex–Leef Migration Team, Martha Reynolds.

and had to take preemptive action. He announced to the Brunch Committee, that, though Martha's methods were immoral, illegal, that he, Eliot, could find no real hard evidence to support any official complaint. He went on to say he had checked harassment and bullying law, company grievance procedures, and found little useful weaponry therein. In fact, Eliot Spenser had read several books on the subject, talked to his lawyer, worried, journalled, even had a sonnet or two written on the subject.
"We have to strike back,"
"Oh, and how do we do that, Captain America[10]?"

Pauline Flak, thirty eight years, five foot nine, one hundred and ten pounds, unmarried, no offspring, executive, with Leef Inc. for seven years, promoted twice to Senior Marketing Manager, said: "Eliot, this is insane."
"What is insane?" Jim Jones[11] asked
"Jim! Our careers are being ruined, and we are being managed out of the company. Did you get your performance review?"
"Yes."
"How did you do?"
"Very well," Jim said.
"I got my yearly performance review last month."
"Really?"
"Do you know how I did?"
"I could only begin to imagine, Pauline."
"Does it really matter?" Eliot said.
"Yes! It fucking matters!"
"Okay, then."
"I got an overall rating of 'poor'."
"How disappointing. I am rather troubled to hear that," Jones said.
"I never got a rating of 'poor' in my entire life, not in this company, nor at any other company I ever worked for," Pauline Flak continued.
"Really?"

10 Eliot had a nondescript middle American accent, which led to the nickname 'Captain America'

11 James Bartholomew Michael Jones, age 51, depressive, private secretary to Philip Sound, also Private secretary to Mrs. Angela Sound recently deceased (Mother to Philip Sound), bitterly opposed to the merger with Xpex; unmarried, interests include botany and the poetry of Philip Larkin and Emily Dickinson, occasionally publishes his own work in journals and magazines; silent, shy, given to moments of hilarious laconic wit, no family, no degrees, education level leaving certificate and six disastrous months in Trinity College Dublin where he suffered his first major depressive episode; a person considered too gifted for the rather minor role he played in his rather uneventful life. Flack was irritated by Jim's lack of savvy in what the Brunch Committee considered rather disastrous times.

Jim grinned infinitesimally at her self-absorbed misery.
"I came into this company to get away from all that kind of job effectiveness analysis. It had a relaxed, almost family atmosphere; despite there are fifteen hundred working here?"
"Really? I never thought that. They were always pushing me," Eliot said.
"That's because you were always too ambitious, Eliot. You pushed yourself. They saw that, and helped."
"Thanks Pauline, that's nice to hear."
"Anyway, this, before it was torn apart, this company was very different. It had a more social, less isolating, atmosphere. I joined Leef because it didn't have the kinds of intensive corporative competitiveness that other places seemed to have. That's gone, and gone forever. I don't want to have to look for another job. I want to stop searching for work every five or six years." Pauline Flak hissed, picking her nails and making a little break in the cuticle where blood emerged and some of the others saw it and felt disgust and then Pauline smiled guiltily and crossed her legs and wished she could hide how she felt.
"It's impossible," Spenser said, "It's not possible that not a single legal weapon could be used against Martha"
"Yes," Pauline said. "Yes."
"God, how I hate Martha Reynolds Brock."
"I know."
"Jesus, she is evil."
"Right. It's like she is dead inside. Like she doesn't feel anything. She gets rid of people without a thought. She is like the grim reaper."
Flak started imagining Martha in some dark room with lights and monks with dead faces asking her to confess she was a witch or had intimate relations with some dark angel. She fixed her carefully pressed jacket, folded her hands, cleared her throat and said:
"Something has to be done."
Jones spoke up.
"A whispering campaign might do what's necessary to solve our issues here."
Nobody paid any attention. Spenser took up what he thought to be the group thinking on the matter.
"An official complaint could boomerang," he said. "I mean native Australians don't want the boomerang to come back."
"They don't?" Pauline asked.
"No, not at all. The average functional aboriginal boomerang is over two metres in length and weighs several kilos.
"That's like some kind of learned factiod. You learn facts. Why do you

do that, Eliot?"

"Sorry?"

"Show off like some kind of undergraduate trying to impress people with how much he knows," Pauline said.

"Fuck you, Flak" Eliot said.

"Or," Jim said. "We could skip all the competitive crap here and piss in the well from which Martha drinks."

"What well?" Pauline said.

"The well of her good name. If we ruin her good name she has nothing."

"I have been thinking about the legal situation." Eliot went on.

"This is a complete waste of time, I might as well be talking to two fence posts with smiley faces painted on them. Is anything I am saying getting through?" Jim asked.

"They have friends in the labour court, you see," Eliot went on, ignoring Jim.

"People they pay to take decisions in their favour. If we were to sue." Pauline finished his sentence for him.

"Who said anything about suing?" Jim said, feeling increasingly irritated.

"We would inevitably lose," Eliot said.

Flak saw his point and nodded.

"So why bother?" Jones said. "Why do something so stupid and expensive as taking a case. Ruin her fucking reputation!"

"Eliot's right," she said. "Might as well turn in our resignations right now."

"Or, you know, we could kill her. We could poison her Kool-Aid." Jim said.

"What?"

"Jones, you psychopath," Eliot began.

"I'm joking," Jim said. "I was … never mind. Perhaps, with a long period of intensive therapy, and a little invasive surgery, you two might shed all the technocratic, brainwashing, procedural bullshit and develop a sense of humour. The solution is to start a whispering campaign! If this takeover fucks up —"

"The Takeover has already happened!" Eliot said.

"On paper only. As I said, if this –actual- takeover fucks up because of her, no matter who they get to replace her the waters are muddied, so to speak, and it's going to be a long while before things get better for the mother company."

"That's a little simplistic, Jim."

"It's not actually, Eliot. It's very difficult and requires enormous

courage, art, and patience. You would never be able to do it."
"I agree with Eliot, Jim. It's a dumb move."
"That's because you want to fuck him, Pauline, and you are hoping I will leave this incestuous little group and let you two get on with your courtship."
"Jim, how fucking dare you?"
"See? Absolutely no sense of humour. I am going back to work now. You people are making me want to kill myself with all this waffle."
"Wait!"
"Hold on, Jim."
"I'm late, chaps. Gotta go. What?"
"What do you have in mind?"
"Ring Sound. At about four in the morning. Sound has insomnia. Tell Sound that Martha is an alcoholic. Phil Sound's father was an alcoholic. Died from cirrhosis. That should start the old globe toppling."
"Wow Jim, that's nasty," Spenser said.
"Yeah Jim, that's harsh." Flak muttered, putting a very small plaster on her torn cuticle.

Then as Jones shambled back to his office, Eliot Spenser imagined Jim Jones calling Sound at four in the morning, drunk and mumbling about a conspiracy and telling him about the Brunch Committee. Jones would do it because it was the right thing to do, Eliot Spenser thought. Jones was too loyal, too decent a human being to do anything else in life except the right thing. Jones never came back to the Brunch Committee. Virtue, Eliot Spenser figured, has its limitations.

But then Eliot Spenser, Accountant, degree in marketing and accountancy, married, one child from a previous relationship, thirty five years old, five feet eight inches tall, just like Pauline Flak, was always was a total idiot. Jones started the whispering campaign all by himself, and, hating his new bosses as much as he hated the world he, an artist, had found himself in, he did a wonderful job destroying Martha.

And Martha went on unawares, not sensing a difference in atmosphere in work; and the Brunch Committee (reduced from three to two in number) went on; and the Joshua foetus inside Martha was then growing a nervous system, developing a working body, was about six centimeters long, had the beginnings a brain, kidneys, testes, liver and something of a digestive tract, and the indentations that would be eyes, ears, and a jaw began developing. Martha was becoming unwell during the morning and part of the day, not so much morning sickness as a sense of fear and uncertainty. She ate and slept more. She got irritable at little things, worried obsessively over her workload, found herself gazing out of her office window across at the Dublin skyline, wondering at the millions of lives and all the concerns and thoughts and dreams and loves of the millions of lives she did not know and would never know, and wondered if she would ever know the life that was growing inside her. Merely a lodger, she thought. And then he moves out. How do I know it's a 'he'? It could be a Dorothy, A Lorna, A Ruth or A Vanessa. Why a he? It could be a she? Inside me right now, she worried, subtle genetic changes could be making the child unable to have a normal life, anencephalic, down's, scoliosis, hydrocephalus, future bulimic anorexic junk head, foetal alcohol syndrome, cancer; some dreaded complex organism eating him alive? Though they tell me all is well. I mean, can I love whoever it is in here? Can I do this? Perhaps some hyper-intelligent freak? Some government experiment gone horribly wrong? I could be subject to experiments while asleep. I could be growing a future rebel who revolts against the status quo and goes to live in some suburb to be alone with her muse?

Actually, Joshua turned out an intelligent, lovable, normal boy. He has brought me nothing but joy. I'm supposed to say that aren't I? It's true, though.

Rumours about Martha stretched like the skin on a drum, all tight and resonant. Rumours that got distorted with the retelling. Rumours, like flies buzzing against a windshield, distorting the view. It was difficult to know what was true and untrue[12]. And they became more bizarre with the retelling.

Polite, smiling, nodding, non-committal silence accompanied her trips to the coffeepot, the water fountain, the canteen, the afternoon drinks to discuss some client, though she thought, I shouldn't be drinking coffee, alcohol, or taking the odd hit of marijuana. After all, Martha thought, I am pregnant. Martha figured things had changed, figured things were wrong, some imperceptible shift in the ether. Probably someone was in trouble. She rang Sound.

"Phil, is there something going on that I should be aware of?"

12 Here are some of the false rumours I learned through interviews for this book: That Martha was a secret alcoholic. That Martha hit her first fiancé, Dr. Richard Smith, with a bat (which was why they broke up). That Martha had some type of shady dossier on Philip Sound. That Philip Sound was the father of her baby. That Martha had connections with a secret government agency that were investigating certain mergers and acquisitions. That Martha had a cocaine nose job and had done time in jail.

"Shouldn't I be the one asking you that? I mean, you report to me last time I checked."

"Phil, no disrespect, but that's not an answer."

"I am hanging up now. Martha, this is absurd. Take a weekend off."

"I can't. I have the meeting with Accounts Reconciliation committee."

"Okay. The offer stands, and no, I hear nothing. Relax!"

And Phil put down the phone and thought about Martha and all he had heard for a long time after.

23.

If Martha had a friend in the office, they might have taken her aside and explained the intricacies of what was rumoured about her, told her there were awful things being said about her, rumoured on the rumour mill. And, as those terrible rumours echoed around the office and along the electronic pathways, little Joshua's heart was beating steadily, his stomach functioning, his liver and kidneys creating and purifying blood and the foetus was sixteen weeks old, he was emptying his bladder regularly, had limbs, lungs, fingernails, and a brain, Martha felt him moving around and loved the feeling and finally decided on a name.

"Did your parents ever think about having a brother or a sister, for you? By the way, I am thinking of the name Joshua for our child"
"No," I said." I don't think they ever did. My mother had a very difficult pregnancy. I think she nearly died having me. And they took a decision not to have a second child. By the way, I hate the name."
"Is that why your Dad doesn't call so much?" Martha was relaxing in the bath.
"I don't think so."
"Really, why then?"
"Dad and I, and Mom when she was alive, we always had a – difficult – relationship. I'm closer to Dad than Mom, but Mom and I drifted apart in my teens and twenties. And then she just died. She just got a really bad headache one day while talking to a neighbour and collapsed. I mean, it's not that I don't call Dad. I do call him. It's not that he doesn't care. He cares. I love him. He loves me. It's not that he isn't excited about what's happening- that we are having a child. It's to do, I think, with, well —"

Between the sixteenth and the twenty third weeks, as Joshua floated blissfully in the watery timeless zone between conception and birth, Martha was lying there deep in the bath, for she took a lot of baths then.

"I think they never got past what happened, when I was a kid in St. Raymond's and afterwards, that's what I think, anyway. I told you about that." I said.

She was there in the bath listening and sensing the rhythms of the child's movements, his sleeping and waking, him being fully formed, developing brown fat to keep warm, kicking a little now and then turning over, and she would rub him to calm him.

"So you did. Things like that happen to lots of kids, and parents," she said. "I mean I don't want you to think I don't feel for you. There isn't a town or village anywhere in the country where kids aren't bullied by someone, especially if they were smart, and you are smart. Too damn smart for your own good, if you ask me, but listen, I have a question," Martha said:
"Hm?"
"How come we aren't married?"
And little Joshua becoming who he became, who he is now, would no longer be distressed, sensing what mother feels by the umbilical that rarely breaks.

"I would marry you in a heartbeat," I said. "But I am not sure you would want to marry me."
"Why?" She asked "Because you sleep around on me?"

And elsewhere the Chief Executive of Xpex Inc., in conference with Philip Sound, having heard the most awful rumours surrounding Martha who was, up to the point she started talking about what a cad I am, lying before me in the warm sudsy bath, chatting away as the baby was lying blissfully asleep.

"Yes," I said. "Because I sleep around on you."
"I can live with that, the poly amorous thing," she said.
"Then you are a fool," I said.
"Lots of couples do. They call it 'cheating' though," Martha said.

...and somewhere, elsewhere, Phil Sound was hearing all kinds of rumours, the first few he ignored and laughed about that rumour Martha was bisexual (which did her reputation little harm, except in more extremist absolutist areas of the company opinion market), that she was, you know, a drug user (aren't we all), an embezzler (untrue), in league with the opposition (whatever that meant), attended swingers partys (I wish), satanic worship (how Goth!), child abuser (palpably absurdly untrue, but, like the taint of communism back in the 1950's, always good for a career killer).

"I want to stop doing that," I said, after we had made love that night.
"What?" She said, in the midst of a sexual high.
"The poly amorous thing. It's not that I think it wrong."
"How politically correct of you," she said.
"I just know that it's wrong for us. I want to be with you. Just you."
"Okay then," Martha said. "We might set a date sometime. That's if you want that. If you don't want that we can —"
And I kissed her and we laughed.
"Yes, we should," I said.

It is, Martha would say, simply extraordinary the kinds of lies liars can construe. And I would say, yes, it is really extraordinary. And people believe the lies. People, she would say, want to believe the bad. That is, if they hate you enough. But, anyway, by the time Joshua was born, her reputation was ruined. Without so much as a shred of evidence a whispering campaign had been initiated, spread, and did its malicious work on her good name.

On the two hundred and fifty second day of her pregnancy, the necessary backup provisional evidence to have Martha removed from the firm of Xpex if she didn't go quietly, was hacked from Martha's personal database.

Baby Joshua was born on the two hundred and fifty third day of her pregnancy. We had quietly married a month before. The moment of Joshua's birth did not correspond with the moment of the rubber-stamping of Philip Sound's decision to fire Martha during the closed sitting of the Personnel Review Board Committee meeting. Martha gave birth to Joshua at 3.30 AM on August 12th. The Committee met twelve-hours later.

Firing Martha didn't matter to us financially. My book had come out long before. We had money. My earnings had tripled. We had started looking for a big family house to live in. Now I had money, I was looking for somewhere safe to hide myself in. We were married. But Martha's brutal dismissal gave Martha a major depressive episode. In other words, she had a breakdown. Personally I wanted to hunt Phil Sound and kill him for what he did to my Martha. But I didn't. I don't know why. I think I stayed away from him because I knew I really might kill him. Though I had gone for decades without touching another human, I knew when pushed, I was capable of extreme measures. I thought of the various forms of punishment beatings. Use of Iron bars. Bats. Wearing balaclavas. Bullets in the knees and hands. I could do that. If pushed in extremum I could be devious and extremely effective and get away with bad things. In a sense my history had proven what I was capable of. So I suppose I was wise to stay away from Phil Sound. And he was wise to stay away from me.

24.

After the incident with Ed Frasier and his crew in the cafeteria, I had an interview with Headmaster Anderson. This was prearranged.

I remember walking towards Francine Seyfert, Headmaster Anderson's Secretary, how she perched herself comfortably in her roomy, high-backed chair behind her desk in the outer office, that office situated between Accounting and Jim Anderson's inner rooms. As I approached, the phone rang.

"Good morning, Headmaster Anderson's offices, how may I help you today? Good morning Dr.. Murphy and how are you? I am sorry; he is in a meeting right now. I know, I know. I will get him to call your mobile as soon as the meeting is finished. Good to hear from you too. Goodbye Ma'am."

The phone kept ringing. It was just before the ten thirty mid-morning break. Francine looked tired, bone weary, as if, for a self-conscious moment, her whole world became compressed into the tiny box that was the shining super-modern prison that was the outer offices between Accounting and the offices of Headmaster Anderson, and she couldn't breathe, couldn't expand her lungs sufficiently to oxygenate her mind, her body, and her organs to remain self-supporting. She looked at the computer screen. Calls that had their numbers withheld or were unrecognizable from the screen in front of her she let go to messaging. Francine dealt only with communications between Anderson's office and staff, government offices, committees and representations from other schools, the occasional visit from high profile donors, ministerial representations, high profile alumni, donation dinners, and the interminable political dialogue that enables a school like this stay in the top five schools in the Irish System. She had that gift of communication that had enabled her to stay fifteen years in her present job. Few students came by, except folks like me, who had an interview, though she could hear, very distantly, from the lofty corridors outside, the rest of the privileged student body passing by, the youthful energy waves penetrating the timeless walls imprinting the structures with their vibrations. Drifting up the stairs and down the corridors in waves of shouts and cheers and chatter and clatter, came the student body, but only a distant echo. Inside Francine could hear Anderson's voice on the phone. She could also hear his damn music, and the sound of his pacing.

The offices she occupied were spacious, high-ceilinged, and, at her time and money consuming request, regularly remodelled. They were filled with carefully ordered files, classic overpriced furnishing, state of the art computing, and tasteful pastel coloured wallpaper and tasteful, none too bright lighting, giving the overall effect of approaching the offices of a timeless power structure, one that had both endured and remained unaffected by the movements of history or the vagaries of politics, yet aware of modern times and not resistant to them either. I remember it. I remember it and I have never gone back, never gone back, till now. Till here and till now.

"Ms. Seyfert?" I said. It was ten-thirty.
Francine closed her copy of The Decline and Fall of the Roman Empire and looked professional and smiling and disinterestedly in control of the headmaster's offices. She had taken to bringing in books these last years to alleviate her tedium.
"How can I help?"
"I could never understand that," my eyes resting on the cover of her 'Everyman' copy.
"I'm sure you will," she smiled.
"Why do they call it Everyman? That's what I can never understand." I shook my head sadly, "That's what I can never understand."
"I ask myself that every day," she said, greeting my warmth, depth of sincerity, and apparently unreflected charm with a futile attempt at humouring me.
"Does it upset you?" I asked, looking at her with tremendous sudden intensity.
"Yes, I suppose it does."
"My name is Gordon Brock."
"Yes, Gordon. How'd you get the black eye?"
"Punched on the way home from school."
"I see. No one from this school I hope?"
"No, some thug from the area I think. A real lowlife," I said.

On the computer screen beside her I saw my name blinking for an appointment, a tiny icon photo beside the appointment time. It was a photo taken of me last year. My face and body was beginning to change quickly. In the photo, I was dressed in a new suit, bought for the occasion. The photograph was cropped from a larger family

portrait that hung in the hallway of our home. Not a good photograph of me, I thought. I don't like it. I don't approve.
"I see I am due here at this time."
"Yes."
"Mr. Anderson made an appointment for me to meet him this morning at half-ten. Well, actually my mother made the appointment with Mr. Anderson. I was not involved."
Francine raised her finger with a smile and silenced me. She called Headmaster Anderson and told him Gordon Brock was waiting and he needed to call Mr. Murphy.
"That's great, Francine. Be good enough to send him in, Brock, I mean." Mr. Anderson said.
Francine put down the phone and nodded to me to head on in. I went to go on in.
"Mr. Anderson will be glad to see you."
"Thanks, Ms. Seyfert. Sorry to interrupt your reading."
"Not at all," Francine replied. I walked past the long glass desk, through the doors and into the office. The carpets, the artwork on the walls, along with the heavy doors, all conspired to seal the sounds between both offices. Inside, everything was different.

Inside Mr. Anderson's office, the floor was of polished wood. There were bookshelves along two walls, and there, in the far corner between two huge arched windows, was a state of the art sound system. It looked like an artefact of alien technology making sounds from its own non-random internal creative force. Jim Anderson was playing music. I remember I immediately liked what I heard.

It was Radiohead. Okay Computer[13], or should I say, Ok Computer. The record that was playing was a voice, a mechanical voice that, by its quiet emotionless tone seemed to depict the greatest pathos imaginable as it spoke of all the good healthy well-adjusted things it did as a good productive person to the hum of mechanical sounds of its own internal universe of unceasing pain and loneliness and alienation. This was the panic office, the voice quietly said. Let everything and everyone remain calm. I laughed. I knew all about the panic office. I was the panic office. I was in the panic office. This is the panic office. Section seventeen may have been hit. I knew that. I smiled. Now hear this. Stay calm and carry on.

13 Released by Radiohead in 1997, the band's third album, covering such ideas as consumerism, social isolation, modern malaise and the growth of the space age, regarded by critics as one of the greatest concept albums ever made, though the band don't like the idea of it being called a 'concept' album.

Jim Anderson the headmaster of St. Raymond's smiled, and finished the sentence he was writing. I listened to that voice on the recording of the album Ok Computer was saying. It, the voice, was talking about a section, possibly a group, called section nine seventeen. Section nine seventeen, had, according to the singing-speaking mechanical voice, possibly been hit. I liked that sound. I liked the voice, the list of things that might make him fitter and happier and more productive. It was a chaotic, frightened, pain-ridden sound that released, relished cold alienated feelings like a sudden chill wind in a long corridor before stepping off the spacecraft on an alien world not alien to its multi-millennial inhabitants. This was the panic office. Nine seventeen. Knock, knock. Time to go. I checked my watch. It was ten thirty four.

The song ended. Anderson saw I had stopped to listen when I came in. This was good. It was good for Anderson. Anderson went to finish the sentence he had been working on, still smiling. Jim looked at his text once more. The trouble was, he had forgotten about this particular appointment.

"Gordon, good to see you!"

"Okay."

"Please come in. Close the door. Sit here."

"I will."

"Thank you, Gordon. Well, how are you today?"

"Fine, thank you, sir."

"Your eye?"

"Punched on the way home from school."

"Which of our bullies did it?" Jim asked.

"I didn't know him. He wanted my lunch money."

"How did he know you had lunch money on you if he wasn't from our school?"

"Maybe someone from our school told him, I don't know."

"Did you contact the police?"

"No."

"You told your parents?"

"Yes. They are looking into it."

"That's a good one. They are looking into it. It's like something you would hear on the radio."

"Yes, but they are."

"Please, sit. Well, Gordon, is there anything you would like to ask? Usually, we might discuss your results, or what you hope to achieve

during your stay with us here at St. Raymond's."
"I don't know, sir. I don't know if I like it here."
"Really? What's wrong?"
"It's so big."

For me, the school was too big. Though my dreams had always been filled with great anonymous half darkened corridors, auguring malevolence, the vastness of St. Raymond's, so many hundreds of students of all ages and sizes, the hive-like noises and factory-like movement, all terrified me, fulfilled my worst imaginings rather than providing a real life catharsis of them.
"Right. Well it's a big school."
"Yes, it is. I don't like that."
"Okay, then."

And here in Anderson's office, with it's strange island-like isolation, despite the hive just outside, attracted me. I wanted to read what Anderson was working on, maybe talk to him about it and about music. I wanted to befriend him. I wanted to talk all day, have a sense of security, an anchor. I didn't want to go back to class. It might be interesting here with this person.

I wanted to talk about my relationships in the school, what I might want to study, history, English, perhaps philosophy. I wanted to go into the arts, but was unsure what I really wanted, that I felt such a profound sense of overwhelming obligation because of my gifts, and that I did not see myself as a university professor, a travelling academic seeking tenure in one college after another until I found a home somewhere. I was so tormented by a sense of duty, a desire to fulfil a destiny that seemed to emanate from outside, from what other people wanted for me. But this was an unsuccessful conversation. It was unsuccessful because Anderson talked and talked, about the school, about his face animated by a forced smiling optimistic determination to draw a clear terminal line over the proceedings that would entertain only a minimal feedback from me. It was, more to the point, unsuccessful because I wasn't honest, either with him or with myself.

"Now, after discussing, in what I would describe as a lively debate with your parents, we have moved you up a grade or two, so you are already with boys a year or two older than you. I understand you are already attending class, right?"
"Yes, Mr. Anderson."
"And no one from this school hit you?"

"No sir."
"You can tell me if they did."
"No sir."
"I would take a dim view of it if they did."
"Yes sir."
"Okay then. I must ask you. You're not lying to me?
"No sir."
"I would take a dim view of one of our students lying to me."
I didn't answer Anderson.
"We do not allow any kind of bullying at this school."
"Yes sir."
"So, we are kind of getting ahead of ourselves here, I know that, but we feel you are well capable of handling the pressure, and we want to build a strong support structure for you. Do you feel there is too much pressure put upon you? Though we expect our students to, of course, do their best, we also want you to learn how to deal with the kinds of expectations and pressures that are put upon our gifted students. Now this is something that will take time."
"Yes, sir."
"I know I have been doing much of the talking here."
"Yes sir."
"Is there anything you'd like to ask, no pressure?"
"I can't think of anything, sir. Can I get back to you on that?"
"Certainly. If you need to make an appointment, ring Ms. Seyfert. Anything else?"
"No sir."
"Thanks for your time and I'm sorry to take you from class. Bye, Gordon."
"Thank you, sir."

25.

My mother was standing outside her house talking with Jimmy, our next door neighbour. They were chatting for about ten minutes now, mainly about his retirement and the weather. It had been a showery day.

"How are you coping?"

"What?"

"If that's the right word? What I mean is, I know it was a big adjustment for some of my other friends when they had to retire."

"Are you serious, Lisa?"

"What do you mean?"

Jimmy tapped his pipe a little, blew into it, and proceeded to fill it with the sweetest smelling tobacco. The bits of burnt out tobacco weed blew away in the breeze.

"I have largely stayed in this fucking job for the last thirty years because it paid for things. I have been waiting for this severance deal for five years now. This is the best thing that ever happened to me. I am selling this damn house, which is nothing more than a money pit and I am getting the hell out of here. You can live cheaply and quietly in Portugal. I am going there and the Missus and I are going within eighteen months. Mind you, I am telling you all of this mainly because you are the kind of person who knows how to keep her mouth shut —"

"Gosh, I was just about to go make a few calls about this, Jimmy. Let everyone know." My mother grinned at Jimmy.

"Don't be a bitch, Lisa," Jimmy grinned.

"Can't help it Jim —" my mother gripped her forehead and shook her head, widened her eyes and tried to focus. Things had gotten a bit blurry and the pain in her temples seemed to sharpen for a moment. The smell of that tobacco was overwhelming. She took a step back, not noticing she had stumbled a little, only to be caught by Jimmy.

"Whoa! What's the matter, sweetie?" Jimmy took her shoulders, the meerschaum stuck in his mouth unlit, and peered into her eyes. He looked concerned.

"Its this fucking headache, I had it all day and it's getting into the migraine zone. I think I might take myself to bed with a nap and some super strong pain killers, and a coffee. I feel nauseous.

"I will call Dave. I didn't like the way you stumbled."

"I didn't stumble. Did I stumble?"

"You most certainly fucking stumbled, sweetie."
"See you later, Jimmy. And thanks."
"I am calling Dave," Jimmy said.
But my mother couldn't hear him.

I think I remember the moment she passed. I was sitting in a bar with a girl I was seeing. It was two in the afternoon and I felt this overwhelming panic and sorrow. I began to tear up and the girl put her hand on my cheek and asked me if I was all right. I said I didn't think so, but I didn't know why. Then, about an hour later, when we were back at her place, my phone rang and I found out.

26.

Dad had been ringing us on and off for the past few months, but our schedules were always misaligned. Then he rang at about eleven o'clock at night seven months into our pregnancy. He never really rang that late. Martha had gone to bed. I was sitting in the half-light of a small lamp, drinking vodka and reading. I answered quickly. There was a phone right beside Martha upstairs and her asleep, tanking up on dreams for the next big day ahead.

"Hi Gordon."

"Hey Dad."

There was a silence there with neither knowing what to say to the other.

"So, how are you?"

"I'm fine, son."

"Is there anything I can do?"

"I was wondering if we could get together."

"What's up?"

"Can we get-together? Son?"

"You don't sound so good."

"Oh, I'm fine."

"Then why ring me up at this hour asking to see me?"

His voice seemed drained of life, modulating the groan and strain of ancient branches.

I remembered the voice of a younger father.

"Do you want me to call up?"

"No. I'll see you in your offices."

"What time?"

"Okay, maybe, I shouldn't see you there."

"Why not Dad?"

"Why don't we meet for a drink, then? Lowry's? About eight?

"Great. What day?"

"Son?"

"What day do you want to meet? Tomorrow?"

"No. Not tomorrow. I have something on tomorrow."

"I see. So?"

"So."

"When Dad?"

"Thursday."

"Dad?"

"What?"
"Eh, today's Wednesday."
"Oh. Silly me. Son?"
"Yes Dad?"
"Do you miss your mother?"
"Of course I do, Dad."
"Okay then."
"That's a really big thing to bring up out of the blue."
"It is, I guess."
You miss her, Dad?"
"I do, son. I do."
"Let's meet Friday. Lowry's. At about eight. And we will have something to eat, and then go for a drink. My treat."

As time and disparate lifestyles and experiences had widened the gulf between my father and I, warmth and affection and the mutual understanding brought about by shared experiences, had been replaced by cool rational appropriate phrases chosen for their lack of commitment to any furthering of our relationship.

"Sure son."

I put down the phone, finished my drink and then began to fall asleep, listening to Glenn Gould humming through the speakers as he played on.

27.

After I walked out of Anderson's offices, walked past Francine Seyfert, walked towards class, and, on the way, two flights down, near a doorway to the yard, I saw Ed Frasier and his coterie lingering in the corridors. Ed was prodding Smudge on his bony chest. Smudge was grinning and gently pushing Ed away.
"This is one of your twisted jokes," Ed said.
"No, it fucking isn't!"
"It fucking is!"`
"Go see, then."
"No! You fucking go see!"
"She is out there in the middle of the yard calling for you."
"She is?"
"She is. Don't be a fucking pussy, go out and face the music."
"You can be a bit of a sadist, Smudge."
"This isn't a time to look good, Ed."
"Fuck you Smudge. I always look good!"
"That's a little, well, gay, Ed."
"So what if it's a little gay, Smudge. You prejudiced?"
"No, my uncle is gay, you know that?"
"Really, is he gay?"
"Sure, he came out last Christmas."
"Anyway, you still owe me from the Frankie Four Faces scene when I was talking to Gordon Moron," Ed said, still interested in what Smudge had to say about his uncle, but wanting to change the subject away from Smudge accusing him of being gay.
"I know, I know. And I'm sorry about that. You should go out now and face her. You're not afraid, are you, Edward? Of her?"
"Fuck you," Ed grinned. "You were always a bigot, Smudge."
Then Ed saw me watching him and Smudge, and the others. He smiled broadly.
"Speaking of the very devil, there he is. Hey Brock! Come here! Someone is here for you. It's your mama!"
"What?" I said. My mother? Here? No, I figured. She would have told me if she had decided to come to St. Raymond's.

This, I decided was a trap. It was not a very good one, but still a trap. It was Frasier's way of trapping me and giving me the works. So I got out of there.

28.

So I ran. At the point I ran like hell away from the bullies, my mother was standing in the yard of St. Raymond's, looking to speak to Ed Frasier.
"Come back, you fucking moron, Gordon is a moron!" Ed and his friends yelled.
I ran and I kept on running, though, no one followed.
"You!" A teacher yelled.
"Sir."
"No running. Your name?"
"Gordon Brock, sir."
"I'll be keeping an eye on you."
"Sir."

Maybe that's a joke about my shiner, I thought.

As soon as I turned a corner there was another stairs I could take to get out onto the main yard. Two students sat at the bottom of the stairs, a tiny chess set between them.

If I hung around the school during break, generally I got beaten up or publicly verbally abused by Frasier or one of his crew (sometimes it was a case of 'mixed doubles', as they called it- one group of two holding me while another duo punched and kicked me) so I had developed the habit of getting out during lunch and break times. I didn't live far from the school, so I could go home if I wanted to. So I escaped by climbing two large deciduous trees, then climbing from the tree branches to a wall, then climbing over the wall, then swinging simian like from one final Acer Pseudoplatanus Sycamore, I dropped onto the pavement, nearly (but not quite) hitting the ground, yes, running. As I climbed I saw a tiny spider suspend itself from a new leaf, its new legs dangling as it went about the business of unwinding its web string.

Unaware I had torn my trousers, I had just decided to go back to school when I heard Mrs. Johnson's voice behind me.
"Hello, Gordon."
"Hello, Mrs. Johnson."
"What are you doing out of school?"
"Nothing, Mrs. Johnson. I forgot a book. I was going to get it."
Mrs. Johnson eyed me sceptically and then smiled.

"I have three sons and two daughters. I have heard these answers before."
"Yes, Mrs. Johnson."
"Your mother, you know, wouldn't be pleased to see you out of school at —" Mrs. Johnson checked her watch "-five minutes to eleven in the day, and, mind you, with torn trousers." She looked suitably frowningly maternal, superior, and disapproving, like an ex-nun maiden aunt, who, in her mind, never left the convent. I noticed my torn trousers. There was going to be trouble over those, I thought.
"Yes, Mrs. Johnson. I have to go. I'm going to be late. I was just going to change my trousers."
"And you were looking for a book too, I suppose," she said.
"That too, Mrs. Johnson."
"You must really think I am naïve, Gordon."
"No Mrs. Johnson. I think you just don't believe me because I am young."

I changed my trousers and ran back. So little time, mere minutes to evade the authorities, I thought, and get back to class. Sweat poured down my back as I ran and avoided the footpath people.

As I approached the gates, there were few students around near the gates, usually a bad sign. There were cameras watching. More cameras than in a casino. I slowed down. I've got to appear cool, I thought. I'll get it if I'm late. Yard filled with sounds. Fight going on, I thought. Who gives a damn? People hitting. Kicking. Who gives a damn?
"Hey Brock?"
"What?"
"Your mother is in the yard."
I looked down the yard. There were only passing students and teachers. The buildings looked so old. Two hundred and thirty years old, plus change.
"Not this one, you idiot, the other one."

The boy spoke from within a group of kids leaning up against the doorway to the physics lab, pointing to the second building. The boy talking to me from the group was Smudge. He looked coldly at me.
"Hey Brock, you deaf or what? Your mother is in the yard! Go check out Mommy dearest"
Then he said in a lower but no less inaudible voice. "What a fucking idiot."
"How do you know what she looks like?" I asked.
"Easy. She's the one with the fangs, the pitchfork and the interest in arguing with little boys in schoolyards."

As they laughed, the door to the lab opened, and they went in.

From the yard, I heard the sounds, roars of laughter, whoops, catcalls. It was hard to know what was happening. Usually in the midst of a crowd like that, some kid would be beating some other kid up, schoolbags tossed aside with onlookers watching the violence and others keeping sketch in case the authorities appeared. The fights usually lasted mere minutes with all the cameras about. It had been me more than once. I hid the bruises from my parents (or at least deluded myself that one can do such things, of course one cannot), talking about falling in the yards when they did notice, and pointing out I was not made of porcelain and they didn't complain when I bruised far more in the house. But you couldn't hide a black eye. It was getting near to break ending. I passed on, pushed through the middle of the bawling crowd. In the middle of it all stood Lucy, my mother. She was pointing and yelling at Ed Frasier. [14]

"Don't you speak to me like that!" She yelled. Frasier's face was red with rage.

"I'll say anything I like, you bitch!" He said.

"Really?" Lucy said.

"You shouldn't be here!" Frasier pointed to the ground. "I should sue you!" Then he pointed to the cameras "You are on camera, you know that?"

"Go ahead. Get your parents in here. I want to meet them. They aren't answering the phone or the door when I call, or write letters, for that matter."

"Who the fuck would want to talk to you anyway? Somebody get a teacher!" He yelled.

"Gordon came home a few days ago. He had a black eye!"

She kept asking me where I got it, I thought. I told her I was in a fight. I had got it on the way home.

"That's my fault?" Frasier countered.

"I think it is. I think it's your fault."

"You think. You have no proof. You have no evidence. You don't know shit!"

"Oh I know shit. You are a punk. And a bully. I think you are behind

14 There were no teachers in the school yard at that time of day, which was singularly bizarre considering this was a schoolyard at break time. I think over these moments over and over and I ask: Where were the teachers? I can think of three main reasons why there were no teachers:

One: they knew about the event and ignored it.

Two: they didn't know about the event and thus avoided it.

Three : they knew about the event, didn't ignore it, and thoroughly enjoyed watching the videos of the event on tape and disc or other electronic media.

this." Lucy looked at him. The crowd hissed disapproval. Someone hissed the word 'Bitch' 'Wagon' 'Haradin'. She ignored the hisser. Mother looked calmly at Ed. A small boy with a torn jacket was pushed forward into the space between Ed and Lucy. Then the boy with the torn jacket, frightened and embarrassed, ran back into the crowd and seemed to disappear into the thicket of boys. Someone punched him on the back on his way through the crowd. After he fell down then got back up, the people lost their interest in him.

Everyone held their breath for Ed to answer. Frasier looked at Lucy, rolled his eyes contemptuously in a way that failed to hide his sense of humiliation, and his friends smiled, knowing that Frasier had one of his unforgettable responses ready. Then Ed said:
"Maybe he got hit with a football! He hit me, you know that?"
"That was an accident! You know that. This is different!"
"Maybe this was an accident too! Look, do yourself a favour —"
"Yeah?"
"Go. You are already going to go to jail. For just being here in the yard. It's a stranger danger moment."

When I look back at what happened that day, considering how really unprotected we all were despite the supposed stranger danger protection propaganda the school espoused, we all could have been put in a transport container and disappeared for the purposes of genetic experimentation; we all could have been abducted by slave traders or axe wielding pedophile, considering what went on that day. There were no teachers. It was almost class time, and no teachers. And the schoolboy crowd cheered. And Lucy was nonplussed. And I grew numb and disoriented and went into shock as I watched the bizarre proceedings before me.
"Call the police! Call the headmaster! Call security! I'm here! The question remains: What happened to my son? What happened to Gordon?" She asked.
"Maybe he got hit with a boot," Edward said to peals of laughter and cheers of 'Yeah!' 'Yeah!' 'Yeah!' "Do it!' Do it!' "Do it!'
"Gordon doesn't do much football," Lucy yelled.
"Yeah, Gordon is a moron!"
To which the chorus responded with:
'Gordon is a moron!' 'Gordon is a moron!' 'Gordon is a moron!'[15]
"That's so cheap and pathetic, Edward. Compared to him, on a level of intelligence, well, you could be his pet."

15 This is a reference to the Jilted John 1978 (Gordon Fellowes) record of the same title.

'Gordon is a moron!' 'Gordon is a moron!'

The crowd kept yelling. I can still hear them. I see their smiling sneering faces, their dull eyes, their stupid mindless shouts. They seemed wrapped up in an ecstatic chant. I was crushed and humiliated. I could never ever feel any level of safety or confidence again in that school. Waves of paranoia and self-loathing engulfed me. I felt dizzy. I was nauseous. I wanted to run away. My body flooded with adrenaline. I was filled with panic. I wanted to disappear completely. I wanted to erase myself from the planet. I hated my mother for doing this to me. I felt violated. I felt bitter. I felt I had been ruined by circumstances I could not control.

Ed Frasier said nothing. He smiled at his friends. His friends smiled back. Lucy knew she had lost initiative in this little ambush. She said,
"Someday this will all catch up with you."
"You know nothing! You don't know your Gordon. He's a bad seed!"
"You are going to leave my son alone."
"Gordon Brock is a fucking dickhead. Actually, as indicated, he is a fucking moron."
"Okay Ed. I've had the conversation with you. Okay? I've given you a chance. I'm going to escalate this. Stay away from my son, are we clear?"
"Is that a threat?"
"It's a stern pointed clear request."

And, without looking at or speaking to me, she left the yard.

Frasier walked up to me and looked me in the eye. There were hundreds of grinning schoolboys watching. They were shuffling. This was the best entertainment they'd ever had. As Ed Frasier walked over to him, the crowd filled the space around him. He looked at me with more hate than he had ever thought possible. The hate terrified and overwhelmed me.
"You are a fucking dead man, Gordon Brock, you fucking moron fucknugget dipshit asshole cocksucker prick."
Ed took off his watch. He put his watch in his pocket. Then took off his jacket, tossed it on the ground. Someone picked it up. Then Ed Frasier went for me saying:
"I am going to fuck you up, you goddam motherfucking sonofabitch."
"Frasier, I —"

I was going to say things to him. I was going to explain myself. Try to dig myself out of this grave, but Ed Frasier, using his index and middle finger bunched together in a tiny fist, poked me hard in the

solar plexus. I groaned. I keeled over, and, winded and in agony. Then something, I think a foot hit me on the head. I watched the grey walls of the school yard spin with a sense that all of this was unreal, a horror that will, eventually, end. I looked up and saw the web of tall windows of the old school buildings stretched out tight beneath lead grey epic skies. The crowd cheered. The bell went. As the bell went Frasier knelt down beside me, and slamming my head against the ground he said:
"I am going to get you Brock. I am going to keep coming for you till there is nothing left of you. I am going to ruin your life. I am going to fucking kill you! You are gonna hurt. YOUMOTHERFUCKINGFUCKINGPIECEOFSHITYOU —"
"Ed! Ed! For fuck's sake man," Smudge grabbed him and pulled him back. I fell down, passed out. The yard emptied.

The bell should have gonged long before then. But I remember the bell at that time. I remember Ed's words and the terror and horror and I remember nothing else except these words:
"You, boy, what are you doing? Are you all right? Do you need a doctor?"
It was Brother Frank. Smelling of leather and Old Spice aftershave.
"Hello Brother Frank."
"Good. Now follow my finger with your eyes, and tell me what happened."
As I watched his index finger move between my eyes, I told him I got hit with a football in the stomach.
"I passed out. And think I hit my head, as well."
"No football in the front yard."
"Yes Brother. Won't happen again."
"It breaks windows."
"Yes Brother."
"You know the rules."
"Yes Brother."
"I see your charitable classmates called first aid when this happened."
"I guess the bell went, Brother."
"Didn't it just, eh? It's no excuse."
"If you'll excuse me, I have to go. I need to go to get something for my head."
"Something like a scan to check for hemorrhages?"
"No, Brother."
"Were you kicked or punched?"
"I felt dizzy, fell down. Football in the tummy."
"You are lying."
"No Brother."

"Don't lie to me!"
"I'd like to go see the nurse."
"I can't tell you how pointless and self-destructive lying is in these circumstances."
"I'd really like to see a nurse or a doctor. And I am telling you the truth, Brother."
"Very well. I shall accompany you."
"I'm fine, Brother."
"I insist."
"I'm fine Brother, thank you for your concern."
I went to run off and Frank stopped me,
"What are you doing?"
"What? What Brother?"
"Walk slowly and carefully."
Frank looked at me with the grim knowledge that I, the boy, had no intention whatever of going to the nurse.
"Some of our footballers are evidently gifted, first division potential. If only they scored as highly in their examinations. Well some do actually."
"Yes Brother."
"Where are you scheduled to be?"
"English Lit."
I had no idea in the wide earthly world where I should have been at that time.
"Go. Go quickly. By the way, who was that in the yard?"
"My mother. I forgot a book."
"I see. What a thoughtful parent. Where is it?"
"What?"
"The book, Mister Brock. You claim your mother, out of the goodness of her heart, brought you a book. Where is it?"
"I don't know, Brother. I wish I knew. It's gone."
"What book?"
"What?"
"What kind of book. History? Geography? Applied Pharmacology? What's your poison, Mister Brock?"
"Nineteen Eighty-Four. Orwell."
"You are worryingly good at concealing, Mister Brock. We'll make a bureaucrat of you yet."
"I'm sorry about that, Brother."
"You're too young for Orwell."
"I see, Brother."
"I can't ensure you go see the nurse. I have an appointment I can't

break and there doesn't seem to be." He looked about the deserted yard with its sweet paper wrappings and thrown away cartons.
"But I will be calling your parents about this in the next hour or so. Rest assured."

I looked sceptically at the older teacher and wondered what he meant by too young for Orwell. My head throbbed unbearably. I could see small specks of white before my eyes. The tiny specks were being systematically transformed into tiny points of light that spun like tiny spiral nebulae within my minds' eyes. I wanted to fall down again, but managed by dint of will to prevent it. I wanted to vomit. But I stopped myself. Then Brother Frank began to see the humour of the situation. The boy was, after all, fine, apparently. Frank pointed to the cameras.

"Big Brother is watching you. I will be keen to look at the footage for what really happened."

A tiny smile played over Brother Frank's thin deeply lined face. He seemed carved out of a dried out knotted branch. His face that of a sun wrinkled explorer. Greetings earthlings. His voice soft and thin and carefully elocuted.
"Yes, Brother."
"Don't draw too much attention to yourself. It attracts the wrong kind of friends. The kind that aren't friends. I notice you have something of a talent for that."
"Yes, Brother."
"I'm serious, Mister Brock."
"Yes Brother. Thank you Brother"

29.

Brother Frank walked away from me. He crossed the yard and climbed six flights of hard polished stone steps. He had made an appointment to see James Anderson. He had little intention of mentioning what he had seen. He had made the appointment to tell Anderson that he and one of the French teachers were lovers. He was going to go on to say that they had been for over a year, that she was pregnant and that they planned to marry. Anderson knew all this anyway. Frank knew that Headmaster Anderson knew this. But he wanted to tell him anyway.

As Frank entered Anderson's office, I went home. I walked the short stretch back to our house and went to my room and looked at the ceiling and felt numb. Then, from the numbness came grief and loneliness and depression, and I sobbed, feeling an overwhelming sense of desolation. This experience of being beaten and excluded was the fulfilment of my fate. It was what I feared most, what I saw in others eyes when they smirked at my strange quirks of character, my odd attempts at humour, or became angry when I silenced them with an answer that came too quick for me to stop it. I was disliked, no I was hated. I felt I was falling into a great void, like a deep well, or an oubliette, and I watched the walls of my room grow taller, and I heard voices from beyond those walls, familiar voices just out of earshot. I was in shock. I was shocked and horrified and equally unable to comprehend what had actually happened. That day exposed a belief in my immigrant status as a member of human society, that my passport would never be stamped because I was and never would be the same as others, and I listened to the silence in the house and wondered where my parents were and the phone rang a few times and I didn't answer it, and then first my mother came home and ran up to my room and hugged and kissed me and we wept together and she asked me how I was and I said I was fine. I said I was fine; 'Mom really, why did you do that? Why did you go into the school yard like that? I have never', I said, 'never been more humiliated. They hate me! They hate me! They hate me!' and she said 'oh sweetheart darling the last thing I wanted to do was to humiliate you I am so sorry, so very sorry about that. Did they touch you? Tell me the truth Gordon,' she said. 'Tell me, did they?' And I said, 'Yes they did, they hit me and they kicked me and I hit my head. I fell and hit my head today,' and she said, 'God that damn school is like a prison camp. We must immediately go to the doctor'

And the doctor examined me and sent me for tests and the results of the tests came back and the test results said I was fine but to be on the safe time we might get another scan and we did a scan and I was fine and I stayed home a week from school and eventually a week later and I was fine there was some bruising, but I should be fine.

I imagine Anderson in his office poring over notes, reviewing his weekly schedule, checking class statistics, reading review papers and educational theory, feeling a scintilla of an unowned burden of responsibility, perhaps fearing he had taken on too much with this job, that all he really wanted was to be alone before the open jaws of a text that threatened to swallow him, the words he tamed and wrote during working hours, words far away from his own true sense of how it was but knew it shouldn't be. Just then, right at that very moment, Frank walked in.

Francine was missing. That was the only explanation as to why he hadn't knocked.
Frank smiled and said "Hello"
"You should knock, you know," Jim said without looking up, switching off the computer screen before him, and closing his notes.
Frank didn't answer. He smiled.
"You don't walk in here."
"I have news, Jim. I'm leaving."
"Holiday season already Frank?"
"That's cute. I'm leaving the brotherhood, and the school."
Jim sat down. For the first time, he saw how shaken Frank looked.
"Sit down, Frank. What's going on?"
"Jim, I have some personal and family matters to attend to."
"I see. Do you really think I haven't heard the rumours Frank, don't be fucking cute!"
"They're true."
"Do you think the people who gave you your job and me my job, will let you work again in a school like this? Eh Frank?"
"No."
"Any school?"
"I don't know about any, Jim."
"Do you think there will be no revenge?"
"What the hell are you talking about? There is no revenge. She is six months pregnant."
"I see. That I did not know. I think that when someone breaks a code

there is naturally a consequence. That's why we are all hypocrites in one way or another."
"That surprises me."
"Who knows about this?"
"I haven't asked around. I would imagine everybody knows about this. People live for this kind of news."
"Who knows you are the father?"
"I know."
"Congratulations."
"Thank you. Has anyone complained to you?"
"People complain to me about a lot of things. I get letters of complaint every day."
Anderson held up a sheaf of unopened letters.
"Oh look, here's a dozen more. Most of them are crap, but I answer them. Teachers come to me for all kinds of reasons. Actually, I have a meeting in a minute or two, so we will have to conclude this later."
"Let them wait."
Jim smiled.
"Has anyone mentioned me? Talked to you about me? I need to know."
"Absolutely."
"Go on."
"You are regarded as an exceptional teacher, and an effective educator."
"I'm touched. I mean the truth, Jim."
"That's the truth, Frank."
"Okay. Anything negative?"
"I am not at liberty to divulge."
"Ah, I thought so. What?"
"I can say I have no concerns. I think, Frank, your departure at this time, is bad for you, and certainly bad for this school. I think you are a superb teacher and a brilliant man. In fact, on a personal note, I regret we never became friends. I certainly tried a few times, as I recall."
"I had a lot on my mind. Anyway, I don't think we are compatible. You have too many friends."
"Your... companion."
"Susan. Don't say 'companion'. It cheapens things."
"Teaches mainly French, also maths to second and third years."
"Yes."
"And this has been going on for about a year?"
"I am fifty-one years old. I imagine it unlikely this happening to me again in my lifetime."

"So you weighed the probabilities."
"I am in love with Susan."
"Ah, Love. How tragic and beautiful."
"Fuck you Headmaster. I'm telling you this because —"

There was a knock at the door. Jim walked quickly over, opened it and whispered something to Francine. There were several solicitors and accountants waiting for their scheduled meeting. They were sitting in the waiting room, looking dourly at their watches. They had other appointments. Jim looked over at them. They stopped looking tired and irritable, and then nodded amiably. Jim whispered something about their having to wait. Francine looked angrily at him. He closed the door. Frank had lit a cigarette.

"You just love getting cancer, don't you Frank? And giving it to me, you bastard."

Jim opened a window.

"I also enjoy teaching."
"Why?"
"I am good at it. So does Susan. I have money. I never needed to continue teaching. But we both enjoy it. So we continued our —"
"Arrangement."

Frank nodded appreciatively.

"Arrangement."
"Let me put it this way to you, Frank. I am going to try to find a way to fix this."
"Well, there are other countries, you know. I might try getting a job somewhere else. By the way, Headmaster, you have a problem."
"I do?"
"Yes. Not the one we are presently discussing."
"No?"
"No, another one."
"Really?"
"I found Gordon Brock fainting in the school yard."
"You found what? What the fuck? When you walk into a room with me that's the kind of thing you say to me first! I had him in here for an interview not too long —"
"I said —"
"Why didn't you tell me till now?"
"Kids get knocked out all the time."
"That's about to change. Every concussion is a huge payout."
"It's not a concussion."
"And it's just downright wrong."
"Oh I agree Headmaster. Personally in thirty years of teaching I have

never once had to strike a pupil. But kids, they fall down. They get knocked about. They get concussions. They faint. They fight. All the time."

Frank looked at the headmaster for a long time, and smiled.

"You, Headmaster are an elitist. To you every child is not precious."

Anderson was indeed snob and an elitist. Frank went on:

"We, and by we, I mean the school staff, clean them up, send them to the nurses' station, and send them to the doctor. For the most part they're fine. It's called childhood and adolescence. Brock wants to fit in, which is ridiculous."

"Not on my watch they don't! Are you insane?"

"No, I am not."

"Have you any idea what parents do nowadays if they find one of their little darlings suffered a concussion? How exposed the school becomes? And you fucking idiot, have you any idea what happens to a kid with an IQ over 170 gets hit on the head?"

"He wasn't hit on the head. He might have bumped his head, or got hit with a ball on the head or hit his head against a wall or the ground. It happens."

"I mean these test results aren't from some crappy internet site. You can't fucking walk away from this!"

"I agree. Look, I had a lot on my mind."

"Look, it wasn't easy getting Brock to come here. He is part of the new breed."

"What is this 'new breed' nonsense? What is this? The Third Reich? He is a kind of statistical anomaly rather than a new breed. They usually go mad those types. Mental health issues. Alcoholism. Depression. Breakdowns. Normal is better. What you are looking for is a nice bell curve of achievers. People like him come and go. You can see the boy is barely clinging to reality as it is. All that faux politeness. He will probably crack up if he isn't careful. A few knocks and bumps might toughen him up, help him integrate."

"Bullshit! And by the way, Frank, you are right I am an elitist. But I also think every child is precious. But all children are not the same. Each has different needs and different abilities. You are mistaking rights with gifts. Brock could do anything if given the right support. Get a fucking grip! If he goes, we are in trouble."

"No we are not!"

"It will look very bad. We have to fix this and fix it fast."

"I think it would be better if we let him go."

"Really?"

"It's sad, but most like him don't make it. There's a lot of bullshit written about the gifted, but most of it is about people projecting their own unfulfilled expectations, and I include the shrinks who write these books."

"Spoken like a true educator, Frank."

"I would imagine we have at least three others like him in the school right now. That being said, I do admit something serious is afoot. I think Frasier did this."

"No shit, Sherlock."

"That Frasier boy is trouble, Jim. Mark my words."

"How is the Brock boy?"

"He came round fine. He's attending class. Frasier is out to get him. I'm calling his parents later on."

"I'll deal with Frasier. And don't call anyone."

"I have already given the Frasier boy a serious warning."

"By the way," Jim pointed cynically to beyond the closed doors of his offices to Francine, the lawyers, the accountants and the school staff.

"What is it, Headmaster?"

"They know."

And Frank smiled sadly, nodded, and left.

30.

I remember this time, and I made notes, endless notes, sketching and re-sketching the scene between Frank and Headmaster Anderson, and then I remember looking at my son Joshua, and how happy I felt. I held my newborn son Joshua in my arms and I felt more love than I ever imagined possible. I loved him more than I ever thought possible. Once a person has experienced that connection with someone, a child, it is never forgotten, indelible. Then, after the incredible joy and euphoria wore away, I worried I was not experiencing love at all, but a chemical reaction. This was part of a scepticism that has never left me my whole life: that nothing was what it seemed, that I could never trust my senses, that I could never know the truth. I wondered where the spiritual selfless love existed in the midst of all that programming. After all, I worried; parents are biologically programmed to love their children, to sacrifice themselves for their children, well, most of them. I did not know what loving meant, but I knew the immediacy of my need to nurture and take care of Joshua, as I knew Martha knew it too. I wanted to do everything in my power to give him all he needed to flourish. I wanted him to be neither clever nor rich nor poor, but happy. I was prepared to pay any and every price imaginable for Joshua's happiness. I was also unsure what happiness was.

But as I write this, I know the power of instinct, how we mortgage what we think to be happiness for those we love and cannot help but protect and worry over. I remember my own childhood, as I remember Joshua and I loved him from the first moment, as I love all my children: born in sanitized hospitalised circumstances, washed and weighed, checked for heart, lung, limb or weight problems, immunodeficiency or any contagious illness, and, as the medical technicians took several other samples for their lab records, the little one screamed mercilessly, hating the loss of his warm dark safe watery universe of sightless sound and breathless touch. But, having been fed by Mommy, cooed and sung to, loved and kissed and cuddled, hearing those voices so familiar from the first moments of sentience in the womb, Joshua fell asleep and dreamed of the warm watery depths from which he had emerged. Swimming and sleeping, saved not drowned, connected to the dark from which he came.

31.

Martha entered through the large automatic security check doors, crossed the pseudo-Romanesque marbled lobby with the traditional knowing, assertive executive demeanour, and took the elevator to the eighth floor. As she climbed into the lift, people started to get calls about her. Philip Sound received the first call. He sent word he wanted to see her.

Word travelled through the ruthless, desperate, middle management corridors and lobbies and water fountains and coffee corners and central processing nodes of endless calculus and speculation and canteens of Xpex that Martha was back. For Martha, it was as though she had never been away.

Martha wistfully looked out the window of her eighth floor office, the carefully polished desk, the clean swept office, clothes stand on which her jacket and coat carefully hung, the filing cabinet carefully locked, the cool clean air from the air conditioner, the microscopically clean carpet with thick pile that seemed to suspend her in a surreal midairness. On her desk sat a paper cup half filled with distilled water. Her office was quiet, for the most part. Occasionally her phone rang. She ignored it.

Martha Brock relaxed, sipped some water and checked her messages and letters. The phone kept ringing. She answered it. It was Mr. Sound's secretary.
"Hi Joe. How are things?" Joe was unresponsive.
"Mr. Sound would like to see you in his office."
"Really, why? I already talked to him." This wasn't true, but she didn't want to talk to Sound just then.
"He asked me to contact you."
"What's the story?"
"Can you come up?" He replied in an incrementally sharper tone.

Joe the secretary was becoming increasingly irritated with this difficult person. It was also time for his coffee break and, somewhat depressed with the endless thankless demands on his time, he had, over the past six months, become inflexible over his personal time. As he was no longer the overworked, ultra-obedient, mindless lackey that Sound enjoyed snapping his fingers at, Sound was thinking of replacing him.

"Okay. Be right there. Jeez, Joe calm down." And Joe the secretary, the executive assistant, went on his coffee break and whinged about Martha to his buddies.

She took the elevator to the twelfth floor. By another complete lack of coincidence, Pauline Flak was in the lift. She was leaving a report in to Eliot Spenser. Eliot Spenser was going to get Martha's job. Pauline Flack was going to get pushed into Eliot Spenser's old job.

Pauline looked longingly at Martha, imagining with loving detail the pain Martha would soon be in, and then turned her eyes so as to stare strategically at the steel lift doors.

"Hello Martha. How are you? Welcome back."

"Great! It's a little strange being back. How have you been?"

"Good, Good."

There then followed a longish awkward silence.

Martha stepped out of the lift. Flak stayed on board and seemed to look lonely and pitying as the lift doors closed.

"See ya."

Martha crossed into Sound's offices. Sound's offices were sepulchrally silent. The secretary who had called her was absent. Sound should get rid of him, she thought. He has a bad attitude. There was no one queuing to see Phil Sound. The door to his office was ajar. She passed through his outer office into his inner office. A glass wall with glass doors separated the two offices. One could at the touch of an invisible switch draw a huge curtain and enclose the room in privacy. The screen was absent today. Sound was sitting at the top of his conference table. The room was quieter than she had ever heard it before.

"Sit down Martha."

She sat down.

"What the hell is this?"

Her emotions had swung from acute joy to deep loathing and fear. Something was terribly wrong.

"The end, I'm afraid."

"Really? What?"

"Yes."

"How very Jim Morrison of you. What the fuck Phil?"

Sound grinned. That's funny, he thought.

"What do you mean 'the end'? Philip? Hm?"

"How much do you want me to tell you?"

"Don't fuck with me. What is this?"
"I'm in a position to offer you a very generous severance package in exchange for your resignation."
"What the hell is this? You can't let me go. I have just come back, walked in the door of the company."
"Look, I —"
"No, Phil, you look. I can sue you. I am just back from maternity leave. You have never expressed any dissatisfaction with my work, with me. And now the very day I come back from maternity leave you want to fire me?"
Sound smiled when he heard her use that kind of language, the word 'sue'. He usually took it to mean the other person was really threatened. He folded his carefully manicured hands and allowed a little silence to linger between them. Her eyes widened. She crossed and uncrossed her legs and he said:
"Firstly, I am not firing you. On the contrary, you are resigning. If you look carefully at your contract it explicitly states that if we reach a mutually agreed position whereby we feel things are not working out one or other of the parties can request a dissolution of contractual obligations. I am doing that right now. You will not sue. You are not that – how shall I put it? -You are not that unenlightened."
"Really?"
"Really."
"Why don't you die in a crash sometime, Phil, eh?"
"Unlikely. This is the kindest thing anyone in my position can do to you right now. It has been brought to my attention that your behaviour is incompatible with your position in this company."
"What exactly is incompatible? I did what needed to be done, what you wanted."
"But you failed in one important aspect. You did not build relationships as you worked. In fact, you made mostly enemies, which is a really stupid move. And those enemies have been busy. This is why I am prepared to offer you this package, and allow you resign. This will never go past these doors, ever. Everyone comes out of this happy, which I can assure you will not be the case if you go legal on this company."
"This is zero-sum[16]."
"Wow, Phil – a maths metaphor. Do you know what that means?"
"It means things will be bad, very bad for you, Martha if you don't sign.

16. Zero–sum game is a mathematical representation of a situation in which a participant's gain (or loss) is exactly balanced by the losses (or gains) of the utility of the other participant(s). If the total gains of the participants are added up, and the total losses are subtracted, they will sum to zero.

It is with considerable regret that I must ask you for your resignation. I have arranged for a sizable severance package to be made available for you. Let me make this clear to you without in any way prejudicing the company's position. You will not sue. Let me be totally clear with you, and I am being very patient here, I am not afraid of you suing. Actually, my lawyer suggests I not use that word, but then again I will lay odds that no lawyer will take your case. It's because you have none. This isn't hush money either by the way. It is exactly what you are due. And not a penny more. I find you have been conducting yourself in a less than professional manner. I am just not happy with you and would ask you to sign this."

"I did this for —"

"Please sign."

"Why. Why are you doing this? No!"

"Let's not make it worse than it has to be."

"Fuck you!"

"Martha, I. Don't take that tone with me!"

"What is this? What are you doing? This was a good thing we had! I did exactly what was expected of me. I did nothing illegal and everyone we fired had to be fired, either because they were incompetent, performing under par, or they were superfluous to company requirement."

"Look Martha. This is our contract. If I felt at any time we weren't working out, I could ask you to resign. That was our deal. You get hugely compensated and we walk away without tears. We weren't engaged to be married."

"No, but —"

"And this is terminal point, Martha!"

"'Terminal point!' Jesus you were always using vocabulary you weren't sure about."

"I have the full right to do this and I am exercising that."

"Fuck you!"

Sound ignored her, inwardly so angry with her he could hardly control his boiling rage. He pushed some papers across the desk, pointed to them, and between gritted teeth said:

"This is a rather overgenerous severance package in my view, but there you have it. Take it and go."

"'Overgenerous' – would you regard it as profligate or just libertine on the company's part, seeing as I have pretty much rescued Leef from a financial disaster zone?"

"If it had been a disaster zone, then why did Xpex buy it? You are talking nonsense. Please let's get this over with. Martha? Please?"

She picked up the paper and wiped her eyes, not able to see what was

printed on the page.
"How much?"
"See for yourself."
"I can't, I can't fucking see, I..."

The figure was substantial. Lots of zeros and when she saw the lots of zeros after the ten that started all those zeros, she signed. She didn't know what or why she was signing but she was signing away any rights to sue, and acceptance of the company's terms, taped by the security people who watched everyone in the firm, randomly taped their conversations and taped even their break times, their emails what web pages they browsed, the times they came and went, and, especially, all board meetings, always watching the watchers watching.

Martha sobbed, tears dripping on the over-polished, over-tasteful, pretentious, overpriced clear glass table that she and Sound were sitting at.
"Don't even think about this. It was inevitable."
He took the signed papers and putting them in a drawer he then locked.
She didn't answer. Then she said after a moment:
"Once word of this gets out, I am finished."
"It won't happen. I promise."
"After all I did, Phil. After all I did for this firm."
"I said it before. I have thought about it carefully and I feel it within my boundaries to say it again, this time with feeling. You left me with no choice. I only wish things had been different."
"Fuck you, Philip Sound."
She went to put the pen down. The pen rolled across the shining desk. It touched against a conference call phone that had a hidden microphone and camera attached. Philip noticed the neat tears dripping from the edge of her chin onto her perfectly fitted suit.

Martha turned to go. Then she stopped, dried her tears again and looked him in the eye. Perhaps, he thought, her rage has gotten the better of her. How stupid, he thought.
Stupid.
"Martha, if you've got something to say, speak your mind."
Martha smiled.
"You're joking, right? You know, Phil, I think I might have just done that. So I say what I have to say, and I end up at the end of this as the

bad guy."
"Are you the bad guy?"
"I was hired to be the bad guy. I was hired so you could be the good guy. I'll never lose this moment. I feel I'll never stop hating you, but then it's hard to hate someone who doesn't feel, doesn't live. You'll get yours."
"That sounds like a threat."
"It's an observation, Phil. You'll die alone, loveless and alone."
Sound smiled, and turned his back on her.

The first thing Martha thought of as she left Phil Sound's office, as things went coldly clear inside her mind, as that cold-clea-primordial-lizard-brain-shock-to-the-system-adrenaline-rush-fight-or-flight-mind kicked in. She wanted one thing. Martha wanted her mother.[17] Wanting the comfort of a woman too disturbed to give her the comfort she always wanted, a mother whose unstable presence had driven her to such high risk behaviour as living with me and working for Phil Sound, was very troubling and probably an indicator of how upset my wife was at that point. Martha remembered what her mother, Isolde, said, in that broken accent, about holding one's dignity in even the most embarrassing situations. Isolde had told her about keeping her dignity when Martha was a little girl. Now she remembered what her mother had told her. Martha wanted Isolde to tell her it was all going to be okay. Then Martha felt nothing. Then the cold clarity left her. She felt hot. Then cold. Sweaty. Definitely going into shock. Perhaps, she thought, I am in shock. I hate it when I sweat. That's it. As though everything had suddenly become unreal. People were talking to her, people she had worked with, people talking to her suddenly from a great distance, she smiled and nodded and went into her office.
"Mummy?"
"Yes my dear. How is it with on this lovely day?"
"Mummy I need —"
"I have spent my morning painting with some of my friends. You know, I am having a party soon. You must come, and bring that lovely man you are living with now. What is his name, Richard?"
"Isolde, please."
"No, no. I am sorry. You are no longer engaged in a long-term

17. Isolde Reynolds was a woman I avoided like bubonic plague. Perhaps that is an understatement. It was more that I avoided Isolde Reynolds as one avoids an arbitrary group of unmedicated homicidal psychotic individuals brandishing high powered fully automatic weapons with an urge to kill and eat their victims, and not necessarily in the order of killing them first.

relationship with that man, a man I might add I never particularly took to, despite his many external appealing characteristics. But —"

"Mummy, they fired me."

"I see. Why?"

"I don't know."

"How?"

"They fired me."

"I will come over if you like. Is that what you want?

"Yes."

"I am leaving on a painting trip tomorrow for six days, and then you will come to the party. I will call over to —"

Martha hung up on her mother. She took a few plastic bags and threw her stuff into it. She opened her computer with a nail file, took out the hard drives, and flushed them repeatedly in the toilet. Then she filled a sink, and tossed the hard drives into the sink.

As she walked quickly down corridor after corridor, disoriented, looking for the main lifts, she looked at the Xpex people, as she passed then by for the last time to leave for home. One of the security types asked her for her mobile phone. She said no. They said they had to take it. That it was company property. She held it up. They snatched it from her. She snatched it back, then threw it out the nearest window, and then walked on, happy she was on the twelfth floor.

It was as though the company faces and bodies were insignificant, were on a slow motion over-dramatized movie screen, holograms, the distant voices of ghosts, flickering figment fragments of light appearing and disappearing, appearing again, then gone.

She had gathered her things, in mechanical android fashion, as though somewhere else someone was operating the controls of her life, left Xpex, and drove home. The severance cheque (if it could be called that) was already in the post for her. She burst through the hall door crying out in anguish and devastation. It was four minutes after ten in the morning. I was conducting group therapy in my offices. The baby sitter child-care professional was somewhere about. Martha threw herself on the sofa and wept. After an hour of uninterrupted crying, she crawled from the sofa and she heard Josh crying. Where the hell was the baby sitter? Sally, the child carer, was upstairs, in the bathroom, sick. She called up. She would be right down. Sally, the child carer, an out of work philosophy graduate who had failed her Master's Degree, was suffering from diarrhoea and vomiting due to a bad take-out meal the night before. Martha had tried, but could not quieten the troubled, bawling baby. Sally, the child carer arrived back, looking pale and angst ridden. She said, sorry, sorry, so sorry, I shouldn't be here what with the stomach, it couldn't be, couldn't be helped. She took the child up and held the baby boy, and, after a minute, Josh stopped crying.

32.

Around the time all this was occurring at, I received a call from Isolde telling me that it appeared that Martha had been (and I quote) 'excommunicated from the heaven of her job' and, though she was about to go visit her daughter, she thought it might be better if I went to see her. I said it would be an hour or so before I could get out of my office and Isolde said that was fine, and so I made a call and got Sally, the child carer on the phone and she said that Martha was upstairs, and that she would go get her. And then after a minute or two Martha came onto the phone.
"Where is your mobile phone?"
"What? You hardly ring me on it."
"Where is it? Its important they don't have it."
"They took it."
"What? When?"
"They fucking took my fucking mobile phone."
"They took your mobile phone?"
"They took my phone. Just as I was going. They took it. I snatched it back. I took it and tossed it out the window."
"Excellent! I love you."
"I also soaked my hard drives in a basin of water. I saw that on television."
"Very wise. I'll be home as soon as I can. Stay where you are and don't answer the phone. Give Sally a few hundred and ask her to stick around. Isolde is on her way."
"It must have taken months to plan."
"Indeed. I think so."
"All the time I was away. It's the same for all of them. They are all the same, all of them are the damn same, and the worst part of it is I have become one of them."
"What?"
"The same thing that I did to other people has been done to me."
"Nonsense, you have behaved honorably. I love you, Martha. I'll come home soon."
"I gotta go."
"I call in a couple of hours."
"Okay sweetie, I love you too.
"I'm sorry I can't get home straightaway. I feel terrible."
"No worries. Talk to you soon."

33.

I got home and we held each other and I felt her fall away from me, crumble. This was the worst moment of our entire time as a couple. I never for a moment thought she could be so fragile and there was nothing I could do to shore up that fragility. We stayed indoors for a few days and she rested and after a few weeks seemed a bit better. I had gone back to seeing patients after the fourth day. I had to. Then Martha went into depression. She seemed to grow more and more tired. She stopped going out. Then, after a few months, I took fewer clients and started another book, only to put it aside. Then she became somewhat catatonic, lost interest in life, and began drinking. I was left with much of the babysitting, took her to therapists who recommended a few weeks convalescence in this or that clinic with various experts, which I duly booked, astonished at the effect her firing had had on someone I always thought to be so much stronger than I. I knew too that, despite the depressive episode she was going through, that something deeper was going on, that a gulf was opening between us, that we were moving in different directions. I watched helpless as no anti-depressive seemed to shift her darkness, no conversation or convalescence renew her lack of hope. We began to move in different directions, and, after those years, we were different people from the two who first met in Bobby Lydon's place.

34.

"Hi Mary. It's Lucy. Lucy Brock. Gordon's mother. What am I saying? Of course you know who I am. Look, sorry. I'd appreciate it if you would call me back. See you."

"Hi Mary. It's Lucy. Listen, can you please call me back? Thanks. Talk to you soon. Bye."

"Mary. Hello there. Lucy, Lucy Brock, here. I have been trying, I dunno for a seven, no, eight days now. Can you please give me a call?"

"Hi Mary. I have been trying for two weeks now. I can't get Larry on the phone either. And I tried the headmaster's office and he isn't calling me back. Please call me."

"Hi Mary It's Lucy, Lucy Brock, what am I saying? We know each other a long time, well maybe not years, but long enough, really. Look, I have been trying to get in touch for weeks now. I also am getting no answer from Larry's phone. And he doesn't seem to be answering emails. I don't know what's going on. Well, I do, really. And I do think we need to get-together and talk this out. I think there's something terribly troubling going on in St. Raymond's and I think that not communicating like this will only result in —"
And at that stage the Frasier's home answering service ran out of time. About an hour or two later my mother tried again.

"Hello? Hello? Mary? Can you? Ok? Ooohhhh, fuucc —"
Klickk.
DIAL TONE.

Mary Frasier, Ed Frasier's mother, after much anxious avoidance of the telephone, saw from the visual readout that the number calling her was once again, Lucy Brock. My mother was trying to get in touch. There was something so infuriating about the persistent ringing of a telephone.

My mother, Lucy Brock, was relentless, immune to the wisdom of circumspection and self-restraint, leaving yet another of those messages saying how it would be really great if they got together and sorted this whole matter out, how this was not good for either of them, how worried she was, how much she thought it might be good if communication might be used and how sad all this made her. So Mary answered the phone.
"Frasier home?"
"Mary, this is Lucy here. Lucy Brock."
"Hi Lucy. I was going to call you, but what with my schedule and Larry's surgeries —"
"I understand. Absolutely. Surgery and whatever. Mary, I wanted —"
"It's been very difficult. We —"
"I can understand."
"I wonder do you, Lucy."
"Mary, I regret greatly all that has happened."
"Thanks. I do too."
"Look I'm sure we —"
"Look, I felt bad about not returning your messages."
"Mary, it's. I feel so bad —"
"And I wasn't —"
"I was hoping we could get-together in the next while and talk."
"Why not?"
Her voice dropped a little at the end of her agreement to meet, as if she truly expected an apocalyptic result from this superficially positive move, as if there really was no hope for an agreement. Lucy heard this and she couldn't stand it, and felt her anger once more ignite.
"I'm sure you have heard about what been happening," she said.
"Yes, I received a telephone call from the headmaster about your allegations."
Wow, a word that's full of legal meaning, Lucy mused, suddenly very angry with this vindictive, petty person who refused to see she had a sadist for a son.
"Eh yes, I received a letter from Jim Anderson too. It seems your Edward was very upset about —"
"Yes Ed hasn't been sleeping much. We have had to take him to a therapist."
"I'm sorry to hear that."
"I see. It's all been very upsetting."
"I confronted him because I know he and Gordy, well —"
"Yes, they were such friends."
"They were?

"Yes."

"As far as I know, they hardly knew each other. In fact I understand there's, you know, bad blood."

Mary didn't seem to hear that. Mary looked wistfully away into the middle distance, as though recalling faintly something of incomparable sadness, her life perhaps. On the other end of the phone Lucy saw her opportunity to take control of the situation.

"We never did figure out what happened, did we, Mary? I tried talking to Ed directly."

"How did that work out for you?"

"Not well, I'm afraid, not well. I have to say."

"I see."

More silence from Mary's end of the phone.

"I want to find a way to fix this Mary, I really do."

"How about not harassing my son in school?"

"How about your son not beating the living shit out of my son."

"Lucy!"

"Look, Mary, I want us to understand each other and I want there to be no more beatings, no more confrontations, no more bullying, and most of all, I want my son to have a happy life."

Mary's voice grew colder.

"Well, it seems we have a very different view of what's going on. Edward denies anything has been happening and, in the absence of proof —"

"Mary, don't go there"

"Sorry?"

"When I hear that kind of talk I hear lawyers opening their pocketbooks…"

"In the absence of anything conclusive —"

"Like Ed's long history of bullying and intimidating…"

"I feel I have to ask you Lucy, to leave my Edward alone."

"That's no problem, and you can take that as done. I will never contact or come within any distance of Ed Frasier. Okay? If that's what you want I will do it. Now, please, before this escalates any more, I think we should sit down together and talk…"

"Lucy, I…"

"So let's settle this. Let's get-together and have a frank and full discussion."

"Okay, Lucy. How about next Tuesday? Eight o'clock? I'll drop over. Will Dave be there?"

"He can be."

"Okay then. See you."

"Bye Lucy."

Dave stood in a pair of shorts and a T-shirt, as Lucy hung up the phone.

"Well?" Dave asked.

"I think Larry is having an affair."

"What!?

"I think Larry is having an affair."

"How do you know?"

"I can't get him on the phone."

"That's absolutely conclusive. He won't pick up, therefore he is cheating on his wife," Dave muttered to himself. What I mean is that might not necessarily imply an affair. Usually you get a second phone, usually a disposable phone, just in case. And you take your calls on that."

"I think he is seeing someone else and I think I know who."

"Nonsense. He is not well. Larry is still ill."

"And that might be the reason."

"Okay, but in the school, just got get back to the really important stuff about our son being tortured," Dave said. "In the school, there are cameras everywhere. There are witnesses everywhere. I'm still really, really mad at you for going into the school yard like that."

"Really?"

"Yep. It was a really dangerous and stupid thing to do."

Lucy took out a plastic bag and opened it.

"You know, I really don't do drugs."

"Yes, very nice. Thanks for your support. Now you are going to browbeat me into admitting it was a stupid thing to do?"

"I don't brow beat you."

Lucy opened the plastic bag.

"Oh, well goodness me. Look at what I have here."

"It's a recording machine," Dave said.

"I even made a recording of my conversation with Mary and with her son, Ed Frasier…."

She took out a slim leather bound recorder about the size of her hand and pressed play. Suddenly Ed Frasier's harsh voice crackled out. It was beginning to break.

"…Don't you touch me! I'm going to go home. I'm going to get my parents, and we are going to sue you."

"No, no you're not. You are going to leave my son alone."

"Your son is a fucking dickhead."

She switched off. Dave grinned.

"Ed Frasier is such a sweet, lovely, charming kid, isn't he?"

"Delightful."

"I think so…I really enjoyed that little schoolyard chat with him."
"A charming individual. You wouldn't hear our boy talk like that. You should have told me. I know you had your reasons, but you should have told me."
"No I didn't have to tell you. I don't take orders from you…"
"Lucy, that's not what I …"
"I know…"
Lucy played a little more of the recording….
"….'What happened to my son? What happen to my Gordon?" She asked.
"Maybe he got hit with a boot," Edward said to peals of laughter and cheers of 'yeah!'
"Gordon doesn't do much football," Lucy said.
"Yeah, Gordon is a moron."
"That's so cheap and pathetic, Edward. Compared to him, well, you could be his pet…"
Dave muttered- "Jesus, what an angry kid, Frasier I mean."
"Right," Lucy smiled dreamily and lay on her back." More issues than —"
Lucy paused for thought, following from his suggestion, what did Ed Frasier have more issues than, issues.
"The Times," she said, and chuckled somewhat too light heartedly.
"Guardian."
"Playboy."
"Hustler."
"Times Literary Supplement."
"See? I was collecting evidence," she said, kissing him.
"Yes, that was extremely cool,"
"And you thought it was a fool's errand."
"Yes, I was wrong. Big time wrong," Dave said. "What are you gonna do? You were collecting evidence, I guess. Very…dangerous. We can't use that. It's against some legal, precedent. I'm not sure, but if we use it, there could be trouble. I'll give the solicitor a call tomorrow."
"We'll build a case against this boy. This will fix him. We could get a court order," she said. He didn't answer. She was smiling and looking into his eyes. She went on.
"Forbid him to come within such and such a distance from Gordon."
Dave shook his head and smiled.
"Not too sure about that," he muttered. "That would make headlines."
"What?"
"Headlines," Dave said. "Oh, oh, ooh," shaking his head

"Negative publicity for us," Lucy said. "Right, not that it matters a damn,"

"And Gordon. Negative publicity for Gordy."

Now Dave was looking out the window, drinking brandy, obsessing about Edward Frasier and trying to envision what was happening to Gordon, what it might do to Gordon in the long run, if he was living his life through his special boy, if he loved the boy too much, if the boy might lose his gifts as he grew older, if the boy might burn out or break down or become just the same as the other former smart kids, smug and lazy and addicted to information. She looked at him and asked:

"What is it?"

"Hum, nothing."

"Tell me?" She said. As if I didn't know, Lucy thought. He is thinking about Gordon. That's all he thinks about.

"That bastard Frasier, the one beating the shit out of Gordy, I hate that kid. Sometimes there's no grey area. This is one of them."

"I know," she said. I know.

"Just going to get ice, maybe a little ginger ale. Want anything?"

"I'm good, thanks," she smiled. "Actually, no. Actually, I'm not good. Actually I want us to go back to the way things were once. When you and I would make love for hours, when we would come home from work and just take ourselves off somewhere, to the Dublin mountains, to the park, to the beach, anywhere, and just hang out, when Gordon was five or six and would recite verbatim from whatever he was reading or remember exactly the sequence of events he saw on television, or multiply any two numbers you gave him, or tell you exactly what was on television any day of the week any time, or remember phone numbers or talk about some science program, all the stuff he does secretly now, all the stuff about himself he loathes and suppresses because he feels a shame at the difference that exists between himself and others. I want to protect our boy. I want this, this life we have, to work. Did he feel that shame because of something we did or something we failed to do? Was it something that happened to him during the time he went to one of the other schools, or is this Frasier kid the real reason behind it all? I want him to feel loved. I want him to just be the beautiful, delightful charming little boy he was anyway, when we would laugh a lot, and you and I actually had some kind of a connection. I want our sex life back. I want us, all of us back together. So if you were wondering why I did what I did in that yard, because I know that why you are doing all that brooding, there's the reason. I did it because I want you to make love to me now."

Dave put his drink away and looked at Lucy for a long time. Then he smiled. His eyes had tears in them.

"I do too, Lucy," he said.

"Good," she said.

35.

The guilt I felt after I began my affair with Lucia, Martha's half- sister, was mostly self- indulgent; a self-hating agony I indulged because I was and am that vain and stupid. See footnote.[18]

I began an affair with Martha's half sister, Lucia, whom I subsequently married after a relatively amicable divorce from Martha, after I went to a party thrown by Martha's mother, Isolde. We were invited to quite a few parties by Isolde. We generally didn't go. We didn't go because I didn't want to. Eventually Isolde came over to us, and, during dinner, expressed her anger and hurt at being slighted in this manner by her own flesh and blood, and that she had never been so treated by any of her ex-husbands or lovers, nor indeed by her beautiful daughter, Lucia, whom we never got to meet, mainly because we never come by to visit. So that was it. We had to go to the next one. And we did.

Martha and I drove to the house on Reuben Street, a huge five bedroomed affair that Isolde owned after her long and acrimonious divorce from her ex-husband Tim, whose name both forever held equally in ignominy and memory, referred to in conversation; discussed, dissected and bitterly regretted. There were little of her ex-husbands past actions, personality, and predilections that her friends and sometimes unwilling acquaintance listeners did not know about. She had painted him into the walls, and when I say painted, I am not speaking in any other way than literally. His satanic portraits hung on the walls like a sacred image, a shrine that might scare away evil, somehow alerting Satan and his passing hordes that there had been, and in some way remained, something much worse living in that house on Reuben Street.

18 I started my affair because I wanted to escape the emotional hell that home had become after Martha got fired. We argued endlessly. She accused me of being happy she had failed in life. I said I did not think she had failed in life, but really I was disappointed in her, angry with her, and feeling as I did, feeling my own self- disappointment projected onto her, I grew as estranged from her as I was from myself. Boredom and contempt crept into my home life. I began an affair because I was bored and wanted stimulation, something to capture my imagination, some meaning to exist in what had become habit and ritual. I felt I was attending to a daily rubric of a life that somehow become empty.

I liked the house, and liking a structure was always important to me. If I disliked a building, I tended to find ways to quickly exit the structure. But not this one on Reuben Street. It had a certain stripped down feel to it, a nouveau Gothic stone, ghostly feel, leaden with time and tormented memory, arches and huge doors, echoes and measured atmospherics, carefully chosen pieces of furniture gleaned at a fraction of their true value, restored lovingly or purchased discreetly from friends, or friends of friends, those in the know who had already restored it and made it special enough for Martha's mother's carefully nurtured uniqueness.

Through the front hallway Martha and I walked, trying to look nonchalant, trying to feign the confident self-possession that would be expected of relatives, successful, moneyed, self- contained, fruitful, loving relatives who were in a successful relationship, who had love and compassion for each other and, by default, for others as a consequence of their own status of having an existential trajectory targeting self-realization. I don't recall deliberately wearing that mask. Fear and annoyance and insecurity made me put it on.

We passed a tall handsome twenty-something Goth boy. He loitered like a wraith about the hallway. He wore a dog collar, well more of a spiked neck band. He was also nose ringed and lip ringed and ear ringed. I wondered if he had taken the full force of some shrapnel. Then I imagined he might have changed his name from Jim or Pete to Antoine or Luciferous. I overheard him muttering about Rimbaud to his beautiful lady friend, who I mused had adopted some odd name with a heavy Latinized subtext, Degana or Agrippa or Apollina. The name Rimbaud caught my ear. The odd couple were either coming or going, I didn't know. Well, I thought, we're all either coming or going, I thought. The heavy metal Goth boy was, as well as talking poetry, giving meaningful butterfly kisses a hair's breath from a lovely blue-eyed long blond haired peach cheeked female, that lady friend bedecked in a dark black rose petalesque flowing dress with the standard issue overpriced Jesus sandals. She was smiling and nodding to whatever incomprehensible theory he was expounding as they stood near some of Martha's mother's sculptures of the female form, tiny breasted, stick legged, wrought in a type of Giacometti style, gazing with cavernous hollowed out eyes by way of ghostly greeting to us, their hands reaching upwards in a cross between stretching straight up to some unreachable height and a tortured fascist salute.

We passed through the hallway, and suddenly Martha turned to me and she said,
"I will be right back, ok?"
"Where are you going?"
"To get a little something to cheer myself up. I will be right back ok?"
"You are going to get cocaine, aren't you?"
"Yes!"
"At your mother's party!"
"She always gets the best weed and the best coke for these gigs."
"And you are going to leave me behind for the evening, aren't you?"
"Coke makes you obnoxious, Gordon. Well, more obnoxious."
"Fuck you."
"You are to stay away from it. I am not spending my evening apologizing for my husband, again."
"Okay, okay. Go!" I said.

And I was alone. Martha was gone, seemed to dissolve into the house. I thought she might have gone upstairs. I decided that feeling abandoned and alone was something I could do without, so repressing the feeling, smiling, I walked into the main rooms, the rooms with tables and cabinets bedecked with black and white candles, fairy lights tacked to the darkened walls, small lamps on sideboards, and more electric lamps, so many small lights posing as centre pieces on small tables packed with finger food and health drinks. On the walls were other occasional paintings, the types done quickly as studies for larger projects, watercolours of sweeping mystical landscapes in pale imitation of the etchings of Blake; other more realised oils of couples in tantric positions, beautiful sketches of lesbian love scenes that arrested me momentarily as party people significantly noticed me studying them. Then, I saw the books Isolde had probably read. I knew she had read them. I opened them and saw her name written on the inside cover: volumes of Anais Nin, Miller, Joyce, Burroughs, Alastair Crowley, Shelley, William Blake, Alexander Solzenitsyn, James Joyce, William Burroughs, Franz Kafka: some of the names that caught my eye. I didn't look too closely. I felt I was probing the workings of another's soul if I looked too deeply into their library, almost a sense of violating another person. But the pictures were there to be seen, and their explicitness to me hid an uncertainty about the human subject; the delusion that were we to all strip down naked in fearless physiological fragility a truth were to be found as to why we were here would be marked on our fragile skin.

Through the soft lights and flickering shades and tinkling laughter, I saw the food, the colourful all-vegetarian dishes. Such good food, I thought, so carefully prepared. Across the party, through the main room's huge, opened, dividing doors, I noticed a fondue set at a table being used by mostly slim monk-like people, sitting and eating and talking and laughing as they nibbled bits of textured flavoured protein, vegetarian sausages, tiny carrots, potatoes and sweet corn with salad, each on small side plates, dairy-free or vegan signage as appropriate. I passed small tables with little cakes and pastries and small carefully cut sandwiches and beer and wine and vodka and tequila, salads and snacks on it, prepared, it seemed, by the guests rather than any expense gone to by the host, for there were so many different styles of preparation, so many different types of crockery, so many different types of glasses. There was such a distinct lack of homogeneity in the food preparation. Anyway, I could see guests bringing their own food, which was being put out into bowls, bowls they brought themselves. She was so cheap, I thought. And she is so rich too.

I could see willowy females and some willowy men. Funny, I thought. The metallic-death-loving-life-denying-Rimbaud-loving Goths Martha and I saw at the door didn't set up a kind of precedent. I expected the room to bristle with leather jackets and steel-tipped, inch-thick-jackbooted, fantasy novel writing, soft-voiced, hypersensitive slightly needy nihilists, but no. These were earth mothers and earth fathers, a product of some benign belief in the goodness and spiritual wholesomeness of the natural world, most of them in these obligatory dark colours for the sake of clearly expressing their individuality, by dissolving into black, hovering in little groups, like escapees from Dante's dreams, their voices exercising a kind of well-elocuted repressed politeness, looking blankly at me as I moved past. Clearly by my demeanour I was not one of them. After I was gone a few paces they resumed their conversation.

The music began. Naturally, because of the sense of premeditated difference, it was nothing one would normally hear at a party, more like at a new-age meditation chant group. It was a music of the forest type, a slow chant, filled with the sounds of wild rushing feelings of freedom-invoking fresh mountain streams, and underneath, deep in the substratum of polyphonic nature sounds, came that hum, a hum building to some type of pseudo primal scream type call of the wild. I gritted my teeth in irritation. Some of the party goers got up and danced. They danced to this chant, holding each other and smiling the smile of people who were happy in this very nice cult, so I fumed to myself. Then, in the midst of the primal scream stream nature sounds, came a single lonely voice that spoke in carefully modulated sincerity. It spoke in hushed, loving, wise tones, about how we were all one with the seas, the skies, the rocks, the stars, for, according to the laws of conservation of matter we were all one, and this oneness could be experienced if we were all only open to the experience.

At that stage I wanted more than anything to get very drunk or very stoned, or maybe both.

Others, sitting about in small, exclusive groups, talked meaningfully to each other, and as I walked out of the main room, down to what I hoped would be perhaps the kitchen, for I had long lost Martha, someone passing with a bottle of wine in one hand and sandwiches in another, stopped me and asked me was I part of the support group. I had no idea what he meant. So, taking a sandwich from the plate, I said no. I looked at him. He was a slim man with a long beard. His oval face seemed to emphasize his deep brown compassionately gazing eyes. I said I had no idea what that was. You are not part of any group, are you he said with a smile. I shook my head. With that smile his face utterly transformed. He positively beamed at me. Though I had met him for only that moment, I was very attracted to him. I wanted to kiss him lightly on the lips, just to see what it felt like, that affection like that for another man might lead me else where, somewhere I dare not go yet wanted to go, simply because I felt suspicious of deep felt unexplored taboos. I loved his thick long straight black hair tied back with deep brown sad circular prophetic eyes and a dark full beard dressed in a T-shirt and jeans and sandals. Okay then he said. Have another sandwich. I took a few and he walked away without saying another word to me.

It was only later on in the evening, after an hour and a half of watching the dancers dance, the talkers talk, and the poets bring half-finished pieces of their mediocre poems out of deep pockets, and read to each other their truly mediocre verses, Martha returned with dilated eyes and an obsequious smile of covert apology. I had found a newspaper and was reading it "as an act of defiance to the fantasists all about," I said. Martha smiled and I looked coldly angrily at her, a barely detectable snarl curling in my lip. Don't smile like that, I thought. I hate it.

"Thanks, thanks for leaving me here amidst these, these lunatics!" I hissed.

"They can hear you."

"Excellent. That's a diagnosis, by the way."

"Gordon, please don't be a jerk."

"Okay, I am going to mumble to myself over here. See that corner?"

"Yes, Gordon."

A few looked at me for a second, and then continued talking. I felt very embarrassed, and my embarrassment made me angrier. Martha looked coldly disapprovingly at me. "These are friends of my mother," she said.

"Figures," I said.

So Martha took me to meet the parent. As no one had either introduced themselves to me, or greeted me aside from the man with the prophetic gaze, Martha took me by the hand and as she brought me through the people that filled Isolde's house, I found myself watching Martha's hips and shoulders lithely shift beneath her clothing, imagining the line of her spine move like a dorsal fin as she cut through the people, so many people, to the object of her introductions, a wave of forgiveness emanating from my watching her like that. She does this to me, I thought, she does this to me, or I do it to myself. She had the newspaper gone from my hand, which was killing my eyes anyway in the terrible tiny lights, and telling me these were people she wanted me to meet. Interesting people. Gifted. Different.

"Where did you go?"

"Upstairs. I said I was going to do some white. So I did."

"I never really understood how your mother gets cocaine for her parties."

"From her police friends."

"I see. That's nice, dear. And are you feeling so much better now?" I asked. And she nodded, and she told me she would show me later how much better she felt with a knowing smile.

"I fear you are turning into my wife." I said to Martha.

"Now that's not funny. I will pretend you just didn't say that, or that you said it because you weren't having fun. Let's talk to Isolde. She'll tell us how we were cleverly avoiding her."

"There's little cleverness in avoiding someone at a party like this. The lights are so low. How come?" I said as we walked up to Isolde.

"How come what?"

"How come there are so many people here?"

"I dunno, Gordon. I don't go to many parties."

Isolde was drinking red wine and smoking a cigar. Martha went up to

her, and threw her arms around her and kissed her. There had been no mention of gifts for her as she had told her children that she did not need gifts and that their presence at the party was sufficient.
"You are, each of you, a gift to me," she said, "a beautiful gift from God, and each day I thank her for it."
"Hello, Mum."
"My sweet," Isolde said. "I was so very rude to you and your lovely Gordon. Though I am glad you came, if only for the indulgence of having you here. Let me introduce you to some people."
"Glad to be here." I said.

Martha was the product of Isolde's first marriage, to Timothy Reynolds, banker, a man she said had the fiscal ethics of a loan shark, a man Isolde later claimed she never loved, but a man she said most certainly loved her, indeed who deified her for her talents, prodigious creative output, and the large sums of money she eventually brought into the family after over a decade's investment in her gifts by Tim. Things went south when it was discovered that Tim had something of a predilection to going on foreign holidays and sleeping with underage girls. Isolde didn't take it to the police. Instead, she sat down with her soon to be future ex-husband and quietly suggested he grant her a divorce, and the house, and some undisclosed rather large sum of money.

Yet she perversely kept the name of her marriage to Tim because, she said, she liked it. She said Tim was special to her. Tim had given her Martha.

As I kissed Isolde that night, on the cheek I might add, I saw an woman with a ravaged face from which beauty shone like the light from that pock marked moon she drew into the background of so many of her drawings.

"Good of you to come. One hopes you are not too put out here in this strange party." She waved her cigar holding tanned hand in an arc sweeping towards then away from the floor, an affected gesture that slightly irritated me, and then brought her hand back to her wine glass. She was of medium height, wearing a pair of black jeans and a gray and white-flecked turtleneck and a necklace that seemed to have some type of small crystal attached. Her white hair was straight and cut short, the type of straight cut one decides upon as a radical measure after wearing one's hair long for such a long period.
"No, not at all. It's fine."

"Of course," she said, "all is illusion."

"All is illusion?" I said. O God, I thought. I won't be able to resist rubbishing her crazy philosophies. "Thank god – what you just said was an illusion."

"I know you do not like when I say such things, Gordon."

"I know you say them to provoke and I know you know deep down that they are dangerous, puerile, fantastic, contradictory ideas, and poorly thought out." I began.

"Really," she said.

"Yes," I said.

"Gordon!" Martha frowned.

"Well when you say all is illusion," I began.

"Yes. There is no way of knowing the truth of anything except by love, except by realizing that it is us, we create our own reality."

"So 'love' is the way we know reality. Now that's really fascinating. Is 'love' a kind of seventh sense that only those initiated really understand? Is this the kind of half baked nonsense you are currently-?"

"Gordon," Martha interjected, "Gordon, don't."

And Isolde talked on:

"You are drunk on your own intellect. You do not understand. You are arrogant and an angry man."

"Why thank you Isolde. I love you too. The reality we see," I continued.

"Here comes the philosophy lesson," Martha moaned.

"We see reality? Who says that?" Isolde countered.

"Okay then," I said. "The cancer some of us get from smoking, the death and life we all experience, the families we have, the children you have (unless you think they are an illusion too) the people we meet, good or bad, the things we think happen to us, actually, according to you, Isolde Reynolds, my mother- in-law, you are saying they are made to happen."

"Made to happen by ourselves." Isolde said. "We make the universe."

"Oh for fuck sake!" I snapped. "Which one?"

"This world we think is real, well, it is real only because we make it real, the omnipresence of the Christ in all of us, that salvation is truly at hand, that love, once again, is all there was." Isolde said, looking smilingly around at her party of dancing, talking party friends.

"That's dangerous nonsense." I said.

"Do you know," she began.

"Know what?"

"Do you know why so many clever people go mad?"

"Because there are so many people like you out there who destroy harmony and peace with psychotic dogmas they force on people?"

"No, Gordon. I have no desire for you to believe me, just accept me."

"There is no relationship between cleverness and madness, that's more nonsense."

"Yes, yes there is."

"No, there is not."

"The really clever go mad because they have ideas they cannot cope with. Love makes things make sense, and it can never be understood."

"To say nothing makes sense is to contradict yourself."

"How do you know anything?"

"I guess I am just lucky, or I must be terribly loving." I said.

"You hide your madness. You have nothing. And now love has failed you."

"I'm not interested in." I said.

"Salvation is all that interests you," Isolde said.

"God, you are so arrogant!"

"Look who's talking!"

"Are you trying to deliberately provoke me?" I said.

"Yes Gordon. I am arrogant. I want you to hear me. You won't find salvation in the arms of a lover, believe me," she said looking significantly at Martha.

"What's that supposed to mean, Mother?" Martha said.

"My only interest is in how things are, not how they should be!" I said.

"Be a man," she said. "Become the man you were meant to be! Not some loser!"

"Thanks for that, Isolde. I think we'll go home now. Great party! Fuck you!"

"I'm sorry." Martha said. "I didn't expect it to go so badly. I'm sorry, really. I feel so bad."

"I'm going home. God, what a bitch! Where did you get that coke?"

"We can't both go home coked up. One of us has to drive."

"We'll get a cab."

"It's twelve miles."

"Don't be a bitch."

"Don't call me a bitch!"

"Sorry, Martha. Where did you get it?"

"Upstairs, third door to the right. We'll do some together later on at home. I can give someone a call."

"No."

"See you later then, Gordon."

"I am sorry. About before." I said.

"Don't worry about it." Martha said.

36.

And I went towards the door, or what I thought to be the door, and out the hallway and saw the crowds and the faces and the bodies swimming past and the lights seemed to blur, and I went upstairs to find the second, or was it the third door, on the right and so many of those doors locked, and I walked from room to room, trying doors to see which of them would open.

And then I walked into Lucia Reynolds's room: small, book filled, smoky, low-lit, double bedded, with a window that looked out onto a disused rail track. I knew immediately this was Lucia Reynolds, a kind of terrifying preternatural certainty that this was the daughter of Isolde Reynolds, Martha's younger half-sister, someone Martha only obliquely referred to. It was as though something gripped me by the throat when I saw her sitting there in that small room, excluded from the party zone, a light dangling above her small oval shaped head like some sword of Damocles, its beam cutting across her pale skin like the last tiny silver of light before everything blacked out. Her eyes seemed the blackest black, like the lens of a huge paparazzi camera; eyes built to pick out the tiniest detail of one's face or body or life, carefully balanced, beautifully made, deeply biased.
"This is a private room," she said unsmilingly.
"I'm sorry," I said.
"Are you sure about that?" She said.

In the far corner sat a huge parrot cage. Inside it a cantankerous parakeet squawked and clattered about its various perches like some aging major general confined to some humiliating home for the bewildered far below her dignity and reduced to bland regular meals and a degrading game of draughts in the afternoon. Lucia, I said to myself, as though remembering some heartbreaking song. This was her room, with Tori Amos singing from the record player and she catlike on a broken down sofa bed smoking a cigarette in a manner reminiscent of her mother. Of course, I thought, if one is not at war with one's history, if one accepts one's lineage, then there is more time for peace. The sofa was draped with a series of throw rugs to give its agedness dilapidation and depression a little camouflage. The whole room, its dim light and old bed and books and smoky feel, was like a scene out of some bed-sit dwellers most poverty-ridden days. The time before making a regular income when one is taking refuge in old

recordings and good novels and booze to stave off the loneliness and odd hunger pangs borne of feeling isolated, away from home in a new area and looking for relationships to fill the void left by family, who were probably far away in another city, the comfort zone of family one had long outgrown. But this was no bed-sit. This was a small room in a huge house in a wealthy area, and this was the daughter of Isolde Reynolds, and Isolde Reynolds was worth a fortune, despite her craziness. Well, I think she's crazy, but then what would I know?
"You look terrible," Lucia said.
"I am terrible."
"The coke is two doors down. Close the door after you?"
"You're Lucia, aren't you?"
She smiled, but still neither invited me in nor offered me one of those dodgy looking chairs near her equally dodgy looking sofa to sit on. I stood at the doorway like some mute schoolboy waiting to be asked in, waiting to be offered a seat. She didn't ask me, so I sat down anyway on a chair with a loose leg, getting used to being on weak legs and unfamiliar footing. At first I thought it might give way from underneath me, but later I discovered it was one of those pieces of furniture one acquires in an imperfect state. Then, after a while, like false friends or intimate acquaintances, the type one, despite oneself, reveals intimacies to, one keeps the piece of furniture because it's just there. It completes one's environment precisely because of its brokenness.

"You are so beautiful," I said. "But you know you are beautiful. You don't wear clothing to accentuate how beautiful you are,"
"Oh please," she said rolling her eyes.
"Nothing that clings, that shows off."
"Why don't you sit down?" She said.
"I have."
"Sit on something that won't break, then," she said.
Her clothes were simple but tasteful, the obligatory individual black, a jacket thrown over the sofa just like I did it, sensible shoes, slacks. I sat on a stool.
"Thank you." I said.
Lucia's beauty was protean, at first crude, a hard turn of her lips on a cigarette as she drew the smoke into her lungs, that cigarette, I thought, that delivery system for nicotine, that weapon of mass destruction, then seeing her casually exhaling the hexamine carbon monoxide pyrrolidine solanesol vinyl chlorine toilet cleaner antiseptic mothballs along with the three thousand eight hundred other chemicals, in a rehearsed, pseudo-relaxed, bohemian manner, the smoke rolling over

the porcelain skin of one who hates the sun, turning the page, and looking for a moment with her fabulous eyes at me, who also was not speaking, watching this strange creature in her room, world-weary, angry, suspicious, alone before thirty years old, that old dull ache came upon me once more.

"I would like to have sex with you, if you want to," I said.

"Well, you are just all charm and seduction, aren't you?"

"Not really."

"No, you are pretty charmless, really."

"I know there is a big age difference between you and me; I'd say about twenty years, and maybe fifty IQ points," I stopped for a second, trying to understand what I was saying.

"Delightful, thanks for that."

But understanding was gone; I couldn't stop myself.

"God, but you are an idiot," she said.

"Very true," I said." I know you are reading, that you are taking a little personal time, not that I haven't heard of any of those books or those writers."

"Yes, you have."

"I have, and most of them are pretty piss poor novelists, with a terribly skewed vision of the human condition. The types of writers trying to spell out and prove to themselves through cultivating a moderately wide, equally disgruntled, unhappy reading audience, some deeply flawed list of cliched reasons why they should do nothing with their lives and feel somewhat satisfied with letting the wheel of life just spin. All those novelists probably need is a good course of suitably prescribed antidepressants, and a non-enabling network of friends, and maybe, just maybe they might write something that actually breaks new ground. I doubt it though."

"I see. Ever think they might be right and that life holds no real meaning?"

"Eh, what do you mean by life? My experience? Yours? Your mother's? Your sister's? The cat's?"

"Whatever. Do you have an answer?"

"I think life's been good to me so far." I said, and she grinned at me.

And I sat there and looked at my hands, then looked at her hands, and she seemed not to be surprised or pretending not to be surprised.

"Why would I want to fuck you?" she said.

"I don't know," I said." I can't give you a reason to want to. But I want to, and if you don't." I said.

"Are you married?"

"Well, yes, very legally, very publicly, in a registry office, to your half-

sister Martha. We have a child together. How could you not know I was living with Martha?" I asked.
"I don't know. I don't see much of her."
"How could you not see much of your own sister?"
"Easy."
"Okay…"
"I avoid her."
"You don't like her?"
"We never got along."
"Why not?"
"I'm not a nice person."
"I hate it when people say that."
"I don't care. It's true. Martha is a nice person. I guess all that disapproval makes for enough righteous indignation to ruin any family. Martha can be very disapproving."
"That's deep. So what do you work at?" I asked.
"I date a lot of older men."
"I see," I said.
Lucia got up off the sofa and walked over to the press and took out a bottle of wine and opened it and offered me some.
"I don't work at anything. I live here. I take casual jobs. I see a few boyfriends. I take my time. I have few plans. Mother will leave me this house. When she dies I will rent out a room or two. Then I will die. I write poetry."
"Doesn't everyone?"
"What's the matter?"
"No matter. I'm okay."
"Do you usually have affairs?"
"No. I mean yes."
"Don't then, really. I like you, Gordon Brock."
"You like me. That's patronising."
"But don't do this because you want to dial back the clock of time."
"Look, I came up here looking for some cocaine."
"Okay," she said.
"It's a talent killer," I said. Like marijuana makes you never finish another worthwhile project. You just sit around dreaming."
As I said all this she moved past me so closely, her proximity an electric force washing through me. The shock of the Atlantic Ocean. The ocean so cold for the swimmer no matter what the season. Tsunami. No, I thought, that's in another continent.
"How old are you?"
"Twenty- eight. Is that entirely relevant?" She said.

"Entirely. Relevant." I said.

I would have done anything to have sex with her. I took the glass and drank, noticing the ink on her thumb and index finger, a smudge of face paint, her sleeves draping like fifteenth century frills over her dark painted fingernails as she gave me the glass, glancing across to that press from whence the wine came and seeing other bottles stashed. The wine was a little bitter; perhaps it was my mood.

"I'd like that," she said after an eon of silent clock watching.

"Like what?" I said.

"To have sex with you," she said.

"I see," I said terrified.

Now her eyes seemed cold, expressionless, cold dark watchfulness with a half smile playing on her lips, as if this was her habitual pose before allowing someone inside her. My eyes are my passport. I looked at her smile. A false smile, I thought, can be identified by an excessive curve on the right side, betraying the emotion leaking from the left side of the brain. How did I remember that? But her smile was steady. She stood up and put her glass on the table beside her and stood in front of me, waiting, giving me permission. I looked at her hips and slowly looked up her body, running my hands awkwardly nervously along her body, imagining her body naked.

"Old man," she said. "Old, old man with weathered face and young vulnerable eyes and long thin hands and long thin body and soft voice and all that cleverness hidden underneath shy, bumbling ways. Are you a hitter?"

"What?"

"Do you hit women?"

"I don't hit anyone," I said.

"Ever steal anything important?"

"No. What are you doing?"

"Wondering if you were telling the truth when you said you weren't a hitter."

"Last time I hit someone I was just fourteen. And it was the first time I ever hit anyone."

I haltingly touched her shoulders and neck, leaned down and kissed her softly and she kissed me, putting her tongue into my mouth and I allowed her explore as though somewhere inside was what each sought, and I felt frightened. Didn't know where to put my hands, like a terrified rookie field medic attending a dying marine. I touched her on her shoulders, along her back, holding her as she wrapped her arms around my chest and drew me to her and I felt safe and my fear diminished and I lifted her up and she wrapped her legs around me and I felt free of everything and she felt it too, a freedom, a sense of something dying that had finally died as it should have died long ago. No more fighting. A sense that something new was happening and she was glad at that moment that she had said yes to me and I felt happy too in the midst of all the insecurities and adolescent shyness and fumbling for neither of us wanted the burden of experience there and then, the disappointments and ravages time and habit wreak on love and hope, and, after we had taken off our clothes and she locked the door and we had sex for a long time, both surprised at how good it felt after such a surfeit of expectation, and we lay there and finished the bottle of wine and talked about nothing of consequence and she smoked some cigarettes, and I took a shower and gave her my number and asked her, if she wanted to, to call me, She said she would think about it, that she too was seeing someone, though she wasn't, but she would think about it, as moments like this are often once only. I agreed, but I wanted to see her again anyway.

"I have to go back to the party," I said, and left and went downstairs and found Martha and said I had to go home.

"I'm sorry," Martha said.

"It's okay, I said, "I'm glad I came. I looked everywhere for you. I rang your number over and over. I thought you had gone home. Then I went out to the car and it was still there and." I said.

"You did?"

"I did."

"But if you rang my number, wouldn't your number register on my phone?" Martha said.

"It certainly should," I said.

"So where were you for all that time?" She said.

"I ended up sitting in one of the bathrooms talking about Freud to this kid who kept asking me if I had ever had an affair. The kid kept hitting on me," I said.

"Really, who was it?"

"Some Goth kid. I dunno. We drank a lot of wine and he kept smoking cigarettes. The cocaine was all gone by the way. You had better drive."

I woke up with the worst hangover the following day.

"You can't drink, Gordon," Martha said. She handed me liver salts and aspirin. "You should accept the fact you have no tolerance for alcohol. You look terrible. But I hope you had a good time." And she kissed me on my aching head and I felt such love and guilt and sorrow and my eyes teared up and I turned my face away and she pulled away gently and went to get me a drink of water, wondering what was the matter with her guilty husband, while somewhere deep down, knowing only too well what was happening.

37.

After being with Lucia I felt happy in my marriage. I felt happy because I had an escape clause. Time spent with Lucia was my escape into another life. And, so long as I had that other life, the one I had built with Martha was a little less intolerable. I had felt trapped, bored, frustrated. With Lucia things seemed reborn for me. My elation at feeling love again, my inner happiness invested the world with an unworn mantle. I was careful to hide my happiness with a sense of irony. I was equally careful not to seem too needy, too guilty, to over caring. I was playing the perfect husband to hide the obvious truth.

But infidelity worked. Martha and I began to be together more often. We would stay in of an evening watching cop shows on television. Or my favourite thing: we used for instance, drive out to places and just walk around.

We both loved Wicklow. I remember picnicking on the Wicklow hills. Little Joshua loved it and squealed with delight. I remember stillness like the memory of lovers, hovered over the forest floor, replete with pine needles and leaves and bits of bark and trees and ants and small furry creatures one did not usually see. The sounds of the wood pigeon, a child's soft giggle somewhere off in the distance playing somewhere just out of sight, all filled the forest air, already thick with summer, filled me with joy.

Down in the dark, beneath the gnarled ancient twisted green and blue and dappled yellows, we walked stoned with the beauty of it all. As Martha and I talked, small splinters of sunlight penetrated Gorgon knots of branches, and it all felt surreal, as if we had stepped out of our lives and were merely visiting another time another place, and, in a moment, it might all end.

The day I particularly recall, the day I describe now, I recall there was little wind, but it was still cool walking along there, so Martha said, and I agreed and smiled. Here and there one might see something move, a flutter of takeoff wing or the scamper of squirrel or a fox. Look I said. Look! I pointed out the beautiful fox, an image that lingered, with its dark look before it went disappearing into the forest, or the squirrel doing its acrobatics, then stopping with Buddha like stillness despite its manic heartbeat, lost in the high branches, trying to merge with the endless wood all about. And Joshua's joy and fascination filled Martha and I with happiness and together we walked along the allotted path, with its designated stops and cute wooden signs to indicate some interesting feature the Irish Forestry Commission had written about in their 'please take one' brochures, and, after an hour of talking, we stopped for sandwiches and the flask of coffee and the orange juice and water to stay hydrated, to talk about the smell of woodbine hovering in the four o'clock summer air and the life cycle of animals. And then Joshua ran suddenly down a path when we were about to explain this or that feature to the boy, running off with his arms outstretched making the noise of an airplane, pretending to himself he was operating a Hawker Sidley Harrier Jump Jet, a machine he had seen in an old comic book, running down the afternoon path with the sun now low enough to cut between the trunks. And there in the distance between the trees the honey sun hovered, and the boy ran off, playing planes, flying like the wood pigeon or the squirrel, running between other families or tourists in neat functional walking gear, tourists with expensive hiking boots and state of the art backpacks and mobile phones, bespectacled lean, blonde tourists with good English and a ready smile as they trekked on, chuckling at the fat boy playing planes with all those glorious curls on his head. It was a perfect day. And Martha and I went home and made love.

38.

Headmaster Anderson wondered what it would be like to have rough sex with Mary Peters the psychologist as they sat there waiting for the Brocks to arrive. As a psychologist Peters was well regarded, and had been used by the school on many occasions previous to this one. She was the one, the right one, Anderson decided, to bring in for the meeting with the Brock family, and especially the boy, Gordon Brock. Mary Peters was about ten years older than Anderson, but still, Anderson considered her, despite her obvious disability of age, an attractive woman. She was physically fit, experienced, knowing, clever, embodied. For her part, Peters saw how obviously Anderson was looking at her. She didn't call him on it. She didn't care. He was a creep.

"How long do you think this might take?" She asked him.

"I don't know, Mary, as long as it takes. This can get messy."

"Do they have proof?"

"I don't know."

"Do we?"

"Do we have what?"

"What? Proof? Proof that what they say happened actually did?"

Francine Seyfert came into the room.

"The Brocks are here."

"Great! Please send them in."

Mary Peters sat smiling, her face set in an inscrutable distant friendly gaze, as Anderson looked at the solemn faces of Mom and Dad, Lucy and Dave Brock. Mary was not there as facilitator. More in the capacity of observer. I remember my Dad telling me subsequently how he immediately didn't like her. Mom didn't know whether to like her or not. Mary knew it, but, deferring to Anderson, she smiled amiably, and made polite conversation about her role in the school, generally, about her other jobs, how long she had been a Department of Children consultant, about her private practice, about her association with the school, whether she had any children, the usual meaningless cover story told by those used to therapeutic interventions, thought Dave. Anderson was deeply uncomfortable with this meeting. A lot was riding on it. For him the tension was all too palpable. Time to go, he thought. And he began his speech:

Anderson:

"Look, I want to thank you all for turning up here at this."

"Where are the Frasiers? Where is our son?" Dave asked.
"I will answer that in just one moment. I realise a number of things about being here. I realise that this is an extremely painful time for you, Lucy and Dave. Gordon will be along in a moment, by the way. I realise that you are taking a considerable risk too, and I honour that. I also realise this is an awkward time of day for all of you, eleven in the morning."
"Excuse me, why are you here?" Lucy asked Mary suddenly.
"Because Headmaster Anderson asked me to come along."
"Headmaster Anderson didn't ask us. He said the Frasiers would be here. Just us, and him and the Frasiers." Dave said.
Mary stood up, suddenly feeling a sense of relief.
"I can leave if you want."
"I would like Mary to be here," Jim Anderson said.
"Maybe we should have brought a psychologist too. Who do you represent in the meeting, Mary?" Dave asked.
"The welfare of the children."
"Okay you can stay," Lucy said.
"Thank you both," Jim said." I think Mary's presence and her participation at this particular juncture will be enormously beneficial. And I am sorry I didn't mention Mary's presence before this. I should have."
"It could be interpreted as deceitful," Dave said.
"I know," Anderson said." I wanted to go on to say that being here at this time means there's an inconvenience factor. I think it's also important that there's no legal representation at this meeting. I know you have an issue with this, and I am grateful we have come to some type of accommodation. This meeting is not just for us. This meeting is for all those involved, and, believe me, I am not trying to tell you all what you want to hear. I know that it is easy to slip into the role of seeing them, especially people like Gordon, or Edward for that matter, as eccentric little adults. That's because this school, St. Raymond's, seeks out the brightest and the best and there is a certain unnaturalness in seeking that particular section of society, rather than a more balanced representation of the demographic."
"We didn't come here for a lecture on child psychology, Headmaster. We have spent tens of thousands of Euros listening to the advice and direction of various doctors and therapists, psychiatrists and psychotherapists. What is the school doing to first of all stop the bullying, and then compensate and heal the trauma?" Dave asked.
"The bullying has stopped, Dave."
"Has it?" Dave asked. "Are we sure about that?"

"Very sure," Anderson said. "We want to find out exactly what happened and we want to restore in these children the values that are central to St. Raymond's."
"What values? The values of over-competitveness and becoming captains of society? Because since our son has come here, that seems to be the ethos. Over-competitiveness, obedience, creating good team players who have a certain loyalty to the old school tie, who help each other out come what may and stay connected to the school no matter what." Dave sneered.
"We want to stop this ever recurring. We want to restore a positive motivation, stop the self-defeating behaviour and return both these boys to desirable behaviours in the best spirit of the —"
"Headmaster?"
It was Francine at the door.
Jim Anderson paused. He looked up smilingly from the group. Lucy looked at Francine. Francine smiled at Lucy.
"Hi Francine, what's up?" Jim Anderson asked.
"Sorry to interrupt," she smiled.
"Not a problem," Jim smiled.
"Gordon Brock is outside."
"When are you interviewing the Frasiers?" Lucy asked.
"They won't be able to attend," Jim said.
"What?" Dave asked.
"Why?" Lucy asked.
"What the fuck is this?" Dave asked.

Jim had received a letter that morning from the Frasier family solicitor, detailing the many reasons why they would have no further dealing with the school, except through legal representation because of the charges of bullying and assault that were being made against Edward Frasier. But he wasn't telling the Brocks that. He wanted to try to talk them down, give me, Gordon, a chance to ventilate, see if there was a way out.
"Have you interviewed them?" Lucy looked coldly at Jim Anderson.
Jim peered at her. What the hell was she playing at in the school yard with Frasier in the first place? He wondered.
"We're all going to get together next week, sometime."
"And will we be at that meeting?" Dave asked.
"We will all meet together at a future date."
"So we won't be at that meeting," Lucy said.
"Jim, do you ever give a straight answer to a straight question?" Dave asked.

"At this stage it's judged better, and in accordance with procedure, that we meet separately. In cases like this, we have something of a procedure to go through."

"So now there is a 'procedure' to go through! I though this was an informal meeting." Lucy said.

"You mentioned little or nothing about there being a 'procedure' to go through," Dave said.

"Is this procedure that we have to go through written down somewhere?" Lucy asked.

"Yeah," Dave said. "If it's written down, could you give us a copy of it, so as we are all on the same page?"

"I will do that. Right now, though, we are going to see the best way through it."

Francine was still standing with the door ajar. I was listening intently outside. Francine raised her eyebrows irritably at Jim, who nodded apologetically to her, and began again to instruct her on what to do.

"I see. Give me another two minutes then bring the young gentleman in."

Jim smiled warmly at the group gathered in his clean fresh smelling office. Dave, my Dad, liked Anderson's office. It was homely, an office filled with books and files, cleaned daily and yet retaining a sense of being specific to one person, a person uncomfortable in his own skin, Dave thought.

Dave looked at Francine as she held the door for me. Then Dave watched Anderson watching me, Gordon, walk into the office. My Dad saw me, his son, for a moment, as others might see me, a slim blond boy in runners, slacks and a white shirt, my voice soft and clear, each word measured, though not self-consciously so, with a slim serious face that in a second could morph into a warm arresting smile, intense watchful eyes, a sense of someone much older than his years, a solitude about me despite the obvious sensitivity and warmth. Dad looked over at Mom. And Mom looked at me, and together it was as if two out of the three of us (the adults) guessed at that moment how Anderson would try to shift this away from the school, and if possible, onto me, Gordon. He would not be successful, at least not ultimately.

I walked quickly and confidently into the room. After hugging and kissing my parents, I walked over to Anderson. Anderson shook my hand and invited me, with great deference, to sit. In a soft voice Jim

Anderson said,
"Gordon, I'd like to, we all would like to, thank you for coming here —"
"Thank you." I said.
"Great, I'd —"
"I felt I had no choice," I said, interrupting Jim Anderson.
"I'm sorry about that. I imagine you, well, kind of know why we asked you here. Of course, you can leave if you want to. Please only stay if you really feel you want to."
I looked coldly at the headmaster. Jim looked calmly back and did not answer. Then I said,
"Yes sir."
"Nothing you say to us here today will go any further than these four walls, Gordon. What we are asking you to do, if you want, is to tell us what happened, your side, if you like. And no one here is judging you."
"Can I ask who this person is?"
"This is Mary. Mary helps us out occasionally."
"Psychiatrist?" I asked.
"She helps us out," Jim answered.
"She is a psychiatrist, son," Lucy said. Mary did not correct them. Lucy took Dave's hand, suddenly feeling alone and frightened and angry at everyone, people she felt might think of her as a bad mother.
"So, Gordon, would you like to tell us what happened?" Jim began, speaking softly and with as little emotion as possible. I shifted in my seat, looking intently at Jim.
"I have prepared a statement," I said.
"You have?" Mary, who had quietly taken over lead position in the dialogue, looked surprised, and then smiled. Releases endorphins, Dave thought. Even babies can smile. They are born with it. It takes an effort of concentration, more muscles, to frown. Dave frowned at his wife.
"I have, yes, Mary," I said.
"Of course you have," Mary smiled. Another little shot of dopamine, I, Gordon, thought. There was so much smiling, so much fear and tension forcing lips to move upwards, teeth to peep out. Mary smoothed her skirt over her legs, folded her hands over her knees, and leaned forward. She looked earnestly into my eyes.
"So, do you have the statement, Gordon?"
"Not here. I have it at home. I was worried it might be taken from me."
"And who might do that?"

"People. Certain people I know. People you know, too."
"Okay then, you can, if you wish, tell us more about that."
"Isn't that the reason why we are here? Surely if I say something here, it has to go further? It has to be taken down in evidence and use against the people who have been bullying me and tormenting me and depressing me and undermining me and torturing me. I mean, if this is just where I give my version of what happened, what's the point? It reduces everything to an opinion. There is proof, I mean there are cameras, you know? And, if there are cameras, there is evidence. I counted fifteen cameras outside the area of the school. These are here for reasons to protect the students from the teachers and from predators. Ed Frasier and his gang are predators. How can there be no footage of what happened?" I said.
"Well, we are here to make sure that doesn't happen anymore."
"I agree with Gordon," Dave said. "Where's the evidence?"
"We are, at present, searching for that evidence. When it becomes available, it will be there for all to see. First of all, tell us what happened."
"You know what happened. I got tortured," I said. "Ed Frasier, from the first day I came into the school targeted me. The first day he excluded me from the society of others because of an incident in a garden during the summer. I had to stop him from assaulting a little girl. He punched me, grabbed me by the balls, kicked me repeatedly, slapped me, had me beaten up again and again on the way home from school, sent me to Coventry, poured cups of saliva down my throat and down the back of my clothing, put dog turd in my school bag, tore up my homework, shoved me down the toilet bowls and flushed, burned my books. That is all I can think of right now."

There followed a long silence, broken by Jim nervously clearing his throat. Mary looking kindly, in her best therapeutic passive aggressive pose, into my eyes, waited for something to happen, controlling the moment with her silent gaze. And I, in the centre of the room, sitting on a newly placed chair, occasionally looking around the room, being smiled at by Mom and Dad, being watched by Jim and Mary, wondering if I could remember what I had written down the night before, what with all the tension and the expectation, tension and expectation being the most difficult thing to cope with, causing so much under performance, knowing that at some stage I would be asked to give an account of myself. I shouldn't have worried, I thought. Frasier had chickened out. Weasel. Frasier's parents hadn't come either. At that stage I didn't know the two families were being kept separate.

"I knew the Frasiers wouldn't come," I said. "I knew it. It's a bad sign. I bet they have lawyers involved by now. And I bet Frasiers' Dad has gotten involved, what with his being a policeman. Its all a cover-up. They are trying to protect their son, trying to hide the truth. Before long, you will be doing the same, Mr. Anderson. Before long he will find a way to lean on you and make you do the wrong thing. That's what people like him do. I knew it from the moment I saw him."
"Try to remember," Mary began, "Try to remember when it started."
"This is a common technique," I said, "used by the authorities. Get the witness to repeat themselves until they make a mistake. But everyone makes a mistake. Everyone will slip, contradict themselves, doubt their own minds. It won't work. Ask yourself whose side are you on. As I said, Mary, it started when I came here; well it really started in the Morrison's garden, with the big fight. I accidentally hit Frasier with a sliothar[19]. Then, when I got to St. Raymond's, it started when I got into the class. Frasier's group. They started calling me names."
"Can you remember the names they called you, Gordon?"
"Gordon is a moron. Gordon Fuckhead. Moron Gordon. It started when I had a fight with Frasier. He grabbed me by the testicles and kept squeezing tighter and tighter and then he grabbed me by the throat. Then Brother Frank came in and broke it up."
"Can you remember where and when that happened?" Anderson asked.
"October 15th at 1.20 in the day, in the canteen." I said.
"I see," Anderson said. I paused. I was feeling upset. I felt I was losing control of the facts. I was embarrassed. I was resentful.
"Do you want to go on, Gordon?" Mary asked.
"Then the next day his entourage —"
"You are talking about Ed Frasier?"
"I am talking about Ed Frasier. His entourage started following me. And the day after. They beat me up, kicked me and punched me, pushed me around and around till I fell down and then they really layed into me. Day after day they kept pushing me. Pushing and pushing. Then one day Ed picked on me in the school yard, saying I had gotten my mother to come into the school yard and accuse him of bullying me. But, you see, I didn't do that. I didn't do anything on him, not really. He just took this hatred of me and he went to do everything in his power to make life hell for me, because I threaten him. That day he kicked me. After that it just didn't stop. He, or one of his gang, would push me in a school line, a line for food, or a line in the library, and you

19 A sliotar or sliothar is a hard solid sphere slightly larger than a tennis ball, with a cork core covered by two pieces of leather stitched together with puckered stitching. Sometimes called a "puck" or "hurling ball", It is used in Gaelic games

fall over and your tray is spilled and then there's a food fight, or you knock someone else's tray over and you get kicked, or punched. Or day after day they follow you and call you names, at first you don't know what's really going on, then after a while you feel it."
"What does it feel like Gordon? What does it feel like to be pursued every day and treated in the way you have just described?" Mary asked.
"Like you don't matter, like nothing you think or feel matters."
"Is that why proof, the camera footage, is so important right now, that it shows you matter?" Mary asked.
"No, Mary I want the bastards who did this to me to suffer the consequences. I don't want another therapy session. I don't want this reduced to just my experience of the events. I know that bullying goes on all the time. I know other boys in the school are being bullied. I have seen it. It's taken as normal. It isn't talked about. It's taken as part of growing up. But it's wrong. I can't take it anymore. My homework has been stolen and copied or ruined. You know I found shit in my lunch box? A flask of coffee poured into my bag? A cup of saliva poured down the back of my shirt? This is torture. This is cruel and inhuman."

And I began to shake, weep and shake. Lucy (Mom) and Dave (Dad) were sobbing and saying how sorry they were, so sorry, how much they had let their son (me) down. How very sorry.

Intermission:

I looked outside, and I saw the trees. Outside, on a lighter note, outside the structure of the school, just across the street, a line of hundred and fifty year old sycamore trees baked golden in the leafy sun. Soon I worried that there would come a time the trees would not survive the ultraviolet. Soon there will be nothing but desertification. God will come down. It will be a divine rapture. An immaculate conception. The trees shyly trembled a little, and then, growing still, let the sun fall on them again.

"So, as you said, you want something done about this, and this is why we are all here, to hear from you. Who hit you, Gordon?" Mary asked.
"Ed Frasier did."
"Ed Frasier?"
I nodded.

At this point the question of Ed broke through the hard core of my hate. I didn't mince words. I realised my hate and desire to get back at

my tormentor, it never really left me.
"Ed Frasier is the devil. He is the fucking Antichrist! He is a scum sucking bottom feeding mother fucking —"

Mary nodded with an understanding smile. I went on:

"When you go down, they hit you everywhere. It's like they don't know what they're doing. If they had a gun, I swear, they would've killed me. There isn't a place that they don't kick don't punch. No where that doesn't hurt, doesn't ache, ache for a time so long I can't talk about."

I smiled in the midst of all my sobbing and crying, so much of it, and the tears and the nose blowing and the handkerchiefs. At last something different in the midst of all the pointless misery and the beating, something interesting and meaningful to talk about.

Nobody spoke. I felt tears all down my face. Lucy and Dave wept quietly. They looked at each other in a horrified understanding of what they had allowed go on.
"Did you ever try to talk to Ed Frasier or any of the other boys?" Anderson asked.
"You have to be fucking kidding, Headmaster!" Dave said.
"No sir," I said.
"Why not?"
"Well I figured he is a lunatic. He hates my guts. Not that interested in rational debate. Anyway you don't want to talk to someone who causes you pain like that. After a while you wake up and all you feel is the pain, the sense that all that's coming to you is more torment, and you learn to live with that. There's no talking to it, no idea that if you explain yourself, try to understand the other boys, and talk to them that they will understand you and you will understand them and an understanding will be reached? They aren't that kind of people. These are the kind of people that are out to get you and make you suffer. They are that kind of people."
"Okay, thank you Gordon. We want to say here that everything you have talked about here has been taken with the greatest of seriousness," Anderson said.
"Considering all you have, been through, Gordon. Is there anything else you would like to say?" Mary asked.
"Yes there is. I don't want to go to this school any more. I hate it. I want to go to another school. I want to go to a school where they don't treat you like this. I don't like it here any more. There must be a record of this. Even my Mom tried to stop Ed Frasier because the school did nothing for weeks and months. And everyone thinks my mother

is some kind of pervert for coming into the school yard like that, but that's the times we live in. And I know she tried to get in touch with you guys but I know there was no answer on the phone and no answer on the letters and it was like nothing happened, but something happened. Something happened here. On your watch. I don't like this place. It lies to its students. It doesn't really teach you anything except it shows you how cruel the world is. I don't need that. I know the world is a terrible place. I always knew that. Teach me something I don't know. Teach me something I can't read in a book. Teach the kids how to be good people. Teach them how to be decent to each other. Teach them how to think for themselves. All this school ever does is teach people how to be a competitor, a good team player, and we fight each other like wild creatures. You're a school, aren't you?"

"Thank you Gordon, for that." Jim said. "I know I will think long and hard about what you have said today."

"Please, Headmaster, Please don't patronise us." Dave began.

"Dave. Don't. Dave." Lucy said.

Jim looked at Mary, who waited with a patience that exceeded any professional requirement. The words I had given her, had given all of them in that room, that morning, as the morning moved into that afternoon, as midday had come and gone and no coffee drunk to break the tension they had somehow grown numb. Though Mary remained grave and compassionate and attractive, in her dark suit and crisp white blouse and pageboy cut, she knew this was a good moment, a moment signifying the faith so many teacher and colleagues and trainers had put in her had not been in vain.[20]

And I remember Mary looked with absolute focus at me. The boy, she figured, seemed to have ventilated, for now. This was no cover story. This was a messy, agony-filled unscripted confession of confusion, of weakness, of a hurt that would possibly never leave me. Perhaps I might be referred to her. The parents seemed hostile, though. They looked out of their depth, and, indeed I can confess that they were. Mary, I imagine, went on to decide that the guilt and self-loathing that Mom and Dad felt could on its own ruin the boy (me), possibly their marriage. A lifetime of guilt and self sacrifice, never really satisfying their own needs, a narcissistic oldest son, a second child, if they ever bother to have one, hating his parents, not to mention me.

20 'Student A2. Student A2, with an IQ of 170, Caucasian male 12 ys old, both parents living, had due to the significant bullying received at a venerable and highly acclaimed school, subsequently under performed. I had occasion to experience the situation, both during and after the bullying episode. Student A2 showed considerable depressive withdrawal and post traumatic stress..." Journal of psychoanalytic studies no. 21- vol 34 June----- pp 241 – 4 by Mary Peters, MA PhD

As I remember now what I was busily imagining and considering what Mary the shrink was imagining and considering, I remember, just then, Francine came back into the room. Francine went to say something. Jim looked gravely at her.

I must talk to her about doing that, coming in like that, Jim noted to himself. Jim Anderson shook his head crossly. Francine nodded. She lip synced 'sorry', and discreetly, embarrassedly, left the office.

What disturbed Jim about all that he had heard was the number of well connected and successful students involved in this disaster. It was as though the entire elite had conspired to break Gordon Brock and, because he was a particularly vulnerable person, they seemed to have largely succeeded. Ordinary pupils would not feel they had anything in common with Brock, thus they left him alone. But it was the mother's arrival and of course Frasier did the trick. And it was the successful and the intelligent that seemed to feel they had something to lose, at least in this case. To deal with this would be to challenge and discipline some of the moneyed and connected members of the school board. If any of this was to get out it would permanently, negatively impact the school's image.
"Would you like to go on, Gordon? Or perhaps you would like to take a break?"
"No, Mr. Anderson, I'd like to go home."
"Well, I think that's all. Thanks, Gordon. If you would like to go home with your parents, we'll pick this up later."
"No!" Lucy said. "No way!"
"Sorry?" Jim looked startled.
"That's it?" Dave said. "I mean that's it?"
"I just said this was not it." Jim Anderson snapped.
"You get my boy to pour his guts out here on the carpet, and you say that's it?" Dave snapped back.
"No that's not all. By no means. I have every intention of taking the strongest possible action, as soon as this is further investigated. We have a zero tolerance for bullying in this school. The reason why this has gone on for as long as it has is because no one brought it to my attention, despite everything you pointed out."
"Ignorance is no excuse for this. This was both violent and abusive behaviour," Dave said.
"I agree."
"Then do something!"

"I am. What do you think this is?"
"I don't want to hear any nonsense about investigations or reports. Reports are what you commission to ensure nothing ever gets done."
"That's simply untrue. I understand you are angry."
"And I understand how you work."
"What do you mean, Dave?"
Dave looked at Jim in a way that frightened him.
"Listen to me carefully, Anderson. I'm on to you, okay? If this isn't immediately resolved, I am going to take action that will bring my complaint to your door in a way you will never ever forget."
"Is that a threat, Dave?"
"You can take it as a mark of absolute certainty that you will be hearing from the most expensive litigator in the city."
"I'm sorry to hear that. Given time and the right methods, I feel we could have fully and happily resolved this."
"I really don't think so."
"Okay? Tell me why?"
"I am not satisfied this has been even initially dealt with in an acceptable and sufficiently serious manner. There seems to be a lack of corroborating evidence from this school, as my son has pointed out. This should all be on video!" Dave said.
"That's a little forensic, don't you think?"
"I don't know, Jim. You tell me."
"I still think we can resolve this" Jim said.
"It's resolved, Jim. We are taking our son out of this school. And we are suing this school."

Lucy looked at both Dave and Jim, trying to find a way of resolving the escalating conflict, her mind failing her, due to fear and uncertainty. Her trip into the school yard had been a terrible mistake. It was a guilt that never left her. And Mom and Dad took me out of the headmaster's office. Mary looked at Jim for a long time.
"Dad, Mom?"
"What son?"
"I would really like a fruit smoothie, more than anything."
Dave answered.
"Sure. We'll go get one. Are you hungry? I think I'm hungry. Definitely could do with a bite to eat. Lucy, are you hungry?"

40.

After the Brocks left, Jim went looking for Francine. He couldn't find her. So Jim called Francine on her mobile phone. Francine hated being called on her lunch break.
"Hi Jim," she said.
"You left early."
"No, I didn't."
"This is not a day to leave early."
"Boss, I didn't leave early, okay?"
"I need you back here."
"I see. Why?"
"Because we have a fire storm raging."
"My lunch break is between one o'clock and two-thirty. It is twelve minutes past two."
"I don't care, Francine. I need you back. Right now!"
"I hear you. I am on my lunch break, Jim. What do you need?"
"Can you get our solicitor on the phone? Set up a meeting for early next week?"
"I take it the meeting didn't go well?"
"Actually, on second thoughts, can you set the meeting up for about eleven in the morning?"
"Sure. I can do it right here. I have the numbers on my phone."
"Okay."
"Francine?"
"Yes?"
"Thanks."
"No problem Jim."
"See you later."

Francine went back to Triple Tall Coffee and Handy Andy Tofu Burger and hand cut chips and ate away, scrolling through her list of contacts, wondering whether an e-mail or a phone call would elicit the necessary response from the lawyers. The fast food vegetarian restaurant Genelli and de Medici, a mere two blocks down from the school, was beginning to lose its serious, thoughtful people in expensive cut casual attire, dancing around each other, struggling to be fed as quickly as possible, as staff with elaborate haircuts carefully secured in jute hair nets, cleaned and served food with only the most environmentally pure products, cleared emptying tables, wiped down surfaces with environmentally friendly disinfectant cleanser. Francine took another bite out of her delicious burger and looked out the window, her view obscured somewhat by A4 advertisements for up and coming bands, poetry readings, and left wing politically inclined discussion groups, and caught a glimpse of the clear blue skies. It was so beautiful. Suddenly she felt happy today. There with her burger and her coffee and her book. She didn't want anything else. That was it, she thought. Why am I always looking for something else? It's nice here. Then, as if happiness reminded her of her duties, she thought of all the calls she had to make this afternoon. They were beginning to bother her. Most of the relevant parties would inevitably be at meetings, or in court, or working on other cases, or the hundreds of other matters involving intense concentration, so they wouldn't take calls if she rang them after lunch. She might get one or two staff or secretaries if she made the calls right now. She would express the urgency of her call, and ask to be transferred to their personal mobile phones, if she called right now, at this awkward hour. Francine took out her notebook. In the notebook she had a list of all relevant duties she had that afternoon. She decided a well placed call at exactly the right time would elicit the necessary response. She took out her mobile phone and began calling.

41.

"What time is it?"
"Uh?"
"What time is it. What time is it?"
Lucy looked at Dave from her position of lying on his stomach, passing him the rolled cigarette of potent weed she was smoking.
"Dunno. Hold on. Let me check."
"Okay, you know what I was just thinking?"
"That you are really stoned."
"No, I was not thinking that."
"I see. What?"
"I was thinking about suddenly remembering the times I used go into your office during lunch hour, or when you were working late, just because I missed you, just because, more than anything else, I wanted to make love with you. And we would make love and it was so good, so good. What happened to those times. What happened, I want to know." Lucy said.
"What?"
"Maybe we conceived Gordon then,"
"What? What are you talking about?" Dave asked, struggling to find his watch, knowing he dropped it somewhere, finding it underneath a chair, along with his shirt and underwear.
"Aah, there you are! Nasty watch, trousers, underwear! Thought you could escape me, eh? Eh?"
My father, having spoken to his clothing as though they were sentient, begins to don them, then thinks it's better to take a shower first.
"One day at your job."
My mother, wandering round the room, mumbling to herself, has located all necessary items of attire, and is watching her spouse bemusedly.
"We never had sex at my job." Dave said.
Both parents stood one metre apart, discussing the location of my conception, stoned out of their minds.
"Yes, yes we did." Lucy said.
"Did we?" Dave said, kind of uncertain at that point.
"We did."
"You sure about that, hm ?"
"Sure. A memorable moment of lovemaking."
"Does it matter, Lucy?"

"Well, you know, Dave, you (she chuckles) you brought it up."
"You brought it up, not me! You are. What time is it?"
"Three o'clock."
"Is it? Is it really that time?"
"It is really that time. Time is totally unforgiving."
"We have to pick Gordy up, Lucy, Sweetheart, Darling."
"Don't you 'Lucy sweetheart darling' me. You are only saying that 'cause you got lucky."
"He doesn't have classes today, does he?"
"I don't think so."
"I'll make some coffee. Can't pick the boy up like this. We did say we were going to pick him up where, at St. Stephens Green or actually at the shrink's offices? Does he have class this afternoon?"
"You know the answer to the first question, and I already answered the second. We cancelled his class this afternoon because we planned dinner at my fave Pizza joint.
"That's why we called in sick today."
"You called in sick. I don't need to."
"Shut up Dave."
"I feel kinda dizzy, Lucy. Where did you get that stuff?"
"I got the drugs from a drug dealer."
Mom looked into Dad's eyes, wondering where he was, if somewhere in her explorations of his body, she could get a twenty on where he was. "What?" He said.
"Nothing."
"What were you thinking?"
"How much time do we have?"
"Fifteen, maybe twenty minutes."
"You know —"
"What?"
"We'll call a taxi then"
"Absolutely. The emergency services will otherwise spend valuable time untangling our ruined screaming bodies from the twisted wreckage of our automobile."
"Shut up, Dave."

42.

If one is a practising therapist, as I was for near on two decades, that is, before I retired on the monies I made from the junk self-help books I wrote, one knows a lot about sexual relations. People, some of them married for decades, all talking about affairs they were having, or had, teach you things. It gets tedious, deeply boring, learning about lies and sex, how people are always surprised at being deceived, guilty at deceiving loved ones, ugly and cruel and heartless people, people filled with self pity. The one thing I learned, though, is where to have affairs. To have sex with someone who is not ones spouse is expensive and risky. Location is vital. So its rather like investing in property. It's all about location. The best place to have sex with one's future wife is actually in one's own office, especially if that office is unmonitored. We did that a lot.

Having sex really helped me think. I knew this more than I ever wanted. I knew I was hopelessly lost, hopelessly confused. I hated myself. I hated my betrayal of Martha. I knew things were irrevocably broken. I knew the intense obsessional love I felt for Lucia was a disease I never wanted to be cured of. I was a lost person, lost in the new life I dimly saw appear before me, there on the floor of my office.

It never crossed my mind to ask Lucia was she seeing someone else, was she marrying someone else, had she been married, was she pregnant, suffering from any serious illness, in good mental health, was rich, poor, happy, a reader, a cinemaphile, did she enjoy golf, horseback riding, football, was she gay. I didn't care. I didn't care for those were things that didn't matter, not there and not then.

Scenes from the poetry of Lucia Reynolds.

Lucia Reynolds, my beloved, who comes and goes from my room as I work on this, mostly reading and washing clothes and writing and talking to our children, Lucia who allows me to take her poetry and use it in this book, who never really knew her father, which is important to know when one is trying to paint a complex poignant picture of a vulnerable, intelligent, sensitive, person one has fallen in love with and subsequently after a long, discreet, intense love affair, married. Her father Julius, had since remarried, was a convert to some fringe millenarian cult, was living in Cork, had three other children of his own, worked in a very successful firm that replaced windows and doors for offices, homes, shops and factories, and didn't want to know her. He never called, never wrote, leaving Lucia desolated and distrusting of other's love and care for her, distant and secretly hypersensitive to rejection, with a lingering sense of meaninglessness, like the tart metallic aftertaste of bad wine, about a world that she somewhere felt owed her something – a life or an identity or a sense of being loved. Perish the thought.

LEAVE A NOTE.

Kiyoko Matsumoto, a 19-year-old student 1933 who committed suicide by jumping into the thousand-foot crater of a volcano on the island of Oshima in Japan, which started a bizarre fashion in Japan. In the ensuing months three hundred children did the same thing. Death by imitation.

In Japan in 1999, 33,048 people killed themselves, the main reasons being either ill health or financial problems. Death by degradation.

Heinrich von Kleist, a German writer and Stanislav Ignaci Witkiewicz Polish writer, and Arthur Adamov, French poet. Death by method unknown.

Ian Curtis, born July 1956. Lead singer-songwriter of seminal band Joy Division, hung himself on eve of Joy Division's first US tour, May 1980

Death by hanging.

Cleopatra, Egyptian queen – death by snakebite.

Kurt Cobain, American rock star. Injected heroin coupled with shooting himself with a shotgun. Death by overkill:

Ernest Hemingway, American writer and Nobel laureate. Severely depressed about his progressive physical illness, he had failed to respond to two series of electro convulsive treatments. Death by shotgun.

35 years later, On July 1, 1996, the model and actress Margaux Hemingway, granddaughter to Ernest, killed herself by taking an overdose of barbiturates, the fifth in four generations to commit suicide. More of the same: severe depression, alcoholism, Bulimia Nervosa. Death by inheritance.

Hart Crane, American poet, 1899-1932. He leaped from a steamboat into the Caribbean. He had bid his fellow passengers farewell, he jumped overboard. Death by water.

Yukio Mishima (Kimitake Hiraoka), Japanese writer, 1970 committed suicide by disembowelment and decapitation (a ritual called seppuku or hara-kiri) as a protest of the Westernization of Japan. He killed himself in front of an assembly, which he had called, of all of his students that he was teaching at university at that time. Some of his students followed his example and did likewise. Death by teacher.

Claudius Drusus Germanicus Nero, a Roman emperor 68 AD, committed suicide by stabbing himself with a sword. His last words being, "ah what an artist dies in me." Death by hubris – followed by nemesis.

Donny Hathaway, singer in 1979, committed suicide by jumping from his room on the 15th floor of New York's Essex House Hotel. Death by gravity.

Sylvia Plath, born 1932, American poet, died 1963 after securing her children from the possibility of being gassed, put a pillow in the kitchen oven and lay down on it. Death by gas.

Lucius Annaeus Seneca, Roman philosopher, dead.

David Foster Wallace, American Novelist, 2009, after a long struggle with severe depression, death by hanging in his garage. Death by depression.

Socrates, a philosopher, who in 399 BC was required to drink hemlock to end his life after being found guilty of corrupting the youth of Athens. Death by hemlock.

Vincent Willem van Gogh, Belgian painter of genius, who in his entire life sold only one painting. In 1890 he shot himself. He died two days afterwards. Killed by life.

Johnny Ace (John Marshall Alexander, Junior), a singer. In 1954, died playing Russian roulette. Death by stupidity.

Cato, Roman Philosopher. Death by IQ.

Janet Elaine Adkins, 1990, was the first suicide assisted by Jack Kevorkian. Death by decision.

Clara Blandick, an actress, (known as Auntie Em in The Wizard of

Oz) 1962. Ended it all by sleeping pills, with a plastic bag tied over her head. She was 81-years-old and had really bad arthritis. Death by choice.

Gordon Combs was a talk show host of a TV programme called Family Feud. He hanged himself on the night of June 2, 1996, with bed sheets in his hospital room at Glendale Adventist Hospital while on a 72-hour"suicide watch." Death by inattention.

Thich Quang Duc, Buddhist monk, who in 1963 set himself on fire on the streets of Saigon to protest government persecution of Buddhists. There is a famous photo of it, I think I've seen it in magazines, or the cover of a Rage Against the Machine Album.

R. Budd Dwyer, a Pennsylvanian politician, who in 1987 having been convicted of bribery and conspiracy in federal court and about to be sentenced to 57 years in prison plus a $300,000 fine, called a press conference and in front of spectators and TV cameras shot himself in the mouth. Death by spectacle.

Lillian Millicent Entwistle, an actress, in 1932 committed suicide by jumping from the 'H' of the HOLLYWOOD (LAND) sign in Los Angeles. More death by gravity.

Joseph Goebbels, a Nazi politician. In 1945 involved a group suicide with his wife, as well as poisoning their five children. Death by fascism.

Hermann Goering, 1946, poisoned himself hours before he was to have been executed. Death by cowardice.

Rudolf Hess, 1987. The last member of Hitler's inner circle. Strangled himself with electrical cord. Age 93. Spandau Prison. Avoidance through Death.

Chris Hubbock, a newscaster in 1970, who shot himself in the head during prime time news broadcast on Florida TV station WXLT-TV. Died 14 hours later. Death by television.

Jim Jones, infamous leader of a religious cult known as the Peoples' Temple. In 1978 he killed himself after watching more than 900 of his followers die from the ingestion of Kool-Aid laced with cyanide. Death by megalomania.

Terry Kath, rock musician from the group Chicago. Died in 1978, suicide playing Russian roulette. More death by stupidity.

Jesse William Lazear, US physician. 1900 . Voluntarily infected himself with and died of yellow fever as part of Walter Reed's research. Death by research.

Vachel Lindsay, a poet, who, in 1931 committed suicide by drinking a bottle of lye (Lysol). Death by lye.

Francois Maurice Marie Mitterrand, former French president who, in 1996, committed suicide by intentionally terminating treatment for prostrate cancer. Death by decision.

On October 5, 1998, Margaret Mary Gordon killed herself by kneeling down in front of an oncoming 105-car coal train in Hotchkiss, Colorado. Ms. Gordon, 46, a celebrity stalker, had suffered from schizophrenia for years. She left a note to mother that said 'I'm all travelled out. I choose a painless and instantaneous way to end my life.' Death by engine.

Horace Wells. He pioneered the use of anaesthesia in the 1840s. In 1848 he was arrested for spraying two women with sulfuric acid. He then anesthetized himself with chloroform and slashed open his thigh with a razor. Death from trying in vein.

Virginia Woolf. Writer. 1941. Suicide by drowning. More death by water. She left a note. Leaft a note. Note. Leaf.

43.

"Daddy!"
"Yes, Josh sweetheart. No. Don't touch Daddy's book! Please, please, please. There's such a good boy. Thank you ! I love you."
"Why not?"
"You mean the book?" I hold the book aloft. "Because it is Daddy's friend's book. You know? And Daddy is reading it right now."
"Why?"
"Because the book doesn't belong to Daddy."
"Okay. Why?"
"The book doesn't belong to Daddy. It belongs to a friend of Daddy. It belongs to Mommy's sister. Lucia. You know Auntie Lucia?"
"Is Mommy's sister Auntie?"
"Yes. Yes sweetie. She is. Auntie Lucia. No, no! Please! Thank you. Did you have a nice day today?"
"We all drew a picture of a train and a star and a flower and a tree and a house and that Thomas threw the ball and hit Suzy and she got a plaster with a star on it, and Miss Blamires was nice and gives sweets and Daddy, Daddy, Daddy."
Joshua is jumping up and down and Martha is laughing with delight at our delightful excited after school little boy who has had so much fun.
"What Joshua, darling, what?" I asked.
"We all ran around and it was nice and then we danced.'
"You danced? That is so cool! Show me!" I said, imitating big surprise. And I thought as I saw him dance how he looked like me and then he also in a way so looked like my mother. Perhaps the shape of the chin and the little trooper was so talkative, so full of fun and so funny.
"That's so good. That is so much fun and so good!" Martha said.
"Yeseee, we danced," said Josh, nodding vigorously and with great seriousness, remembering dancing with the other little boys and girls as ring a ring a rosy, that great bubonic plague nursery rhyme, that should be politically incorrect and excised from the minds of children, was played and all the boys and girls joined hands and danced around in circles and acha acha we all fell down and all the children fall down and everyone laughs.
"Like this," said Josh. And then Josh delighted Mommy and Daddy by doing a swaying movement with his little hips that imitated a dance, a movement custom built to delight Mommy and Daddy, who laughed and hugged their little boy and everyone went back to a cooling

dinner.

"Okay then Joshua darling. Come on and eat . I have dinner here and Daddy has cooked it and here we are. Eat up eat up," Mommy Martha says. "Eat up like a good boy." And we all ate up.

"Gordon, are you eating with us or is your life to be taken up with David Foster Wallace? It extremely rude and irritating to read at table."

"I - I am pretty hungry. Sorry. Let me have a plate of stew. Thank you." I said, "So- you obviously didn't kill someone in your job today."

"No. Should I?"

"Well, you were really furious. You are home pretty early, aren't you?"

"They are flexible. This is really nice, Gordon."

"This is nice Gordon!" Josh says.

"Thank you, but call me Daddy, ok?"

"Yes dear!" little Josh said as he imitated his mother and we all laughed and Joshua roared and banged his spoon on the table and I frowned at him and waggled my finger and I said

"Now, now, little man," and he stopped and said

"Sorry Daddy," and I said

"Don't worry about it" and he said "Okay Daddy", and I felt such hearbreaing love for him then that I knew I would die for him if necessary.

And we ate and after a while the conversation picked up of its own accord and we talked and Martha talked about her boss and colleagues.

"I know," she said, "It's only a junior management position in Harvey and Joyce, and I know when you have a position like that you are going to get a world of grief because that's why they hire you–to take on a world of grief."

"Right." I said. "It's been a long time. And I know it must feel like a real climb down from the kind of work you did before, and I know I have said it a thousand times, but you need to be really gentle till your strength builds."

"I know, and the whole music industry is filled with criminals, I mean if you aren't a mobbed-up type, you are going to get your legs broken, inevitably."

I felt like scooping out my eyeballs and eating them with the intense, frustrated, enraged tedium I felt listening to her talking about her job. I tried to go to my happy place, which is where I am having sex with her half-sister in a cabin deep in a wooded area, a cabin I had bought and had quietly renovated and extended for the purposes of going there to word and write and think for a bit. I guess getting the place was yet

another symptom of my increasing separation from Martha. And she went on talking:
"I mean, Gordon, I process the requests, supervise the clerical staff who were all imbeciles, see that the clients were well looked after, and make sure the company was paid. It's basically a knowledge management system."
"Knowledge management systems?" I asked "What's that?"
She looked at me with cold serious eyes for a second, then looked down at her food and said.
"You're supposed to be some kind of genius. Surely you know what that is."
"Well, I don't. I am obviously not that embarassing thing. So tell me."
"Knowledge-based systems are the computers and other storage data which contain the collective information a company has as a resource, the information it has and uses to make a profit- Wow, that was condescending of me, sorry about that," Martha said.
"I see. Hum. Ho hum. Don't worry about it." I said.
"Okay, I am sorry."
"It's okay Daddy, I forgive you." Joshua said. We chuckled.
"That's very nice of you, sweetie."
"Sorry for what?" Martha asked.
"Ranting. It wasn't a good thing to do. Look if it takes from home life in the least I will quit. We don't want a repetition of the Xpex incident."
"Sweetie, you weren't ranting."
"Yes, I was," Martha said. "I was talking and talking about my job. When I should have told you what really happened today."
"Oh?" I asked.
"The truth is I got a phone call today,"
"And?"
"I got a phone call telling me that Philip Sound is dead."
"Philip Sound, I know that name."
"You don't remember who Philip Sound is?"
"The name is familiar."
Then I remembered.
"Oh, I remember," I said.
"Apparently he had been having an affair with a colleague, Pauline Flak."
"Wow, really?"
"Fucking her in the back office twice a week."
"Hey, do you really want to talk about this kind of thing with our little-? I mean... later honey, okay?"

Joshua looked bemusedly at us and ate his stew rather sloppily. Martha went on obliviously.

"He and his lovely wife split, a year or two after."

"I see, well, just a thought, but, hey where did you hear all this gossip?"

"After I got the phone call, I made some other phone calls to a few folks who would still take my calls and the filled me in. Apparently it was a very nasty acrimonious split, physical fights and a nasty civil lawsuit. She was, or at least at the time, very publicly embarrassed that someone so well known would be seeing someone else under her nose and none of her friends told her. So they went their separate ways. And then, one night, Phil was out walking the dog and an articulated truck hit him. Crushed his head like a melon. Did you know a melon is the same density as a human head?"

"No dear, that's delightful, and I am sure our offspring is delighted to have that image in his mind at such a young and tender age, don't you?"

I shuddered, imagining Sound's big melon head being squashed under the huge wheels of a passing truck. Death by weight.

"Saw it on a cop show. Hmm, death's too good for that son of a —"

"Okay, knock it off honey; please, you know? There being a minor present."

"Right. Horrible topic. And we are moving on."

"Praise Zeus for moving on," I said.

"What's with all the sarcasm?"

"Sarcasm?"

"I mean what's going on with you?"

"I am a bit frustrated."

"Sexually?"

"Martha, not in front of —"

And I looked at her as Martha talked and I could not stop the anger, wishing she would stop, even though I was smiling and nodding, and somewhere inside I could feel the edifice of my admiration for her crumbling, sounds of falling masonry in my mind.

And we ate our stew, and like so many things Martha and I made together it was a thing of beauty, and I admired my beautiful boy and in admiring him I was that little boy watching of Mommy and Daddy and his banging of his spoon against his plate when the adults seemed to be distracted from he, who was the centre of the universe, the beautiful one, the chosen one, and Daddy smiled and told him what a good boy he was, eating potatoes and vegetables, and that he will grow up to be a big strong clever man, just like Daddy, oh yes.

44.

"This is a really beautiful-whatever the hell it is." Lisa said.
"I think its called a house, but don't quote me on that," I said.
I had, as I mentioned, bought a small cottage/cabin at the foot of a mountain by a small woodland in Kerry. I had refurbished it, then added an extension. It was warm, dry, freshly painted, reliant on solar power, and self contained.
"You like it?"
"I do."
"Nice," I said.
"It's cosy. Safe. Secluded. The views are, beautiful," Lucia said.
"It's a shepherd's cottage," I said.
"It is? Romantic." Lucia asked.
"Yes, I think so" I said. "There were a lot of sheep associated paraphernalia when I was clearing it out. I think the poor fellow passed away in his sleep in the bedroom. Sad really. Well no, not sad. Nice way to go."
Lucia was looking out the window.
"Sure. Is that a squirrel? "Lucia asked.
"That's a squirrel. I call him Charlie."
"Is that a good name for a squirrel? How about Snickers the squirrel?" Lucia asked.
"Ha ha! That's good!" I said. "Charlie is a cheeky little fellow."
"No, no. Snickers the squirrel is a cheeky little fellow. Charlie is a cliché kind of name. There's more of a sense of usurping copyright and challenging large multinationals by taking that name and using it."
"But I have called him Charlie for years and years."
"Squirrels don't live for years and years, Gordon. That's not the same little fellow."
"Oh, how sad!" I said.
"Sorry about that, lover. I thought you were supposed to be some kind of genius? You should know that."
"Apparently I'm supposed to know everything and miss nothing, which is impossible. And I hate it, because it's a cliche. And there is nobody who can do that, except Kim Peek, and he has no corpus collosum."
"Who?"
"The chap they based Rain Man on."

"I see."

"You see Charlie, or Snickers?" I said, suddenly changing the subject.

"I do."

"You can walk up to him and he won't run away till you get within two or three metres, and then Charlie just scampers up a tree. It's funny."

"That's funny."

"It's funny."

"Are there many farms?"

"I don't know. How come you are so interested?"

"Just curious."

"You seemed bored the last time you came here."

"I don't know. It was raining. I think I had a nasty cold, and I think we were having an argument."

"Okay, doesn't matter. I think you pick fights when you are bored."

"Maybe I do."

"Oh, you do, Lucia."

"Okay. We have established that. Let it alone, Gordon. What I mean to say, I'm not sure I will be able to come here after the wedding."

"Lucia,"

"What?"

"Why are you getting married?"

"We talked about this."

"True, but I still don't feel happy about it."

"It seems like the right thing to do."

"Okay."

"I think I am in love." Lucia said.

"It's not a natural state, marriage."

"It is something I really want to do. Will you come to the wedding? Please?"

"I have to. I am married to your sister. Does your future husband know you are here?

"No."

"Don't you think that says something. I mean, you have snuck off to see me and be here, away from your future husband, a few months from your wedding? I don't think it's —"

"I know."

"Sorry. Are you hungry? I was going to make a nice stew."

"Where do you buy your groceries?" Lucia asked.

"I bake bread. I buy in stuff and I freeze a lot of stuff. I buy in canned goods. I use solar energy, cuts down the bills."

"Well, do you get much work done here? "Lucia asked.

"Sure. I bought it originally to work here. But I really come here to get away."

"So you come here for peace?"

"I have a need for solitude. Peace and quiet and regularity."

"Do you ever worry about your sanity?" Lucia asked.

"No. Help me prepare the vegetables."

"Okay. What do you want to do afterwards?"

"We can watch television. Did I tell you I found Joshua drunk?"

"How old is he now?"

"Fourteen. They grow up so quickly. It seems like yesterday he was, well, a tiny boy. Did I tell you I found him drunk?"

"Wow. I started drinking when I was nine," Lucia said.

"He has been stealing liquor. I think stealing the odd beer or whatever is okay. But getting drunk."

"You think?" Lucia asked. "I got drunk a few times as a kid. A few times. I don't particularly remember feeling drawn to alcohol."

"Yes, I am sending him for therapy. I think he might be-."

"Might be what?"

"I think he might be drawn to alcohol."

"And therapy will cure him of that?"

"Therapy is not a cure, exactly. More a way to understand what is going on. I might have him down here afterwards, or during the time he goes to therapy."

"Does he know about here?"

"Sure. But Martha doesn't come here. And neither does he."

"I see."

"I'd like you to think about coming here. After you are married."

We had started preparing the food. We were standing beside each other preparing vegetables and getting things ready. It was getting late in the afternoon. A fine rain fell for a while. Then it stopped. Sunbeams shone through the gaps in the trees. Suddenly everything looked new again.

"Do you have a phone?"

"Yes."

"I mean, do you have a phone here?"

"I said I do. Look, you are cutting the carrots too small. They will go into mush in the stew."

"Well if you're such a fucking carrot expert you can do them yourself!" Lucia said, tossing the carrots down. I frowned at her. She took back the carrots and continued cutting them.

"All I was saying. Doesn't matter. So what's he like?"

"Matty? He is great."

"Where did you meet?"

"At a bar."

"And?"

"And we got to know each other, had sex, went on holidays together, dated, met each others parents, he proposed and I accepted."

"Marriage is an unnatural state."

"Want to go for a walk?"

"Sure. Did I tell you that Joshua is showing signs of alcoholism?"

"You did, Gordon. Let's take a walk and let the stew, well, stew."

"How's the poetry coming on?"

"I'll read you some after we get back, after we eat."

"Did we put enough potatoes in?"

"I think so. We can always have bread with the stew, can't we?"

"I suppose. I'm worried about Joshua."

"I know."

45.

JOSHUA AND SEÁN ARE DEFINITELY NOT HAVING SEXUAL RELATIONS

The first time Josh walked into Seán O'Gorman's offices he was somewhat struck by the Spartan nature of the room. There were no pictures, just plain white walls, no computer screens, no books, and a window view of a big garden where a huge sheepdog occasionally played ball with Seáns partner or just lolled in the sun. In the distance, the netting of a pitch and putt course made the view a bit oppressive. The netting reached thirty foot into the air so as to prevent golf balls smashing the neighbours' windows. Though Joshua didn't know it, at the back door there was a large bucket of golf balls that Seán used give to the local kids to sell back to the pitch and putt club what were always looking for their golf balls back.
"HI Joshua,"
"Hi," Josh sat down on the surprisingly comfortable chairs.
"So, I am glad you decided to come in," Seán said. His eyes were boring into Joshua, looking for micro reactions.
"I felt I had no choice."
"Why?"
"Well, the kinds of pressures that would be put upon me if I didn't come in would be terrible."
"What makes you think you didn't have a choice?"
Joshua didn't answer.
"What happens here is confidential."
"I know."
"Do you?"
At this point Joshua got up, obviously extremely irritated, and, without another word, left. He didn't come back for three months. Seán didn't say a word to Gordon. Then, late one night, just as Seán was about to go to bed a very drunk Joshua rang.
"Lo, lo hello? Hello there you mincing queen of therapy, I need to see you."
"Josh. It's late. You are drinking and dialling."
"I know. I —"
"Come in tomorrow at four. I will see you then."
O'Gorman assumed that's what Josh wanted. To come back. Josh didn't turn up. The he rang the following day.

"I want to apologize."

"I want you to know I am billing you for non-attendance. Next Tuesday at three. Last chance. Don't waste my time, Joshua."

He turned up and sat for an hour. No one spoke. The following week he asked:

"Are you gay?"

"Yes."

"Are you attracted to me?"

"Yes."

"Would you have sex with me?" Joshua asked.

"Are you gay?" He asked Joshua.

"I don't think so."

"Are you sure?"

"I am mostly hetro."

"Well, I am glad we cleared that up. Anything else?"

"You didn't answer my question."

"It's not a good question. I am in a permanent relationship. You know my partner. Also, for god's sake, you are a client!"

Josh didn't speak. Inside he had lived with the a sense of overwhelming inadequacy for so long it had wedded itself to his sense of identity. He wanted to express himself to this hairy giant haystacks of a man, whom he should really not be seeing as his therapist.

"Why did you call that night?"

Josh didn't answer.

"Well, we will leave it at that will we for today?"

"What? What the hell is this? My hour isn't up!"

"How about next Tuesday same time?"

"Fuck you!"

"I'm sorry?"

"This is a tactic."

"What kind of tactic?"

"A tactic to get me to talk! Fuck you!"

"Okay then. We have twenty minutes. Let's sit for awhile."

"Okay then," Josh said, feeling more anger at O'Gorman than he ever thought possible.

"I am so, so pissed at you right now."

"Why?"

"You are playing mind games with me."

"If you feel that way, Joshua, then don't stay. Tell me why you called me late that night."

"I don't know."

"Then you are wasting your time here. You don't want to talk about things. Maybe you should think about —"

"I drink too much," Joshua sobbed. Seán let him cry for a moment. Then he asked:

"Okay then. How much is too much?"

"A lot," Joshua said.

"Ok, then. Now it really is time to call it a day. Next week then? Same time same place. Take a moment to compose yourself."

"Okay."

Joshua took four tissues and blew his nose loudly.

"See you, Joshua," Seán said. And Joshua nodded.

46.

Anyway, Josh went out to that poorly constructed, over-priced, standard issue two large bedroom with a box room house, deep in the predatory tall grass of suburbia, where Sean Kept and office, and Josh would be really scared going out there, walking around, smoking cigarettes, looking at his watch, feeling watched, feeling exposed, carefully measuring out his time so that he might not be too early, which would be an issue in therapy, or too late, another issue open to discussion and interpretation, afraid lest he meet another patient which would be intolerable (he did), or forget to pay (he did twice). He went there once a week, feeling deep down that this was a waste of time, looking at the books and files filed away, and the pretty view of the garden just over Seán O'Gorman's mountainous shoulder, and hearing his heart pound in his chest, and the sweat creeping down his back. It would be about around four in the afternoon, and the session would begin with Seán saying:

"Well, how are things?"

And Joshua would sit on the chair, looking at O'Gorman, with O'Gorman's beautiful, huge, ancient, knotted, craggy-cliff face before him, looking him in the eyes, and Joshua, as usual, refusing to lie on the nice comfortable pseudo leather black couch, knowing there was a point to all this being here, and telling the truth, knowing he was there to get better, better than before, become healthier and better adjusted, less anxious or depressed, less aware of the overwhelming sense of futility that seemed to cloud his life.

"My father is a bored and frustrated man."

"I don't think he loves me."

"Why am I alone?"

"I know my mother loves me. I feel it."

"I go from one job to another. Nothing interests me."

"Things come so easily to my dad. He just does stuff."

"Why do I have no friends?"

"I think my mother suspects my father is having an affair."

"I drink because I am depressed."

"I don't feel lovable."

"I am terrified of my father's intelligence."

"I feel I have no purpose in life."

"Can you help me?"

47.

O'Gorman had been addicted to cigarettes since he was about ten years old. He had begun stealing cigarettes from his parents about then, running off, and smoking them somewhere private. By the time he was in his teens he couldn't go two hours without a cigarette. He knew it was a matter of time before they killed him. He was forty five years old and about the time Joshua began to see him that the smokers cough he had always had became persistent and unremitting he would wake in the wee hours convulsing and needing a glass of water which Greg would give him, looking worried and begging him to see a specialist. He didn't need a specialist. He knew.

O'Gorman was initially diagnosed as having a 'shadow' on his lung. After a chest X-Ray, then a CT scan, which helped to locate the abnormal spots in the lungs, the doctor inserted a small tube, a bronchoscope into O'Gorman's mouth and down the throat, to look inside the airways and lungs to take a biopsy. The shadow was shown to be a tumor the size of a golf ball. Then they found a secondary in his liver, then in his lymph nodes. The cancer spread through his body. Greg, his partner, was inconsolable. O'Gorman knew he hadn't much time left, and his oncologist and his GP were both reluctant to speculate, so he kept working, kept seeing people as long as the medication worked and the pain and weakness and weight loss, didn't impede his work (it did of course). And then he found a way of telling Joshua, as he told all his other patients, when the time came to refer them on to someone healthier.
"You don't seem well"
Josh said to him one day as O'Gorman started coughing and wheezing again. That was when O'Gorman saw his chance.
"I have cancer."
"Cancer?"
Joshua was horrified.
"Cancer. Yes."
"That's terrible. I'm sorry, Seán. Do Dad and Mom know?"
"Yes."
"You have cancer? Where?"
"Lungs, mainly. My liver. I haven't much time left."
"When were you going to tell me?"
"I wanted you to benefit from being here."

"How…how long do you…have?"
"Not a lot of time. Let's do some real work here, Joshua."
Joshua tried again with an even more personal question which O'Gorman readily answered.
"Weeks, months?" Joshua was tearful and deeply upset.
"I am not sure. Not long, I think." O'Gorman said.

Joshua looked at the floor for a long time, not knowing what to think, never having known anyone who died, being too young when his grandmother died, and then Dad didn't talk about her so much now. Then he stared at O'Gorman's black, slightly old shoes, shiny in parts, and then scuffed in other parts, and how small his feet were for a person so large in so many ways. And then, after a while, O'Gorman said:
"How does that make you feel?"
"What kind of a question is that?"
O'Gorman smiled one of his lofty inscrutable smiles. And then they sat in silence for a few minutes.
"I don't think I should come here anymore,"
"Okay, so, why not?"
"Does my Dad know you are sick?"
"Yes."
O'Gorman did not avert to the fact that this question had already been asked of him.
"He never told me. Bastard!"
"I suppose he was waiting for me to tell you myself. I wanted to tell you myself."
"I don't think I should come here anymore."
"Why?"
"What's it like?" Josh tried to look coldly at O'Gorman who thought 'something eating me inside.' Life like a cancer, eaten alive, like having a bad marriage, or a bad job, or owing money to the mob, or owing a drug dealer, or having one of those slow death day jobs, or starving to death while others do okay.
"How do you think it's like?" O'Gorman uncrossed his legs.
"Don't handle me, don't fucking handle me."
"Is that what you think? That you are being handled?"
"I think so."
"Who else handles you?"
"My Dad."
"Your Dad handles you. How does your Dad handle you, do you think?"

"He knows everything."
"What's that like?"
"You can't win."
"What does that mean?"
"Every time you say something, or give an opinion, it gets corrected. Or he finds a flaw in your argument."
Joshua gritted his teeth, angry for feeling suddenly so hopelessly sad.
"Go on…"
"Fuck you, you fucking queer!"
"I love you, Joshua,"
Joshua sat in silence, looking at O'Gorman looking at him, and then looking at O'Gorman's shoes and Josh hated the silence and the way O'Gorman monolithically sat there gazing, waiting and waiting. But he decided that if O'Gorman wouldn't talk first, why should he? But Joshua talked first.
"Why are you manipulating me?"
"Manipulating you?"
"Yes, you are!
Seán didn't respond.
"You are!"
"How?"
"Using your illness against me. Just sitting there."
"What's wrong with two people just sitting here? What upsets you about that?"
"Why are you trying to outsmart me?"
"Who said anything about anybody trying anything on you, Joshua? Manipulate you? Outsmart you? I am not doing that."
"I could get my Dad in here and he could kick your ass in an argument."
"What?"
"I said."
"I heard you. Why would you want your Dad here to do that?"
Joshua didn't answer.
"Is this something to do with your dad being smart?"
"Yes. I mean, no!"
"Is that an answer? I am sure you have lots of friends who have smart parents. Doctors, scientists, lawyers, professors."
"Because he doesn't understand feelings."
"But he is a psychotherapist."
"Yeah, go figure." Joshua said.
"Tell me about your father."
"No."

"Why do you not want to talk about your Dad?"
"Why are you using your illness against me, to get me to talk?"
"I have told you I am terminally ill. I have told you there is an end in sight. How is that manipulation? I mean, that is not something I can hide or protect you from."
"Why are you using your pointless death to help me?"
"Pointless? Talk to me about your Dad. Is he trying to outsmart you?"
"Yes, I mean, no. My Dad is a fucking dickhead."
"Is he really a fucking dickhead?"
"Why did you tell me you were dying?"
"It's important. Death is important. Just like having a father who is too clever for his own good."
"Did I say that, Seán?"
"No, I said that."
"Okay."
"What do you think about what I said?"
"Innocuous."
"Okay. Why is it innocuous?"
"I am kinda embarrassed for you. I think my Dad is wasting his money here."
"Your father is always winning arguments. What does that mean to you?"
"Why are you using your pointless death to help me?"
"Pointless?"
"Are you going to tell me it means something?"
"I am not telling you anything. Why pointless?"
"If it doesn't mean something, then it musn't mean anything."
"Talk to me about your Dad. Is he trying to outsmart you?"
"Yes."
"How does that make you feel?"
"Stupid."
Then Joshua began to cry.
"Okay. I see."

Joshua was confused, anguished, mind out of order, bats in the belfry, mind on the blink, like waves of rage and pain throwing his suddenly tiny body on a great boiling sea.

O'Gorman looked at the boy's anguished face; his tear filled eyes; and answered slowly carefully. There would only be one, maybe two more sessions before Greg wouldn't let him work anymore.
"Maybe you don't want to live, O'Gorman."
"I do. I want to live. I can't, though."

"It's all so pointless..."
"What is?"
Joshua continued crying.
"What you said about my death- pointless. Is my death pointless? Is your father's brilliance pointless? What does it do to a person to live with someone like that? Does it kill you?"
"So you are okay with this? Dying like this? I should go…fuck you!"
O'Gorman's voice lost its calm impassivity. He leaned forward a little
"There isn't much time", he said. "One's time should be carefully spent."
"Thanks for the Grandpa Walton nugget of wisdom. It was worth all the thousands spent on coming here."
O'Gorman smiled. The boy was funny.
"And we'll leave it there for today. Now, I am not free next Thursday, however this Tuesday is good, about four?"
Joshua got up and walked out, leaving the money on the table. O'Gorman took it. "I'll be back" Joshua said.
"I doubt it," O'Gorman said.

48.

O'Gorman had been worried. Worried and terrified, and getting sicker. He went through his days stoned, for the most part, on morphine. He had checked himself out of hospital to die at home. For the most part O'Gorman had felt only sorrow and anger at the prospect of dying, of saying goodbye to Greg. He never thought it was possible to feel such love, such overwhelming passion for another person as he felt for Greg, but now he knew it was time to say goodbye, he began to feel happy. He knew the end of the pain of living, the end of his pain was in sight. Greg would be well looked after. Greg would have no financial worries. Seán knew there was no escape from this. Aside from the pronouncements of doctors, he knew what the pain in his chest signified, the deep coughing, the weakness and the nausea and the hopelessness, depression, longing for God. He was getting thinner and thinner, and even he could smell the smell of death in the room and the cycle of medication and sleepless nights, weeks in and out of hospital, waiting for something to happen, was so tedious. He wanted it to be over. There was nothing occupying him. Lying there, talking when he felt able, listening to music, watching a show. The cancer had weakened him, and his reason seemed so much less reliable now. Seán lacked the strength to care, to concentrate, and, even if he had something to care about, he wouldn't have time to complete the thought properly, or indeed the project if he wanted to do something useful. Only those who have time, he thought, feel the joy of anticipation. Then, after so many visits from friends and relatives, he began to be gripped by that strange mixture of fear and anger and guilt and euphoria and that slowing down of time which affects those who know they are going to die know, as every moment of staying alive is that mixed blessing, that angry happy anguished reminder of the loss of everything they once had.

Martha and I went to see him. Martha walked into the room to see this ghost as she called him afterwards.
"Oh Gordon, he seems so sick. It's terrible."
And she wept and we held each other and O'Gorman with boiling eyes so desperate for love, the thin sallow face, bony hands that reached up to hug her and she smiled though the tears and hugged him and kissed him and Josh stood there shyly, and really didn't know what to say.
"I'm thinking of going home, back to Greg's mother's house,"

O'Gorman said.

"That's a good idea, I think. What does Greg say?" I said.

"He thinks it's a good idea. And Greg's mom and I are very close."

"When do you go?"

"Next week."

"Why don't you go to a hospice?"

"I'd rather not. I would rather die this way."

So Greg and he went down to recover with Greg's Mom.

Greg's Mom, Phyllis, had a big house in Wicklow with a view of lush green hills, welcomed them, and they were happy and relieved, and though O'Gorman had lost all the weight and had been so sick, he had survived thus far.

"Less weight to carry around. And frankly I haven't the energy to lift it all."

A week into the stay O'Gorman got up at five in the morning to go to the bathroom. Lately urinating had been painful, possibly an infection he had contracted. He urinated very gently, feeling a dull ache across his chest as he urinated, still sore, he thought, imagining what it might be like inside his lungs for the briefest second, then he went back to his room. Greg was sound asleep, strangely calm after all the months of trauma. O'Gorman stood looking out at the hills and could see the first light, the tiniest crack of light coming through the hills, and it gave him such a joy, tears welling in his eyes, seeing the light and the branches and hearing the birds, something he had heard and yet never heard before. The pain in his chest got quickly worse, couldn't breathe with the agonizing stabbing pain stretching along his arm and chest. He began to feel faint, struggled to a nearby armchair .The last thing O'Gorman saw as he died was Greg's face, weeping, calling to him, crying out in a voice growing ever duller, fainter and the light that he saw, the beautiful light from the dawn and the birdsong and the trees through the window, getting narrower, like Greg's face until the beautiful void opened up and O'Gorman smiled, tried to tell Greg he loved him, failed, and that was all.

49.

GOTH BOY

Josh sat in an early morning coffee shop drinking a really unhealthy drink containing alka seltzer, some liver salts and three aspirin, along with a giant coffee. It would make his hands shake, but he would be better by eleven in the day. He looked up on the shop display. The doughnuts looked good. He ordered a couple. He had a craving for something sweet. He kept seeing the tombs he had slept beside all around the coffee shop, between the tables and the chairs. Maybe it was an after-effect of the alcohol mixed with the dope. The drugs swam like sperm through his blood and bones mating with his brains, multiplied multiverses in the hall of mirrors of his mind. Looking at the imaginary tombs and their dead inside, he remembered hearing about some genetically modified weed, something made by the government, something that gave the purest of pure highs, a clean floating flying. Then he imagined he saw O'Gorman, his dark deep eyes, the eyes of the ruined god, dark crystalline, sad beyond imagining, his voice saying the words "the purest of pure highs". Suddenly he felt intolerably sad. He wept silently into his napkin and toyed with the doughnut. He remembered the grave. After the funeral, after they buried O'Gorman using the liturgy of a faith he had long lost, after he looked down and saw the darkness of the soil cover him, Joshua buried his feelings for him with the coffin, buried himself alive with the dead. After O'Gorman, everything stopped. I shall be there soon too, he thought. Joshua didn't care anymore. There was nothing to care about. He felt the days merge into a matrix like continuum; fuse into an impenetrable time. It was as though each moment acquired an infinite density. Each moment was hard and cold and abstract. Each moment was dark like a diamond, made cold and beautiful only by the light, only for the light to turn to dark.

"Hello? You can't sleep here. I'm sorry. Hello?"

He sounded broken-voiced and looked acne-faced and greasy and had nervous rabbit eyes, scared in this franchised dawn coffee shop. And, as the night's black chiffon slid away into the horizon, he waited there, knowing he was afraid of the unbearable uncertainties of his future, that he could never do what his father could do, that he could, for a little time, wait here in the coffee shop as the door opened again, and three people in impeccable business suits came in sparkling with energy, talking of the estimated arrival times of reports from accounts section, ordering cappuccinos and breakfast bars. They had just come from the gym, and they looked like gods with their combed back hair and clear skin and cheery smiles. Joshua watched them with their certainties and their self-confidence and envied them and drank down his coffee and left the mutilated doughnut, finishing his aspirin and alka seltzer and tossing the paper cup over his head. A little left over drink splashed him as the shop door closed behind him. He was on Grafton Street. Most of the big stores were closed, shop shutters like forbidding fallen portcullis. A little rain fell as he walked on, looking for a morning taxi or bus that swung down along the walls of Trinity College, crossing the Suffolk Street bottleneck. Newsagents were open, but he decided not to get a newspaper, feeling vulnerable, fearing having to deal with other people, rather following the bottleneck into Dame Street, seeing a taxi, a cantankerous taxi driver across the road at the Dame Street taxi rank reading a tabloid, waving indifferently to the curly headed kid who, even from a distance, looked wasted. He couldn't live like this. He had to get a steady job. So he applied for a job in an insurance company. And he got it. Within five years he was in a junior management role.

50.

SO, ANYWAY, MARTHA AND I DIDN'T LAST LONG TOGETHER AFTER O'GORMAN DIED.

Martha stood up. She put away her working shoes, put on slippers and put the vacuum cleaner back in the downstairs cleaning closet beside the back door. Martha looked at her hands. Clean under the see-through rubber gloves. No nails broken. I can see my hands, I see they are fine. I had a manicure a few days ago, and a pedicure and a facial and a massage. Suddenly she was a tireless pursuer of perfection, a relentless manager. That's what I do for a living: I manage. She stood up and washed her hands. Then she dried her hands and put the radio on. She sat in the downstairs room and listened to the radio while doing breathing exercises, something not recommended by the professional meditation course-giving gurus, or indeed the wildly successful books they write. The title of the particular book that Clodagh in work had lent her was called Dream your Life into Healing. It centred on visualizing one's idealised life into reality.

The dream of the breathing exercises is imagining a bright clear light at the centre of the centre that you conceive of as your being as you inhale allow the light to expand inwards till it apprehends the light of the universe, a calm relaxed better sense of self, calmer fitter happier, a peaceful calm ocean of light. Yes, that's the way the higher cleansing of the chakras, of the spirit, of the inner self, the inner child, the Christ-self within. Consciousness the healing light that reflects the light of the universe.

She was always cleaning. What made her clean things so? She had cleaned the house. She had cleaned the house when she had people to do that. I have a job. More than that I have, well, I had a life. She had cleaned the house when the house was already clean.

The radio was giving the news right then, followed by the weather, followed by racing tips, and a preview of the night's play. Could not follow the words. The retention and the processing of such statistical data were becoming a matter of considerable strain to her. A little frightening. Usually statistics were her bread of life. She could absorb spreadsheets of them with frightening ease. She switched off the babbling radio and listened. Nothing. I'm upset. I can tell I am upset by the way I have difficulty processing things. My mind is elsewhere. Processing turbulent emotions deep down.

She went into her bedroom. She sat on their very best bed and carefully listened. Nothing. Tiredness eased nervous tension. If one was too tired and disconnected to agonize then things were not so bad. Instead of suffering, one slept, the feeling of tiredness gave respite from fear and uncertainty. She listened throughout the house. She waited for the specific sounds of my imminent arrival, my car's crunch up the driveway. After all these years still the same. One hears things. She knew anyway. The difference between suspecting and knowing is possession of your husband's girlfriend's underwear. How she had acquired this incriminating piece of evidence is still beyond me. One way or another, Martha would have found out. More damaging than the weed one's girlfriend buys is the presence of her underwear in one's weekly wash. It smelt of her, that faint reminiscent odour of tobacco, woodbine, Fleurs Du Lis perfume, and honey soap, unmistakable under all those carefully lathered showers I took. She imagined her skin, impossibly soft with the olive oil texture of youth, her eyes looking hungrily up at him as they had sex, feeling all the intensity that she could no longer give him. And Martha wanted to die. She curled up on the floor in foetal position and longed for death. It hurt so much, after the shock came the pain, the afterbirth of realization, so much pain, an ocean of suffering, adrift in the freezing waters of loneliness. Some think suffering is hot. No, she thought, it's cold. It's dehumanizing. It's like hypothermia. It kills you quietly. It chills from the inside out.

The phone kept ringing. She didn't answer. The phone never rang that much. She sat there and listened to it ringing as she curled up on the floor, wanting to die rather than feel all this rage and hurt and betrayal and the sense her life was a lie.

Soon after this Martha Reynolds and I parted.

51.

PEOPLE OFTEN ASK ME IF I HAVE ANY WORDS OF ADVICE FOR DIVORCED PEOPLE.

Here are a few simple admonitions based on my own experiences.

When, in the course of human events, it becomes necessary for two married people to dissolve the bonds that once united them, it is a self-evident truth that the world is full of toxic marriages. So, if you have to divorce, then do it. Why add to the number for the sake of propriety?

It's important not to kill your spouse. It's messy. It involves a lot of unnecessary complex planning. Finally, it is rarely worth it. Many people who kill their spouses feel they have achieved something worthwhile, namely revenge, or even a sense of emotional satisfaction-a sense they deserved it. This is not true. Taking revenge on your spouse, be they really evil or not, is an utterly futile move. You will go to jail. You will feel a lot of guilt. In certain countries they have the death penalty for that kind of thing. Also, the family or loved ones of your spouse may seek to exact revenge upon you. Few ever really get away with it. Anyway it's wrong. Your children will think less of you for it.

Assuming you follow me on my strict admonition against violence, I think it is important to know your ex-spouse. I never really knew Martha, that uniquely luminous person I did not properly honour. I knew her in relation to my needs, which were all-consuming needs, cynical needs, egotistical needs, rapacious, avaricious, thoughtless, excessively intellectual needs.

Assuming you follow my line of thought on the issue of knowing your ex-wife, and, as everybody lies, one might mistakenly think one needs to do what is necessary to know your ex-wife or husband. This is an illusion. A need to control a desire to cling to what is left of one's self respect and deny the profound embarrassment and humiliation that comes from a failed relationship. Don't do anything immoral. Don't break the law.

Do not obtain copies of her communications and analyse them. Do not follow your ex-wife. Do not keep a record of her movements. Do not seek out the men your former wife is dating and congratulate them on their excellent choice of sexual partner.

Do not request heartfelt conversations with your former wife in order to reach some kind of understanding, the kinds of understanding perhaps one didn't achieve during the time of being married to them. It causes confusion and engaging in unwarranted sexual relations with them.

Do not have sex with your ex-wife. It's deeply confusing. I used call her up and we would meet and talk for hours. She wanted us to get back together again. I explained that though I enjoyed the sex with her when we got together, I was no longer in love with her. This caused something of a negative reaction from Martha.

Do not explain to your ex-wife that you are going through therapy as you are being divorced. Do not explain that you are trying to let go of the pain you brought into your former marriage to her, the very toxic element that ultimately ruined the relationship. It might devastate her. Do not say something like what I said that my new partner and I were going through intense counselling and therapy, sometimes in groups, sometimes separately, sometimes just talking things out either with each other or with Martha.

Don't waste time. Time is money. Nobody likes a penny pincher. After all few things cause more rage and hate than one spouse ripping off the other one simply because the letter of the law says they can. Better to reach an amicable financial arrangement than an adversarial one. Be generous, but be reasonable. I gave away vast sums of money to Martha, though she had her own money. She used give the money back.

It's really important to avoid your child growing into a psychopath or an addict or the kind of angry ungrateful needy self-loathing upwardly mobile ruthless self-serving jerk who is incapable of loving or being loved or maintaining a long term relationship without feeling trapped or mistrustful, someone who will blame you for everything that will go wrong for them in later life. I really cannot repeat this enough. The kids know- and they never forget.

52.

My divorce from Martha was one of many break-ups, failures of reconciliation, with so many people stretching back to boyhood, to the events with Ed Frasier, who tried to kill me. Mom and Dad, as I said, took me out of the school. But Ed Frasier was himself a victim of circumstances. Larry his father took executive action against his son.

Here is how it happened:

It happened when Ed came home after football practice as Larry Frasier, his father, sat in his study looking out the window.

Earlier that day, Larry had received a call from Headmaster Anderson.

"Hello?"

"Larry Frasier?"

"This is he. Who's this?"

"Jim Anderson"

"Who? Oh yes, of course. How's it going?"

"I was wondering if you might be willing to drop by and meet me today with regard to an issue relating to Edward."

"I heard there was trouble. I haven't been well."

"I heard you were injured on duty."

"Yep."

"I hope you are making a full recovery."

"Well..."

"Would today be too early to meet?"

"Today does seem quite sudden, Jim."

"I know, sorry about this."

"What's going on, Headmaster? I mean I was aware there were problems with Edward."

"That's what I wanted to talk to you about. Ten minutes, maximum."

So they arranged a meeting, and Larry dropped by for what turned out to be something a lot longer than the ten minute maximum meeting that Jim had promised during the call, as he over the telephone assured Larry he was only too well aware of his injuries, the stress and exhaustion involved in healing mentally and physical, and that he, Jim, would not have called if it weren't a matter of the highest importance.

"Thanks for dropping by."

"I was wondering how you're feeling. I mean after your injury."
"Much better, thanks Jim."
"That's great. Can I ask how it happened, if that's not too much to ask?"
"I was injured on duty. We were making an arrest in what we understood to be a nice neighbourhood, and I got hit with a table leg."
"Oh my God!" Jim said.
Larry looked carefully into Jim's eyes, measuring the gaze, wondering if he meant his words. Yes, Larry thought. Anderson was really shocked.
"I know, the assailant, a fifty year old psychiatrist, missed my head by half an inch. I know. Psychopaths can be so psychopathic."
"That's really shocking."
"Would have probably killed me. I needed surgery, you see. Look, Jim, if you don't mind."
"It means a lot you came," Anderson said.
"I'm worried about Ed, have been for a while."
"I see. Well, we really have a problem here."
"It's just I am almost back on duty, only a week or so to go, and there is so much catching up, you see, and I still have a touch of post-traumatic stress,"
"Oh dear, if this is too much."
"Not at all, it's only a bit of PTSD. I am very worried about Ed, and I wanted to hear what you have to say. I know we have spoiled him a bit and I regret that, so, tell me, what's going on?"
"Okay, I think we have a serious problem. Ed is, if you will, the leader of a group of bullies, and if this isn't stopped, we could have serious trouble in the future. He is a kind of puppet master."
"Puppet master, for god's sake, that's a bit extreme!"
"Don't get me wrong, Jim. I like Ed, and Ed is really good for the school in a lot of ways. Your son is a top sportsman, a superb student who works hard, a person with sufficient social skills and intelligent enough for others to look up to as a leader, but not so bright as to alienate the group. He seems to have something of an indomitable need to dominate. Put it this way, he's not exactly a good example to others, and maybe you can tell me why, because I have my best people on it right now and they are at a loss. Ed has his friends, well, doing things, beating up kids. Taking stuff from them."
"Do you have anything on camera?"
"It never happens on camera."
"Never? Everybody makes mistakes. That's how we catch people and put them in jail."

Jim shook his head.
"Really, Larry. It never happens on camera. We have been searching for weeks. We have no evidence. We we have a few pushes and shoves, but nothing we can really work with."
This was a lie, of course. Much of the evidence was being destroyed, or at least never surfaced.
"Even the smartest and the most resourceful. Always. It's how cops catch crooks or it's how crooks get away."
"Ed is smart, as I said. I have my people on it, if you understand. It's a matter of time before the evidence emerges. I have spoken to your wife Mary, but Mary won't accept what I'm saying."
"I hear you. We lost our first child, and then we had Edward and he was doted upon by her, and I think it has spoiled him somewhat."
"I understand, Larry."
"I will speak to the boy, but I have to say, in the absence of evidence, I wonder if I can in conscience —"
"Larry, I would not be talking like this if I did not have the gravest concerns."
"I understand."
"I'm in the position whereby I am waiting for hard evidence to come in and, once it does, I will have no option but to take action."
"What kind of confidence would you have that hard evidence is on its way?"
"I would say, Larry, that I have every confidence that good evidence is on its way. It's coming like Christmas is coming."
"I see."
"Now, if you were to take action yourself, Larry, it would prevent me from —"
"I think I understand what you are saying to me, and I ask you not to worry."
"I mean Larry, what could I do if someone came to me with hard evidence saying your son punched a boy three years his junior, knocking him down, and then kicking him? Someone with video, for instance on their phone."
"My son, my Edward, did that?"
"I can't prove it, Larry. It just might be the reports I'm getting. And I am profoundly sorry to be sitting here telling you this. I did mention this to Mary, but she became upset and refused to, well, have any further meetings until you had fully recovered and both of you could decide on a course of action. I know this is early, but I had to tell you. I had to take action."
Larry's shoulder began to hurt at this juncture, probably from holding

it tense while listening to Jim.
"I understand, Headmaster. This is very serious indeed. I'm hungry, sorry I get like this sometimes. A craving for food."
"Have some fruit." Anderson said, taking a bowl of fruit from his desk and offering some to the detective.
Need to take a break, Larry thought. Decide on a course of action. Hungry.
As Larry took a banana and an orange, Jim noticed the slim pistol holster protruding beneath his brown tweed jacket. There it sat over a crisp professionally ironed white shirt. He noticed from his open necked shirt he wore a snow white T-shirt.
"Why do you bring a gun here?"
"I feel safer with it."
"Are you allowed to have your gun with you off duty?"
"Sure, if I feel I need to have it with me."
"I'm being nosy, I know."
"You write all those books too, don't you?"
"I do."
"Writers are always like that. They want to know everything, even things they should never dream of asking."
"I'm sorry."
"You haven't offended me, not at all. I'm going to go home now and rest up. Then, when Edward comes in, I am going to have words, you know? He might not be in tomorrow, or the day after. He might be a bit too upset after the words I have with him. I want you to let his absenteeism go."
"That bit of absenteeism we all might slip through the net for a day or two. After two days, it goes back on the record."
"I think then, Headmaster James Anderson, we have what you might call an understanding. I'll give you a call in a month or so and we'll see if we need to take further action to end this unhappy episode."

There was an awkward silence during which Larry wondered if Jim was recording the discussion. The meeting ended with a warm handshake and Larry continued to worry as he walked through the crowds of boys who were shouting and passing from one class to another as teachers raised their voices and shepherded their students from one class to another, in the gorgeous cold clear sunlight that came through the windows of the hallways intersecting one classroom after another.

After he got outside and walked the grounds collecting his thoughts, Larry stopped to look at the new sports hall. It stood pristine, a magnificent blend of reinforced glass and steel, shaped like a large birthday cake, protruding, as a very modern anomaly arrogantly protrudes, amidst the surrounding older, darker stone, labyrinthine halls and floors and schoolrooms, all added to and rebuilt and refurbished over the centuries with a seemingly endless supply of donor money from grateful former students and former students and government officials, all proud of the extraordinary record this school had held for the last century and a half, all wanting association with an institution that brings out the best in their sons, a ticket to the furtherance, not only of their career, but of the country itself. It was a kind of preparation ground for the future mandarin class. He wondered if his son wanted that, or what Ed really wanted. Maybe all his son's rage was the frustration he felt at being squeezed into a uniform he did not want to wear.

Larry drove home slowly, climbed into the bath for an hour to think, and waited for Ed to get back from wherever he was. He thought of the day, as he thought so often of the day he went to make that arrest, the arrest that caused his injury, the injury that led to such a long period of convalescence. He was arresting a psychiatrist for sexually abusing her daughter. It was to be a straightforward matter, and, as they knew of the dangers of taking straightforward matters for granted, no chances were taken. His team had profiled her carefully, had planned everything, brought backup, had the house monitored, waited for optimum time. Psychiatrists, so they reasoned, were not known for their physicality. This one was always up early, her daily full schedule of patients, usually beginning about eight-thirty. Larry and the team of arresting officers called at six-thirty. She was sitting in the kitchen. When she saw the police she ran into her study, and taking a heavy mahogany table leg that been leaning against a bookstand for no apparent reason, as things are left around a domestic abode for no good reason, brought it down upon Detective Larry Frasier's head, with the full intent of killing him, so the other police present claimed. But Larry saw it coming and moved. The table leg, as it came down vertically, glanced instead against his cheek, breaking his cheekbone, and as it made full contact, smashing his shoulder blade. The psychiatrist was disarmed and restrained. All he remembered was the look in her eye. She wanted to kill him. She wanted to go back to her life of sleeping with her twelve year old daughter and seeing patients. Remembering this as he splashed about in the bath, he began to weep once more. The people in evidence had showed the table leg to him after he got out of hospital. They had weighed it at four pounds, three ounces. Under interrogation, the psychiatrist explained she was throwing out an old table she had no use for. The rest of the table had been collected for disposal. That one table leg was all that was left. She stood on a chair as he came into the room looking for her. He would have suffered a fractured skull if he hadn't noticed a slight movement out of the corner of his eye. A slight flicker of movement seen from the corner of his eye and Larry instinctually moved sufficiently for the table leg to miss his skull and crack against his shoulder.

Ed came in late. Two hours late. Larry heard the clump clump clump sound of his football studs against the polished, varnished hardwood floor boards. That boy moves like a storm trooper. Dammit. I told that kid to take his shoes off and shower in the shower room, he thought. I spent a fortune getting the floors done. Larry went down to him. He was putting his clothes into the machine.
"Hi Dad. How was your day?"
"My day went fine. I had a good day. Did you have a good day, son?"
"Thanks. Yeah."
"Are you going to take a shower, son?"
"Sure Dad."
"When you are finished, could you knock in and see me?"
"Sounds bad. Everything good?"
"Not at all. It's a surprise, son. See you then."
Larry went back to his room and opened The Decline and Fall of the Third Reich. He was in the lifelong habit of re-reading books. After thirty minutes of reading, he realised his son was avoiding him. After another thirty minutes, he heard footfalls. The knob on the door turned. The door opened. It was Edward, freshly showered wearing a fresh pair of jeans, his house runners, and a shirt that said 'surfs up, dude'
"Hi, son. Come on in. How are things?"
"Great, Dad. What's going on?"
"Nothing. Come on in. Close the door will you. Thanks. No, there's nothing going on. Nothing at all. Come on over here."
"Jesus."
Edward's face froze in fear.
"There is something I have to tell you, a kind of message that I have to give you. Something I want you to remember forever. Can you understand that there are messages like that?"
"Dad, I have no idea what you are talking about."
"I know you are afraid of me."
"Dad, I am not afraid of you. I love you."

"You love me."

"Yes."

"So why are you taking your anger and your fear of me out on Gordon Brock and so many others?"

"What?"

In an insane moment, in a blind moment's rage, Larry punched Ed on the forehead with the base of his hand. It was the smallest of movements. It seemed impossible to punch someone so hard and stand so close to them, a mere inch or so away. It felt something like the impact of the spine of a heavy volume, not hard like a piece of wood, but something soft and almost pliable, like a thick Shakespeare or a Bible. Edward fell back hard on the carpeted floor and lay there for five minutes unconscious, his mouth partially opened, his ivory teeth peering out like little jewels hidden in a dark cave, the whites of his eyes showing like eggs, one moment appearing and the next disappearing behind Ed's moving eyelids. Larry looked at him. Larry had hit him with his left hand. I hit him. Had to do it, he told himself. He'll be out for a bit. This was something that had to be taken care of now, before the boy got too big to take on, before he became completely unmanageable.

Edward woke up with his father sitting on a straight backed chair looking at him, neither compassionately nor cruelly, his flinty skeptical eyes watching Ed, missing nothing. Edward didn't know what to say. In fact, he was unsure exactly what had happened, and, if something had happened, the speed with whatever it was had happened, was completely overwhelming. Then, slowly, by the spontaneous evolution of insight, Edward understood what had happened. His father was bitter. He had been hurt. He wanted to hurt back. Edward smiled savagely, showing his sharp white teeth.

"So, you get hit by a little old lady who is hot for her twelve year old, and nearly killed, and you take it out on your own son. Is that irony, or just child abuse of the saddest kind?"

"I hear you've been beating up geniuses."

"What?"

"You heard me, son. You've been beating on people so smart they make you look stupid, or feel that way. It doesn't matter what they can or can't do. It doesn't matter who or what Brock can or can't do. He is irrelevant. He is a dot on the landscape. What matters is you. You are my son. And you can't hurt people to feel better. Brock us just something that stands out that you can hit."

"N-no." Ed said, trying to say what his father wanted to hear. But Larry saw that his son was trying to placate him, and such displays of weakness enraged Larry.
"Don't insult my intelligence," Larry said, feeling an uncontrollable rage beginning in him once more.
"I don't understand."
"You do."
"What?"
"You do understand, and I have to say this is really irritating me. I'm talking about Gordon Brock!"
"I never touched him."
"Don't bullshit me!"
" I'm not!"
"It's a terrible thing. Bullying people."
"You mean Brock? He is a fucking dickhead. Brock thinks everyone is an idiot, except him and a few teachers."
"Yet you hit him, didn't you?"
"I did."
"It was a terrible thing to do."
"Okay."
"I wanted to talk to you."
"I'm definitely listening."
"About your future."
Ed nodded tearfully.
"I have learned, son, and you will learn, or you and I will part company forever."
"Learn what?"
"I will not have a bully in my house."
"Dad, I —"
"I will not support one and I will throw you out on the street to rot in some gutter, before I let this go on. And don't think I won't."
Edward was standing three feet from his father.
"I want to tell you something, please Dad."

Ed opened his mouth to speak once more, to tell his father that he was breaking his sacred oath as a black belt, that the rumours he had heard about a dispute between himself and Brock were unfounded, that he respected Brock's gifts, that he would never ever pick on someone smaller than him, that he was hurt and humiliated and very angry at a father he loved and venerated.
His father grabbed him by the throat in a choke hold. Then he let go. Edward gasped for breath.
"I hate you," Ed said.

"Hate me then. But stop torturing people."

"You are one to talk, beating suspects till they talk!"

"I have never done that, son. Never! A good detective doesn't need to torture. I am sorry I attacked you. It was wrong of me. But I am trying to get through to you, Okay?"

Edward nodded. He was seeing spots before his eyes.

"Listen to me. They are presently amassing evidence against you in St. Raymond's, you know that?"

No answer.

"I asked you a question. Did you know they were amassing evidence against you in St. Raymond's?"

No answer.

"Did you know that? Make an effort to answer."

"No."

"They are. They are going to get you unless you stop. Understand?"

"Yes."

"Okay then."

Larry's voice had dropped an octave.

"People like you go on to beat their wives, their children, their friends and enemies. That is, if you don't change your behaviour. Until now, I never hit you, never in your entire childhood, and neither did your mother. You have no reason to behave as you have towards Brock. It ends now. Do we understand each other? Now, go."

53.

Ed went to his room, slammed the door, and beat his bed and pillow as he wept in rage. He was, aside from his father, alone in the house. After the initial rage subsided, he sat for a while and looked out the window into the garden. His father had wandered out to the garden and was looking at the pear and apple trees, seemingly lost in thought. Larry sat down on the garden seat, and, looking lost and deeply guilty for what he had done to his son and profoundly worried, stared at the trees for a long time. And Ed looked down at his father and as he did, Ed noticed tears rolling down his cheeks. Young Frasier's fists were clenched in a rage he feared he would never be able to control. He reached under the bed and, taking out a clear plastic two litre bottle, he poured himself a cup of vodka, drank it down with a trembling hand, then had another, then lay on his bed, shaking with fear and rage and a sense of violation he had hitherto never experienced, waiting for the warm feeling of the alcohol to kick in. He had always lived in fear, in a nameless fear of an impending overwhelming force he could never control, that all the power and knowledge he could amass would never erect a barricade tough enough to protect him. He looked at the ceiling, at the walls filled with photographs of his favourite places, holidays beachside resting in the shade of the too hot sun, or snowboarding where he broke his ankle more severely than when playing rugby the year before, beaches, girlfriends, pictures of his mother and father in Cahirciveen where his parents had, only three years ago, bought this ruined farm as an investment, rebuilt it, and rented it out during the summer to pay for the mortgage, and now were able to use it as a family retreat for eight months of the year. The rest of the time it was still rented out at a substantial profit. Edward had taken so many pictures of the gradual reconstruction of this house, and, as he got drunker and wept more, he looked at the pictures and found he really hated the fucking old house with it's pretty farm look and it's nearby animal sanctuary and hedges and old trees that twisted by old roads into and indeterminable distance, especially when it rained and the days would pass and all Ed would have on his hands was time and the vision of the rain and the movies he would watch by himself and books, so many books to read, so many books he read, passed through his hands to alleviate the boredom. He took a video disc out of a box of discs he hid underneath a floorboard underneath a small bookshelf. He looked at it, checking it and found it as pristine as ever, and then put it into his computer. It was a movie. He began watching the young man have sex with his best friend's mother, a fantastically attractive older woman with beautiful peach-like skin, powerful hips and shoulders, arms that held the willing, enthralled teenager, well muscled, suppled toned shaped to optimum form, being perhaps twenty years older than the young man, who was already having his penis sucked by this exceptionally skilled beautiful powerful woman in the recently removed business suit, that just happened to be the mother of the best friend of the young man in the movie he was watching. Ed took another mouthful of the vodka, locked the door to his room, took some tissues, and began masturbating. He had already watched, so he remembered, in the first movie frames, the woman take off her business suit with a thrill of anticipation, saw her wooden acting as she walked through the bad movie sets, the equally bad movie lines with irritation, but when she touched the teenager, and when he touched her, Ed stopped disbelieving, for he believed what he felt. She had watched this young man for a long time, so she said. She had just come in from the office to find this young man, her son's best friend, watching a movie as he waited for her son to come home from a camping trip. Smudge had given Ed this disc a few days before. Ed watched it as though it were his first time. He liked this woman in the movie. There seemed to be nothing she wouldn't do. She made him feel confident and safe in this high risk imaginary situation. She knew what she was doing. She made him feel good. Afterwards, when Ed felt better, less angry, he called Smudge.

"Hey there!" Smudge said.

"Where are you?"

"I'm at a friend's house. What are you doing?"

"Getting drunk," Ed said.

"Wow, on your own?"

"Well, you're not here."

"I got company, if you understand me."

"Sure. I got a question."

"Sure. What up?"

"Whatever happened to Brock,?"

"Gordon Brock? I dunno. Why are you so curious? That got all legal. I thought the whole thing was hushed up. I thought your dad got involved."

"It seems that he is still trying to ruin our reputations. Yours and mine."

"The little fucktard!"

"What do you say we have a word?"

54.

Jim Anderson watched Barton and Todd, Solicitors, finger the handles of their cups of freshly percolated coffee for a while. Todd and Barton and Anderson were watching, in the continuous present of camera footage, Lucy Brock's confrontation with Edward Frasier in the main schoolyard. Then, after what seemed a brief exchange from the perspective of the overhead cameras in the main schoolyard, Lucy began to walk away. Then, after a few steps, she stops. Then she turns and says something to Frasier in front of all his friends and a gradually gathering crowd.

"There is Gordon Brock, just walking into camera view on the left," Jim said.

"And Lucy is his mother," Todd said.

"Exactly," Jim answers, irritated at the obviousness and stupidity of the questions. They continue to watch as Lucy walks past her son without seemingly saying a word.

"She said nothing to him,"

"It looks that way, doesn't it?" Jim said, pointing to the screen, as though guiding an advanced class through a particularly abstruse differential calculus problem.

"Now, it's at this stage that Frasier turns on Brock. There he walks up to him, there, camera on right." Jim waved his finger as Frasier stands on screen, toe to toe with the much smaller, younger Brock, and there, in front of the entire school, proceeds to beat him up, punching him in the stomach, the shoulders, knocking him to the ground.

"Where were the teachers? You have security guards?" Todd asked.

"There was an announcement. One of our staff members announced she was about to have a baby. There was a little get-together. The schoolyard was unattended for a few minutes."

This was a lie. A lax indifferent attitude had developed towards the monitoring of the school since the installation of the cameras and the hiring of the security guards. No one wanted the responsibility of being put in the position as a potential witness against the school, their employer, if there was an incident.

"I see," Barton said.

As with most fights, it was over in less than two minutes. The time stamp on the video said it was almost the end of break time. The crowd dispersed in response to the bell, programmed to ring on the hour. As the crowd dispersed, Gordon was lying on the ground. A

minute passed. Brother Frank arrived. He knelt down beside the boy. Brock got up, and, after a brief exchange, walked off towards the school building. The screen went dead.
"The rest is inconsequential," Jim said.
"I'm sure we all agree that what we have seen is not, shall we say, inconsequential. Who else knows about this?" Barton asked, thinking St. Raymond's exposure lawsuits, not to mention the near incalculable loss of reputation and consequent future losses to the school.
"A couple of people."
"Two, four, how many? Try to be specific."
"Some members of the staff, reliable types."
"I see. I never met the types, who, having you by the testicles, were reliable enough to resist buying a decent set of vice grips. I ask, are we looking at the only copy? What I am trying to say is that, if we are not looking at the only copy, you are in so much deep shit, such a world of fuckedupness, and Mister Anderson, we would advise you to simply disappear, take up writing travel sonnets on the Faroes, or baking cookies somewhere, because your career, as well as this school, will be carved up and sold off as real estate." Barton said. His voice is so soft, Jim thought, it's almost inaudible.
"To the best of my knowledge. Yes, this is the only copy."
"Naturally," Barton intoned, "I would exhort you in the strongest possible terms to release this copy, not only to the parents, but to the police, and begin a full investigation into the systemic errors that allowed this to occur. We have just witnessed something of a serious assault, with possibly life altering consequences."
"Naturally," Jim snapped. "But today I really don't want to commit career suicide, destroy the reputation of a school with a history like this one, and —"
Barton continued on with his intonations, ignoring his client's meanderings.
"If we are not looking at the only copy, and other copies come out, we are looking at a very expensive, rather clichéd situation, aren't we?"
"Do tell."
"The school will, metaphorically, take you down a laneway, and do it execution style. What about the pictures on the net?"
"Bad copies, taken on mobile phones. There are no pictures of the fight itself." Anderson said.
"The media coverage will wreak the kind of carnage you could only dream about in apocalyptic literature."
"Okay, I think I have been thorough. Really very thorough." Anderson said.

"That's all we need to know."

"All hard disks have been cleared down with a military encryption wipe."

"Wonderful. I love that tech speak. It's so efficient. So you got rid of the evidence."

"Any electronic fingerprints also have been wiped. All backups have been disappeared. All personnel have been checked for an appreciation that no such incidents as depicted here ever occurred, and, finally, I have been authorised to spend whatever monies are necessary to —"

"Did the staff alert you to this incident?"

"No, no they didn't"

"Who alerted you to this incident?"

"No one, I heard Lucy Brock was in the school yard. I logged into the security system, checked the files, and saw what happened after she left."

Another lie. Todd stopped him, raising his hand pleadingly.

"Thank you."

"Who copied and cleaned up the files?" Todd asked.

"I did." Jim said.

"And you did a good job?"

Anderson nodded, trying to suppress his rising irritation with the cross questioning.

"What about the program you used to do the military wipe on the hard disks?"

"I replaced my computer last week."

"I see. Is there any evidence you purchased the program you used to clean up the files?"

"No. I downloaded it, using another program I acquired free of charge. Then I got rid of the machine."

"Who else knows about this?"

Anderson answered on, searching for inconsistencies and incompleteness's.

"Brother Frank knows something, but then it's near impossible to keep anything from him. He's at least as smart as young Brock. I think, though, he has his own troubles."

"And we don't care and really don't need to hear the rest of that sentence. Okay?"

"Sure, sure," Anderson said.

"Let's just say we never saw this, and that poor kid, who, by the way should be either dead or permanently brain damaged."

"How do you know?"

"Know what?"

"About possible brain damage?"

"How do you know he was injured?"

The lawyers didn't answer. Anderson smirked.

"He's neither," Anderson said. "And he is actually exceptionally gifted, as I say, and he has left the school as a result of this affair."

"I see," Barton said.

Jim began to see the world the way Barton saw it. It was a world, not of what one knew in one's heart to be the case, but what could be evidentially asserted to be the case.

"What about medical examinations?"

"Well, you need to be more specific."

"Is he permanently affected by what happened?" Todd asked.

"I have the results here."

Jim slid the file across his desk. Todd and Barton looked through the file together. It was a thick copy of what was undoubtedly a thick original file. Gordon's parents seemed obsessed with their offspring's health. He seemed to have incurred no permanent damage.

"It's probably the product of a mix of luck and genetics that —"

"As far as we, in St. Raymond's, can judge the medical report, though troubling, is not enough to allow for suit to be filed against the school for whatever their team decide to be the most advantageous charge or charges."

"We would agree. However this footage is a problem. Have the police been involved?"

"Not yet."

"Why not?"

"I have a strong sense the police won't be involved."

Todd looked coldly at Anderson.

"How prescient. I take it then, you talked to the police?"

"The matter is being dealt with, as I now speak."

"That's very cryptic."

"What I am saying is, that I spoke to Frasier's father. He is having a quiet word with the Frasier boy, and letting him know the consequences of continuing to behave in the way he has been behaving. I don't know the specifics, but —"

"What about witnesses?"

"Certainly a few admit to seeing a couple for fist fights between the two parties, but nothing like what we see here."

"So you don't need us, do you?"

"St. Raymond's always needs the advice and support of people like you. I have been brought in, gentlemen, because this school is in a state of dangerous transition."

"Really. I am an alumni myself," Barton said.
"Once a prestigious school, as far as I can gather, with a reputation for severe discipline, religious conservatism and high achievement,"
"Rather unfashionable now?" Todd said.
"Elitism is unfashionable." Anderson answered, pointing to the video. "Mr. Todd, we are trying to change this school's image, tone down the image of a school that provides only leaders and shakers in the light of a hugely altered demographic, where schools are springing up in the suburbs like weeds, where we have to seem attractive to the new middle classes, we have to not only seem gentle, but be gentle."
"What about the boy?" Barton asked.
"Ed Frasier? He'll be fine. He will get the shock of his life from his father, but believe me, he will be fine. He will come back a far better behaved, far wiser, young man."
"Brock. We mean Brock," Barton muttered angrily.
Todd looked once more at the purloined medical file and meditated for a moment at the difficulty of acquiring the medical records of a minor.
"Brock will be fine."
"Really?" Barton asked. "Congratulations on your medical licence, Jim."
"You're funny!" Anderson said coldly.
"And how do you know he will be fine?"
"I have every confidence. He has very caring very loving parents. And he has left the school. The best thing for everyone is to put this behind us, file it away if you will. And, heartless though that might sound, we believe it to be true."
They smiled.
"Thank you for your time. We will be in touch," Barton said. And they left, quietly closing the door to the room after them.

55.

THE END OF THINGS

It was three in the morning when Martha came home to find me waiting for her. I was sitting in the hall smoking a joint and drinking brandy from one of those fragile universe shaped brandy glasses. I looked at her and said hello. I caught my reflection. My eyes seemed to burn like storm lanterns from within my ragged face, my voice softened by the tobacco and the brandy.

"I, I —" I began.

"I always loved you Gordon, you know that?"

"I know that. But you always competed with me and compared yourself to me and hated how being with me made you feel and as a result you always demonised me and blamed me for your unhappiness. I hated and I loved you. Sometimes I wanted to kill myself."

"Really? When was this? Where is all this coming from. This is bullshit,"

She said.

"This can't go on. I can't stand this endless conflict over your sense of self loathing and inferiority. I can't stand being blamed for things that don't work out for you. I can't stand being made to endorse your projects because the price of not endorsing them is the withdrawal of your love and being made feel less than a person because I think you are making a mistake."

"That's all you ever did. You never did anything else except undermine me and insult me and hurt my feelings, in one way or another."

"But it's also true that I have never been fair to you, Martha. Or true to you. I have never been a good man or a kind man. I have never been the right man for you. I never gave you what you really needed because I wasn't able to. I have been preoccupied with my own boredom and the lack of anything that really engaged me in life. I have fallen in love with your half sister. You are better off without me. I assure you, Martha, I will make you financially secure for the rest of your natural life."

"I don't need that, not from you."

"It's the one thing I can promise, whether or not you choose to remarry."

"How long did it take you?"

"Sorry?"

"How long did it take you to get that speech right?"
"I don't need to practice speeches. It's not a speech, and I swear to you."
"How do you expect me to believe anything you say to me?"
"I don't know."
"I knew you were having an affair."
"I know."
"I knew you weren't happy."
"I know. I am sorry I failed you. I am sorry for everything."
I stood up unsteadily, tried to place the brandy glass beside me as I stood up, failed, took the brandy glass with me on my journey to her centre of gravity, walked awkwardly over to her, raised my eyebrows and opened my lips as though to speak, failed, put the butt end of the marijuana cigarette between my lips, for a moment reminding her of an emaciated Edward G. Robinson, raised my hand in oracular intent, then let it fall. She walked towards the stairs.
"Stop," she said. "Please stop." I stopped. "Please stop."
"I have. I've stopped."
"I mean to say. Stop. I mean stop."
"Stop? What the fuck are you talking about?"
"This. All of this" Martha said. "It has to stop. This torture."
"Torture?"
At this point, I stumbled against a chair I didn't see, fell over, let go the brandy glass, spilling brandy and glass down, then breaking, then projecting the fragile vessel across the floor, it smashing against the wall, ricocheting fragments back across the hall towards Martha and I, fragments of glass were directly under my knee as I fell, the glass penetrating the fabric of my suit and into my lower leg. I stood up quickly, fixing the chair and sitting upon it.
"Sorry, sorry," I said.
Her eyes flooded with tears. This was the end, the end neither had wanted to admit. I was shaking and sitting on the chair, my eyes like coals, bloodshot with the dope and alcohol, oblivious to the glass having its fragmentary effect, cutting into skin and muscle.
"What do you want to do?"
"Split up. The money. House. Stuff. Split."
"You want a divorce?"
I nodded, weeping on the chair at the foot of the stair. A dark stain crept from beneath my knee through my grey suit, which suddenly seemed less dapper than before.
"Gordon, I —" She saw a small piece of glass jutting from my knee. "Hold still," she said.

I touched her head tentatively, touched her hair as she tried to remove the glass. She brushed me away.

"This will require plasters, disinfectant, and the deft use of a tweezers," I said. "I shouldn't have done that."

"It doesn't matter. It doesn't matter."

"I shouldn't have done that"

I drew my hand back and let her take the glass out. She went upstairs and got a tweezers and some plasters and fixed up the cut. I always bled easily, my once young blood now awash with grief and self-pity and guilt, rich dark red blood filled with all the things someone my age shouldn't eat and drink. Bad blood, I thought, twisting my face into a grimace I thought was a smile. I remembered all the things, my boyhood, school, tutors, university, meeting Martha at Lydon's, our affair, our falling in love, the lovemaking, the birth of Joshua, the home together we once but no longer had. In a flash I experienced all we had done together, all the possible futures together now gone.

"If you ever do that again, I'll —"

"Do what? Do what?"

Then she turned and went upstairs and I stumbled after her, saying how sorry I was, how sorry.

"I love you," I said.

And she turned around after eight steps ascension and in response she hit me, her face twisted with hurt and sorrow and anger, and I let her hit me and though I was bruising, I stood back from himself and watched her grief and savage hurt emerge like a Mister Hyde from inside her. And when she could hit me no more, after she had imprinted on me a tattoo of the torment I had caused her, she put her arms around me and held me and wept and reaching for my lips, kissed me. And there on the landing, amidst the torment and the blood and the ruined suits and torn clothing we made love for the last time, our cries and tears echoing through the empty house, we made love. I moved out soon after that, forever; the matters placed in the hands of the accountants and the lawyers I had so often complained about, but who so effectively worked for us both.

56.

DEATH ROW EXTERNAL RECREATION AREA

"Well, shave my pubes and call me a pop tart! It's Gordon Brock! Smudge!"
"You know it is. Let's say hello," Smudge said.
"Brock, how long has it been? A year?"

Ed Frasier and Smudge walked up to the Stephens Green park bench I was sitting on. I was sitting there reading in the hot sun. I had been sitting there by the water near the band stand. I had been thinking about how my parents would find me here with the ducks and the birds and other avian and non-avian forms as I read under a tree by the pond. They would be really angry. Now I was terrified of Frasier and terrified of Smudge.

"Brock? How's it going?" Ed said. Hey Smudge, this is the fuck that sold me out to the authorities. Did you know, Brock, I had to see a therapist? Did you know my old man took a swing at me? He accused me of bullying you."
"You did. And you are very lucky we didn't take matters further. Now fuck off or I will call the police!"

I wound up in Stephens Green because I wouldn't stay put in the austere mahogany of Dr.. Rita Murphy's offices and waiting area, where her secretary, also confusingly called Rita 'Call me Rita' had smilingly, firmly insisted I stay. But I wouldn't call her Rita and I wouldn't stay. I didn't like either of the Ritas. I wanted to sit in Stephens Green, despite the fact it made me lonely and depressed. I was feeling somewhat vulnerable and confused after therapy. I had to see the sky.

And while I was seeing the sky, seeing the sky and reading, I met Ed Frasier and Smudge. It had been years since I had seen them, and it was as if it had been only yesterday. We were all older, taller. I was in a different school, fifteen years old, Frasier sixteen or seventeen, I expect, near the end of his time in school, and, as always, I was still as terrified and angry with him as I had ever been, there in Stephens Green, just across from Dr.. Rita Murphy's offices, leaving notice with Rita (the secretary) that I would be there by the main bandstand, not expecting that, when I looked up, and to see Edward Frasier with his smartass, 'shaved poptart' remark and Smudge.

An American tourist, who was eating a toasted cheese and tomato bagel and sipping a double skinny latte, noticed the godfather moment between Ed Frasier and I, then got up and left.

"Gordon, I wanted us to reach an understanding."

"I see," I said.

"You know the difference between you and me?"

"I have a future and you are a complete bastard?" I said, lamely trying and failing to think of something suitably confident and devastating to retort, wishing I could think of something witty and brilliant, after all I said to myself, isn't that your whole identity? Witty and brilliant? But I was suffused with fear, wanting to run and run, just a frightened, bullied teenage kid.

"Look at you," Ed said. "No friends, alienated from family that doesn't understand you, sitting out in the park reading books for company. It's pathetic."

"Better than stalking people. I have people who love me"

"No Gordon, you have people who keep you stable and maintained."

"You always needed to hurt people Ed. For all the reasons you or I couldn't begin to understand. But I have met at least one of your parents, and, to be honest, I am not surprised. I always wanted friends. I always wanted acceptance, and you have such a good radar for what people want, and you made sure I didn't get it, at least for the time we were in the same school. The only reason why you don't have a police record for assault or whatever, is that, at the time, my parents thought it would traumatise me too much. You have people who love your exam results and your sporting talent. That's all you have. What you do."

"You have been spreading lies about me."

"No, no I haven't. What lies?"

"Gordon, I want you to stop ruining my good name, or I will take action."

"Do you want to tell me what kind of action you are threatening to take?"

"I want you to tell the relevant authorities I didn't do anything to you."

"Go fuck yourself!"

"If you don't, I will tell the police your Mom used take me into a toilet in my house and suck my cock until I came right into her mouth?"

"Don't you speak like that about my mother, you fuck!"

"Then, Gordon, after I report that, I'm going to get really nasty. I'm going to say she shoved her finger up my ass and I used cry out in pain.

Now, my Dad's a cop. One word to him about that and the reason why I beat the shit out of you so often becomes clear, doesn't it Gordy? Eh? Now you read whatever bullshit you like into that, but you know as well as I do that shit's gonna stick."

"Look, Ed, it's been fucking years! Nobody cares about it now. What fucking difference does it make? Eh? What happened to you, Ed? You have a nice accent. You have money. But you may as well be down a lane way with a rubber hose beating some loser for an unpaid tab."

Ed visibly flinched. Then he resumed his previous script.

"But anyhow, loser, you think long and hard about what I said. All it takes is a report and then the whole machinery comes into place and then suspicion falls on your folks. Your parents will be taken in for questioning. You will be taken in for questioning. Reports will be filed. Lawyers will be hired. You know, suspicion never goes away. Neighbours and friends stop calling. Your Dad and your Mom won't get promoted. You might even have to move house. And then, word will get out if you move to a new neighbourhood. They won't want child abusers in the new neighbourhood. So you know what, Gordon? You will probably have to move to some fucking remote town. Your Dad will have to take a job as a low paying real estate agent, and your mother take in laundry or do baby-sitting. And, well, you can forget about your Mom ever getting a job again, not even as a cleaner, even if her record is expunged or sealed. Why? Because Ireland is a small country. And word has a habit of getting out, you know. For instance, my Dad can make a phone call to any police station in the —"

I interrupted Frasier at this point.

"I know the drill, Frasier. I am familiar with what happens to people who have been wrongly accused of wrongdoing. Believe me it's not going to happen. Believe me Ed, I want you to know that I know the kind of person you are. I know nothing will stop you."

"Oh really?

"Yes. You are like Satan. People like you teach people like me what not to be. But in the end you have to be defeated, because nothing will ever stop."

"Yeah, very, I dunno, Dante?"

"Maybe Milton," Smudge said.

Smudge had interrupted both of us at this stage.

"Gordon you look well. You know, Ed, I think he is looking well, rested, relaxed, calm."

"Fuck you, Smudge," I said.

"Fuck you too, Gordon is a moron." Smudge grabbed me by the back of my neck and began to squeeze. Smudge had long, thin, strong fingers, they that coiled around the object of their grasping.

"Let me- let me go!"

Smudge let me go. Then Ed grabbed me by the throat and dragged me into some bushes. I felt the pressure build in my temples, searing pain in my forehead. Right then, in Stephens Green, I feared my neck might break, or that a vein in my head would suddenly burst and I would spill blood all over the ducks and the pavement and the shoes of passers by. I began to see my field of vision narrowing. Then Ed Frasier, throwing me down in the twigs and leaves in a small copse in the middle of Stephens Green, punched me in the stomach, kneed me in the groin, then stood up, and kicked me in the head.

"Ooh, nice one, Centurion!" Smudge grinned.

I would like to point out this is the murder attempt that Ed Frasier mentioned in Arthur's pub on Sackville Place twenty odd years later, when we met that Christmas. Ed was at least two stone heavier than me. Ed was, and I think remained for many years afterwards, an excellent athlete. At the point of impact, my head popped forward. And then there was nothing. Unconsciousness for an indeterminable space. Then I stood up. Automatically. Then I puked. Then I passed out. I woke up with Ed and Smudge smiling at me. Smudge clapped me on the back and smiled.

"You know, I think he has healed, Ed?"

Ed grinned.

"Smudgers, I think it's because he comes from a good home."

"You think?"

"Definitely. Our friend Gordon Brock has made his recovery due to having the resources necessary to actually get well. It's a combination of good parenting and a little therapy. Next time, I might kick harder. I want a letter from you Brock. Are we clear?"

I nodded.

"You know something, Ed?"

"What Smudge?"

"I think we have killed the buzz of Gordy here getting away from St. Raymond's and more importantly, from you and me. Isn't that right? Gordon?"

"We should form a band and call ourselves the Buzzkills."

"You are a loser."

"Let's go Ed, we have things to do."

"I hope, Smudge, Ed, when you die, you both die slowly, and alone."

Then I turned to Edward Frasier. I wanted to kill him, make him die slowly too.

"If I retract the things I told the headmaster at the meetings, they won't believe me. Do you think these people are stupid? It's got to be some kind of partial retraction."

Frasier looked away worriedly for a few minutes.

"Okay, you are right."

I nodded. He looked across and the ducks and saw a child lean over by the water's edge and, with a fat little hand, toss crumbs for the gobbling ducks. Her mother held her other little hand. Frasier interrupted.

"Say it was a kind of rough and tumble. That, because of your sensitivity and desire to get out of St. Raymond's, you said it was bullying. Say you found the whole experience of class work at St. Raymond's, so overwhelming, and you are terribly sorry. It was a breakdown of sorts, something like that. I can't have my reputation ruined like this – not because of scum like you, Brock."

"I am going to get you Ed Frasier. I am going to destroy you."

And I walked away and left them there amidst the sun and the ducks and the lunchtime people.

"Can you believe that guy? Like, he threatened us?" Smudge said. "Actually he threatened you. He probably sees me as a side kick. I mean we could bury him in a recycling bin and no one would be the wiser."

"But we won't. A line has to be drawn."

"So why did we, you know, go up to him?"

"Because he has to be made retract."

"Do you think he-? He could have gotten us expelled, or sent to jail," Smudge said, lighting a cigarette.

"Not a chance. We were careful," Ed said. "I just don't like the fact he made formal accusations. It gives Anderson something to work with."

"You worry too much, Frasier. That thing is deader than my parents' marriage. Want to go get a drink? I know a place."

"You do? Why didn't you tell me before?"

Smudge picked up his bag and walked off, expertly holding the cigarette in the manner he remembered James Dean doing in one of the old movies he liked to collect on disc.

"Are you buying?"

"We'll share the cost."

"Yeah."

"Hot today."

"Yeah," Smudge said. Hot today.

I settled elsewhere, and allowed my rage and trepidation feed his absorption in going back to reading. After about twenty minutes my mobile phone rang. I looked at the caller identification.

"Hello?"

"Son, where are you?"

"In Stephens Green. I missed you."

"Shouldn't you have stayed in Rita's offices."

" I was getting freaked out in there."

" I see."

"Listen, I need to talk to you about writing a letter."

57.

THE LETTER

St. Raymond's School
25th August--

Dear Mr. Anderson,

Since I have left St. Raymond's school, I have taken a considerable time out to re-examine the direction my life is taking and I feel I cannot properly continue my life unless I set the record straight on some matters pertaining to the accusations I have made regarding my being bullied by certain parties at St. Raymond's. In writing this letter to the school, I would like to make it clear that, though I did experience some pushing and punches from certain parties I named during interviews I had in the presence of you, my parents, and Dr. Mary Dunne, it was not to the extent I may have intimated. I feel, having had time to consider the matter more detachedly, that my excessive sensitivity in temperament, the feeling of being overwhelmed, after existing in a relatively small school that catered in a more exclusive manner to my needs, and my need for a greater personal space, may have led to feelings of persecution and unwarranted accusations of bullying and beating. I was simply unused to the culture of a school with its more robust expectations from an individual of my temperament. Further to this, I would like to say that I regret any possibility I may have affected negatively the reputations of any teachers or students in the school, or indeed wasted your valuable time. That was not my intention, but the product of the extreme stress I was under during my time there. I have discussed this matter at length with my parents and advisors and would like to take this opportunity to thank you for the entirely sensitive way this matter was handled and to, once again, unreservedly apologize for any misunderstanding between us.

Yours truly,
Gordon M. Brock.
(The M stands for Michael, my grandfather's first name)

My father was very angry about that letter. Though we argued about it, I sent the letter anyway. We received an acknowledgement from Anderson, thanking me for my candour and honesty and how it showed real character, that he would discuss the matter further with the relevant people and may at some stage in the future call upon me and my parents for further discussions.

58.

RAGING AGAINST THE TEEN

As far back as I can remember, and I had a very good memory, I know my father was not a man who became angry often. That day, the day I sent that letter he was more angry than I had ever seen him. He left the house and drove away and sat in his car at the top of Howth Head looking out on Dublin Bay. It had begun to rain. Rain had followed rain, day after day, for five days. It was weather that was very depressing. I imagined my father sitting out in his car on that rainy day. The clouds moved across what had once been and silver and blue horizon and obscured the view of Dalkey Island and the knob of the Martello tower below. Mist descended like some loathsome shroud killing the freedom of the panorama my father had all to briefly enjoyed. The elements are out to get me, Dave feared. Before him the heather began to shiver in the wind and rain. Hiding from the elements, Dave sat in his car and smoked a cigar and listened to the radio. His mobile phone rang once more. It was Lucy. They had finished screaming at each other for two hours about the letter I had sent to Jim Anderson. I showed him the letter – after I had mailed it.

"What the hell is this?"

"I was thinking over everything that happened."

"Do you honestly think we believe a word you have written?"

"I think you should. I think I imagined things to be a lot worse than they were."

"So none of this really happened?"

"No. None of this was as bad as I imagined."

"So you lied to us. You lied to the authorities and you weren't really bullied?"

"No. I mistakenly interpreted normal school rough and tumble as egregious bullying."

" 'Normal school rough and tumble'."

"Yes, Dad."

"You call getting punched and kicked like that 'normal', eh?"

"I took what was said to me to heart and allowed an aggressive boy to push my buttons."

"Answer the goddam question, you little smartass!"

"No, I shouldn't have been kicked and punched. That was wrong."

"So do you think this letter is truthful? Do you!?"

I didn't answer.
"Answer the question, Gordon! I will dance attendance to your every whim and desire for books and music if you tell me the god's own truth in this matter. It is critical for our relationship."
Mother spoke:
"Gordon, please make an effort to answer your father. We know you have an answer for us on this one. You have answered so many other difficult questions."
I made an effort to answer:
"I think that I have exaggerated matters."
"You do?"
"I think, I was bullied, to an extent. I was pushed around. I was kicked, as you mentioned, but not to the extent I spoke of in the headmaster's office."
My father said: "So you are all right now. You weren't really kicked and bullied and spat upon. You weren't really tormented and teased relentlessly. You weren't really followed around the school yard punched and kicked."
"Seeing as you put it like that, Dad."
"Well, son. Maybe you would like to tell your mother and I exactly what happened, because a couple of years ago, you seemed to have put on something of an Oscar-winning performance in front of the Headmaster and his pet shrink. And, seeing as there is something of as dearth of physical evidence, well you see what I am getting at. I am not a solicitor, but you have exposed us to a horrible lawsuit for defamation of character or something like that with that dumb letter of yours."
"I think I was pushed around, a little bullying did happen."
"So, you were bullied. That's not what you're saying here."
"I think I might be saying that what happened was not exactly as I described."
"God Damn it! I want a straight answer from you, or so help me!"
"Dave!" Mother said. "Enough!"

So, Dad had strictly forbidden the letter be sent to Anderson, but it was gone. I said that was a denial of my fundamental rights to free speech and self expression. Dad took the letter and destroyed it before me. Lucy then accused Dad of bullying me. Dad told Mom to stop demonising him and turning him into some type of male stereotype. She said she wasn't turning him into any stereotype and that he should stop acting like his own authoritarian father. Dave said Lucy was as passive and manipulative as Lucy's own mother, and to look at how many marriages that behaviour had ruined. (He was referring to Lucy's mother's tendency for intrigue and gossip in her children's marriages, and that Lucy's marriage to Dave was the only one left intact). Lucy said she was sick of being made feel insignificant. Dave said he was sick of being hurt by Lucy and he was sick of her. At that stage, I burst into tears told them both that what he, Dave, had destroyed was only a copy, and the original had gone by registered post that morning. Dave, enraged beyond reason, slapped me across the face, and told me I was a manipulative lying, deceitful, little bastard and it would be a cold day in hell before he forgave me for telling such lies to the authorities and, if what I had written were ever properly investigated, he could not protect me. I told my father I hated him and he would never understand how important that letter was, and I ran to my room. Lucy looked at Dave, slapped him hard across the face, called him a bastard and went to her bedroom. At that stage, Dave left the house and drove up to Howth Head with a box of comfort cigars he kept for emergencies.

The phone rang once more. He switched it off.

Dave settled himself in his car and watched the rain spatter the windshield, and the clouds move overhead, deepening the grey, the wash of rain increasing until the clear vista of the bay from the hilltop, the expanse of sky and infinity of ocean, was gone, only a few feet from the car visible, that and the clouds of smoke from the cigar Dave was smoking alone. He listened to the rain outside, the wind picking up, and noticing there were no other cars or people running for cover in a place the offered precious little cover, he began to feel the thrill of being safe from a storm raging just outside the steel box he was hidden within. This was a big four wheel drive. High off the ground. Stop a tank. Stop a buffalo, he thought. The wind and the hills like rumbling buffaloes. And the stars like tears. The rain like stars. The clouds breaking. He decided to sit it out. After all, he figured, it was a matter of time before it passed. The stars like tears. Breaking from the eyes of sky. He wondered when he would start forgiving the boy. Soon maybe. He didn't know.

59.

NIGHTWATCH

At night, sleepless, unable to think or read, I started stealing out and sitting on the wall of Ed Frasier's house, my presence shrouded by trees. I was watching everything. I was an instrument of recording. I was waiting. I was looking for an opening. I was sitting there with a flask of hot chocolate, lights go on, and lights go off. Trash taken out, dog fed, laughter, television on, off, sitting in front of screens, eating, drinking, washing, dressing. I sat covered by convenient undergrowth. I was sipping hot chocolate. I wanted to find a way into that house. I spent hours watching lights go on and off, and hearing the odd conversation about missing slippers and 'guess who died on the golf course just last week?' and 'no I don't want to watch that programme', and 'I hate you', and 'let's have sex', 'no the kids are asleep' and 'what's that noise?' Then, lights out after the kids long gone to bed and then total darkness, and I would steal up to see if any doors were left open. But they weren't. Best to turn up after two in the morning, I thought. Safer then.

I saw my shoes were not right. Forgot about that, I thought. If I went inside the house right now, I thought, then I would leave impressions. Distinct impressions. Better to leave some impression rather than no impression, like when the forensics team wear white suits and foot covers when entering a crime scene. Not to leave a trail is significant in itself; it shows a forensic awareness, taking self conscious countermeasures. But not my size. If they know my size then I am a prime suspect. They could measure the size of my feet and then determine the intruder was of a specific age and then of a certain height. My feet were small. They were small and slim. If I were to put on shoes of an older person, then my own movements would be hampered. If I were to find a pair that would fit over my shoes, then destroy them, that would be useful. They would fit snugly if you will, lest I flop around in my floppy shoes like Bozo the Clown. Big problem. I could crash into something. Make a mess or a noise. I need to practise outsize shoe walking. I would be carrying a weight on my feet. Get discovered if I were not deft on my toes despite the footwear poundage. Have to find a way to do this. Have to think out a plan. What am I doing here? How come I'm so tired and can't sleep? I'm going home. So I went home and came back ten days later. I had spent time thinking. Thinking and drawing plans. I came back after I found correct shoes that did the right job.

I stood outside Ed's home. I looked at my watch. Couldn't see it. I turned on my teeny tiny flashlight. Two-thirty am. Good time. Chances are everyone's asleep. No lights on. I walked to the front door. Front door light automatically switches on. OOOh scary. I look for possible cameras. No cameras in sight. Though I had checked this before, it only took an hour's work in the afternoon to install security cameras. I stepped back from front door of Ed Frasier's house, breathing heavily, beginning to realise the danger I was in. I saw a cat hop off a wall, some people pass along the top of the lane. No, I thought, they didn't see me. I came by bike. Put on a track suit and my runners and my parka and I cycled here. Three miles in the middle of the night. Passed no police. Cars and small knots of people on their way home. Suburbia. Feel sleepy now. Fighting urge to doze. Want to snuggle up in bed. I am too tired to make a move. It doesn't feel right. So I go home and come back a few days later. And I do the same thing again. I wait until it feels right before I act.

I went home, out the back door and acquired my rucksack that I had left there after I noticed my bedside light had thrown a tell tale shadow on my curtains. I had the light positioned so that, as I entered from the back gate, I would notice a shadow in my room from the back lane and garden. I guessed it might be my father, judging from its size.

I don't know why he never asked me. I am as sure as I can be it was him, yet he never mentioned it. I opened the back door discreetly and collected the rest of my stuff. I once again checked to see if my equipment worked properly for the job I had designed them. I had two pieces of a fishing rod that locked together. I also had the broken-off handle of an axe. I checked the fishing rod connectors once more to see if they locked tightly together. They did. I took out a roll of tape and bound the rod, omitting to bind where the two pieces of the old fishing rod interlocked. Then I took the axe handle and bound it too in masking tape. I held it once more in my hand for weight and balance. It was good. Left was best, I felt, not right. Finally I checked my notebook for the numbers. I had watched the alarm being set in Frasier's house five or six times. They had changed the numbers. I was almost sure I had all the numbers. A few more monitoring sessions and everything would be ready to got. Then I hid my stuff away and went to sleep.

60.

THE BEATING CONTINUED BUT MORALE DIDN'T IMPROVE SO MUCH

The most effective acts of terrorism take time and thought. As I was superb at taking my time and thinking clearly, I decided to take the terrorist route. Terrorism, I figured, is a method of asymmetric war. It's designed to inflict maximum damage mostly in terms of shock and awe when you don't have a huge supply and logistics network and your opponent is more powerful, better supplied, and probably more skilled than you. It's meant to destabilize a government and economy. It reduces, when effective, an opponents self-confidence. I wanted to destroy Frasier's self-confidence. Terrorism is a method deployed when an opponent is more powerful. Frasier had the law (his father) on his side. He also was bigger, stronger, and had more resources available to him in terms of friends and establishment contacts.

Insurgent groups, when they plan an act of terror, usually work in four discrete groups. The first amasses information. The second make basic preparations. The third advances preparations and runs final checks. The fourth turn up to do the job. Clearly secrecy is a big issue. If your network is not locked down, and spies terminated, then your network is threatened. I didn't have secrecy problems when I stalked Ed Frasier. I did it myself, and nobody knew about what I did to him until now.

As I described, I watched his home late at night, learning the movements of the various members of the household, their comings and goings, the habits of the house dog, who appeared to be somewhat poorly sighted, despite being rather young. I was going to discipline Frasier. This was not because he bullied me, not because I hated him, but because he was going to ruin my life. He was going to ruin my life by hurting my mother's good name. It would ruin all our futures and hurt my future good name.

It was two-thirty am. The Frasier house was all dark. The moon shone full on the silent house. Chances are everyone's asleep. No lights on. I walked to the front door. Front door light automatically switched itself on. I looked for possible cameras. No cameras in sight. I stepped back from front door of Ed Frasier's house, breathing heavily, beginning to realise the danger I was in. If I was seen right now by anybody, I was finished. I heard movement. Then I saw a cat hop off a wall. That's ok, I thought. Then I heard some people pass along the top of the lane. Can they see me, I thought? No, they didn't see me. They couldn't have seen me. I am out of their field of vision.

I had put on a track suit and my runners and my parka and I had cycled here, same as all the other times. Three miles in the middle of the night. Passed no police. Cars and small knots of people on their way home. I had two pieces of a fishing rod, and the broken off handle of an axe. I checked the fishing rod connectors once more to see if they locked tightly together. They did. I took out a roll of tape and bound the rod, omitting to bind where the two pieces of the old fishing rod interlocked. Then I took the axe handle and bound it too in masking tape. I held it once more in my hand for weight and balance. It was good. Left was best, I felt, not right. Then I had a pair of my Dad's old gym shoes on to mask my footprints. Finally I checked my notebook for the numbers. I had watched the alarm being set. I was almost sure I had all the numbers. One can never be certain of everything.

On this, the thirty-fifth non-consecutive stakeout night, I saw that the back door to the Frasier residence was left unlocked by Larry, Frasier's Dad, who was a Garda. Some policeman, I thought. I waited till everyone had long gone to bed, till the lights were long switched off.

I fitted my Dad's shoes on, and I walked up to the back door and tried it. I was right. It was unlocked. As soon as I opened it I heard the alarm beginning its quiet countdown beep. I took out my notebook and shining my light on the keypad, punched in twelve-thirty-one-zero-five, and the alarm switched itself off.

I listened for a while. No one had stirred. The dog padded up to me and sniffed me. I gave it a pet on the snout and led it out the back garden, gave it some doped dog food (two sleeping pills mixed with nice meaty chunks) I had prepared. Then I sat and watched. Within ten minutes the dog was asleep. I waited another sixty seconds just to be on the safe side, feeling little beads of sweat trickle down my back. Stillness. They were all asleep. Next, I had to judge just where Edwards's room was. Not sure of that. Certainly upstairs, I thought.

Time to take the next step.

I went upstairs, slowly, looking for the quietest areas of the stairs to tread upon, not that I knew myself to be a particularly heavy treader, or a person carrying a lot of poundage, but I was aware that, even in the deepest sleep, an unfamiliar sound in a familiar space can cause someone to wake up for no reason they can pinpoint. I was now on the top of the stairs and I saw three doors. This must be the bedrooms and the bathrooms. Funny, I thought, I expected more rooms, as though I should be confronted with a network of rooms. A labyrinth. Into the unknown.

I tried the first door. There, in the half-light, lay Larry and Mary, husband and wife, Policeman and Nurse, asleep in each other's arms, a silhouette of a loving couple slipping into the deepest stage of night-time subterraneans. Ah, I thought, behold the happy couple. I closed the door and moved on. The second door was the large bathroom. Someone had left the light on. It had a huge cast iron bath on legs, a roomy shower, as well as a bowl and bidet. I checked out the bidet, squirting it up and watching the water splash, chuckling to myself, beginning to enjoy the intruder mind-set. I liked the checkerboard tiling and the fact that when one switched on the light, a fan quietly hummed to take out the steam and smell and ensure a quiet circulation of fresh air. Good design, I thought. The next room has to be Ed's, I thought. I put up my hood, checked my gloves, and checked the fishing rod, giving it a couple of preparatory swings. Good to go. Job to do. I reached for the knob. Then I opened the door. Onward.

When I got to Edward's bed, I looked to see if he was asleep. Moonlight peeped through the curtained window. I put down my rucksack beside the bed, took out the axe handle, and hit Ed across the frontal bone on his forehead. To prevent a scream of pain, I put my hand over Ed's mouth. That should immobilize him, I thought. Hit him hard. Then I stuffed some cloth into his mouth. Important thing is that neither of us should speak, and that he doesn't see me.

This first blow was successful. It knocked Ed unconscious. Then he woke up suddenly. He began moaning softly. I taped Ed's mouth, ensuring his nose remained uncovered. Then, I peeled off a few layers of blankets, allowing a sheet and a blanket to separate the air from Edwards green pyjamas. I looked at Ed Frasier writhing there. Ed, dazed and semi-conscious, had no idea what was happening. Then, taking the fishing rod, I began beating Ed, swinging the stick as hard and as fast as I could, avoiding the head and the stomach area to minimise permanent damage. Ed tried to scream and tried to move, tried to see who was hitting him so hard so fast, but I had the room in darkness and as Ed tried to get out of bed, I hit him again with the axe handle, immobilising him. As I hit him harder and faster, I felt the rage and the hate I had kept inside since my tormentor had begun targeting me, this dark god, this incarnation of all the hate and prejudice and rejection I had seen in Ed's eyes and body language, heard not just in his voice, but in the voices of those who did not understand or accept me, as though it were my fault I were not the same as all the rest, as if it were my fault my IQ were higher. I felt it coming like an orgasm, water falling in a great arc, a spray in the rainbow sky, felt it flow into my mind and my shoulders and arms and fingers, giving me cold, endless power and accuracy, clearing my mind of guilt or remorse and the potential for error that such self-awareness brings. I stifled Ed's struggling arms by taking the broken axe handle and smashing it against his wrists and hands as he tried to reach to his taped mouth as he tried to peel off the gag. Then, exhausted with agony, and delirious with pain, Edward Frasier gave up, and he lay surrendering to me on his bed and let me beat him for another minute or two. Then he passed out. Finishing up after my victim passed out, checking him for a breath and pulse, I collected my materials, took off the gag, and replacing it with another fresh one after removing the piece of cloth I had stuffed into Ed's mouth, cracked him on the Adam's Apple to silence him for a little longer, and left by the same door as I had entered, putting the alarm back on. Luckily it was the same code by which I had gained ingress. I thought that rather sloppy. I'd have chosen another code, I thought, as I took off my father's old runners and put them in my rucksack, and got on my bike. Then I remembered the dog. I walked over tot he dog. He was still asleep. If I cover the dog in the cold with a sack or something I will be leaving some type of psychological forensic trace, I thought. So I left it.

I cycled home, put my bike in the shed, locked the shed door, took off my shoes and tip toed into the front room and lit a fire. I put everything in the rucksack, including the rucksack onto the fire and watched it burn.

Then I went upstairs, took a long shower, went to bed, and slept soundly.

61.

My father was never much of a cook. When he did cook, he made bad omelettes, which we all ate and complemented, because he was invariably sensitive about his cooking skills.
"Enjoy, my love."
"You make a lovely omelette," she said, slicing another segment.
"Thanks very much. I do like to cook," Dave said.
"You do, do you?"
"Er, yes." Dave said
"Why?"
Dave looked at her and wondered what she was getting at. She grinned at him.
"Relax Dave, enjoy the food and let's —"
"Let's what?"
"I dunno let's get the shopping."
"Yeah we should get the shopping. There was damn all in the fridge this morning."
"Hmm."
They ate in silence for a few minutes. News papers were rattled. The silence was intrusive. Then Dave asked:
"Where's Gordy?"
"In the television room."
"I see. What's he doing in there?"
"Cleaning the fireplace."
"What?"
"He's cleaning the fireplace in the television room."
"Why?"
"The Murphy's are selling," Dave said.
"So Gordon is cleaning the fireplace in the television room because the Murphy's have decided to sell their house. How do you know the Murphy's are selling. Is it in the paper?"
Dave smiled and he nodded, and showed Lucy the advertisement.
"That house is grossly overpriced," Lucy said.
"I have another piece of news."
"What?" Lucy stopped eating her omelette.
"You are going to love this."
"I am?"
"I was having a drink in Madigan's, Middle Abbey Street last night, just after the group meeting, and I came across Joe Underhill."

"I don't know any Joe Underhill."
"He's actually Dr. Joe Underhill. You don't know him. But you do know his new main squeeze."
"I do?"
"You do. You go to Pilates with her once a week. She is a friend of yours. As I recall she was here last month for a meal and afterwards you two went to the theatre together."
"Virginia Murphy?"
"Virginia Plain as I like to call her."
"Dave, that's horrible. She is a lovely person, and extremely fit."
"Evidently. She has been seeing Joe Underhill for the last six months, and do you know something else?"
"I have this psychic intuition you are going to tell me."
"Don't be cute."
"Even if I ran screaming out of our house, declaring you a baby eating axe murderer, you would run after me and tell me."
"Lovely image. It's strange she never told you."
"Actually she did."
"She told you?"
"Right."
"I see. And you saw fit not to tell me."
"Dave, she swore me to silence," Lucy said.
"How nice. Now people are swearing their friends into lying for them."
"I know she has been unhappy for a long time. She met Joe at a bar one night and afterwards they got together. Sorry to ruin your news."
"That's not what I heard."
"What?" Lucy said.
"I heard they met at a picnic, so Joe told me"
"Does it really matter where they met? Couples usually can't remember exactly, or they romanticise where they met. She is having a wonderful time, and she wants to marry Joe."
"That's not what Joe told me."
"Jesus."
"Well, Joe told me it was a casual thing. That they are having all this sex every so often despite the fact they are both married, and it's great and wonderful and secretive and he expects it will take its own course once their respective permanent unions pick up where they left off. It was all a kind of pleasant interlude in a series of mediocre marriages, you know?"
"I see. That's a little sad and cynical for me, you know, Dave?"
"Sorry, but you should have told me, sad and cynical or not."

Lucy stood up and put her hand on Dave's chest and smiled.
"I can't be expected to remember every bit of gossip about people's extra marital affairs. You forgive me then?"
She kissed him for a long time and pressed their foreheads together.
"I might find ways for you to earn your forgiveness. It might involve a lot of concerted effort on your part."
"I'm sure, but you will agree it's nice to know if one of our circles of friends is seeing someone other than their spouse."
"It is. Sorry about that."
"Not to worry. Luckily I didn't say anything?"
"True, is there any more coffee? Dave?"
"Then I know what to be discreet about. Do you want me to go back? Start again? Writing?"
"I guess," Lucy said.
"You know what the worst part of all of this is?"
"What? I was looking for coffee. Oh, there it is."
"Physics."
"Physics?"
"Yep. The bad use of science to explain stuff. Laws of thermodynamics. Everything turns to crap. The worst part of all of this is the kids. That the children involved are irreparably emotionally scarred and end up sullen, emotionally stunted adult children who cannot commit or trust? Or, maybe if you keep trying you might get better and not give up like big child?"
"No, it's much worse than that."
There was a crash from the other room.
"What is that noise?"
"I think Gordon is still in the television room. Gordon?"
"Yes, Mom?"
"You okay sweetie?"
"I'm good, a little tired. I had a disturbed night. I just noticed the fireplace hadn't been cleaned. Just dumped the stuff and vacuuming the rest."
"Good for you. Hungry?"
"A little."
"Fancy some omelette? Before school?"
"Why not?" I said.
"Are you all right?" Dad asked.
"I'm fine."
"You look pale. Kind of tense. Actually, son, you look ill."
"I think I had a lot of bad dreams last night."
"Really. Did you sleep at all?"

"Yes."

"So how did you go back to sleep after you woke up?"

"I put some music on and read till I fell back asleep."

"Good."

"Dad, I wanted to say I am sorry."

"For what?"

"I am sorry I sent the letter."

There was a long silence while Mom and Dad looked at each other. Eventually Mom said something.

"Dave, Gordon just apologized to you and me."

"I know that."

"So?"

"It's okay, I guess," Dad said. "I'm glad there have been no long term repercussions, that's all. I mean I never really accepted that the Frasier kid wasn't after you. I know in my heart that he was. I just was so upset when you defied your mother and my wishes."

"Enough talk. Breakfast. School in fifteen minutes! Your mother will be driving you today."

"Okay," I said." But I would rather take my bike."

62.

There, in the night, as I beat him, when all Ed could hear was the swish of the stick through the air and the thud of it landing on his body, muffled by the placing of bedclothes over him, I thought afterwards how lucky I was that he had not died. One blow in the wrong place and I was looking at a murder enquiry. Then I recalled how doctors are sent in to patch up torture victims, examine them for heart issues, or a predisposition towards hemorrhage.

Ed tried to scream, but, as I said, the happy release of a scream, the promise of the death of a pain that stretches out to infinity, I denied him, by the careful application of a gag. When I, the assailant, unknown subject, was finished, I replaced my stuff in my bag, checked the floor, and quietly left, putting the house alarm back on. Ed didn't hear me either enter or exit. Ed heard no noises, no tell tale signs of someone in his room, not even a sense of something wrong, and no vibration of an ancient antenna from his lizard brain.

The attack commenced when he was sound asleep, his eyes moving backward and forward, recreating scenes from his day, meetings with friends and girlfriends, classes attended, distorted landscapes of memory and desire creating complex psychic artifices and artefacts decodable through the key of self awareness, love and memory of dreams denied. Then, the first blow came and the dreams disappeared, replaced by a flash of white light, and then a silence, then nothingness. Ed re-awoke to the feeling of boiling pain, as though each blow raining on his person was delivered with a white hot rod of steel and each impact burning through his flesh, ripping it out, and leaving only bone and consciousness in the great desert of loneliness that was his room at that time.

Ed wanted to negotiate. I saw it. He wanted to, for one second, see who this was, but if Ed turned his head, I hit him in the face, and around the eyes. I didn't blind him. I didn't maim him. I did nothing other than hurt him for the time I was there, in the intimacy of all that occurs between torturer and victim. In that room, I was his personal hell, and I have never forgiven myself for what I did to him.

I often thought that I broke him. Maybe Ed wanted to apologize, to write down in detail whatever it was I, the torturer, wanted him to say, expound on television for the entire world watching to see, that he, Ed Frasier, was a monster, was a killer, was a worm, was worse than filth. But I didn't want him to apologize. I wanted him to suffer. Ed learned the consequences of his disobedience, by broken bones and hairline fractures, and a bed filled with the blood from a hundred cuts. My intention was to scourge him for his sins.

As I silently beat him, I thought of Edward Frasier's other victims, those he had beaten and bullied, for his undoubted skill and ruthless intimidation did not emerge fully flowered from some void. It was a delicate sapling requiring love and nurturing and the proper educational environment. Thus, I felt I was doing something of a service to the community, ending the reign of a tyrant. Then I left.

After the event, Ed wept. He was numb and immobile. He felt himself bleeding, but not as though life was leaving him, more as one is cut while working or playing and the bleeding continues until bandaged. He felt the imminent agony approach, as one senses a terrible unendurable storm coming. It was only by early morning that he could scream, and when his father and mother witnessed the scene in their son's bedroom, called the police and ambulance, they too screamed. As it had been such an elaborately planned and executed cold blooded crime of passion, police forensics found nothing, no DNA worth using, no fingerprints, no trace evidence, few fibre traces, no signs of forced entry or exit, no evidence of anything other than a horrible beating administered with ruthless cold efficiency by what was evidently a clever assailant. But they all suspected Gordon Brock, for no other reason than he was someone smart enough to do it and to get away with it.

Larry Frasier, for instance, had no doubt whatsoever :

"Anyone else would have left evidence. The very fact that he didn't leave evidence, the very fact that the assailant got in and out without so much as leaving a hair, means it was him. It's an absence that can only be filled by Gordon Brock."

"Detective Frasier, sir, who is Gordon Brock?"

The young police officer Larry was talking to was sitting with him while other police were questioning Mary, who was too hysterical to make any coherent sense. A doctor was in the process of recommending bed rest and would later sedate her for a few hours.

"A kid I know. My son bullied him, tortured him, and made his life hell."

"Sir, I. . ."

"Don't 'sir' me."

"Okay, sorry about that, Larry.

"What's your name? I usually know, you know, most people."

Larry looked for a while at the tall young officer in his late twenties, still with the unthickened frame as would befit his build of a young man, crew cut hair shorn so thin one could barely discern its chestnut brown, dark blue eyes, perfect uniform, clearly out of his depth, wanting to support, wanting to make a difference. Probably did remarkably well during training. Pencilled in for promotion. So long as he doesn't mess-up. I was like that, once, Larry thought.

"Seán, Larry, sir." Seán had answered the telephone call from the Frasier house." I'm, I, I just want you to take a moment. We have counsellors on their way."

"Thank you, but I already have a counsellor, and I pay her an absolute fortune. I'm going to the hospital now. I want to see how Ed is doing."

"Yes sir. If you don't mind, I'll come with you."

"As a matter of fact, Garda, I do mind."

"Sorry Larry, I'm following orders in this regard, but I would like to accompany you if that's okay," Seán said.

"Why not?" Larry said.

As they drove through the evening traffic, Larry talked:

"I have been thinking, Seán," Larry said.

"Yes, sir?"

"Take for instance, the way the assailant got into my house. Someone gained access by knowing both codes. In other words, the code to put the alarm on, and the code to put the alarm off. That takes some doing. Most crooks are not that careful and filled with foresight. Nor are they that patient."

"Well sir, some are. But I take your point. Most aren't."

"The fact that the person concerned went to that level of trouble puts them somewhat ahead of the herd. Now they drugged my dog with a common enough type of sleeping pill. They got into the home of a decorated police officer, me, went right past my bedroom where I was asleep, down the hall, and taking weapon or weapons, beat my son so badly that he will be in hospital for a while, and yet did no permanent damage, except the psychological damage of course. My son has no idea who hit him in the first place, because the first blow presumably knocked him out enough for the assailant to gag, bind him, and put on a blindfold. Now that takes fast work. Then they administered the punishment beating. Why would someone administer a beating like that and take nothing. No money, jewelry, nothing? And they got away with it. And they will get away with it. Know why? Because I guarantee you that forensics will not find a single fingerprint, a single hair or fibre, nothing other than my son's DNA in that room. Do you know why? Seán? Do you?"

"Because Gordon Brock did it? Sir?"

"Yes, Seán. Only Brock could have conceived and executed a plan like that. And we can never ever prove it."

"Do you have a video surveillance, sir?"

"No Seán. I don't. Normally crooks don't break into police homes."

"You would be surprised, sir."

63.

Lucy saw Rachel Morrison wearing a halter top in the extremely long queue in Halter and Ridges exclusive lingerie shop off Grafton Street. Dave had seen there was a sale and mentioned it to Lucy, told her to go get herself something nice. Anyway, Lucy wanted to buy some nice underwear as a treat for herself, something she did despite her denial of it, to make herself feel prettier. Rachel was queuing two people to the front of Lucy. Lucy studied her carefully. She looked beautiful, if beautiful was the right word. She looked desirable, which was something that didn't bother my Mom so much. It was then that Lucy saw Rachel waving at her, signalling that she was about to be served and that she would wait for her to say hello. It was only when Rachel smiled broadly and hugged her that Lucy knew something was terribly wrong.

"How have you been Lucy? It's been an eternity. I don't know why I haven't called you. Well, actually I do. I was afraid to. I'd love to have a coffee with you. I need to talk to you, in confidence of course."

"Sure, Rachel, no problem, I'd love to take coffee with you. There's a nice place round the corner. I thought I saw you in the shop there, but you looked so distracted I didn't want to, you know"

Lucy smiled weakly, trying to conceal the fact she had been actively avoiding her, wanting to make her purchases and hide in the undergrowth of the crowds and make an escape home to the quiet of a life she had finally managed to restore to some semblance of equilibrium. When they settled into the coffee shop, the cream spiralling in Fibonacci curls in the centre of the cups, it was anything but comfortable, anything but the settled environment, conducive to the kind of dialogue Rachel clearly wanted. The coffee shop functioned as a sandwich bar for local office workers, the large passing trade making for a constant clatter of foot and vocal background.

"You seem a bit, you know, I mean —"

"I know. I wanted to apologize to you; I mean, it's part of my ten steps."

"Apologize for what? I have to say I'm kind of surprised. You don't need to apologize to me. No, I don't think so."

"Well, after that day."

"Sorry?"

"The day. In our garden, when Gordon got into the fight with Edward Frasier, and Alan of course."

"Well, now Rachel, that wouldn't be my understanding of events by any stretch of the imagination. Gordon is pretty passive when it comes to any kind of violence. He isn't afraid to express his opinion, I know, and people misread his endless stream of ideas and opinions as a kind of, I don't know, maybe condescending arrogance, but its not. He just has all this stuff going on inside and he wants to make a connection, that's all. And that is strictly as far as it goes."

"It's pretty far, sweetie," Rachel smiled an excessively hostile white toothy smile evoking careful dentistry, reminding one more of a predators' signal to run rather than the smiling warmth of an old friend. Lucy looked at her and saw, despite her show of teeth, no smile in Rachel's eyes, and felt that sadness deep down in knowing she had been mistaken in befriending this person in the first place. Lucy went on,

"He is actually pretty unsure of himself, you know. He loves to help if he can, and as you know, he is especially fond of Jenny. Once he bonds with someone, he stays bonded. He never forgets. How are Alan and Jenny? I haven't seen them in —"

It was then she realised what Rachel was apologizing for. She had cut them off. She hadn't had a thing to do with Dave or Gordy or herself since the incident in the garden. They had been erased from their social circle, and thus from the potential advantages of being in the Morrisons social circle might afford them.

"Good. Good. They are fine, really —"

"You cut us off."

Rachel looked at Lucy for a while, and looked down embarrassedly.

"I did. I am sorry."

"You bitch."

"I am. Drunk or not, I am a bitch."

"Why?"

"Why what? Why am I a bitch?"

"No! Why cut us off? What's going on?"

"I'm not sure. I was ashamed of myself. For not being there that day. I wanted to apologize. I feel very bad. I have been going through a rough patch, the other half and me. I think I was ashamed of how bad it had become between us. I didn't want perceptive people around picking through the guts of our messy lives."

"Okay, I guess. I'm not that perceptive, you know. Actually, Dave and I are pretty self-absorbed. And Gordy is kind of lost in his own process pretty much of the time."

"Well, he seems a bit out of it, you know."

"It's very difficult. You have to be sensitive to Gordon's needs a lot of the time, though its not out of selfishness, you know."

"I know."

"I guess you could be dying in a ditch and we wouldn't notice. We are nice people, you can tell," she grinned ironically.

"No, you are really good people, honestly," Rachel smiled in return.

They laughed a little and returned to the background noise, the uncomfortable chairs, the constant movement, the mediocre coffee, and the condescending staff.

"I don't know about that." Rachel said "You guys see a lot."

"So you were hiding a rough patch? Is that it?"

"Right. I was humiliated. My self esteem took a nose dive. I wanted to hide the truth."

"Dave and I go through rough patches all the time. Try having a gifted kid and you feel like killing either yourself or the kid or your husband half the time. The rest of the time you wonder if this strange creature you love and cherish is really for real."

"I could imagine. I think Alan was always a bit jealous of Gordon. I think so much of his energies are directed towards pleasing others. I try to get him to focus on his own needs, not selfishly but —"

"He gets that. All Gordon wanted was acceptance and bit of friendship and fun. He doesn't get that much."

"That was a rough day in the garden."

"It was."

"Something bad happened. It changed things, though I could never really get to the bottom of it."

"Rachel?"

"What?"

"Are you drinking?"

"No."

"Okay, thank god. That day. In the garden, it was just a fight, though that Ed Frasier is a bad one. I confronted him in the school, he was really obnoxious."

"You obviously haven't heard about what happened to Ed Frasier."

"Really? Is he a friend of Alan?"

"Not especially. They hang out a bit in school. Listen, you should know this. Ed Frasier was attacked and beaten in his own home."

"What?"

"He was in hospital for weeks, I think two weeks. You didn't hear about this?"

"Good Lord! Is he okay?"

"His parents took him, I think, to Spain. They have a place, or are renting a place out there. He has some broken bones, but he is going to be okay. I think it made the news, at least the newspapers. He was in bed one night and someone came in and gagged him and beat him with a handle of an axe or a two by four, a real paramilitary style beating. Went on for however long. Then the psycho who did it just left, no trace. Alarm on. And the parents didn't hear a thing. They are all completely distraught. I don't think Larry will never be the same again, I mean after he was attacked he had a breakdown and now his son, the same thing happening to his own son in his home and he asleep, it's terrible, just terrible. Whoever did it is going to rot in hell or in jail, I don't care."

Rachel started weeping uncontrollably.

"Rachel!"

"Sorry, sorry,"

Lucy got out of her seat, went around the tiny table and held her, surprised at Rachel's reaction. She hugged her for a while, a kind of awkward self aware embrace across the coffee table over the debris of discarded half finished coffee cups, taking her hands from where she held them at each temple between her clear forehead and close cropped hair.

"Thanks, sweetie." Rachel said.

"So how long have you been seeing Larry?" Lucy asked.

Rachel didn't answer.

"Rachel, I think maybe we should go, okay?"

Rachel nodded.

"Sorry, Lucy, I don't know —"

"Sure. No worries, sweetie. Would you be very uncomfortable in a bar?"

Rachel shook her head.

"Larry thinks Gordon did it. He told me."

"Told you what?"

"That Gordon was the assailant. On Edward."

"I am not even going to dignify that with an answer."

"What?"

Lucy leaned forward, and said.

"Rachel, you are a bitch. You're an incredibly selfish person, and a terrible doctor. It's a miracle you haven't lost your licence. You've certainly been sued often enough."

Lucy took her bags, leaving Rachel there dumbfounded, looking bewildered, eyebrows raised, her hand half off the table as though trying to touch something intangible, aware she had told Lucy something, yet not quite sure, for in her moment of weakness, in her need to find comfort, she had betrayed herself. But Lucy was gone.

64.

YOUNG GORDON BROCK'S CONFESSION

Godammit. I know I planned it. I want to set it straight. This Frasiergate. I wanted to tell the truth, but my guilt's my curse, and it's death in life. I waited and waited and one day I stood in the kitchen and saw Dad was on the phone to Mother. The phone was on speaker. Mum sounded upset.
"So, when will you be back?" Dad asked.
"I am going to have a word with Larry Frasier."
"What?!"
"I am going to have a word with Larry Frasier."
"What the hell are you doing talking to that prick?"
"I had a chat with his lover."
"Who?"
"Rachel Morrison, she all but told me they were seeing each other."
"Really? Wow."
"Apparently Ed was attacked in his own home. They think Gordon did it. I am going to have a word with Larry."
"I though the was in Spain or France, Larry, I mean. What's this nonsense about Gordon?"
"Did you know Ed was attacked?"
"No. If I had known I would have probably mentioned it."
"He was. And Larry is blaming Gordon."
"We should call the lawyers on this. Really, that's absolutely insane. Gordon wouldn't ever hurt anyone."
"I know. I'm going to deal with this."
"Jesus, Lucy, if you go in there with all guns blazing; you are only going to ruin things for us."
"Trust me. I know what I'm doing."
"Fine, but if you fuck it up, be it on your head!"
"Thanks for the vote of confidence, Dave."
"No problem!"
That's when Dave disconnected from her. I was standing in the kitchen doorway as he slammed the phone over and over in the kitchen counter in frustration, cursing and swearing to himself.
"I did that thing."
"Sorry son?"
"I beat the living shit out of Ed Frasier."
"What?"

"He was going to accuse Mom of performing fellatio on him."
"What?"
"He was going to say that Mom gave him a —"
"Okay, I get it. What else?"
"And then he was going to report it to the police. Making a formal complaint. So I wrote the letter we fell out over, and I sent it to the school, retracting my complaint. That's why neither the school or Frasier never took his complaint against Mum any further. The letter, though rather hamfisted, did kill any kind of real investigation. But that wasn't the end of it. I knew Ed had real control over us. I knew that if he wanted to, at any time he could hurt us, me or Mum or maybe even you. He needed to be shown who he was dealing with. I knew he was a psychopath. I couldn't prove it. I couldn't prove any of this. The school did such a good job of cleaning up the evidence against themselves, their negligence or whatever, but they conveniently left us exposed to a huge lawsuit. So I had to write the letter and I had to deal with Frasier. Nobody else would. I knew Frasier had no real moral compass, no real interest or empathy in others, And I knew what so much of what he was doing was motivated by jealousy, and he was jealous of this family. So, as I said, I had to take him out, had to take some kind of effective preemptive action. I staked out his house for a couple of months and learned the routine of the house and his family and I watched the alarm codes being put on and off. I wrote them down and learned them off, wore shoes over my own, made myself forensically invisible, gagged and bound and masked him and beat the living shit out of him for as long as I had energy. Then I left the house as silently as I had entered, came home and burned the clothes in the fire. I reduced everything to ashes and flushed the ashes bit by bit down the toilet. Oh and I took a shower and put the clothes I was wearing on during the day in the wash. I know you might think this is, well Dad, I don't know what you might think. You might think you were being taken for a fool, that you feel humiliated that all this went on in front of you, and I feel terrible. I am telling you this because I can't take the guilt for what I have done. I don't believe in God so I can't confess."
"You don't believe in God?"
"No," I said.
"But you choose to play God, judge, jury and executioner."
"I felt I had to protect the family from a monster, but I couldn't involve you at the time. If you had any knowledge or mother for that matter, you would end up in jail for child abuse or whatever, so you couldn't have any knowledge. I was in a conundrum. None of the

systems were working. The school, the courts were naturally blocked from us because of Larry Frasier, who hates my guts, and punched me out, would make sure through his connections, and the fact he is considered a hero, would make sure whatever case we might be able to drum up would surely blow up in our faces. I just wanted you to know. I am sorry."

"Maybe this is something you might have mentioned before your mother went to see Larry Frasier."

"Well I got some of the call. I know."

"I assume you heard all that has gone on by phone."

"Yes, I said that. He has no evidence."

"No evidence? How do you know that for sure?"

I couldn't answer.

"Try to answer."

Dave went on.

"They say every action leaves some trace."

"I took forensic countermeasures."

"How? What countermeasures?"

"Gloves, Masks, use of plastic. Other peoples shoes all destroyed. Reduced to ashes. Drugged the dog. My actions were the lesser of two evils."

"Okay then, sometimes by leaving no traces whatever you tells a big story in itself."

"You can't prove a presence by an absence."

"Gordon, you have done a bad thing. A very bad thing. And it will probably stay with you for a long time. And I am sorry about that. Two wrongs don't make a right."

"Dad, it was the lesser of two evils."

"Yeah. You said that. I have heard that argument before. Like when they dropped the bomb on Hiroshima."

"That was different, Dad. That's a simplistic. That was a totally different situation!"

"Really? Was it really that different son?"

"Yes, Dad. I think so. The Hiroshima bomb was dropped based on predicted troop losses, plus the length of the war."

"Okay, stop! It's just, I don't know how I am going to explain this to your mother. It will break her heart. I am very sad, very angry, and very disappointed, and I would like you to go to your room and think over what you have done. Okay? Go! Now!"

65.

So Mum came home and Dad told her what I had told him and she was appalled. Lucy and Dave looked at each other, kissed, then, after pressing their foreheads for a moment in the empty kitchen, listening to the dull click of each second passing, she said.
"I have something."
"I see."
She took out her recorder.
"You brought a recorder, how did you know to bring one?"
"I didn't. This one is new."
"You bought it."
"The other one is upstairs. See? This one is smaller better, records better and for a longer time. I am taking my recent obsession with things technical to the next level."
"I see."
"Stop saying that."
"Saying what?"
"'I see.' You keep saying that."
He didn't answer. All Dave wanted was to know what had happened.
"I would like to know what's going on."
"And you shall, my husband. And so you shall."
She switched on the recorder. At first there was the sound of muffled voices, crackle and hiss as though some type of high powered electronic devices in the vicinity were interfering with the quality of the recording.
"Well" Dave said.
"This is helpful."
"Don't be cute."
"I'm not —"
"You are too. Sssh!"
"I mean…"
"Dave…"
"Did you read the instructions before you started fooling around with new devices?"
"Oh shut up, Dave!"
"Well I'm not the one who screwed up the —"
Just then voices came from the recording device. It was Larry Frasier.
"Jesus, you really went to see Frasier?" Dave said, as the recording started. Lucy stopped the machine.
"I did. I went to see Larry Frasier."

"Why?

"You will find out. Okay, now hear this —"

66.

WHAT WAS RECORDED ON LUCY'S YAMA Y7GBH1 POWER RECORDER – ENHANCED

Larry Frasier: "You come here and you think you can make me believe that your kid is incapable of hurting other people. Well you are in for a shock. I am going to get you."
Lucy Brock: "You are going to 'get' me?"
The recording continued:
"I am going to get you." Larry said.
"That's a very scary threat. I came here as a friend." Lucy said.
"No you didn't! You came here to gloat! You know what your son did."
"Look who's talking!" Lucy said. "And by the way, Larry. I came here to make peace!"
"Oh yeah? Well —" I didn't come here to fight with you or do anything other than try to stop this cycle of violence. We don't want this to degenerate into a kind of feud, whether it is fought out in the courts or through each others careers or passed on from one generation to another. I am not delighted. I am very sorry. It hurts me to hear of things like this happening."
"It hurts you!"
"It hurts me, Larry."
"You hypocrite! I am going to fuck you up. I am going to ruin your life. I am going to get into every detail of your life and if I find anything, anything, I am going to destroy you and your husband and everything you hold dear. Do you know why? Because you are here to cover up and…" Larry said.
"I really didn't. I think what happened to your son is beyond anything I could imagine. I know from what happened to my son that the hurt will go on for a very long time. I think whoever did this."
"Your son did this!"
"Really. Any proof? Any evidence?"
"There is no fucking evidence Lucy. There is no fucking evidence because only someone of exceptional gifts could come into my house, get past whatever security, past the dog, get into my son's room, beat the living bejaysus out of the boy, and get out clean."

At this point Dave couldn't keep silent.

Dave Brock: "He actually let you into the house? Larry let you in? How come you don't have any recording-?"

"Sssshhh!"

Dave kept talking and talking over the continuing exchange of continually rising intimidating voices.

Lucy irritably signalled for Dave to be silent. Dave went on.

"This is you and Larry?"

She switched off the recorder.

"Yes Dave."

"Did you intimate you know all about?"

"Yes Dave."

Then she switched on the recording.

"Then, let's be hearing this."

"I really fucking wish we could, you know? You really need to hear this. Okay? You need to shut up and listen okay? It's really important."

"Sorry, sorry. I just can't believe my ears."

She tracked the recording back a bit. Then she pressed 'play'.

The rest of what was recorded on Lucy's Yama Y7GBH1 Power Recorder – enhanced

"I am going to fuck you up. I am going to ruin your life." Larry said.

"Larry, you don't know what you are saying. I will come back another time." Lucy said.

"We have known each other a while now. You are a calm and thoughtful man. A good man. You don't know what you are saying. I will leave if you like. I'll come back in a few days. I wanted to assure you in no uncertain terms that our son is a peaceful gentle boy who would never raise a hand to another person. He prefers the company of adults and books to that of other children, and whatever he alleges your son did to him; we will find a way through this." Lucy said.

"I know Gordon did this! That little psycho could have killed my boy!" Larry said.

"You do?" Lucy said.

"Right!" Larry said.

"Okay, Larry, I have tried and tried and tried to get you to calm down and you won't calm down. I have asked you to talk to me and we will peacefully listen to each other. And I think I am just tapped out. So let's look at this. Where is your evidence, Larry? Tell me, I want to know. If you are so convinced, where is your search warrant? Why haven't there been police combing through all my worldly possessions? I mean I know you are a talented policeman and you know me. We have known each other peripherally for years. The fact of the matter is that all you are doing is jettisoning years of experience and training because you

are convinced yourself that a kid half your son's size and a few years his junior has committed a horrific act of violence," Lucy said.
"Don't. Don't-patronise-You —" Larry fumed through gritted teeth.
"As I said so many times before, we have known each other for years. I think what's happened to Ed is terrible, and I can only begin to imagine what you and Mary are going through right now. Actually to be honest, I do. I know what it's like. Because I went through it over a longer time scale with Gordon. Day after day, knowing things are wrong, terribly wrong, and it's your entire fault and you feel powerless and nobody really doing anything. But I am not going to go there. Not like you. You are supposed to be professional. You are supposed to take a long careful look at things. Not jump to conclusions. I am really worried about you," Lucy said.
"Don't tell me my job! I can make you understand in no uncertain terms." Larry said.
There was the sound of a crash, the sound of something being broken. Dave wanted to know what that sound was, but he kept quiet.
"Get the fuck out of my house!"
"I know Larry. I know." Lucy went on. "Look, sweetie. Take it easy."
"Out! Get the fuck out!"
"How is Mary by the way? I left a few messages for her and I don't see her around so much. I think she might be a bit depressed. I get that way myself. You know a husband away so much, and of course a lot of resentment can build up when someone gets sick. We all have our bad times and we tend to say things when they are unwell, as unwell as you have been. You know I ran into Rachel in a boutique..."
"That is none of your fucking business. Leave, leave now!"
"I know I am sorry. I was buying lingerie, and who did I meet, but Rachel Morrison! It's been something like; oh well years and years since I have seen her, since that incident in her back garden, maybe more. She is looking well. You know something she is very concerned for you and for Ed. She was upset, very upset. Definitely. Oh and you know? That's why I dropped by. She told me what had happened, the first I heard. No one rang or phoned or mailed or anything. Strange. You know, I got to thinking why she was so upset. And I think I know."
"Get out! Get the fuck out and don't ever come back!"
"Give my very best to Mary. Tell her I will always be a friend to her."
"If you ever come back here, I will arrest you for stalking."
"Take your hands off me, Larry. You are losing control. I'm leaving!"
Then there were the sounds of a scuffle and then a crash. Then the sounds of footsteps and the sound of Larry shouting. Then the sounds

of a car starting up. Then the sounds of a car radio and the engine in the background. Sounds of traffic. Then the sounds of Lucy fumbling with the controls of device, breathing heavily and cursing to herself and the device gets switched off.

"What was that?" Dave asked.

"He pushed me against a coat stand. I fell over onto it. Then I ran out of the house. Now we can go to the lawyers. They will make it clear we have evidence that he made threats against me."

"I think so. As I said, he could have snapped you in two."

"He nearly fucking did, Dave. He nearly did."

"You do know that Larry is right. That our boy did that. Everything that lunatic said about our boy is true."

"The kid had it coming."

"Jesus! Lucy! Do you hear yourself!"

"That bastard, Ed Frasier. I know it's terrible, but someone had to stop him. Its hard to believe Ed was going to accuse me of doing that to him."

"The thing is, you really don't know what to believe. Gordon is so good at making stuff up, so good at constructing an argument, you don't know what is true, but I have to say I do think Ed Frasier would have made that accusation, I really do."

"I do too."

"Maybe this is for the best. What are we going to do about Gordon?"

"I think we are going to have to have a long chat with him and see what's best for us all, Okay?"

68.

I overheard the conversation, and the recording, and I knew that, though my parents would never betray me to the authorities, though they believed me when I told them my reasons for attacking Ed, though we talked and talked about what happened, why I did it, what I felt and thought, how betrayed and how hurt they felt, I knew they disapproved of me, and thought less of me for what I did. I was not the idealised, gifted, tortured, ethical saint they perhaps wanted. Perhaps I too wanted that image for myself. Instead I was as much a monster, it appeared, as my tormentors, and I hated that about myself. It was why I believe, I have not lived up to my potential, why I have been lazy and self-serving for much of my life, why so many of my relationships have failed. True, I finished school. True, I went to college. I took a PhD in Psychology. I became a psychotherapist. I got married to Martha. True, I wrote books and I became wealthy. True, I became involved and fell in love with Lucia, got divorced and remarried to Martha's half-sister Lucia. As is customary for divorced couples in these days of well-adjusted relationships seeking reconciliation and meaningful dialogue, Martha and I eventually sought out each other, and became friends, for our own sake and for the sake of our son Joshua. Lucia and I rebuilt and extended our house down in Castletownberehaven, what with Lucia and I having two children born, one following another within two years, Samuel then Frank. Martha even came down with her new love for Christmas, and she and Lucia get along quite well now. I think the fact that both of them are exasperated with me in differing ways helped somewhat. As said, Lucia and I had two children, the second being born three years ago. Martha dotes on them like a favourite aunt.

And then, two days before Christmas twenty years after the evening I overheard that recording between my mother and Larry Frasier, I met the person who destroyed my life and, who, because of his malevolence and psychopathy, gave me this one thing, this one expression of myself that has remained untainted since that day in the garden with Alan and Geraldine Morrison, and Ed Frasier, who told me the truth that Christmas shopping day. Hence, this.

69.

JOSHUA REYNOLDS BROCK GETS KICKED UPSTAIRS.

Joshua became an insurance broker, a successful and rather good one. One loves ones son. He was a functioning warm caring person, but a part of me though what he did was meaningless, he had become, like the rest of workaday humanity, an economic cipher, a mindless functionary drained of life day by day and destined mainly for the grave after a tedious life. This didn't stop me loving him more than words here could ever express, but I couldn't help how I felt.

Joshua told me what happened the day Joshua Reynolds Brock was promoted

It was about noon. Lauren McBride, Department Head, confronted Joshua at his desk. She normally never spoke to Joshua, except to make his life more difficult by making more demands and giving him more work, through her designated lackeys. Lately he had been considering leaving the job and finding work elsewhere. He was well-qualified. He was equally well-connected. Here in this company there was too much grief, too much work.

"Joshua, could you step into my office for a minute?"

Lauren McBride's carefully manicured index finger had depressed the cradle of his phone. She had disconnected Joshua's customer. Joshua looked at her. His eyes widened imperceptibly. He felt his empty stomach contract in further mounting anxiety.

"Leave your computer switched off."

"Okay, but we are losing because of this, you know?" He said. "And that was a-a Major Customer you disconnected."

"You don't deal with Major Customers. What are you doing with Major Customers? You are barely here a year."

"It was one of the names you gave me to check out."

She looked at him coldly, and smiled, deciding to forget his impertinence. He followed her after switching off his computer. Her office was on the fifth floor. They rode the lift silently. Then they walked through her busy fifth floor department into her office. Joshua closed the door and stood before her. He looked at her coldly, realizing that every clichéd rumour he had heard about McBride was true.

"Sit down."

"Right."

Two others were sitting, waiting in her office. The slim black Venetian blinds were lowered. Then the room seemed smaller.

"Joshua, this is Mike Silver from personnel. And this is Judy Newman from Braxton and Finn associates. They help us now and again, with people."

"Hello."

Joshua said.

"Hi Joshua."

Mike said, giving him a professionally polite wave and a chilly smile.

"Joshua."

Judy said, nodding coldly and looking back to McBride.

Joshua feared the possibility of a handshake. It was unfounded. McBride leaned back on her leather chair and took the emotional temperature of the silence. Arctic conditions. And Joshua looked at the cheap Picasso print above and behind McBride's chair. He hated it. It mocked him. She was staring at him. Maybe she put it there to see how I would react.

"You like it, Joshua? The painting?"

"It's terrible. I hate it. Too many colours."

There was a small smile playing on her lips. She did not smile often.

"We want to promote you. We want you to take over the Major Customer Portfolio for the coming financial year. You will be made executive level AA with a consequent salary, office. We'll take you out of the hamster maze down there and put you somewhere quieter. We like what you have been doing. That's why we rode you as hard as we did. We needed to see what you were made of…"

She pointed at him

"At the end of the year there will be a review. If you do badly, you keep your present grade, but lose this position. If you do well, your life becomes a little more complicated and financially solvent. We look after those who look after us."

"I see…"

"Don't screw it up. I'll be watching. We'd like to keep you, if you'll consider staying."

"Congratulations Joshua," Mike said, smiling a steely smile.

"Well done Joshua!" Judy said, sounding rather happy in a Ronald Mac Donald sense of being happy.

Handshakes happen. Sometimes there is nothing one can do. Mike and Judy looked radiant. They left the office. They made calls on their phones. They faded into the corridors. He never met them again. He wondered if they worked for some shadowy government spy group.

Joshua was dismissed. He went back to his desk, shaking, heady with fear and adrenaline highs. He rang the Major Customer McBride had disconnected him from. He told no one about the promotion. No one asked him. If he had told them, then the sycophants would gather. It was to be announced in any event.

Joshua had a very boring girlfriend called Penny. Penny's mobile phone rang.
"Where are you?" Joshua asked.
"I'm at home. I was making notes. I fixed up the place. It was such a mess."
"Great."
"You sound funny. Are you drunk? Are you back taking those strange tablets I have bullied and manipulated you into no longer taking?"
"Kinda."
"Why?"
Joshua's voice lowered to a whisper:
"I've been promoted! Can you believe it? About an hour ago I was taken into McBride's office and some suits from personnel were there. I was made an executive level AA"
"That's fantastic!"
"It eases a burden," Joshua said.
"We can save it for when you leave." Penny said, feeling euphoric.
"You can finish your thesis. I want you to. Please say you will." Joshua responded.
"We could pay a mortgage quickly and check out some places we always wanted to see, go somewhere." Penny said.
"You could take a Doctorate and go for a department job you always wanted. Don't tell me Penny you didn't want it. Don't tell me, because I know you did. I know it!"
"I love you. You're a genius." Penny said.
"I'll talk to you later. I need to make some calls. We're going out tonight."

70.

After the meeting with Frasier, I sat sitting in my hotel room for hours. I had called Martha. I started doodling, making notes, reading with the television on in the background, thinking about trying to document everything, and how impossible that was. Then I checked out of the hotel. I started for home. I was driving for an hour or so when I noticed I had missed calls. Then the phone rang. It was Lucia

"I have been trying to ring you."

"You have?"

Sometimes I don't hear doors, phones, approaching footfalls, bells, alarms, and other sundry signifiers of proximity. It's a problem.

"Yes."

"So has Joshua. We were worried."

"About what?"

"Where are you?"

"I am driving. I have the autodrive on. Should take a few hours."

"What's the traffic like."

"Surprisingly good. It's not raining and there's only a little ice. So I should be home about eight or so. Why were you worried."

"I just wish you would answer your phone when it rings."

"Sometimes I just don't hear it. I am sorry about that."

"It's very annoying. You know that. What if it's an emergency?"

"Is it an emergency?"

"Joshua got promoted."

"Really? That's very good. Actually in truth I know. I was chatting in the hotel room to Martha. She called and she told me the news. He is a good lad."

"It's really wonderful."

"I must give him a call straight away."

"Call him right away. I think he and Penny are going out to dinner."

"He is a wonderful kid. Well, he's not a kid, but you know what I mean. How are the little ones?"

"We all miss you."

"I miss you too, my love."

"As do I. How did your trip go?"

"Well, Lucia, you are not going to believe who I met, on O'Connell Street, just outside Easons."

"Who?"

"I'll tell you all about it when I get home."

"Do tell, Gordon."

"Ed Frasier."